ROGUE ANGEL

Jeff Rovin

St. Martin's Paperbacks

ROGUE ANGEL

Copyright © 2005 by Jeff Rovin.

ISBN: 0-312-93694-X
EAN: 9780312-93694-5

Printed in the United States of America

St. Martin's Paperbacks edition / June 2005

St. Martin's Paperbacks are published by St. Martin's Press, 175 Fifth Avenue, New York, NY 10010.

10 9 8 7 6 5 4 3 2 1

CRITICAL ACCLAIM FOR JEFF ROVIN AND *TEMPEST DOWN*

"Terrific, a riveting, relevant, can't-stop-reading-it drama! Plan on an all-nighter when you pick up Jeff Rovin's latest techno-thriller masterpiece."
—Joe Buff, author of *Tidal Rip* and *Crush Depth*

"Rovin emerges as a thriller writer in his own right . . . the subsequent yarn has all the fast pacing, state-of-the-art technology, and knowledge of international intrigue that this kind of thriller requires as well as characterization and ideological balance rather better than most of the competition. Looks like Rovin has a future in the genre."
—*Booklist*

"*Tempest Down* . . . follows the finest naval traditions . . . a satisfying blend of heroism and opportunism. A highly recommended, fast-paced read."
—Douglas De Bono, author of *Rogue State*

"An exhilarating high-tech adventure. From fighter jets to gliders, from cutting-edge submarines to foreign destroyers, the reader is in for a whiplash ride, propelled by Rovin's insider knowledge of international politics and the military. Watch out, Tom Clancy."
—Gayle Lynds, author of *The Coil*

"Stand by for a fast and furious technothriller roller coaster with nail-biting action."
—Capt. David E. Meadows, U.S. Navy, author of *The Sixth Fleet* and the Joint Task Force series

"The stuff of high drama and nail-biting suspense . . . more important, however, is his cast—large, varied, and compelling, composed of believable, understandable characters to worry about, even those you don't always like . . . Rovin gets the people right and produces his best yet."
—*Kirkus Reviews*

"A vivid page turner, loaded with suspense. I felt as if I was in the action, terrified, and waiting to be rescued."
—Allan Topol, author of the national bestseller *Spy Dance* and *Dark Ambition*

"Jeff Rovin's *Tempest Down* weaves three techno-loaded story lines together into a mind numbing, deadly contest under the ice in Antarctica that build to a searing, gripping, slam-bang climax. Don't miss it!"
—Chet Cunningham, author of *Hell Wouldn't Stop* and The Specialists series

St. Martin's Paperbacks Titles
by Jeff Rovin

Tempest Down

Fatalis

Vespers

ROGUE ANGEL

Prologue

ONE

Pearl Harbor, Hawaii

On most mornings, Major Tom Bryan loved getting up before sunrise. It was usually the best time of day.

There was always sweet expectation in the air, like the rich smells from the kitchen before Thanksgiving dinner. You couldn't pick out everything so you just enjoyed it all. That was true whether Bryan was in suburban Philadelphia, where he'd grown up; in Corpus Christi, Texas, where he was stationed with his LASER—Land Air Sea Emergency Rescue—teammates, or here, on the terrace of the Active Duty Visitors Quarters at the Hale Koa Hotel on Oahu. Just prior to dawn the stars were especially bright, since only the most brilliant of them could hold out against the expanding glow on the horizon. The sky grew fresh with new color and the air was cooler and cleaner than it would soon become. A man's concerns and solitude, inevitably amplified by the darkness, were given a good backhanded slap by the sun and chased away, at least for a while. The portents of night were replaced by the potential of a new day.

And there was wonderful quiet and a sense of solitude. The thirty-four-year-old Bryan was not a loner. His life was his team's and their lives were his. But it was nice to have this time to himself to savor the new day. Mornings were also enhanced by the fact that Bryan was usually rested, alert, and ready to put his shoulder against new challenges and to learn from them.

Yet this day was not like most mornings.

Major Bryan was awake before sunrise—significantly before sunrise—because at four A.M. he and nine members of his Land Air Sea Emergency Rescue team would drive to Naval Station Pearl Harbor, where they would board a Martin P6M-2 Seamaster. The vintage 1959 flying boat had been rebuilt for a touring display of classic Navy aircraft. The pilot, a Korean War veteran, grabbed any excuse he could to take her up. This mission was one of them. LASER operatives would take a short flight inland and, at six A.M., from the aircraft's service ceiling of 12,000 feet, they would jump— onto the caldera of an active volcano. The target was Waianae, located just a few clicks from Pearl Harbor.

The "lava leap," as it was dubbed by Captain Paul Gabriel, was one of General Benjamin Scott's more inspired ideas for a training mission. They always had a big drill scheduled for the first Monday of every other month. Until now these had been on the water—in a mothballed C-9 Nightingale that had been crashed into the sea, in a capsized military ferry, on a hot-air balloon gondola carrying containers of incendiary materials. The latter effort simulated a Japanese plan from World War II to firebomb the forests of the American northwest. LASER disarmed the devices at sea in case anything went wrong. All of those exercises had been designed around dummies. Today's would be no exception. Five mannequins would be pushed from the aircraft ahead of the LASER ops. Their job would be to stabilize any wounds and recover the individuals. The volcano locale would give them a chance to work in a hostile and changing environment. It would be good training if the multiservice crew ever had to deal with intense-heat situations such as a forest fire or burning building. It was a good idea. But Bryan had jumped before. He knew that the thermal currents were strong in the morning, and would be stronger still at the crater of a volcano.

Bryan stood in a blue jumpsuit sipping very strong Kona coffee and looking at the sea. The major had never been to Hawaii. The LASER team had arrived the night before on a C-17 that had flown from Corpus Christi to Hickam Air Force Base. It was dark when they drove from Hickam to the hotel and Bryan had not had a chance to see any of the island or their target. He still hadn't, really. The water was black, like oil, with a few spots of light from ships, planes, and coastline structures. The breeze was tranquil but invigorating. It was scented with an odd mix of salt air and bananas from a grove directly below his fifth-floor window. It was odd to think that in less than two hours Bryan would be jumping onto the rim of a spitting, hissing, bright red-and-yellow cone of fire. If the wind were blowing toward the sea this morning the major would have been able to smell the pungent fumes. Black grit lofted by the small eruptions coated the island side of the hotel. The volcano comprised the bulk of the west part of the island. When Waianae was awake—even just stretching a little, as it was now—Oahu knew it.

The phone beeped. Bryan answered even though he knew it was the automated wake-up call General Scott had left for his team. Of course, Benjamin Scott would already be up. He liked to review mission plans until the team took off. In this case he was probably checking with the Pearl Harbor Meteorological Center, making sure the winds were not too severe. He would also talk to the United States Geological Survey Hawaiian Volcano Observatory to determine whether the volcano had become dangerously lively during the night. Scott would get up-to-the-minute information on the lava flows, since he did not want his people to touch down and find themselves trapped. Bryan's number two man, six-foot-five-inch Marine Captain Gabriel, disapproved of these checks. If there were a real emergency, they would have to jump whether or not conditions were moderate. That was why few team members had been extensively briefed about the volcano. In a fast-break situation, they would not have much time to cram.

Bryan saw both points of view. He still sided with General Scott. If any team member had a weakness, a drill was the place to find it and work on it. If the ladders or radios or any of the equipment had a flaw, or if there were a better way to configure components, the team needed to discover that before lives depended on it. If the drills Scott came up with weren't 100 percent simulations, they were close enough. Especially when things did go wrong. Months earlier, the Air Force sank a destroyer for retrieval practice. Scott's team obtained permission to go onboard to try and rescue dummies from the flooding engine room. When the damn thing submerged prematurely, the LASER Ops had to save themselves.

The dummies didn't make it.

Bryan slugged down the last of his coffee as he moved from the window. The beverage had cooled quickly in the chill morning air.

"You call yourself a hot liquid?" he joked as he poured it in the sink.

Now lava—that was a hot liquid. It was imperiously unaffected by the air. It took an ocean to stop it, causing the lava to cool and harden into a "bench" when it hit the sea. That was how the coastline of Oahu expanded. Bryan had acquired a profound respect for the stuff during briefings back at Corpus Christi.

The team would be wearing heat-resistant neoprene hazmat suits and flame-resistant hoods for this mission. The temperature of lava in the tube and on the ground averaged two thousand degrees Fahrenheit. If the volcano suddenly became more active, the risk would be dramatic. Fountains of lava could shoot as high as three hundred feet, chucking up soccer ball–size stones and massive splatters of molten rock. Superheated "tephra jets"—steam blasts created when the cool sea came in contact with lava—not only generated lethal heat but produced hydrochloric acid mist when the chloride in the sea salt interacted with the hydrogen in the water. This lava haze, or "laze," was as corrosive as battery acid.

The hazmat masks were designed for nuclear, biological, and chemical situations, so they would protect the team from the fumes. The suits would afford some protection from the acid. Since the only way out would be on foot, that was important.

Bryan never ate right before a mission. Hunger made him a little cranky and that gave him an edge. The only things he needed before facing each day were a shower followed by fifty fingertip push-ups to strengthen his fingers and get the blood surging followed by a long, slow shot of caffeine. After that, Bryan was awake, focused, and ready. Yet he was also aware that what they were doing was dangerous. He was not concerned for himself, but for the other members of LASER. If they were not top-of-the-class professionals, General Scott would never have seconded them from their particular branches. But being a front-rank radio operator or demolitions expert did not mean you could jump or swim or haul ass worth a damn. That was what the daily drills back at the naval air station were about. That was what these missions were about. Though all of that put a burden on General Scott and Major Bryan, there were no options. They never knew when the team might be called upon to help a military unit in jeopardy, or where that might be. Several months ago it was in Antarctica. Tomorrow it could be the Rocky Mountains or the Negev Desert or an earthquake-stricken embassy in the Far East. LASER had been conceived to respond in what the Department of Defense designated VRDSs—versatile rapid deployment situations. Unlike Delta Force, the Navy SEALs, and other special operations units, the LASER team was not designed to conduct covert ops or engage military adversaries. Their enemies were the elements, places and situations where the environment itself was hostile.

Bryan went to the closet and pulled his Air Force windbreaker from a hanger. Although Bryan was Army, Scott's wife, Wendy, had given him this microfiber jacket after LASER returned from the South Pole. Wendy, a retired captain, said it was the warmest windbreaker he would ever wear.

"Even the Coast Guard uses it," she insisted.

Probably without the 12th Air Force insignia on the chest, Bryan thought, but he didn't mind. Wendy Scott was proud of her service. He was proud to wear her winged star symbol.

The major swept his key from the night table—an old-fashioned metal key, not a card—and tucked it in his pocket. He would leave it at the front desk, since he did not want to end up with brass slag in his pants if things got hot. Their gear was already loaded on the Seamaster. A 6×6 soft-top truck would be waiting at the front door to scoot them to Pearl Harbor.

Bryan went downstairs. Several of the other LASER members were already in the lobby. They saluted when he arrived, then did so again when General Scott came down. Scott shared Bryan's enthusiasm for mornings, and was openly eager when he told the crew that the drill was a go.

"It's a one on the Volcano Explosivity Index," he informed them. "That's considered 'gentle.'"

"How high does the scale go, sir?" Army Lieutenant Woodstock Black asked, perhaps inevitably. The twenty-nine-year-old was the LASER team's demolitions expert.

"The top position is nine," Scott replied.

"Which would be described as what?" she asked.

"Megacolossal," he replied.

"I like that," she smiled.

"Out of curiosity, what would a two be?" Captain Gabriel asked. Also a predictable question from LASER's strategic officer.

"That is considered explosive," Scott replied. "Obviously, the local geologists have no way of knowing whether Waianae will get there today, but that's always a possibility. Lieutenant Kodak will be watching for signs of increased activity and will keep the major informed."

Kodak was a reconnaissance specialist whom Scott had plucked from the SEALs. He was good. He also wasn't a geologist. Scott had him Web-tutored by a geologist on the flight over, just as he would be in an actual crisis. Hopefully, that would be enough to spot the danger signs.

Within seven minutes all members were present. Scott led them to the courtyard and the waiting soft top. The sun was just peeking over the eastern horizon, turning the oil back into water. It was more green than blue, not what Bryan had expected. He looked toward the east and got his first real glimpse of the island. In the distance were misty peaks and green foothills, with spots of color from copper and rust-colored tile roofs. White-walled hotels shone ruddy in the early sun. Palm trees and exotic red Ohi'a shrubs dotted the hillsides, while here and there a solitary albatross circled above. But the flora and fauna were not what made the strongest first impression on the officer. Between the rising sun and the LASER team was a fine charcoal mist, airborne particles coughed up by Waianae.

This was a drill. Many aspects of it were controlled.

Many, but not all.

Gentle or not, the volcano was real.

TWO

Waianae, Hawaii

General Scott was more anxious than usual.

With most drills there was room for things to go wrong. The sixty-three-year-old Scott tried to plan them that way. Water usually gave you a few minutes to get out of a confined space before it dragged you down. You could rest during a climb or abort a dive or a jump. And the time they did an underground rescue scenario in an abandoned mine, there had even been an alarm, of sorts. Timbers that Scott had always thought supported the shaft actually did nothing of the kind. They were an early warning alert. If the rock walls shifted the beams shifted and creaked.

Fire was different, particularly the kind of eruptive, liquid fire the team would be facing. It was not forgiving. But this was an area where they needed to drill. Military units could be caught in forest fires or seismic events. LASER needed experience working in those environments. A volcano gave them both.

The ten LASER operatives taking part in the drill were quiet as they rode the short distance to Pearl. That was not unusual. The drills were always held in the morning, when the soldiers were fresh but not yet alert, and rarely chatty. Major Bryan and Captain Gabriel were usually the sharpest of the group. The unofficial slogan was, "Once a Marine, always a Marine." Implicit in that was a readiness to fight 24/7.

Bryan and Gabriel were sitting across from each other on the wooden benches, warped by decades of sea air, that lined the back of the truck. Neither man seemed aware of the bumpy ride. They had never been to Pearl Harbor and Gabriel was becoming visibly agitated as the piers, vessels, and green grass of the port became visible through the windshield.

"This is hallowed ground," the forty year-old captain said as he sipped a Dr Pepper.

Bryan nodded.

Gabriel looked at the major. "You feel it too?"

"I do. Pretty strong."

"Yeah. And right now I'm wanting to kick the heads of the sumbitches who made it that."

"Already taken care of," Bryan reminded him.

"Nah," Gabriel said. "We got 'em in big brush strokes. You know what I'm bettin'? That some of those bastards are still around, livin' happy in little country cottages with sunny days on the other side of rice paper walls, sittin' in nice silk robes, paintin' landscapes and drinkin' tea and enjoyin' the families that these boys never got to have." He chucked his massive chin toward the naval station. "It ain't right."

"Possibly," Bryan agreed. "But wiser minds in the field at the time made the deal they did. I have to lean on their judgment more than a little."

"They were tired of fighting. They had Russians to think about. If they had been thinking clearly I'm sure they would have hunted every one of those animals down." Gabriel turned his big, innocent-looking blue eyes to General Scott. "What do you think, sir?"

Scott was sitting beside Bryan. He looked toward the naval station. The white of the offshore *USS Arizona* memorial shone against the bluing sky, commemorating over a thousand young fatalities.

"I think that for sixty-four years, longer than I've been

alive, those people in their cottages have had to live with the echoes of what they did—if not for the hurt they inflicted on us, then for the cowardice of the act and the hell it brought on their nation," Scott said. "The stigma of failure is with them each night when they go to bed, it's waiting for them when their sleep is interrupted by ghosts, and it's there when they get up in the morning. It's living rot, captain. And those kids and grandkids you spoke of? They live with the smell of that. Posterity reeks of it." The general's dark brown eyes stared out to sea, back through the years. "The men out here died heroes, remembered and revered. I think everything is just the way it should be."

Bryan and Gabriel both looked at the general. They were emphatically silent.

"Except for one thing," Scott added. "We should be thinking about the present and the future, not about the past."

"Right, sir," Gabriel said. Because that was all there was left to say.

If the captain was still feeling spiritual about the attack, it did not show when they reached the base. The truck stopped beside one of the older piers along the outside of the cove. Gabriel was efficient, as was the rest of the team, as they double-timed down the wharf to the waiting seaplane. Their gear was onboard and Gabriel and Lieutenant Black went through the three large hazmat bags. These contained the suits and ropes they would need to secure the victims and hike away from the crater. The bags would be dropped ahead of them.

Army Sergeant Major Tony Cowan and Coast Guard Master Chief Petty Officer Gunther Wingate—"the Dummy Squad"—checked the five mannequins that would be used in today's exercise. The two men laid the figures on the floor beside the forward hatch. The equipment bags were also there, with self-deploying chutes. The mannequins were dressed in fatigues that had been treated with a calcium zinc molybdate flame retardant and would be ejected without chutes on the first pass. Unlike the hollow plastic dummies used in water exercises, these figures were made of silicone rubber. They would suffer no more than a few scratches and small gouges when they hit the mountainside. The figures were also all female. LASER Quartermaster Mary Land had procured them from a website that sold "love dolls." There were quite a few jokes about that, including a gag marriage proposal to one of the figures from Army Sergeant Bernie Kowalski, the team's structural analyst and expert in the terrain they would be visiting. At least, General Scott hoped it was a gag. "Leighanne," as the mannequin was nicknamed, was wearing a vending-machine engagement ring.

During the SOP extraction exercises—named for "sack of potatoes," which was used to describe the disposition and handling of unconscious, dead-weight extractees—Scott warned the group that no dummy was to be given preferential attention. The general was surprised to note that while no one actually looked at Kowalski, all eyes seemed to drift in his general direction, a peripheral scope-out.

The men finished checking the dummies. When they were done there were no longer any smirks, no mock kisses, just sharp efficiency. Kowalski broke out the relief maps of the caldera and unrolled them on the floor. Everyone gathered round. The sergeant was fascinated by how all things were built, the earth included. Although he was not a degreed geologist, he had enough self-taught knowledge to instill the confidence of both Scott and Bryan. Kowalski reviewed the areas where the crust was thickest, where the lava flow was most active, where the smoking vents could obscure vision. He reminded them about what he called "crunchy rocks," jagged, black metamorphic rocks that seemed sturdy but were extremely brittle. A wrong step could fracture a crunchy and drop a LASER operative down a cliff or into a hole.

When they were done, Air Force Lieutenant Jen Marinelli reviewed the parachute safety checklist with the team. They opened the chutes on the wide floor of the Seamaster and examined the vent and suspension lines, the bridle, and the canopy. Then they packed it all away and slipped the chutes on. A Pearl Harbor crewman shut the hatch, which was to Scott's left. He stayed behind to serve as jump coordinator, or JC. He was dressed in a brown flight jacket and matching leather gloves. It was comfortably cool in the cabin now; when the door was opened the temperature would plunge to near-freezing. The LASER Ops strapped themselves into the vinyl-covered fold-down seats that lined the fuselage and the Seamaster taxied from the pier, thumping from side-to-side. Four powerful Pratt & Whitney J75 turbojet engines— mounted atop the wing—howled, causing the fuselage to vibrate as the plane surged forward. Behind them, the frothy white wake was like mighty twin contrails as the ungainly, pelican-like aircraft climbed from the sea. It banked almost immediately to the east.

No one spoke. The roaring engines made that inconvenient. A passenger would have to leave his seat, cross the fuselage, lean close to someone's ear, and shout in order to be heard.

As the plane reached five thousand feet, the JC motioned the LASER "Dummy Squad" to the hatch. The navigator would give them a countdown to position, the JC would open the door, and the dummies would be ejected. The plane would make a tight circle and return to position. Then the team would leave the aircraft. As Cowan and Wingate went over, Marinelli popped her harness and rose. She was ten on the jump list, after the Dummy Squad. The rest of the team was seated in jump order. Bryan was number one.

General Scott looked at the faces of his team. Many of those faces were extremely young. He would even describe a few as innocent. They had gone straight from high school to the military and had not seen much of life. Nonetheless, they had a sense of purpose about them. Some of that came with them from the farm or the suburbs, from the city or the rocky coastline. Some of that came from training, from associating with resolute and professional men. He could see it in the eyes, which were strong but compassionate. He saw it in the stern set of the mouth. No one chewed the inside of their cheeks or sucked on their lips, not just because they could bite them if they hit something or if something hit them, but because any anxiety they felt was folded away and secured like a flag at sundown. A number of these people had been on the Antarctic mission, when dozens of lives were saved because they were at the top of their game.

Young or not, they understood the importance of their work. For many, this would be a career. For some, it was simply a chance to acquire new skills before moving on to something else. For others, it was a time to try and understand what was important and what was not. That was perhaps the greatest gift the military provided its special operatives and combat veterans: inner peace about most things. When you've waltzed with death, either leading or following, a long line at the supermarket or a tailgater on the freeway doesn't seem quite as upsetting. Even illness becomes a set-back and a challenge, not a defeat. You realize that the ulti-mate tragedy, the loss of someone close to you, has to be kneaded into the routine of life.

And you get to do things and see places most people don't, Scott reflected, *like the underbelly of a polar ice shelf or the throat of a volcano.*

A green light came on above the hatch. The JC held up two fingers: The dummies went out in two minutes. The LASER Ops would follow five minutes later. That's how long it would take to make the tight circle and return to the point. Scott looked at his pocket watch, which had belonged to his grandfather. Scott had carried it through Korea and Vietnam. He didn't need to know what time it was, but at moments like this he liked to feel connected with Quinn Scott. Growing up in Wabash, Indiana, Benjamin Scott first learned about warfare from his grandfather, who had lost an eye at Château-Thierry in June 1917. The five-year-old had learned it was a terrible but necessary thing. He learned that because some men were willing to risk their lives—"and sometimes their eyesight"—little boys could sleep safe in

their beds. After hearing that, Scott never took a night's
sleep for granted.

Scott rose. He grabbed the red canvas strap that was
hanging above the seat and faced the hatch. The general was
not as relaxed as his people. He was a point man, an officer
who liked to be the first one in. Leading a unit from behind
went against his nature. The major watched as the green
light went off and a blue light came on. The JC held up one
gloved finger and cocked a thumb toward the cockpit, which
meant he was about to open the door. The Dummy Squad
held the handrail beside the hatch. When the plane had leveled off the airman tugged back the latch and slid the heavy
door aft. Bright sky and cold air rushed in, causing the dummies' uniforms to flutter wildly. Cowan and Wingate released the handrail. Each man picked up a dummy. The JC
stepped aside and Cowan stood in the hatchway. Wingate
would pass and Cowan would toss. Both men waited until
the red light came on.

The dummies went out quickly and efficiently, Leighanne
being the last. Kowalski blew her a near-invisible little kiss
as she flew out back-first. The equipment bags went out after
the dummies. The chutes were on timers that would open at
one thousand feet. The bags were supposed to land on a
slope five hundred yards from the crater. The team would
collect them and put on the hazmat gear before moving in on
the dummies.

The JC shut the hatch and the lights above it went dark.
The plane banked sharply to the east to make its turn. The
airman faced the jumpers and raised his right index finger,
turning it in upright circles and then pointing to the port
fuselage. That was the signal for the LASER Ops to put on
their crash helmets and line up. In case of an eruption, each
of the white helmets had a small blue strobe light in back so
they could be located amidst the smoke. Each jumper also
carried a high frequency point-to-point radio so they could
communicate with the aircraft or with anyone who might
become separated from the group.

Because the Seamaster was not equipped with a jump line, the soldiers held on to the handrail. Cowan and Wingate helped each other into their chutes, then took their places in line. As they did, Scott made his way to the cockpit. The door was shut to keep the wind from buffeting the air crew. The general picked up a black phone hanging beside the door.

"Captain Rockefeller, what's the status of the Chinook?" Scott asked.

"On the pad and ready," the pilot replied. "Would you like me to patch you through to the pilot?"

"No thanks, Captain," Scott replied.

The Chinook was the big twin-rotor helicopter that would recover the team when they reached the rendezvous point. LASER Operative Captain Tyler Puckett was at the controls. If anything went wrong, Scott wanted one of his own men piloting the rescue craft. Puckett had studied the air currents in the area, as well as graphs showing the way air had moved during previous explosions. The Chinook was capable of operating in volcanic air temperatures which averaged 120 degrees directly above the flows. But heat wasn't the only problem. In addition to laze, Puckett would have to avoid "vog"—volcanic fog, a blinding, suffocating combination of sulfur dioxide, oxygen, air moisture, and sunlight—and white-out, the result of onshore winds mixing these various clouds into a caustic, impenetrable soup.

Hopefully, as Puckett told the general when they spoke at five A.M., none of this would be an issue. The volcano would remain gentle and the Chinook wouldn't have to collect the team until they were ready.

The Seamaster leveled and swung back toward the point. Scott made his way back to his seat. The LASER Ops looked like dancers in some surreal ballet, hands on the barre as they shook out legs and stretched arms and limbered themselves for the jump. Scott wrapped his hand around the strap and faced the team as the green light came on. The JC flashed the two minute signal. Lieutenant Marinelli went down the line once to make sure everyone was ready. She took her place as the blue light came on. The JC held up one finger, then raised his left hand as a stop sign. Everyone grasped the handrail and moved close to the fuselage as the airman opened the hatch.

General Scott took a fist of air in the face. He raised a hand to block it and looked over at Major Bryan. Scott couldn't see the major's eyes through the tinted visor of the helmet but there was no missing his big smile. The short, muscular officer loved high-risk situations. Yet he was cautious when it came to endangering the lives of others. That was what made Bryan a great field commander.

The general gave Bryan a thumbs-up. The JC was still holding up his hand. When the red light came on, the airman stepped back, swept his hand in a clockwise circle that stopped sharply at nine o'clock—facing the hatch—and Bryan went out. Each of his LASER teammates followed in turn, without hesitation. When Jen Marinelli had jumped, Scott went to the hatch and looked out. Squinting into the wind he saw conical canopies begin to unfurl. He immediately picked out Major Bryan; because he was on point, Bryan's white canopy had a red circle in the center. Scott watched the higher chutes being tugged in different directions, the jumpers spilling air from the sides to guide them closer to Major Bryan.

The general stepped back as the airman closed the hatch. His face relaxed as the wind released it. While the Seamaster turned and headed back to Pearl, Scott made his way to the cockpit. Once the LASER Ops landed, Major Bryan would give the aircraft's radio operator a head count and a mission status report. If there were problems, Scott would call in the Chinook. Assuming everything had gone as planned, Scott would return to Pearl and go directly to Communications Shack C, a small facility located near the Chinook pad. LASER's radio operator, Army Corporal Jefferson Emens, would also be in contact with Major Bryan. General Scott would follow the team's progress from there.

Now that the hatch was closed the general opened the cockpit door. The pilot and copilot were on a slightly raised platform with the radio operator/navigator at right angles on the starboard side. Despite the age of the aircraft, all the equipment in the vertical console was state of the art. All were wearing headphones and looking at the radar screen as he waited to hear from Bryan.

Suddenly, there was a muffled bang from somewhere behind him. It was like a paper bag being popped in the distance, barely audible above the screaming engines. That one big burst was followed by two more, which were even louder. At first General Scott thought they had come from the aircraft, perhaps engine trouble. He actually hoped they had.

The radio operator was instantly alert, not because of what he heard but because of what he saw. The radar screen was full of small blips, as if a flock of birds had suddenly flown into view.

Straight up.

All had not gone as planned.

PART ONE

Water

ONE

Fuzhou, China

The heavens were rich with stars, making the sky a paradox: as brilliant as it was dark. It was a view that always reminded Dr. Christine Chan of a letter her older brother had sent to her when she went off to college. Lieutenant Commander Bruce Chan of the Republic of China People's Liberation Army Navy had been on an extended year-long mission on-board an aircraft carrier.

> At sea, we are surrounded by water we cannot drink. At night, we sit beneath a million suns that provide no light. It seems to me a very strange way to have designed a world. I hope one day you can explain to me why it is so!

As a geologist, Dr. Chan understood why the ocean was salt water and starlight did not reach the earth in significant quantities. She could explain the mechanics but she could not explain the logic.

Perhaps *"one day"* she would, as her brother had written. That is, if she survived her apprenticeship.

The young woman was crouched on the grassy edge of the oceanside cliff. In front of her, on a concrete slab, was her backpack and laptop. The computer was jacked into a six-inch satellite dish which was mounted to the slab. The screen gave her a ghostly iridescence. If there were boats close to shore they could easily mistake Chan for one of the demons her father carved for a living, with her white, twin-peaked wool hat for horns and the ends of her long tasseled scarf dancing fitfully behind her like wings.

It was well after midnight and the scientist was three hundred feet above the East China Sea. The howling winds swallowed the sounds of the unusually tranquil waters below. Tall, brittle grasses grew around her. The constant winds had bowed them permanently toward the north, which made them like many of the academics she worked with: prickly to approach but easy to leave. But leave them she would, gladly, just as soon as she finished the readings.

The scientist did not enjoy the outdoors. This was especially true here, at night, where the elements were raw and unpredictable. When she joined the Academia Beijing's Institute of Earth Sciences (IES) one year before, Dr. Chan expected to be working in an air-conditioned laboratory. She was a metamorphic geologist who had been hired to study rocks. Through them, she was supposed to ascertain the force, movement, and regularity of earthquakes of the past. But IES Deputy Director Leng believed that a scientist could not know the earth if he had hands that had not touched dirt, eyes that had not been bitten by dust, and hair that had not wrestled the winds. *"An earth scientist has to feel the earth underfoot,"* he once told her. The twenty-seven-year-old scientist did not agree. But she did not argue. Working for the IES guaranteed endless professional challenges and job security. Chan did not want to endanger that. Her parents sold handmade ceremonial masks of dancing demons to tourists in the village of Tungkang. When sales were poor they always had firewood but they didn't always have food. Happily, Chan's brother had asked a continuing education liaison officer in the navy to help her get a scholarship to the National Chinese Ocean University. Otherwise, Chan would still be in Tungkang, carving frowning, wild-eyed faces in wood and modeling them for foreigners.

Besides, even on warm and blustery nights like this, Chan had to remind herself that being employed by the IES was more than just work. It was an honor. Founded in 1928, the Academia Sinica is one of the oldest and most prominent educational and research facilities in China. Twenty-five distinct institutions are housed in three separate facilities—one in Beijing, another in the south in Kunming, and a third in the far northern city of Mishan. These institutions study all branches of science and technology, though the Institute of Earth Sciences is arguably the most significant.

Fuzhou, situated near the Ryukyu Trench, shares a transition zone with the Manila Trench. Due to the instability of the underlying Philippine sea plate, the region is one of the most geologically active on earth. Recently, the United States and China initiated a détente program called Plate Boundary Observatory–Far East. PBO–FE has access to dense instrumental coverage in and around China, but incorporates data from American instruments throughout the South Pacific. The purpose is to try and forecast earthquakes in the region to save lives. The United States was hoping to network in seismological instruments based in Taiwan to create an even larger network. Thus far, Beijing had refused; China did not recognize the status of the breakaway nationalists. But if recognition were ever to come, it would probably come through the baby steps of programs such as this. The influx of American funding allowed the IES to expand and created the position Chan held.

Chan's slender-bordering-on-bony legs were cramped. She stood and stretched as she waited for the data to appear. The bright screen attracted small, dark moths. They were the reason for the wool hat and scarf. She did not like insects. When she was growing up, termites were frequent visitors to the Chan home. They had been everywhere: in the masks, in the walls, in her bed. When she went outside there were mosquitoes day and night and gnats at sunset. She did not mind sharing the world with other species but she did mind sharing her personal space.

Chan squatted again and watched as the numbers began coming in. This remote station was part of the BACS array—Broadband Array in China for Seismology—a system of sensors sunk deep into the earth and seabed. These were attached to 24-bit digital recorders that broadcast data from beacons and buoys throughout the East China Sea and into the Pacific Ocean. Seventy-eight sensors were anchored in the seabed or utilized computerized star charts linked to automated Location Adjustment Engines to stay within specified regions on the surface. Once the information had been harvested the recorders were cleared. The main purpose of the BACS program was to pinpoint the source and parameters of earthquakes throughout the Pacific Rim, particularly offshore events.

Twice each week, Chan came to the Fuzhou dish after work—a drive of two hours—to collect the data and also to run a systems check. The water and sea air were corrosive and if any of the regional buoys was inoperative she would be able to execute diagnostics from here. The IES had insisted that each station be a dedicated system when a scientist in Beijing was found to be stealing data. In theory, enemy scientists could still pluck information from the BACS sites. But they would have to be at each dish to do it, and those facilities were password-protected and monitored by surveillance equipment. In case she were ever accosted by a spy, Chan had a cell phone as well as a wireless Internet connection. Within minutes of receiving a speed-dial alert, help would be dispatched from the local police station.

However, no one believed that would be necessary. In response to increased Chinese aerial and naval maneuvers in the region, F-16A aircraft attached to the 427th Tactical Fighter Wing in Ching Chuan Kang made twice-daily passes along this section of coastline. Offshore naval patrols were also ongoing. Chan did not fear mainland Chinese as much as she did the sea spray that soaked her when the direction of the wind changed.

She waved bugs from the screen because she was impatient and felt like attacking them, not because it did any good. They were back within moments. She looked at the data which came in the form of both numbers and waveform displays. The graphic representation consisted of red, blue, green, and yellow lines representing different strata. The scan covered an area that stretched from east of the Hawaiian islands to northeast of the Philippine Sea. The lines were straight, not a sawtooth segment in sight. In twelve months, Chan had never seen a reading so even.

Suddenly, the calm blue center line on the monitor began to jump. The wind and the bugs seemed to vanish as Chan bent closer to the laptop. She checked the reference points and used them to bring up an inset map. The fluctuations were originating at the fringe of the Hawaiian Ridge where it intersected the Emperor Seamounts—a string of underwater volcanoes that parallels the western coast of North America. Chan waited to see which way the underwater shock wave moved: toward the South Pacific islands or to the nearer North American continent. The direction would be indicated by a spike up or down, respectively, along the blue line. Earthquakes tended to roll one way or the other, not both.

Much to Chan's surprise, the wave moved in two directions, southwest and northeast. Moreover, the blue line quieted after just seventeen seconds. Temblors in this region usually lasted twice as long. That meant something underwater had given way, stopping the tectonic movement cold like a stubborn carrot in a blender. Perhaps a landslide resulting from the collapse of a shelf.

Almost at once the yellow line began to move. That meant there was unusual movement in the ocean's middle geostrophic currents, the currents tied to the earth's rotation. These sweeping, powerful currents controlled over 50 percent of the water volume of the Pacific Ocean. It was probably a rush of seawater and detritus into the earthquake zone that had caused the plates to lock up. Most likely a downward flood of water into a fissure at the subduction zone. If that were true, this brief earthquake could have catastrophic ramifications.

At almost the same moment, the red line at the bottom of the graph began to dance, mostly toward the bottom. Those signals were coming from rift zones beneath the surface of the ocean. The young scientist leaned closer to read the bottommost extension of the spikes. They were coming from eleven kilometers below the sea's basaltic layer. That would put it in the Mohorovicic discontinuity, the boundary between earth's relatively thin crust and its thick mantle. It was in this region that a great deal of the Pacific region's volcanic activity originated.

A major geological event was taking place, one that would affect hundreds of thousands of people.

Though it was late, Chan put in a call to Dr. Leng. He would want to go to the IES and watch for the aftershocks of this event. It was probably *too* late, she thought as she speeddialed his home phone number. The disturbance would be registered at seismology monitoring stations in other nations, but that was not going to help the impact zone. Nothing could.

TWO

San Diego, California

Two years ago, in a commencement speech he gave at the United States Naval Academy in Annapolis, Rear Admiral Edward Redmond Parks remarked, "Early human history was not just carved in stone. It was also written on water by those who refused to accept the limitations of the land."

From the earliest days of civilization, when Polynesian seamen reached Easter Island on rafts and Vikings sailed long ships to North America, man's progress has been dependent on, and proportionate to, his mastery of the seas. Nowhere was that more evident than in the area around modern-day San Diego, where Parks served as commanding officer of Naval Base Coronado. Though the region's first settlers came from Asia across the Bering land bridge twenty thousand years ago, their conquerors came by sea from Mexico, Spain, England, and even Russia. The ocean was the only access to land that was bordered on the east by murderous deserts and expansive mountain ranges.

Beginning in the middle sixteenth century, seagoing explorers and soldiers sailed small caravels into the great natural harbor. They brought more than the search for a new home or new business opportunities. They carried gunpowder and disease, new foods and farming methods, and

Franciscan faith to give the natives salvation and give the adventurers hope when supplies were scarce.

In 1774, larger galleons began bringing the first colonists and livestock. The settlers themselves brought new wars, different faiths, and the training to create fresh science for familiar necessities. All of it came in a stream of invention that continued past the doorstep of the twenty-first century.

"Yet as Joseph Conrad once wrote, the sea has never been a friend to man, only an accomplice to his restlessness," Parks said at the end of his commencement address. "Never lose your love for the sea or your passion for sailing. But never lose respect for them either."

If Rear Admiral Parks were to give that same address today, he would have additional words to say about history. And if he were to give that same address tomorrow, he would have more to say about respecting the sea. A great deal more. That was not something he could have imagined, sitting in his office at Naval Base Coronado, the largest aerospace-industrial complex in the United States Navy. The fifty-seven thousand acre facility consists of Naval Air Station North Island and Naval Amphibious Base Coronado. NAS North Island also operates Naval Auxiliary Landing Facility San Clemente Island and Outlying Field Imperial Beach. Since its inception in 1917, the naval command has been one of the largest employers in San Diego County and its outlying areas.

Fifty-one-year-old Rear Admiral Parks remembered the early 1960s, when the Naval Air Station was half its present size. When anyone with a means of transportation could go to the long, inviting beach. When San Diego itself was so small and centralized he could stand on the steeply sloping roof of his home on Ivy Street, near the northern end of Balboa Park, and look for miles in every direction without seeing a tall building, a construction crane, or gridlock. Back then the city was known primarily for the naval station, its zoo—and as a jumping-off point to Tijuana, which was twenty minutes down the freeway.

Parks had watched San Diego grow from a pleasant, lolling town of 570,000 to a vibrant city of more than 1.2 million people, the second largest in California. Part of that growth had been the continual expansion of the naval facility, which brought more and more infrastructure to support the young families. Part had been an exodus of firms from the high-rent, traffic-congested Los Angeles area. And part had been the explosive growth of agriculture in general and wineries in particular. Pharmaceutical research was also a huge growth area. Parks had a thousand-dollar bet with Captain Mel Penn of Naval Station Long Beach that San Diego would overtake Los Angeles in both population and as an economic power by 2010.

Parks was calm as he sat at his desk, awaiting a rerouted webcam signal from the aircraft carrier USS *Edward Hidalgo*. That would come in less than five minutes, at stage 1001 of the objective scenario. This was an important morning for the military, for the nation, but he had lived through many important days. There was never an experiment that went as planned, a test that went exactly as you hoped. But even failures taught us things and the next try was always better.

Parks looked out at the harbor. He was proud of his town. He was there when it made its first sounds like a man, and here it was vital and strong and holding its own among the great cities of the nation. And then there was the sea. When he was a young boy the Pacific Ocean was only "a beach." He did not conceive that the ocean went beyond the horizon and around the globe and down much deeper than his father could stand.

The rear admiral's office was located seaside, in the heart of the complex that housed COMNAVAIRPAC—Command, Naval Air Force, U.S. Pacific Fleet. There were three large windows that took sunlight from morning until late afternoon. Though it became savagely hot during the summer, he never dropped the blinds, and preferred to open the windows and cool the office with sea breezes rather than air conditioning.

That was the only option his beloved Uncle Dick had serving on a PT boat during World War II. If it was good enough for Petty Officer Second Class Richard Breen, it was good enough for Eddie Parks.

Besides, Parks had a dazzling view of the bulk of the fleet, which was harbored on the inland side of the island, as well as the city beyond. He refused to shut the blinds on that. As a fine midmorning mist beginning to lift from the harbor, the gunmetal hulls offered a virile counterpoint to the delicate flakes of light that bobbed across the harbor and the white and sand-colored hues of the buildings beyond.

The San Diego boom was especially apparent along the waterfront, an area that used to be crowded with run-down boathouses and sheds, crumbling docks, and unsavory bars. It was dominated now by high-rise hotels and condominiums, arts centers, office buildings, and the imposing harborside convention center. There was constant activity above, below, and around these structures—an endless flow of air traffic coming into San Diego's Lindbergh Field; yachts and pleasure boats in the bay; and automobile, trolley, and pedestrian traffic along Harbor Boulevard and the Pacific Coast Highway. Almost directly across from his office was a center of the tourist trade, the magnificent *Star of India*, a three-masted vessel built in 1863 and the oldest seaworthy iron vessel in the world. It was now a maritime museum. Like the navy, San Diego respected its heritage. But the eyes of both were also fixed on the future.

The sun had arced well above the Coastal Range that ringed San Diego County to the east. The ivory walls of Parks's office had a healthy, glossy glow. His collection of vintage U.S. warship lithographs were hung in the shadows, away from the direct sunlight. The vessels were dimly seen and seemed to move in the dark. Below them, on the low bookcases, were gleaming models of aircraft that represented the navy's long-standing commitment to air power. Many of these models had been tested in wind tunnels before full-size versions were constructed.

The centerpiece of Parks's collection was an original model of the *Spirit of St. Louis*. Both the model and the plane itself were built by Ryan Airlines in San Diego. Charles Lindbergh's historic May 1927 journey actually originated on North Island, not far from where Parks was sitting. After several test flights over Mission Bay—flights which had been witnessed by Parks's grandfather Sullivan—the aviator flew the plane east to undertake the New York to Paris crossing.

It was a very different time, Parks reflected. His brown eyes narrowed in the bright sunlight. The gentle wind coming through the windows stirred his short salt-and-pepper hair and caused the short sleeves of his white shirt to flutter slightly. Not quite eighty years ago, all it took was a can-do pilot and a band of resourceful, mostly self-taught engineers to make aviation history. Now it took hundreds of specialists and tens of millions of dollars. *And with all our experience, the odds of success are no greater today than they were in 1927.*

Parks looked at his watch. It was 9:58 and change. The rear admiral left-clicked the computer mouse to minimize his screensaver, a montage of family photographs his great-nephew had made. Parks logged on to the secure webcam link that would show him what was happening above the target area in White Sands, New Mexico. He two-finger-typed his password, then waited for the system to load.

A different time? he thought. When he was ten years old, he was copying artwork from comic books like *Sgt. Fury and his Howling Commandos* and *Star Spangled War Stories.* Even if personal computers had been in existence, Parks wouldn't have been designing and executing computer software. The captain wondered if it was good or bad that everyone was becoming a specialist and every tool was becoming so specialized. In Lindbergh's day, when something broke down it could be fixed with wire coat hangers and chewing gum. In the air, if necessary. Parks once met a World War I fighter pilot who had lost his landing gear while he was in the air. Another plane had to fly close with replacement tires, which had to be put on in-flight. Now, the only thing done entirely by hand was building sand castles and other structures on the beach at the other side of the island.

A distant, muffled rumble shook the office slightly. Parks looked up from the computer. The lithographs rattled on their hooks and the models wiggled on their stands as though they were revving for takeoff. Parks assumed that it was an S3B Viking taxiing on nearby runway Alpha 7. The jets were part of the increased antiterrorist surveillance conducted by Sea Control Squadron 29. They were equipped to detect and strike surface and underwater vessels.

Parks glanced out the window. The S3Bs were powerful aircraft. But even the 9,275 pounds of thrust generated by each of the two TF-34-GE-400B turbofan engines would not cause the rising noise he was hearing.

Or the sights he was seeing.

THREE

Wreck Alley, California

The USS *Edward Hidalgo* had arrived at N 32°46.174', W 117°16.140' three hours before first light. Darkness was an absolute necessity for what the science team was undertaking. Nighttime conditions were not a requirement of the experiment itself but rather the security surrounding it. The GAP, as the project was code-named, was going to change the dynamics of national security. The U.S. government wanted to make sure that this final test was completed before the existence of the GAP was announced to the world.

The entire program, including the final air-to-air live fire test, was the responsibility of forty-six-year-old Captain Bob Flynn. It had been the proudest, toughest assignment in Flynn's quarter-century with the navy. The captain would miss the GAP terribly when his role was completed, yet he couldn't wait for that to happen. It would be sweet to have a life again.

Flynn was Chief Scientist, DoNDEM/VAL-D—Department of Navy Demonstration and Validation Division. The GAP had been Flynn's baby for six years, begun as an idea conceived by the man who was standing beside him on deck, Lieutenant Commander William Van Hart. The thirty-nine-year-old aeronautical engineer was the head of New Avionics

at the Basic Research Division at Naval Base Coronodo. The
GAP had recently finished extensive and comprehensive
tests at the inland Naval Warfare Assessment Division facility, under the supervision of test pilot-turned-scientist
Dr. Hank Hathaway. NWAD was a top-secret facility that
had once been a prison, and before that a resort—which
was how Hart had described the project itself. Equal parts
gleaming delight and miserable drudgery. It had been
launched as part of the new United States Aeronautics Initiative, funded by a huge military budget bump that came
with the establishment of the Department of Homeland Security. By this time tomorrow Flynn, Hart, and Hathaway—who
was back in Coronado—hoped that the GAP would have
proved itself as viable as it was innovative. Additional testing
and the creation of final production designs would be shifted
to the DoNOD-D—Department of Navy Operational Deployment Division. There it would become the project of Commander Arthur Callahan. Flynn liked the commander and
knew he could handle all the attendant pressures and joys.

Before that could happen, however, the GAP had to match
at least 95 percent of its objective scenario, as the navy
called it. There were 1,963 separate components in the field
test, some of them hardware and software functions, some
of them mission goals. If more than 5 percent of those elements failed, the test had to be redone and possibly recon-
ceived. Though the toughest parts lay ahead, Flynn was
optimistic. In the nearly five hours since H-hour they had hit
99 percent of 988 functions.

The broad-shouldered naval officer stood on the bridge of
the Nimitz class carrier. With him were Hart and the *Hidalgo*'s commanding officer, Captain Carolina Burdo. The
forty-two-year-old commander was standing between the
two men. She was almost a head shorter, but her sun-darkened
skin and dramatically dark eyes made her seem larger than
the two relatively pale six-footers. The three officers were
watching a computer monitor as the rest of the bridge crew
saw to the operation of the flattop.

This morning, Burdo was doubling as Officer of the Deck, a function normally performed by an officer of her designation. She had told Flynn before departure that since there were guests on her bridge, and as they were conducting a top-secret operation, she wanted to make sure they had everything they needed.

"And also that you don't touch anything you aren't supposed to," she added with a wink.

Ten other people were tucked into the small, horseshoe-shaped command center. The senior helmsman, who was responsible for steering the ship; the junior helmsman, who did the actual steering; the lee helmsman, who interfaced with the engine room; two lookouts; the boatswain's mate of the watch, who supervised the bridge crew while the commander ran the ship; and the quartermaster of the watch, who was seated directly behind them at the navigation and communications deck with the chief engineer, the radio operator, and two aides. They faced forward, their heads above the consoles, reporting on changes in temperature, barometer readings, and sea conditions. The command center was soundproofed so that even with jets taking off or missiles being fired, everyone would be able to hear everyone else.

The captain's computer monitor was mounted to the command console on a swivel arm, which could be adjusted depending upon the position of the sun. The objective scenario counter was at 999 and holding at 99 percent efficiency. In just a few seconds it would begin relaying real-time images from the field. Beside it was the freestanding GAP-Link. Hart was at the controls. The silver-white console was the size and shape of a speaker's podium. There were two computer keyboards on top, one atop the other like a pipe organ, with a monitor above them. The GAP-Link was bolted to the floor of the bridge and jacked directly into the *Hidalgo*'s electronics, through an array of cables that hung from the stand and sprouted from the base. Hart and his team had been making changes to the program and wiring all week. If everything worked the way it was supposed to today, someone was going to have to deconstruct the damn thing and figure out *why* it all worked. It was a problem that Flynn, Hart, and the team back at Coronado hoped they had to face.

Flynn looked across the sunlit waters to the west. The windows of the bridge were tinted to block glare and ultraviolet rays. It gave the sky and sea a slightly pale, even unhealthy look. Yet it still looked alive, the sparkles of sun resembling thousands of luminous sea creatures. The night before, when they were having dinner in San Diego's Gaslamp District, Rear Admiral Eddie Parks had told Flynn that he never tired of gazing at the sea. Parks said that even though the Pacific Ocean was always the same—regal—it never looked the same.

"She's like an empress with an endless array of robes and countless subjects," Parks had told him.

Parks had a reputation for being something of a historian of the sea. Flynn did not have that level of passion, or Parks's poetic bent. He was interested in fancy hunks of sailing and flying machinery. Still, Flynn was rarely at sea and he wanted to seal this moment in his memory. The captain had been on board the 4.5-acre flight deck before sunup. Though he couldn't see the ocean he had enjoyed the salty sea air. Now the sea breeze was gone, replaced by the slightly metallic taste of machine-cooled air. Instead of a seductive whisper there was the drone of the ventilator. But the view from the bridge tower, seventeen stories above the surface of the Pacific Ocean, was humbling. There was nothing but smooth, blue-green water to the horizon with only a Venezuelan tanker, the *Miranda*, crawling across it. DEM/VAL aerial reconnaissance had made certain that the tanker was the only ship in the region, and she had been advised to come no closer than fifteen nautical miles to the *Hidalgo*. The marinas along twenty-seven miles of coastline had also been told to avoid the region for the day. Wrecks Alley was a popular diving spot because of the numerous ships that had gone down here over the centuries, due to accidents or during squalls. There was also an extensive artificial reef system designed to grow the fish population, made of shattered concrete slabs and pillars from coastal construction sites as well as the remains of an old bridge that had once straddled part of Mission Bay.

It was a perfect moment of serenity.

And a brief one.

"Mr. Bundy, get me a sounding," the captain said.

"Yes, sir," the quartermaster replied as his console beeped.

"What's wrong?" Flynn asked her. He looked at his watch. They had twenty-two minutes to go until things started to pop.

"I don't know," she said. "We feel a little thin."

"Thin?"

Before Burdo could explain, the QoW said, "Commander, we have a red communication from NaPOM/SAD."

NaPOM was Naval Pacific Oceanography and Meteorology Center. SAD was the Seismology Analysis Desk.

Captain Burdo picked up a red phone, the nearest of three on the communications console to her right. The white phone was farthest from her, for nonsecure transmissions. The center blue line was for secure transmissions. The red phone was for emergency communications.

"This is Captain Burdo."

Flynn and Hart exchanged quick looks. They watched the commander for a hint about what might be going on. Her expression was impassive. That didn't mean anything.

A commander was supposed to be calm in an emergency. Flynn was not. Some people felt anxiety in the belly, some behind the eyes. For Flynn, it was the back of his neck. The flesh there grew warm, then hot, as Flynn considered reasons NaPOM would call. The earthquake-watchers did not know anything about the White Sands test, so he could think of only two reasons they would be contacting the *Hidalgo*. First, a seismic event had struck Coronado and would impact either communications or their return to port. Flynn could live with that. Second, that an underwater disturbance of some kind might impact on their own presence in this area. If that were to happen within the next five hours it would not be so good.

It bothered Flynn that his first thoughts were not about people in whatever the danger zone might be. They were about the safety and security of the project. There was a name for that: the Ahab complex, when the whale mattered more than the crew. Flynn had once gone to a lecture about it on base. The speaker, Dr. Mike Fuggett, cautioned officers to maintain perspective and objectivity at all times. Becoming obsessed with a mission could turn a measured, long-term victory into a Pyrrhic victory or even a loss. Someone in the audience said that shellbacks should be exempted because they were all naval officers. Flynn thought that was funny at the time.

Captain Burdo continued to listen. As she did, she looked out at the horizon, toward the tanker. Her expression was still neutral. Flynn wondered if she suffered from the Ahab complex. If this test were aborted, it would be months before they could reset and reschedule everything. What if tens of thousands of people perished in a terrorist attack because the GAP were delayed? It could happen. But there were nearly six thousand sea and air crew on board the *Hidalgo*. Was it fair to risk their lives for a what if? If there were some kind of crisis, nothing in Flynn's experience could compare with what Captain Burdo might have to decide.

After nearly a minute, the commander hung up the phone. "Mr. Thurston?" she said to the boatswain's mate.

"Captain?"

"All quarters, storm prep alpha-one."

"Storm prep alpha-one, sir," Thurston repeated.

Flynn and Hart swapped looks again but they did not ask questions. The captain would brief them when she could. Flynn knew this much. In naval parlance, "alpha" meant "expedited action." And "alpha-one" was more urgent than that. It meant "do what you can before the bottom falls out." At

sea, the usual alpha trigger was a storm. But this was probably not a weather situation. The call had come from SAD,
and Captain Burdo had not consulted her quartermaster,
whose station had all the sophisticated meteorological
equipment. Flynn also doubted that they were needed for a
rescue mission. An all-quarters alert meant the crew had to
secure or relocate on-deck equipment before moving to duty
sections below. At the same time the bridge had to decide
whether to try and outrun whatever this was or to muscle
through it. Retreat to safe haven was preferable.

"Captain, sounding reports four percent decrease in ERH,"
Bundy reported. ERH was the elevation of a ship relative to
horizon. Typically, that meant a vessel was sinking.

The captain turned to the lee helmsman. "Mr. Glimcher,
full-about and top-speed return to port."

"Full-about, top-speed homebound," the helmsman repeated.

A klaxon sounded, a warning to the crew that the ship
would be making a sharp course alteration. Crane and winch
operators would need to take the maneuver into account
when attempting to secure loads or lines.

Finally, Captain Burdo turned to her guests.

"Gentlemen. Coronado SOSUS reports that a magnitude
eight-point-two earthquake occurred today at 09:17 hours
along the Emperor Seamounts."

"Eight-point-two?" Hart said.

SOSUS was the navy's Sound Surveillance System, an
array of underwater hydrophones that detected seismic activity. These acoustic devices were over thirty years old.
They were not as sophisticated as the broadband detectors
being used by most seismic institutions.

"What about the shock wave?" Flynn asked.

"The Thetis-7 weather satellite reports that an oceanic
anomaly is moving toward our position from the southwest,"
the captain went on. "The object is traveling at near SS." Her
matter-of-fact tone made the observation more chilling.

"You're saying a wave is headed toward us at close to supersonic speed?" Hart said.

"It was clocked at mach .93," Burdo told him. "It's still four hundred miles away but Coronado reports a five percent drop in the coastal sea level, apparently caused by a backwash situation. That's what I was picking up on when I asked for a sounding. Our buoyancy just didn't feel right. The rock-docs don't know if that's as low as the sea is going to go, but we've got a very uneven sea floor beneath us. Lots of room for sudden swells and dips. I suggest you initiate an abort countdown in the event we lose contact with the—"

The captain stopped, head cocked as if she heard something. A moment later the ship dipped; to Flynn it felt like a scaffold sagging. And it sounded like a sackful of marbles being shaken faster and faster. The edgy roar quickly overtook the sound of the ventilator and the distant hum of the carrier's steam turbines. Very soon it matched the volume of the alarm. The bridge crew had to shout to be heard. The three officers looked back toward the horizon.

The carrier was already executing its thirty-three-knot turn to the northeast when the horizon suddenly rose.

"Captain!" shouted the helmsman. "The bow is four degrees off-horizontal—five, six, rising steady!"

"Half-speed," the captain barked.

The helmsman slowed the ship. He continued studying the global positioning screen to his left. The device created a real-time chicken-wire graphic representation of the vessel as well as the sea and the horizon.

"Mr. Hart, bring her down in the target zone," Flynn said.

"Yes, sir."

Lieutenant Commander Hart stood with one leg extended to brace himself against the sloping bridge. The command screen automatically froze after five minutes, locking the user out. Hart's fingers trembled as he typed in his password. The lieutenant commander was not the coolest operator in the navy. That was not the reason he had been seconded to the GAP. He was a brilliant engineer, one who knew what was at stake. Especially if they lost control of the GAP.

Hart input his code and the screen became active once again. The menu required a second password before Hart would be allowed to "enter the GAP," as they called it. Of necessity, the program was written so that an abort command could not be entered easily. Hacking into the uplink would not work, since the GAP was designed to request secret information stored in its onboard data bank before it would change its programmed responses. That program was dedicated and locked and could not be read from the ground. The information was in the heads of Hart and Flynn. If anything happened to them, the only way to get it was for authorized personnel to access either this GAP-Link unit or the backup at the lab. Once the trial was completed, Flynn intended to lock in this data and send the backup computer to the Pentagon for safekeeping.

"Nine degrees off-horizontal," the quartermaster said.

"ARDaRS online," the captain said.

ARDaRS was the Automatic Roll Dampening Rudder System. The computer control compensated for ship instability faster than the helmsman and his team could manage. Flynn knew the command put extra strain on the rudders, but the ship had to be steadied.

"ARDaRS engaged, continuing to roll," the helmsman informed her. "Eleven degree tilt."

Movement was ever-present onboard a ship and Captain Flynn had gotten used to it quickly. He'd spent a lot of time running in the waterline along the beach, where shifting sands coupled with undertow had refined his sense of equilibrium. But this degree of tilt was not only disorienting, it was also close to the limit the ship could tolerate. He was glad they had bolted the GAP-Link to the floor.

"Twelve degrees—thirteen."

"Send inversion alert, copy to base," Burdo said. There was finally a trace of tension in her voice, but there was also steel in her eyes. The captain sat in her command chair so she wouldn't fall.

The klaxon went from a liquid *wah-wah* to staccato bursts that came in sets of three. Suddenly, the GAP-Link computer screen went black.

"I lost the uplink!" Hart shouted. "What happened?"

Flynn looked at the monitor. The power light was still on so it was not an electrical failure.

"Sir, the dish couldn't compensate for the tilt," Chief Engineer Lieutenant Stribling said from the NAV-COMM. "Correcting now."

"Quickly, please," Hart said under his breath. It was more of a prayer than a request.

Flynn put a reassuring hand on Hart's shoulder as the scientist held the sides of the GAP-Link to steady himself. Though the sea continued to move, the ARDaRS was doing its job. The carrier had stabilized at roughly fourteen degrees to starboard as it continued its turn.

Flynn looked out at the sea. The horizon was also locked at an angle in an opposite direction from the slope of the *Hidalgo,* creating a wide inverted V with the bridge. The ocean was clearly flowing away from them though the breakers continued to roll toward them. The captain felt both pride and fear that their experiment was still out there, presently under no control but its internal guidance system.

A bell sounded on the bridge. It reminded Flynn of a fire alarm. It was a proximity warning from sensors in the keel.

"Mr. Bundy, what have we got beneath us?" Captain Burdo asked the multitasking quartermaster.

"Sonar shows the aft screws closing on a solid mass portside—thirty feet below us and stationary," the quartermaster replied. "It's oblong—looks like it might be one of the artificial reefs."

"Full stop on turn, full ahead!" the captain said.

The carrier was not equipped for speed or sudden stops. But its clockwise motion was carrying the vessel toward something that could damage it. The captain had to do anything she could to try and minimize the impact.

"Mr. Hart, uplink restored!" Stribling said.

"Thank the sweet Lord," Hart muttered as he began typing.

"As soon as I'm finished praying to him, I will do that," Captain Burdo remarked.

The commander smiled and so did Flynn. It was a brief but comforting moment for them both. Hart was too busy watching the monitor to respond. A moment later the GAP-Link started talking to the target again. The lieutenant commander re-entered his codes and waited. Flynn felt a little better than he had a few moments ago. They did not want this test getting away from them.

The alarms were coordinated so that there was no overlap, but there was also no respite. A seasoned ear would be required to make sense of it all. Yet despite the clamor there was a disturbing stillness on the bridge. Hart, Burdo, and her crew were applying a great deal of thought, activity, focus—and prayer—into seconds that seemed to last much longer.

"Captain, we're receiving an SOS from the *Miranda*," Bundy said. "She's going over."

Flynn shot a look toward the horizon. The captain grabbed her binoculars from a clasp to her left. In their excitement they had forgotten about the tanker. The vessel was a sleek gray expanse silhouetted against the blue sky. It looked like a freeze-frame of a surfboard that had just bucked its rider.

"Response, sir?" Bundy pressed.

"Tell them we cannot release our rigids at this time," Burdo replied. "Copy base. The Coast Guard will have to handle this."

"Yes, sir."

That was a tough call. The "rigids" were rigid hull inflatable boats, were used for rescue and reconnaissance. In an emergency, the boats were also used for evacuation. By declining to send them—because release was problematic or she wanted to hold them in reserve—Burdo might have been condemning the tanker crewmen to death.

"Captain, we're closing on the underwater object—we're not going to clear!" the quartermaster informed her. "Six seconds to impact."

"Sound impact warning!"

A moment later all the bells, beeps, and horns were superceded by silence. Then a siren, reminiscent of an old air raid alert, filled the ship. This one was loud and caused Flynn to wince.

The huge vessel was still pinwheeling through its turn, albeit slower than before.

The captain gripped the padded vinyl armrests of her command chair and sat back. Flynn stood by the side of the GAP-Link, at right angles to Hart. Both men held the platform at the top of the stand. The lieutenant commander seemed oblivious to everything else as he waited for access to the GAP program again.

The first code was accepted. Hart immediately typed the second.

An instant later everyone was whipped to starboard as the carrier struck the submerged object port-side aft. The *Hidalgo* slowed but did not stop. Flynn heard the sound of grinding metal as the rudder mechanism tried and failed to keep the vessel from listing further. After a moment the carrier tilted another ten degrees to starboard in one jarring move. Flynn was thrown hard against the stand but he didn't fall over. He grabbed Hart to keep him from being tossed against the helm.

"I'm offline again!" Hart shouted as he struggled back to his station. This time he was visibly agitated.

Stribling did not offer an explanation. The young man was too busy trying to keep the ship's onboard functions from failing.

"I need help!" Hart yelled.

The lieutenant commander was staring at the monitor as though he were trying to will it on. His mouth was taut and his eyes were bordering on wild as he drummed the sides of the keyboard. There was nothing Flynn could say or do to help the scientist. The situation with the GAP was *that* critical.

"Emergency stop, status report all stations," the captain said.

An emergency stop was different than a stepped shutdown; it was like turning off a computer by pulling the plug instead of letting it exit all functions. Both electronic and mechanical systems could be damaged. Since the *Hidalgo*'s mechanical systems already were being damaged, the captain had made the correct call.

There was an OR—Order of Response—for an allstations update. The helmsman was the first to report, since structural integrity and mobility were his responsibility. As the bow of the carrier fell silent, he told the captain that the engines had been shut down. Sounding audibly relieved, Glimcher also informed the captain that a hull scan revealed no breaches. That being the case, they should all be safe if there were no further tilt. Flynn knew that aircraft carriers were designed to withstand and right themselves after a knock of one-third off the vertical. If the ocean settled for a while and there were no significant damage to the engine, the *Hidalgo* might be able to move off the submerged object.

The other stations reported functions normal, save for communications. Bundy said that all uplinks had been severed pending realignment of the carrier's two primary and two backup satellite dishes.

"We need to talk to our device," Hart said urgently.

"We also need to stabilize our position and get out of Wreck Alley," the captain said impatiently. "Mr. Stribling, what is the situation with our uplinks?"

"They're all down and we're showing possible gear jams," he said. "I'm checking on it."

"Christ," Hart said.

"I want to talk to Rear Admiral Parks as soon as you get any of them running," Burdo said.

"Yes, sir," Stribling replied.

"Captain, I don't think you understand!" Hart protested. "We're going to need every second we can get with the uplink, if not to regain control of the experiment then to turn it over to—"

"I understand, Mr. Hart!" Burdo snapped. "Now you hear me. I need the rest of the carrier group out here so we aren't stuck on the reef when the ocean comes back. If it does, we're going to lose more than your experiment!"

Hart turned to Flynn. "Captain, what do we do?"

"We wait," Flynn replied. "As soon as we can we'll contact the lab and have them take over operations." He was speaking with a level of confidence he no longer felt. Because of the secrecy of the project there had been very few options to begin with. This situation, completely unplanned-for, had left them with none.

"Captain Flynn, won't your onshore team take charge?" Burdo asked.

"They can't," Flynn replied.

"Why not?"

"We would have to cede control by code fed directly to the onboard computer. If the device doesn't hear from us for sixty minutes, it will talk to them. But not until then." Flynn looked back at the dead black monitor. That would be forty minutes too late.

"I see. I'm sorry," Burdo said.

Hopefully, base command would alert all facilities in the region to button up.

Hopefully, nothing would happen to the second computer.

There was a sudden clang, then a twisting sound on the starboard side, like a fat cable being turned too tight. Everyone looked in that direction, the captain half-rising from her chair. There was nothing but sea below them.

There was a low *beep*. The helmsman grabbed headphones from a hook and pressed one to his ear.

"What've we got, Mr. Glimcher?" the captain demanded as she sat back down.

"It's a loose bird," he said. "One of the Prowlers."

"Where?"

"In the elevator," he told her.

"Injuries?"

"None," the helmsman said. "They hadn't finished stowing her on the hangar deck—deck command is reporting that the elevator has been compromised. The cables may have broken."

The captain braced herself on the chair and rose again. She looked starboard, craning to see aft of the bridge. "I don't want heroes. Get the people clear—"

There was a louder, much deeper-sounding clang. This time the ship vibrated like a tuning fork.

"Elevator number two has come loose!" Glimcher said. He was practically yelling as he put both headphones over his ears and pressed them to his head, squinting as he listened. Flynn couldn't tell whether the helmsman was struggling to hear or whether it was an expression of pain. Perhaps both. "The platform is dangling," he went on. "We have two men overboard."

"Tell Lieutenant Commander Roche to get his personnel out of there!" the captain ordered.

There was a second heavy clang. It was followed by sharp snapping and grinding sounds.

"We've got multiple situations of aircraft instability!" Glimcher said. "Cables are giving way in the hangar and the planes are piling up starboard."

They heard the crashes as dull thuds below deck. The carrier rattled with each strike.

"Clear that level *now*," Burdo ordered, "and have evac leaders prepare their teams for—"

The carrier shuddered violently and the captain was tossed forward. She hit the command console, then was thrown to the right as the carrier went over. The weight of the planes piling against the starboard side had destabilized the *Hidalgo* beyond the ability of the rudders to control it. Flynn was thrown over the GAP-Link and Hart dropped on his back as the command center was upended. Flynn hit the ribbed rubber floor and slid against crewmembers who had fallen before him. The lights died, along with the hum of the ventilator and the beeps of the equipment. The only sounds Flynn heard were the shouts of the men and the awful, throaty rending of metal as the aircraft carrier rolled onto its side.

FOUR

San Diego, California

Rear Admiral Parks called NaPOM/SAD the moment he saw the sea level begin to drop. The Director of Emergency Response, Lieutenant Frederick Lynch, told him there had been a major deep sea event with an anomaly racing toward the Southern California coast.

"You mean a wave?" Parks asked.

"Sir, I mean we're looking at a wall of water like the one that hit Indonesia. It could be anywhere from ten to one hundred feet high," Lynch told him. "We're trying to get an accurate satellite read. We've got layers of obscuring clouds right now."

"Time of impact?"

"At nearly four million feet per hour we're looking at landfall in about fifty minutes."

"Landfall where?" Parks asked. He felt very sick deep in his gut.

"Preliminary projection has the strike zone reaching from Ensenada, Mexico, to Imperial Beach," Lynch told him.

That was an eighty-mile stretch of coastline stopping just short of San Diego. The naval base was sure to take some of that. As he spoke with Lynch, he sent an e-mail alert to base officers to transfer as many Pacific Fleet functions as possible to facilities north of Coronado.

This can't be happening, Parks thought. He felt as if he'd suddenly slipped into a dream, one in which his brain was screaming for him to *do* something, yet he was moving in slow motion. Parks couldn't evacuate the entire base in time, nor could he afford to have thousands of personnel pouring into the streets of San Diego. There would be panic enough in the city when word spread of the oncoming wave.

"Does *Hidalgo* have the alert?" Park asked.

"We are giving it to her now," Lynch informed him.

Parks thanked him and hung up. The rear admiral had two orderlies. His aide for routine base duties was Lieutenant Michael Ragusa. The twenty-eight-year-old was in a small room adjacent to the rear admiral's office. Parks's assistant for the GAP was Dan Goddard. The twenty-nine-year-old security technician was located in Building B, Administrative Services. The GAP laboratories were located in a secure underground research center at the rear of the building. If Parks needed on-site eyes and ears, Goddard could be down there in eighty-nine seconds. They'd timed it.

Goddard called to inform Parks that they had lost contact with the aircraft carrier.

"What's the radar tell you?" Parks asked.

"She's still out there. We're just getting zero telemetry."

"Stay on it. If you reach them, tell them we're putting the CG on alert, rescue prime hold," the captain told him.

Since the *Hidalgo* was not leaving U.S. territorial waters, the vessels of the carrier group were portside in stand-down status. Rescue prime would have them ready for sea in a half hour. "Hold" meant they were going to stay in port. There wasn't enough time for the carrier group to get to the flattop, let alone perform any kind of assist and rescue. The best they could do was sail immediately in the aftermath, assuming the base itself did not take too bad a hit.

As Parks asked Lieutenant Ragusa to contact carrier

group deputy command onboard the destroyer, Goddard came back on the line.

"Sir," Goddard said, "we're back in contact with the carrier—she's listing and returning to port."

"Listing how bad?"

"Thirteen degrees, sir."

"What about the GAP?"

"Lieutenant Commander Hart is sending an abort signal. He's ordering her to hibernate at the target area."

"Thank you. Put me through to Captain Burdo," Parks said.

"Yes, sir."

Parks waited. Hibernate was an emergency shutdown mode that took only a few commands to activate. That presumed, of course, that the link was stable and communication was uninterrupted.

A moment later Goddard said, "Sir—we've lost *Hidalgo* again. Also, I just received an e-flash. The Coast Guard picked up a distress call from a tanker further out—she's on an inversion course."

Parks knocked the screensaver off his computer. There was an e-mail alert from NaPOM/SAD. Parks ignored that. He knew what the message was. He clicked on the red-flagged e-mail from Vice Flotilla Commander Jackson O'Neill, 11th USCG District, San Diego:

Received at 09:43 hrs live distress signal from
Venezuelan tanker *Miranda* location N 33°22.162',
W116°11.121' reporting capsizement. Attempt to con-
firm met automated response, then silence, suggesting
major systems failure conforming to event profile. Likely
a result of major seismic shift recorded 26 minutes
prior along Emperor Seamounts. Two Seahawks dispatched at 09:45 for flyover and recovery. Vessels
in region should return to port or relocate north
beyond Carlsbad seawall at best speed to avoid ad-
verse conditions.

Parks immediately contacted Captain Howard West at NB Coronado Search and Rescue. West had just received the e-mail alerts from NaPOM/SAD and USCG. In case the base took a hit, he was busy preparing to relocate as many airborne assets as possible, as quickly as possible.

"I also got your e-mail alert about diverting Pac Fleet functions," West said. "Will there be a general evac?"

"No," Parks told him. "I want you to put as many civilian and nonessential personnel as possible onto the aircraft you're moving."

"Is that all?"

"Yes."

"With respect, sir, we may take a pretty big hit—"

"We may," Parks agreed. "But more people may die in a general panic than in tsunami backwash. If we chill, there's a chance the city will stay calm. Besides, captain, this is what sailors do. We hunker down in a blow."

"Yes, sir."

"Meanwhile, *Hidalgo* is in trouble," Parks went on. "How many Knights can you get out to her?"

Knights were the dual-rotor CH-46 D/E Sea Knight helicopters, the workhorses of the navy.

"I can field four right away."

"Do it," Parks said. "I want an assessment ASAP and extraction of loaner personnel if necessary. The carrier is out of communication so you may have to put personnel on the bridge. Tell the pilots that whatever Captain Bob Flynn needs gets priority."

"I'm on it," West told him.

Parks hung up. It hurt to do that. Crewmen might be trapped or injured. But they needed to keep control of the GAP. If the *Hidalgo* didn't have an uplink, one of the choppers might be able to provide it.

The rear admiral hung up and looked out at the sea. The ocean had gone out about twenty feet. People along Harbor Boulevard had stopped to look and in some cases to jump into the muck the receding waters left behind. Parks felt a little better about his stay-put decision; it would have been difficult for anyone to get off North Island in any case. Police in choppers and highway patrol officers had begun arriving to chase people out of the harbor bed and off the road. It was like a hurricane: despite the obvious danger, people still went to the shore to watch the big waves. Off in the distance, on the San Diego freeway, Parks could see cars starting to make a reverse commute away from the city.

Undoubtedly the media had picked up what was happening and was advising people to go north or inland.

Parks rose. He took his jacket from the hanger behind the door. If something happened here he did not want to be found in shirtsleeves. Given the magnitude of what was happening, there was still one consolation. The people he had in the field—Flynn, Burdo, the officers serving under West in the NBCSR—were well-trained. With the exception of Flynn, all had been battle-tested in the Middle East. If anyone could ride this out, it was the GAP team and its support personnel.

The phone beeped. Parks snatched it up.

It was the copilot aboard the Sea Knight on point. They had just taken off and he could already see the *Hidalgo*.

What he saw was not good.

FIVE

Wreck Alley, California

What the crew of the CH-46E saw gave the name "Wreck Alley" new meaning.

Cruising at just under two thousand feet, the CH-46E was flying west across the sea at 145 knots. It was followed by three other Sea Knights in tight two-one formation. From above they resembled a diamond, an illusion heightened by their sunbathed silver-white exteriors.

Lieutenant Justin Cobb, copilot, was on the radio with Rear Admiral Parks. To his left was Captain Spencer, the pilot. Lieutenant Gomez, the crew chief, was in the main cabin to help with whatever recovery effort was required. He would be assisted by Lieutenant Junior Grade Boranza, the crew mechanic. The two crewmen were by the cabin hatch, just a few feet past the cockpit. All four men were patched into the Sea Knight radio.

The sight of the ocean pulled back from the shore had been arresting. The dark, glistening mud of the sea floor had been visible for as far as he could see in either direction, and for twenty or thirty yards to the west. It looked like a garbage dump, with everything from traffic cones to broken furniture to small craft and water sports gear half-buried in the pudding-smooth sand and twining seaweed. Dead and dying fish were everywhere.

But the enormous aircraft carrier turned completely on its side was unlike anything Cobb had ever expected to see. The scope of it was astonishing. At first, the *Hidalgo* was just a gunmetal silhouette against the sky, smooth sides with jagged projections like a futuristic submarine from a science-fiction movie. The shallow water was lapping softly against its sides, serene and unaggressive. Only when he looked at it through his binoculars did the object look like what it was. The most unnerving thing about it was not the sight of the massive ship overturned. It was the specks scrambling across the hull like termites on a log.

"Rear Admiral Parks, there are crewmen on the port side hull of the vessel," Cobb said. "They appear to be moving toward the flight deck."

"Can you see the bridge?"

"Negative, sir," Cobb replied. "The tower decks, from the pri-fly down, are completely submerged." The pri-fly, or the primary flight control section of the tower, was situated above the bridge.

"There is something in the bridge we very much need to recover," Parks said. "I need you to get as close as you can. See if you can find Captain Bob Flynn or Lieutenant Commander William Van Hart. They'll tell you what to do. I will keep this channel open to advise you if they are unable to assist."

"Yes, sir," Cobb replied. "We're heading there now. Rear Admiral, do we know what's happening out there? In the Pacific, I mean?"

"A tsunami is rushing inland," Parks said. "It will hit the coastline south of us in about four-zero minutes. They're going to take a beating. We do not yet know what impact it will have on our immediate vicinity."

"Understood, sir," Captain Spencer said. "I'll inform the Coast Guard, have all ships moved from port or anchor."

"Thank you," Parks said. "They will remain at anchor until notified."

There was nothing else to say.

Before switching back to an internal communications channel, Spencer informed the other pilots that he would be breaking off from the group. He ordered them to recover men from the sea first, then move to the men onboard. Each Sea Knight could hold twenty-two additional passengers. Assuming the point chopper would be allowed to take on passengers, they could rescue eighty-eight people—out of a ship's company of 3,200 sailors and an air wing of nearly 2,500.

Lieutenant Cobb tried not to dwell on that as they raced toward the carrier. There were about two or three hundred crewmen on the hull. They were using ropes and torches to try and get to personnel who were trapped either in structures on deck or inside the vessel. Others were tending to sailors who had been injured. At least the vessel did not appear to be sinking any lower. Captain Spencer shot them all a mental salute as he moved from the rest of the Sea Knights. He could not afford to descend too low. Some of the crewmen would have a very precarious hold on the hull. Rotor wash could dislodge them.

"Mr. Gomez, you heard the rear admiral's orders?" the captain asked.

"I did, sir."

"I need you on the bridge of the *Hidalgo*."

"Yes, sir," Gomez replied. "Putting the wetsuit on now. Lieutenant, what is the wind speed?"

Cobb looked at the digital anemometer. "It's knocking on twenty-two knots," he replied.

"We'll do the ladder," Gomez replied.

Though it would take longer to climb down than to rappel, it would be easier for Gomez to return. That was especially true if he recovered personnel who needed to be helped up, or equipment that had to be carried.

"Captain, do we recover personnel while we're waiting for Mr. Gomez?" Boranza asked.

"If they can make it to the bridge tower, yes," Spencer told him. "We can't leave the lieutenant."

"Testing," Gomez said into the microphone of his face mask. "Able, Baker, Charlie, testing."

"We hear you," Cobb replied. He looked back through the open cockpit door and Gomez gave him an OK sign.

They were about a quarter-mile from the stricken vessel. Boranza attached the rolled aluminum ladder to the eyehooks inside, on the floor. Then he put on goggles. Even at this height, the windblown sea mist would be blinding. When Cobb gave them the go-ahead, the men opened the door and tossed the ladder out. Gomez opened a packet in his equipment belt and attached a half-inch-diameter steel safety line to the top rung of the ladder. Spencer gave him the go-ahead when they reached the target. Boranza helped his crewmate out and the lieutenant hurried down. The ladder torqued clockwise in the wind. Boranza did his best to straighten it.

Cobb studied the area with binoculars as he switched back to the rear admiral's channel. "Sir? This is Sea Knight Seven at the *Hidalgo*."

"Go ahead."

"Our man is on the way down to the bridge," Cobb said. "The bulk of the tower is underwater, and possibly under the seabed as well. I see casualties and debris in the water. Lieutenant Gomez is about twenty feet from the site—"

Suddenly, the helicopter received an emergency, all-frequencies bulletin from NaPOM/SAD.

"Attention all ships and aircraft," said the female voice. "An aftershock one hundred miles east of the original Pacific epicenter has spawned a secondary wave that is moving swiftly northeast. The tsunami will generate a pressure field that is expected to raise tides to twice their present height. It will be followed by backwash from the sea that was drawn away by the original seismic event. We expect the secondary wave to impact the coastline twenty minutes later."

Cobb switched to intercom. "That means we'll get it out here first," he said to Captain Spencer.

The pilot nodded once, gravely, as he watched the horizon.

Cobb looked down. Gomez had reached the foot of the bridge tower. He was just a few feet from the flight deck access door. The lieutenant attached a second hook to a pipe and released the line he'd attached to the Sea Knight. *Hidalgo* crewmen were crossing the sloping hull to reach the ladder. Gomez signaled "two-two" to indicate chopper capacity, then turned his attention to the bridge. The *Hidalgo* crewmen began to organize a group of those who most needed medical care.

Lieutenant Cobb wondered if they had any idea what had happened—or what was coming.

A moment later there was no question about it. Still looking down, Cobb saw something at the top of his eyes. He looked past the three Sea Knights that were buzzing nearby. Their ladders were down and *Hidalgo* crewmen were being helped onboard. Beyond, Cobb watched as the two Coast Guard Seahawks headed toward the capsized tanker. He turned the binoculars toward the Venezuelan ship. He could make out spots of yellow here and there against the darker silhouette of the tanker: the rubber escape dinghies.

As Cobb watched, the small boats began to bob straight up and down, each with its own separate rhythm. "Captain, I think something is happening out at the tanker," he said.

Spencer glanced out. "Probably outgassing from the tanker," he said. "There may be a rupture."

"Right. I don't see crude, so it must be air."

Suddenly, a huge bubble of air and oil rose from beneath the dinghies. It tossed them aside, hung on the surface of the sea for just a moment, then burst as the tanker moved through it.

On its side.

SIX

San Diego, California

"Sir," Cobb said, "the tanker is coming toward us!"

Rear Admiral Parks was standing behind his desk, leaning on his knuckles as he listened to the voice of the copilot over the speakerphone. Parks's orderly, Lieutenant Ragusa, was standing in the doorway. He had just briefed the lab and was listening in, taking notes.

"Explain," Rear Admiral Parks said.

"We saw a huge burst of oil," Lieutenant Cobb replied. His voice was excited but there was no sense of panic. "We think the *Miranda* was struck from behind and ruptured. Then a wave seemed to roll under it from the horizon and lift it up."

"What is the tanker's disposition—"

"Hold, sir!" Cobb shouted. After a brief silence he said, "Sir, the *Miranda* just came apart! She broke in two forward the stern, about where we saw the oil breach the surface. She just folded forward and now both parts are spinning like bastards. The larger part is heading toward the *Hidalgo*."

"Where is your recon man?"

"Lieutenant Gomez is underwater, about twenty-five feet down," Cobb replied.

"Did he find anything?"

"Not yet, sir. The bridge was caved in, there's a lot of debris. He was still trying to get to the command console."

"Get him out," Parks said.

"We're kind of helpless, sir," Cobb replied. "Gomez climbed away from the ladder to get inside the bridge. He's picking his way back."

"Were there other survivors?"

"There are a lot of crewmen on deck. We're trying to get as many of them onboard as quickly as possible."

"Any from the bridge?"

"So far, sir, that's a negative," Cobb replied. "They appear to be coming from the hangar and crew decks."

Parks felt his spirit crash. He did not feel the loss of his coworkers. Not yet. But he did feel the seaborne aspect of the GAP slip away.

"Keep me informed," Parks said. He looked at Ragusa. "Get the lab on the line."

"At once, sir."

The orderly went to his office as Parks waited. They had prepared for electronic breakdowns and for the loss of personnel due to illness or accident. They had even prepared for the loss of one link, though not with the unique circumstances that left them unable to transfer command to the second.

"Dr. Hathaway on three, sir," Ragusa said.

Parks told the orderly to monitor the communiqués from the Sea Knight, then switched lines. Sixty-two-year-old former test pilot Hank Hathaway was not the world's most accomplished team player, but after leaving the Air Force he became one of the most experienced aerodynamics engineers on the planet. He and Parks didn't always agree on how to do things, but Hathaway invariably deferred. As Hathaway once put it, "You don't argue with the man whose head is in the noose."

"Dr. Hathaway, have you got *any* control there?" Parks asked.

"We're talking to the Angel but it's not listening," the scientist told him. "Have you heard from Flynn or Hart?"

"No, and we may not," Parks replied with some finality. "What can we do on this end?"

"We need Hart's password," Hathaway replied. "Otherwise, it will be another thirty-six minutes before we can take control."

Parks looked at his watch. "The test starts in eleven minutes and terminates seven minutes after that," he said. "How will our bird react if there's no signal to tell it what to do next?"

"It will turn around and head for home," Hathaway said, "or at least, where home was. Before that happens, though, we should be able to recover control from here and direct it to a new landing site."

"Have you been following the NaPOM/SAD alerts?"

"Yes. My understanding is that we probably won't catch very much of the wave," Hathaway said.

"Maybe not, but we can't risk losing power," Parks said. "The emergency generators are seaside, and if the main lines go down—"

"They could be hit too," Hathaway said.

"The second wave is less than three miles from shore. It just snapped a tanker in two. We have to relocate the GAP-Link B."

"That's a bad idea," Hathaway said bluntly. "If we disconnect, there will be a window when the Angel is on its own. It will go in patrol mode."

"We'll tell potential targets stay clear of the area," Parks said. "If we lose the second GAP-Link, we'll have *no* way to talk to the Angel."

Lieutenant Ragusa leaned back into the office. "Sir, Cobb reports that the carrier's just been hit."

"Get started, Dr. Hathaway," Parks said.

"We'll pull the electronics last in case you change your mind," Hathaway replied.

"Good idea," Parks said as he switched back to the Sea Knight's line. He hoped he was wrong and that the heaviest impact was wide of the base.

"—have to pull back!" Cobb was shouting. "The spray is like a waterfall shooting up!"

"Lieutenant, what happened?" Parks asked.

"We got hit with upwash from the tanker as it approached, but we saw the wave behind it!" Cobb yelled. "It's the whole damn ocean, sir. The sea is coming back with a wave piggybacking on top of it."

"How high?"

"The wave itself was about fifty feet, stacked on fifty feet or more of returning surf."

That sounded like the smaller, secondary wave NaPOM/SAD had just reported.

"It's like we were watching from a pit!" Cobb went on. "Right now we can't see anything, sir! We don't even know if Gomez is on the ladder or not. We told the other choppers to withdraw but we're hanging on, trying to see through the shower. I've never seen anything like this."

"What's the bearing of the wave?"

"It came straight off the horizon due east!" he said. "And I'm sorry I'm yelling! It's louder than hell's cymbals out here!"

"You're doing fine," Parks assured him. "Lieutenant Ragusa will stay on the line with you."

Parks clicked off and got Hathaway back on the phone. "How long until you can get the GAP-Link out?" the rear admiral asked.

"Another fifteen minutes," Hathaway replied. "We just started—"

"You haven't got that," Parks said. "Can you send the key data somewhere?"

"That would take the same amount of time," Hathaway said. "We tried downloading to a backup disc but the DoD firewalls weren't cooperating."

All top-security projects for the Department of Defense required passwords that changed daily. For systems that were not Internet-linked, like the GAP, the passwords had to be obtained through channels. The time factor worked against them doing that as well.

"Sir!" Lieutenant Ragusa said over the telephone intercom. "NaPOM/SAD has revised its threat assessment to San Diego. The police and fire departments are relocating coastal residents inland."

"Alert all commands, get our people out," Parks said. The situation had changed. He had the right but no longer a reason to keep people here. "Tell them I want everyone on people-moving detail. Trucks and cars are to pick up civilians and help with the general evac."

"Yes, sir."

Parks got back to the speaker phone. "Dr. Hathaway? What *can* you pull from the lab?"

"I don't know!" he replied. "The civilian team saw the NaPOM update and left. I can't blame them. We had just started disconnecting the entire GAP-Link setup, electronics included. We won't have time to go through a proper system shutdown so I don't know what data may have been lost. We'll have to worry about that later."

The operative word was "worry." The GAP was designed to ignore attempts to communicate with it outside a very specific protocol. As bad as the tidal event was, that did not worry the rear admiral as much as an out-of-control GAP. The wave was a one-time event. A rogue angel could be catastrophic.

Lieutenant Ragusa leaned into the office. "Sir, we've lost contact with the Sea Knight!"

"Do we know what the problem is?"

"No, sir. I've put in a call to Port Operations—"

The phone beeped and Ragusa left to answer it. He returned a moment later, his expression severe.

"Port Ops radar reports that Sea Knight has vanished, sir."

SEVEN

Wreck Alley, California

The two sections of the destroyed tanker scudded across the ocean, tumbling in all directions. They kicked murky, oil-laced water ahead and above them and trailed two gully-like wakes, each over twenty feet deep. Metal projections and great slabs of hull plate were bent back and pulled away from the separate sections by the force of the forward thrust. Behind the shattered vessel the sea was a foaming slope, with a towering wave along the top. The sea below was moving as fast as the breaker, giving it a perpetual curl as it rushed inland.

The tanker's forward section and smaller aft piece struck the aircraft carrier in quick succession. The larger wreckage was riding bow-up when it hit the aft keel. The tanker folded over the larger flattop, causing the flight deck to invert even more and sending large, ugly chunks of debris in all side-ward and upward directions. The second piece of the tanker hit the forward section of the overturned carrier. The impact caused the bridge tower to snap at the base, allowing the carrier to turn completely over. The tanker section skidded over it, striking the forward end of the blind Sea Knight. The cockpit was severed, the rotor flopping wildly off center as the battered nose segment dropped into the sea. The aft section hung in the air for a moment, suspended by the rear rotor, before angling toward the water. Rescued seamen were dumped from the midsection as it fell, the rotor spitting spirals of water skyward before being swallowed by the sea. A moment later the ocean rolled over the carrier, finishing the inversion and then continuing toward the shore.

The water surged toward the coastline, its thick white fingers clawing ahead, its broad blue back carrying pieces of wreckage, upending the sunken vessels and detritus in Wreck Alley, and snapping chunks of the artificial reef from the exposed sea floor. The ocean drummed as it approached, echoing off the distant mountains and filling the basin with a continuous roaring echo. The ground shook for miles inland. Fists of water broke away as the ocean floor rose and ledges and hills offered more, if brief, resistance. The wave was diminished in height but not in fury as its platform eroded. Massive plumes of mud were shoved ahead as the ocean closed in. The sea cascaded over itself and the rising seabed.

The headland and promontories of the great harbor created a bottleneck for the ocean as it neared, forcing more and more water toward a smaller and smaller section of coastline. The upward spray was magnified, becoming so forceful that circling police and fire helicopters as well as the news choppers beyond were compelled to withdraw. There were no boats at sea, and those at anchor were splintered on contact. These were mostly pleasure boats, tour ferries, and a few fishing ships. The bulk of the military vessels had been relocated to the far northeastern side of North Island. Most of the aircraft, too, had taken off.

The structures of the Naval Base itself could not be moved, obviously. Seawalls and jetties surround Coronado. They took the initial hit, most of them falling as the ocean rolled over. The elevation of the island caused the wave to flatten considerably. But it was not enough. A fifteen-foot-high section of the ocean hammered the southernmost buildings, buckling steel-reinforced cinder-block walls and crushing the furniture inside, rolling the few vehicles that remained and driving them into surrounding structures. Satellite dishes were pulverized and fuel storage tanks were split. Debris carried by the sea did damage as well, bouncing here and there before burying itself in rooftops and tarmac, in newly flooded basements and sub-basements. Each impediment caused the tsunami to dissipate a little more.

The sea spread itself across fifteen hundred acres of the island. However, it did not remain. Its anger spent, the ocean flowed back and the natural sea level returned. Secondary waves calved from the tsunami came ashore along several miles stretching from the Civic Center to the airport. They damaged aircraft and coastal buildings, pulverized wharves, uprooted trees, and shattered large sections of Harbor Boulevard and the Pacific Coast Highway. Vehicles that had not been able to get away were washed away. Most of Seaside Village, a collection of shops and restaurants, was overrun and dragged into the sea. The magnificent *Star of India* was lying on its side, its three masts shattered across the parking lot beside its berth.

But the bulk of the city was spared.

In a way its founders had never anticipated, Naval Base Coronado had helped to save San Diego.

EIGHT

San Diego, California

For Rear Admiral Edward Parks, history continued to be written on water—as well as under it.

There was a Jeep outside the rear admiral's office. When the wave crossed the horizon, Parks told Lieutenant Ragusa to start it up and he would follow. Parks then opened a locked drawer in his desk and quickly began flipping through computer diskettes containing commands that would allow him to access his private files from remote sites. As he pulled the ones he would need, he called Dr. Hathaway. The scientist said he could hear the water coming and was leaving; Hathaway apologized for not having finished the work on the GAP-Link. Parks told him not to worry about it, just to get out of the laboratory. Then the rear admiral hung up and joined his orderly. In retrospect, it had seemed a silly thing to do, hanging up the phone. In just a few minutes the building might be underwater.

Save for the incoming ocean the area around the command center was eerily quiet. Even the winds were still. The wave itself was audible in the distance, like a fast-running bath. Parks and Ragusa joined the tail end of a long line of vehicles making their way from the base. Dr. Hathaway pulled up behind them. There was no impatience, no visible signs of anxiety. Just humming engines to break the stillness—the promise of mobility, of flight, of some sense of control, if not the reality of it.

There were still at least thirty vehicles in the slow-moving line when the water came ashore.

From his vantage point Parks couldn't see the wave, but he could hear and feel it. Roaring like a bank of jet engines, the water hit the island so hard the ground shifted in all directions at once, causing windows to pop, signs to topple, and trees to list. Beyond the command complex Parks saw shards of wood, brick, and metal fly over the rooftops ahead of a massive spray. The debris was not being carried by the wave itself but had been hurled skyward by the initial impact, catapulted in a high arcing trajectory. It crashed onto the rooftop of the command center. The water that followed came down in huge droplets that splatted noisily wherever it fell. The drops, too, had been driven skyward by the initial slap against the land. The rest of the wave arrived as a low, sloshing flood. It knocked over the structures on the southwestern side and carried them across the island in big, jagged chunks. Local island transports, like motorboats and golf carts, were among the wreckage that washed inland.

There was nowhere for the people in line to go, nothing for them to do but watch the flood. The water thinned as it spread in all directions. The streets created spillways that drained into the harbor; and the buildings, with their many sublevels, sucked up a lot of the raging water. By the time it reached the main gate the wave was barely six inches high. It punched and shoved the cars one into the other and caused several to spin around, but it did not overturn them.

Parks caught glimpses of faces that had been locked in shock. They were no longer frozen. In less than three minutes the only sound Parks had heard were shouts from personnel who were stuck in the base and the crackle from short-circuiting electrical outlets. A few small fires broke out in areas where equipment had sparked or power lines had fallen.

And there was the wind. The tsunami returned winds to the island, but unlike any the rear admiral had ever experienced. They were unusually cold and moving first in one direction, then another. Even this relatively small shift of the sea was strong enough to affect air currents.

Parks and Ragusa left the Jeep. They organized the remaining forty-odd drivers into search parties covering all sectors on the periphery of the water. Going any farther would require boats, life jackets, and other tools they did not possess. When the personnel had left, Parks, Ragusa, and the tall, spindly Dr. Hathaway looked for a way to get back to the southeast side of the island. They wanted to see what had happened to the laboratory. The roads were blocked with debris and the remaining structures were in danger of collapse. Finally, the three men passed the long-term vehicle storage building. Inside they found a cherry picker that belonged to Drydock Operations. Lieutenant Ragusa found the keys and drove it outside. Parks climbed into the basket and raised it, which enabled him to see across the island.

Virtually nothing was left standing. A few foundation walls poked through the water here and there; ironically, so did a few twisted fire hydrants. All the streetlights were snapped off near the base.

Parks also spotted several bodies twisting in the wind-blown current. There was no way of knowing whether they belonged to base personnel or had been washed in from the wrecked vessels.

"What do you see?" Hathaway shouted over the wind.

Parks lowered the basket. He stepped out. "Nothing good. We need to talk to Beaudine."

The men got back in the Jeep and went to one of the battleships which had been moved to the northeast side of the island. Parks asked the captain to organize an immediate search-and-rescue operation for the bridge crew of the *Hidalgo*. The captain was reluctant to recall crews that had been dispatched to the base itself but Parks told him this was a priority A-red situation, a matter of national security. That took precedence over any other activity. While the captain assembled an offshore recovery team, Parks and Hathaway were taken to his quarters. While Hathaway sat by the computer and loaded the rear admiral's CDs into the captain's computer, Parks stood beside him and used the secure phone to contact Brigadier General Beaudine. The commander at White Sands had been following the events in San Diego.

"The loss of both GAP-Links leaves us with not very many choices and only one priority," Parks said.

"The Angel," Beaudine said. "Before we get to that, though, what do we do about the test?"

Parks looked at the analog clock on the cabin wall. The test of the GAP was scheduled to take place in seven minutes. He glanced over at Hathaway. "Doctor, what happens if there are no targets to hit?"

"Bad news," he said, shaking his head vigorously as though wishful denial would make the problem go away.

"Meaning?"

"The Angel's default setting will kick in," Hathaway replied.

"It'll come home early?"

"Yes," Hathaway replied. "We don't want that. In the absence of a return beacon, the Angel will presume there has been an attack against the home base and the survival systems will take over. The test will buy us an extra fifteen minutes to try and figure something out."

"Is there a chance that missing the test will cause some other default system to kick in?" Parks asked.

Hathaway shook his head. "The Angel will assume the threat has been neutralized, possibly by another Angel outside its recognition sweep. It will continue with its basic program."

Parks told Beaudine to proceed with the test. The rear admiral also asked the brigadier general if he had any thoughts for an emergency response. Beaudine knew the Angel's capabilities as well as he did.

"Recover the *Hidalgo* GAP-Link," Beaudine suggested. "See if the command data can be salvaged."

"Bill, that really doesn't help me—"

"I know someone who might be able to do it," Beaudine assured him.

"Who?"

"LASER, the team that saved the Kings Point submarine crew under the south polar ice," Beaudine replied. "I know their CO. If you want, I'll see about getting them over there."

Parks had heard about the daring rescue. The logistics were different but he was not in a position to refuse assistance. "I would welcome any help they can provide," he said.

"I'll get on it," Beaudine said. "Do you have access to an uplink?"

Parks glanced toward Hathaway. The scientist had successfully accessed the White Sands webcam. "We'll be watching the test," Parks said.

The rear admiral gave Beaudine the direct number to the captain's secure line, then sat on the captain's cot. The quarters were spacious by seagoing standards, roughly ten-by-twelve, but the room seemed like a prison. The rear admiral had never felt so helpless. There was nothing he or Hathaway could do save sit and watch the live feed from White Sands.

And hope that the test failed.

The webcam sent a silent picture that ran thirty frames a second at an exceptional resolution. Even though it was just a stark blue sky dropping to a dusty stretch of horizon, Parks could see low-lying vegetation, birds, and even close-flying insects in great detail. Two hundred yards distant there was also a black dot. In a corner of the screen, a pop-up display offered telemetry from the Angel. Hathaway accessed the data and minimized it to a bar across the bottom of the screen. His creation was talking to him; Parks could only imagine Hathaway's frustration at not being able to talk back.

"I'm sorry I couldn't get the Link out," Hathaway said.

"I told you before there was nothing else you could do," Parks replied. "This was not something we had anticipated."

"No. We had a primary and a backup," Hathaway went on. "That should have been sufficient."

"The SEALs have a motto: 'Look twice before you leap.' The DoD has never advocated triple redundancies. We all thought this was enough."

"Not all," Hathaway reminded him. "As late as last week Dr. Gati was still insisting that we should have a portable device—"

"And Admiral Austin shot her down. I know," Parks said. "I also know that security concerns made that precaution a reasonable one. The GAP-Link is not something we want to have in unfriendly hands."

"Ironic, isn't it?" Hathaway said.

Yes. It was. The Angel could be just as deadly on its own.

The webcam was on a tripod anchored in the sedimentary rock of the Tularosa Basin to keep it from being knocked over by the sometimes fierce winds that whipped through the resting range. The only military personnel on-site were in a bunker a quarter-mile to the south. One was a video technician, who was taping the event on two digital cameras: one in real-time, the other in slow motion. Naturally, there were no aircraft in the region.

Parks and Hathaway watched as two tawny marks appeared above the horizon: the low-flying V-TX drones. They had taken off from the Testing and Evaluation Strip 3 and were traveling at a height of five hundred feet. One was the size of a small business jet, punching forward at 500 miles an hour; the other, a single engine airplane tagging behind at 240 miles an hour. They were being joystick-controlled from a 3rd Wave Working Group Center, a building where non-Army groups and outside agencies ran equipment tests. The drones were camouflaged to match the gypsum of the test area.

As the jet sped toward the webcam it suddenly dipped hard to port, then to starboard. An instant later the jet folded hard in the center with nose and tail sections both pointing up. It looked as though it were a longboat snapped in two by a whale. The entire assault happened in less than two seconds. Momentum caused the pieces of jet to continue forward and down. As they fell toward the camera they were crushed into hundreds of smaller fragments, as if the remnants of the whale attack were now being chewed apart by piranha. There was no explosion, no fire, no smoke. Just particles of metal, plastic, rubber, and fabric floating to earth like volcanic ash.

The airplane flew along the same trajectory. Because it was smaller and traveling considerably slower, a different attack pattern was employed. Both wings were hit simultaneously, stitched along the fuselage from back to front. That caused them to snap from horizontal to vertical. They stood upright for a moment before being chewed apart from wingtips to bottom. At the same time the fuselage of the aircraft began to disintegrate. It exploded in large continuous puffs from nose to tail. Within seconds the entire aircraft had been reduced to incredibly small pieces and was snowing its components onto the stark wasteland below.

The men waited. A few seconds after the second aircraft fell the black dot rose from the basin. It was a twelve-gore nylon hot air balloon, just six feet in diameter, filled and launched remotely. Homeland Security was afraid that balloons, laden with toxins or radioactive material, could be released offshore and sent into coastal regions; when the balloon came down, so would its lethal cargo. The black balloon was expected to reach a height of 800 feet before the air currents began to sweep it well off its horizontal axis.

The balloon was spotted and destroyed at just 200 feet, moments after launch. The twelve panels folded outward from the top like a peeled banana and the entire package simply dropped. If it had been a real terrorist balloon, the contents would have fallen back on those who sent it.

Hathaway looked back at the rear admiral. "Two hours ago that would have made me cheer," he remarked.

"I hate to say this, Doctor, but I'm impressed," Parks said. The Angel had performed magnificently.

"Luckys," Hathaway muttered.

"What's it doing now?" Parks asked.

Hathaway studied the readout. "It's scanning the target zone, searching for aerial activity."

That was all the Angel was programmed to identify. If someone had emerged from either craft they would not have been attacked.

"The scan is finished," Hathaway said. "The Angel is turning."

"Which way?"

"Toward home," Hathaway replied.

The flight took two hours. Some time before then the Angel would have exhausted all attempts to contact one of the two Links. It would continue to broadcast telemetry but it would not receive any.

What it would do then was something Parks did not wish to contemplate. His only hope now was that Beaudine could get this LASER group to San Diego—and that they were as good as he'd said.

PART TWO

Fire

ONE

Waianae, Hawaii

One moment Major Tom Bryan was dangling beneath his canopy, a warm, dry wind rushing past him as he stole looks at a lemon yellow sun rising over the Pacific. The next moment, instants before he hit the ground, there wasn't much to see except dark or ruddy dust. The air was a great deal hotter.

There was no question about what had happened. The volcano had chosen this moment to change its status on the volcano explosivity index. The question was what to do about it. The team was lucky to have been so close to the ground: the area above the drop zone was peppered high and low with ejecta the size of bowling balls. Bryan could see the rocks burning red as they flew by.

The major's landing was not pretty. The rising heat and lack of visibility made it difficult to control the chute relative to the ground. Bryan made a knee landing on gritty soil and fell forward, the chute collapsing in front of him. Fortunately the winds were not very active at ground level and he was able to use the cutaway handle. The main canopy and risers came free of the harness and lay where they had touched down. Bryan ignored the sharp pain in his knees as he scrambled to his feet. The air around the crater was filled with pasty white smoke; it had a chalky consistency and

stuck to the faceplate of the helmet. He wiped it off and
continued to knock it away with side-to-side swipes of his
hand as he looked around. The volcano was thundering to
his left. It was a constant rumble punctuated by deep, loud
pops like cannon fire that literally shook the ground. Bryan
turned his back to the crater and walked away. He was on a
thirty-odd-degree slope, though he did not know which
direction it faced.

"This is Bryan! Count off!" he shouted into his headset.

The LASER Ops responded in jump order. Some of the
team members were just landing, others were still aloft.
None of them was sure where they were.

Two of the team members did not respond.

"Wingate! Kowalski! Do you read?" Bryan yelled.

Silence.

"Anybody see them?"

No one answered. Hopefully, the two had only landed
badly and were knocked unconscious.

"Switch on hi-beams and partner up," Bryan ordered.

The hi-beams were laser lights mounted to the top of the
helmet. They pulsed once every second.

"General Scott?" Bryan said.

"I hear you, Major," the general said. "I've already contacted Captain Puckett. He lifted off immediately. We'll coordinate an exit point when he can assess the situation."

"What does it look like to you?" Bryan asked.

"All I see in your area is a churning cloud of white blowing east," Scott told him. "The initial blast seems to have
spent itself. I don't see any more projectiles and I can't dis-
cern any lava flows."

"We'll watch out for them, sir," Bryan said.

"How is the air?"

"Breathable around the crater. I don't know what it'll be
like inside. Hopefully, we can find the hazmat bags."

As the major spoke he looked around, trying to spot a
beam. He saw a pair to his right, crisscrossing like flashlights in a heavy fog. He moved in that direction. Two LASER

Ops emerged from the thick mist—Lieutenant Black and Captain Gabriel. Their powder blue jumpsuits were a dull, floury white. They seemed unhurt. Gabriel held something up as he emerged from the smoke.

"Found this, sir," Gabriel said triumphantly, which was the way he said most things. It was one of the hazmat bags.

"Excellent. Break out the gear."

Gabriel set the bag on the charcoal-gray earth. The three operatives crouched around it. Gabriel passed a suit to Bryan and another to Black. He pulled one out for himself. The ground was vibrating slightly.

The major climbed into the fully encapsulating olive drab hazmat suit, which was puncture- and tear-resistant. It had the texture and weight of a raincoat lined with lead, a virtue of the nine layers that protected the wearer from toxic and corrosive gas, liquid and solid chemicals, and bacteriological infestations. Even the seams had been double-sealed to prevent any kind of leaks. As he suited up, the other LASER Ops were reporting that they had linked up in groups of twos and threes. No one knew quite where they were and, as yet, no one had seen the two missing operatives. Given the conditions around the crater, that was not surprising. Cowan reported finding one of the other hazmat bags.

Bryan slipped the protective hood over his helmet. Ordinarily roomy, it was snug and uncomfortable with the crash helmet but Bryan needed to be in touch with the other operatives. He took a five-liter aluminum oxygen cylinder from the bag. It had a rubber sleeve to keep it from overheating and twenty minutes' worth of air. The major also took a half-liter water bottle from the bag and drank all of it. He grabbed another bottle and stuffed it in a deep pants pocket. Then he removed the coiled nylon rope from the bag and slung it over his arm.

"Gabe, Woody, you two go left and right," Bryan ordered, pointing in those directions.

"Where are you going?" Gabriel asked.

"That way," Bryan said, pointing back up the slope.

"Into the crater," Gabriel said.

"Have to."

"I'm going with—"

"No!" Bryan snapped. "I need the perimeter scoped out—"

A voice interrupted. "Sir, it's Marinelli. We found Wingate. Looks like he fell back and hit his head. He's coming around."

"Good. Clear him out. I want everyone to walk away from the crater." Bryan looked at the other two. "Except Gabe and Woody. I'll stay in touch. Whoever finds Kowalski, holler."

Gabriel and Black nodded and set out in opposite directions. Bryan faced the slope and started toward the crater. He was perspiring heavily and his visor began to fog. He stopped, removed the hazmat hood, detached the faceplate of his helmet, and continued. Even his feet were sweating.

"Puckett has the crater in view," General Scott reported. "We also received word from the Hawaiian Volcano Observatory. We've got a two on the VEI. That first load of rock is all we should see from this one. But there will be a lot of toxic smoke and lava flows around the crater."

"We'll watch where we step."

"They said to watch for smoke coming from the ground," Scott warned. "That will probably be lava punching through to the surface. The hazmat suits won't offer much protection from that."

"Not true, sir. I'm sweating enough to cool Three Mile Island." He reached the slender ridge atop the slope and started down. "Does the observatory have any idea how long this will last?"

"None. It's part of a major seismic event that started somewhere in the Pacific and kicked out in two directions. A small tsunami just hit Naval Air Base Coronado in San Diego. A larger wave is headed toward the coast to the south."

"Was there much damage?" Bryan asked. Talking helped him to focus. The smoke was thicker here and it was getting tougher to breathe, to stay alert.

"The southwest side of the base took a pounding, but apart from the harbor the city was spared," Scott told him. "The second wave is expected to hit a section of coast stretching from Imperial Beach down to Tijuana. Evacuation is under way. Hopefully, the water will strike the lean mid-section."

Bryan didn't answer. He was busy breathing.

"Major, how are you holding up?" Gabriel asked.

"Still standing," he forced himself to reply. "Marinelli? How are things with your group?"

"We're all here now," she replied. "It's getting clearer as we go lower. I can hear the chopper."

"General, anything from Puckett?" Bryan asked.

"Nothing yet. Thermal vision isn't going to help around the crater so he's looking for the hi-beams."

"We'll keep our heads up, sir," Marinelli said.

Bryan stopped and slid the oxygen tank under his hood. He pressed the vinyl facemask to his mouth and took a long hit. As he stood there, the smoke cleared slightly ahead of him. He thought he saw a dark shape lying on a mass of red rock. The clothes were smoldering. He ran forward, his heart racing more from the heat than from anticipation.

It was one of the dummies.

Bryan swore to himself. His temples were pounding now. The air around the volcano was actually cooler than being under the hazmat hood. At least the rumbling had subsided somewhat. He took another gulp of oxygen, put the cylinder in a free pocket, then shouted, "Kowalski! Where the hell are you?"

"Sir?" he heard from somewhere in the pit.

"Kowalski?"

"Yes, sir." The voice was flat and nearly swallowed by the low but insistent grumbling of the volcano.

"I can't see you," Bryan yelled. "Keep talking—yell so I can hear. Tell me where you are!"

"I'm in a not-good place!" the sergeant cried.

"I need more than that!"

"There's blackish crust with holes in it. That's all I can see, except for lava flowing about five feet down one of the holes right beside me. Hot as unholy hell. I'm sitting on two of the dummies."

"Can you see my hi-beam?"

"Negative, sir."

"Are you in smoke?"

"Some," Kowalski answered.

Sergeant Kowalski was probably somewhere along the opposite slope; the thick central column of smoke was in the center of the crater, the direction in which Bryan was headed. He shifted to the right and walked along the side of the crater. His left hip was hot and he realized it was due to the water bottle. The contents were heating and the plastic was starting to go soft.

"Some of that smoke may be coming from my own ears," the sergeant complained. "I really screwed the pooch."

"You had a bad break," Bryan said. "We all did. How bad are you hurt?"

"Dr. K has no freakin' clue. I landed on my right leg. Either it's broke or twisted up real good. Good thing I know the terrain, huh, sir? I can tell you exactly where I won't be moving."

"The things you said helped get me here," Bryan replied. "What happened to your headset?"

"Dead, sir. I had to raise my foot with my helmet or it would have fried. The heat torched the headset and hi-beam."

There was soft ground and Bryan stumbled. He broke his fall with his left hand, knee, and forehead. He felt the heat of the rocks through the multilayer neoprene. The ground had to be about one hundred and fifty degrees. Bryan got back up. The radiant heat was burning his eyes. He put the hazmat hood back on. As he did, he noticed that his hi-beam was off. The light had been damaged when he fell.

Fuck was all that came to mind.

"Sir, I'm melting here!" Kowalski yelled. "Shit! *Shit!*"

"What's wrong?" Bryan shouted. He had to lift the bottom of the hazmat hood in order to be heard.

"One of the dummies just caught fire! I've got to get off! Ow—damn."

"You okay?" He looked around frantically. Where the hell *was* the guy?

"Better than the motherfuckin' dummy," Kowalski answered. "I managed to push it away. It's toast."

"Is there something you can use as a crutch?"

"No—hold on. The other one is starting to smoke! My ass is gonna be next."

Bryan began to run. The ground was unsteady and the smoke was churning toward him again. Thin streams of lava were beginning to push through cracks in the earth to his right. He thought he heard the chopper but the roar of the volcano was building again. It was difficult to tell the sounds apart.

"Give me a landmark to look for, anything!" Bryan yelled. He felt like an idiot for having broken the hi-beam.

"Lava!" the sergeant yelled. "A stream of it."

"Are you still moving?"

"Can't. My freakin' leg hurts too much—I'm screwed."

"No, you're not," Bryan replied.

A stream of lava, the major thought. He looked down at the flow. It was crawling from the center of the crater. "Kowalski, how wide is the lava stream?"

"About six inches."

"The flow here is half that. I'm going to follow it inward."

"Sir, get out before the whole thing blows!"

"Would you?"

"No."

"Then shut up," the major said.

The cracks widened as he walked deeper into the caldera. He couldn't see far. He had to do something that would let Kowalski see him. Stopping, he crouched on the smoking base of the crater and removed his hood. He took off his helmet. "General, I'm going to try something. I may be out of touch after this. I'm going to try to signal Puckett somehow."

"Major, what—" Scott began.

That was all Bryan heard before he removed the helmet. He pulled out the headset, slid the rope from his shoulder, and threaded it through the holes that had been cut for the earpieces. He tied a knot.

"Kowalski, I want you to tell me when you see the smoke start to move around you!"

"Move, sir?"

"Yes. You'll know what I mean!"

Standing, Bryan let out about five feet of rope and began to swing the helmet to his right, vertically. The smoke began to swirl beside him in a rapid clockwise pattern.

"Sir, I see something!" the sergeant cried. "The smoke is moving to my left, like you turned on a fan."

"I'm going to move!" Bryan shouted. "Tell me what's happening!"

The major started walking to his right, watching every step. The ground had burst in spots like a hot dog on a grill. Lava filled the fissures slowly and he had to step over them. The heat was growing more intense and he reached for the water bottle in his pocket. The plastic was soft enough that he didn't have to stop and open the cap. He just poked a hole through the side with his thumb and aimed the stream at his mouth.

"It's coming closer, sir!" Kowalski yelled. "I see something moving around."

"That's my crash helmet," he said.

Bryan peered through the smoke. He had to blink hard to clear the sweat from his eyes. There was a powder blue shape in front of him. It was sitting on a mannequin.

"Leighanne, I presume?" Bryan asked, pointing toward the mannequin as he approached.

"No, sir," Kowalski replied. "She was the one who caught fire. Burned my ass."

Bryan kicked the dummy away and squatted beside the sergeant. There was blood on Kowalski's jumpsuit and greasy dirt on his face and hands. Bryan handed him the water bottle and Kowalski drained it.

The ground was still trembling and the crater was coughing more and more gray smoke. That meant underground forces were building and causing rock to be pulverized and added to the mix.

Bryan grabbed Kowalski's helmet. The radio op was right. His headset had been fried in the fall. *So much for raising the general,* Bryan thought. He thought of tossing the oxygen into the fire to try and catch Puckett's eye. But the explosion would be lost in the belly of the eruption. He slipped the helmet on Kowalski's head, then untied his own and put it on. Even the shattered headgear would afford some protection from falling rocks. Panting from the heat, Bryan took the sergeant's arm, draped it around his shoulder, and rose slowly. The sergeant winced dramatically but did not complain. They began moving toward the rim of the crater. Bryan was afraid to put Kowalski across his back. He wasn't sure of his own strength in this heat, or if the ground would be stable enough to hold their combined weight.

The particulate smoke was sinking lower and lower to the ground and he had to follow the river of lava toward the slope. The molten rock, a dull red, was just below the lip of the ground. He moved away from it, to the right. Another fissure had opened there, just a few feet away. Gray smoke was chugging from that one. It did not look as if the crater would remain solid for very much longer.

"Anybody out there?" Bryan yelled.

No one replied. The major didn't think they could even hear him.

Kowalski coughed hard. Bryan looked at him.

"We're going to make it," he said.

"I know, sir."

The major looked back at the slope. It didn't seem very much closer. The ground was getting mushy and the river of lava was burbling up to the surface now, spilling over the sides of both fissures and crawling toward them. Bryan picked up the pace, even as Kowalski became heavier. The air, too, became thicker and even more difficult to breathe. Ash was now part of the powdery mix. Kowalski had stopped hacking. He was unconscious. Bryan paused to give him oxygen, hoping he would wake and carry his own weight. The sergeant revived after a moment.

"I'm . . . good," Kowalski said.

Then the air ran out and Kowalski slumped forward. Bryan dropped the bottle and continued struggling ahead.

This would be a good time to find the third hazmat bag, he thought.

Suddenly, ahead, Bryan saw a figure in olive drab. It was walking sideways from the left. There was another figure beside it, and another beside that.

"You sons . . . of bitches," Bryan gasped.

The LASER Ops were conducting an hour hand search: they were walking hand-in-hand, doing a radial sweep of the crater. The lightest member, Sergeant Major Cowan, was on the inside some ten feet away.

"I've got them!" Cowan shouted as he neared. He released the hand of the operative beside him and ran forward.

"They would . . . send the leader . . . of the dummy squad," Bryan wheezed as Cowan arrived.

The operative didn't seem to have heard him. The sergeant major grabbed Kowalski while the short but powerful Lieutenant Renny Kodak threw an arm around Bryan's waist.

"You won't need this," Kodak said, pulling the rope and helmet from around Bryan's arm.

The major hadn't realized he was still carrying it.

The four hurried toward the rim as the surface of the crater came apart behind them. Smoke rolled over them as hands reached down, grasping and pulling. Then they vanished into the smoke. Bryan stumbled, then felt himself being half-carried, half-dragged forward. He began to feel a little cooler, though it was more than just leaving the hot caldera of the volcano. There was a strong wind coming from above. The major could still see only smoke, but the wind sent the gray clouds curling in strange figure-eight patterns, up and down and around again. That was one difference. The other was that there was a little more clean air than before.

It tasted damn good.

Bryan's temples were still throbbing and his mouth was gunpowder-dry. The dehydrated officer shut his stinging eyes. He felt himself being moved around. He tried to help but his limbs didn't want to cooperate. They were weak and shaking.

"Just relax, sir!" someone said.

He opened his eyes. His vision was caked. "Who's there?"

"Marinelli, sir."

"How is . . . Kowalski?"

"Looks like he damaged the articular cartilage in his right knee. He's dehydrated and has burns on his legs, thighs, and butt. Apart from that he's okay," she said.

"Leighanne . . . did that."

"Did what, sir?"

"Burned his butt," Bryan said.

"Of course she did, sir," Marinelli replied. He moved back. "Close your eyes, major."

Bryan obliged. He was too tired to argue. A moment later he felt himself rising. The air was cleaner and there was light ahead. Either he'd been rescued or he was dead. Whichever it was, he was liking it.

TWO

Pearl Harbor, Hawaii

General Scott knocked on the door of the private room at Branch Medical Clinic Makalapa.

"Come in!"

The voice on the other side of the door was strong, but that did not surprise the general. It would take more than an active volcano to take down Thomas Bryan. Scott opened the door and strode in.

The hospital cot was cranked up slightly. Major Bryan was lying on his left side, his back to the door. He was watching a portable DVD player on the night table. There was an IV drip in his right arm and big white bandages taped to his neck, back, and shoulder. The rest of the flesh on his upper body, what Scott could see of it, was apple red. Bryan had suffered second-degree burns not from flame or lava, but from the major's own vaporized sweat.

Bryan paused the DVD and craned around when the door opened. His expression was vaguely uncomfortable until he saw the general. Or rather, until he saw what was under each of Benjamin Scott's arms.

"Two of the survivors wanted to thank you," Scott said, holding up a pair of badly scorched dummies.

Tom Bryan's face flushed until it matched the color

of his torso. The look of discomfort quickly became a self-conscious grin. "They don't look so good," the major pointed out.

"And no wonder. They were blown from the crater by the initial blast," Scott explained.

Two months earlier, Major Bryan had been in command of a LASER training operation in the Gulf of Mexico. The assignment had been to rescue dummies from a sinking destroyer. Things went wrong and the vessel went down before the LASER Ops could reach the engine room, where the dummies were trapped. Though all the operatives got out, Bryan considered the mission a failure because none of the dummies had been saved.

Scott set the mannequins against the baseboard. "Kodak and Black found them when the team was bringing you back to the chopper. They wanted me to tell you the dummies were recovered in a daring rescue but—you know me."

"The Big T and nothing but the truth, whatever it costs," Bryan said. "Tell Kodak and Black I appreciate the thought."

"You can tell them yourself," Scott said as he walked to the other side of the bed. "You think I'm going to let you lie around here?"

"I hope not," Bryan replied. He nodded toward the DVD player. "They make you watch stuff. Evil stuff like 'Better Care of Your Heart,' 'Diet Don'ts,' and 'Your Recovery.' That sort of thing."

"Classic brainwashing technique, perfected by Stalin in the gulags," Scott told him. "A captive audience with nothing else to do. You read what they've left you. You listen to whatever's on the radio, watch whatever's on TV."

"This isn't a prison camp. What's wrong with cable?"

"The base gets money for this. PEF—patient education funding."

"Seriously?"

Scott nodded.

"Jeez. There's always an angle."

"The Pentagon is nothing but," Scott reminded him. He

pulled over a chair. "Can *I* get you anything? Water? OJ?"

"A Famke Janssen flick."

Scott smiled. "Apart from the videos, how are they treating you?"

"I feel cut off," Bryan said. "I'm not even sure how I got here. I don't remember much after Cowan grabbed me."

"The sergeant major says you were barely conscious then. Captain Puckett got to the site, circled, and saw the hibeams," Scott informed him. "They worked just like they were designed to in a fog or low cloud situation. Puckett was able to follow them in through the smoke."

"That's good news, at least," Bryan said.

"*Damn* good. And before you start pissing and moaning, Tom, this operation was a success. A big one. It didn't go the way we expected but the equipment worked, the rescues worked, the team was able to adjust quickly to dramatically altered circumstances, and everyone got out." He jabbed a finger across the room. "Including two of the dummies."

Bryan smiled. "Speaking of getting out—"

"Moses says you'll be able to leave as soon as you're rehydrated. That should be tomorrow some time."

Marine Lieutenant Moses Houston was the team's medic. He traveled everywhere with the LASER Ops.

"What about Kowalski? I *do* remember he was pretty banged up."

"It could've been a helluva lot worse," Scott replied. "He didn't break anything. He did have a few more burns than you came away with—mostly on his legs and butt, apparently from that doll catching fire—and a mild concussion. He'll be laid up three to four days, though we'll have to move him before that."

"Why?"

"You two aren't enrolled in Tricare, the base medical plan. We'll have to take you back to Corpus Christi ASAP."

Bryan scowled. "You're kidding."

Scott raised his right hand. "Nothing but the Big T.

They need the rooms for scheduled surgeries, births, and emergencies."

"How many emergencies do they have here?"

"More than you'd think," Scott said. "They just reintroduced hand-to-hand combat after years of weapons-only training. Lots of guys getting themselves hurt."

"What, with sprained wrists and jammed fingers?"

"We've got a badly banged up Kowalski," Scott reminded him.

"And burns."

"Nothing that absolutely needs to be cared for here," Scott said.

Bryan shook his head. "I hate this interservice bullshit."

"There may be some of that, but frankly I think everyone's a little edgy because of the volcano. They've been ramping up their outreach program to deal with possible injuries to the civilian population."

"I see. Y'know, I've been listening for our friend Waianae," Bryan said. "I haven't heard him complaining."

"He's quieted, but no one knows if that will hold. The tsunami situation has played out as expected in California. But there will be aftershocks along the Pacific plate and no one knows how those will impact either region." Scott's cell phone beeped. He pulled it from his belt. "People are afraid new waves may head this way or that the volcanoes could be seriously active."

Scott looked at the phone display. The caller was Lieutenant Stacey Sayles, the general's chief of staff at Naval Air Station Corpus Christi. Scott excused himself and walked into the hallway to take the call. He did not like involving LASER Ops field personnel in conversations that did not pertain to them. There was no point filling their head with distracting issues, personalities, and bureaucracy—the kind of BS that helped stoke his own furnace. The only reason General Scott had landed the LASER command at all was because he had lost his temper with a French officer. The exchange got him bumped off the career track at NATO.

"Yes, Sayles?" Benjamin said.

"Sir, I have Brigadier General Beaudine on the phone. He wants to be patched through."

"On an unsecure line?"

"I mentioned that, sir, and yes."

That was surprising—and disconcerting. Scott couldn't imagine what would be that urgent. "Put it through," he told her.

Scott had served with then-private first class Will Beaudine in the 31st Infantry regiment in Vietnam. Grunts like Scott and Beaudine who were part of the infamous HELL duty tours—Hot, Endless, Lethal, Lousy—deep in enemy territory ended up either sliding a gun barrel between their lips and squeezing the trigger or becoming lifers with a few physical tics and mental lacunas to show for their experiences. The men and their wives had a terrific time when they saw each other two or three times a year, at military functions such as the annual Army band concert in New York City. Scott couldn't imagine what was so important that Beaudine had to talk to him right away. He hoped the general's wife Norda wasn't ill.

After a moment Sayles said, "Go ahead, General Beaudine."

"Ben?" the deep-voiced general asked.

"I'm here," Scott replied. "Is everything all right? You, Norda—?"

"We're well," he replied. "This is a business call. Your aide told me the LASER team is in Oahu."

"Yes. Half the team is here on a training mission, the rest are back in Corpus Christi."

"Can you take LASER to San Diego? Today?"

"I suppose that's possible," Scott replied. "The ones that are still ambulatory."

"How many aren't?"

"A few. Tough training mission," Scott said. The general was surprised by the urgency in Beaudine's voice. Among HELL veterans, the commanding general of the White

Sands missile range had one of the cooler furnaces. "I heard what happened along the coast there, but I assumed the place would be overrun with emergency personnel from Northern California and Arizona."

"It is. But we need big guns for something important. Your team is uniquely qualified to do what needs to be done. You've got the diversity and field experience. Will you go there?"

"Of course," Scott replied. "Can I ask what the Army's interest is over there?"

"I can't tell you that right now," Beaudine replied. "I'll have NB Coronado contact Pearl to arrange for transport. How long will you need?"

"Two hours to pack 'em up here, an hour to get the rest of the team airborne from NASCC," he replied.

"Let's do it. And Ben—thank you."

"Sure," Scott replied. "Will, can you tell me *anything* about what we're getting into?"

"We'll talk about that over a secure line when you're en route," Beaudine told him. "All I can say now is this: LASER is the only game plan we have."

THREE

Pearl Harbor, Hawaii

Major Tom Bryan liked working in the shadows. He did not like being kept in the dark. When General Scott walked back from the hallway and told Bryan that the full LASER unit was heading to San Diego, the major was surprised and pleased. If people were in trouble, he wanted to help. The general did not know yet why they were being summoned, only that the request had come from a good friend who ran the White Sands Missile Range. It seemed a strange juxtaposition, the Army testing range and the San Diego Navy base, and Bryan was surprised that Scott accepted the "ETC" sign-off—explanation to come.

Bryan was curious and he was also challenged by the impasse. There were channels and there were back channels in MSI—military strategic information. Usually, the two led to the same place. Bryan always felt that you learned more faster at the bottom than at the top. There were no filters, no agendas. Just a lot of dogfaces, on site, doing their jobs. All the guys the general had come up with were now top brass. The major was not so lucky. He still knew—hell, he worked with, was still one of—the people who got their hands muddy.

And liked to complain about it.

When Moses Houston came by to check on his patient, Bryan did two things. First, he told the medic that if he weren't released for this mission he would prove his fitness by breaking the man's arm. Houston wasn't moved. The doctor did, however, agree to let Bryan out provided he spent as little time as possible on his feet and drank at least a quart of water an hour. The major agreed.

The second thing Bryan did was borrow Houston's cell phone. His own cell was back at the hotel and the hospital room phone could only be used by Tricare members who entered their account number. Bryan called General Scott to say he would meet the team at the hotel. Then he called for a courtesy car from Pearl to take him there. Finally, he phoned Ensign Davis Galvez, a LASER operative who had stayed behind in Corpus Christi. The twenty-four-year-old demolitions expert, a protégé of Lieutenant Black, had grown up in Southern California. Though he had been stationed at the Naval Construction Battalion Center, Port Hueneme— which was well north of San Diego—he had trained with a number of men and women who were stationed at NB Coronado. The major caught Galvez as he was boarding the team's C-130K Hercules transport for San Diego. Bryan asked the ensign to call anyone he knew at Coronado to try and find out what was going on.

The answer came back before Houston had finished filling out Bryan's release papers. The base had been evacuated shortly before the wave made landfall. All Galvez found out was that an aircraft carrier had been overturned two miles offshore. Reportedly, the flattop had left before dawn without the rest of the carrier group. That was unusual.

Bryan dressed and left his small, spartan room. There were broken blisters under the bandages and it hurt to move. His ears were ringing from the noise of the volcano and probably would be for another day or two. But he was in a lot better shape than Kowalski, whom he visited before leaving the hospital. The sergeant's right leg was in traction and his backside was on a foam pillow with a hollow center, to keep pressure off the burns. His head was bandaged and his eyes were bloodshot. The structural engineer was still groggy.

"You're making just as little sense as you did in the crater," Bryan said as he stood over the younger man's bed.

"I have a fuckin' concussion," he said, then added contritely, "Sir. An' I'm dry as a raisin."

"I know. That's why you're going to a hospital in Los Angeles tomorrow while we muck around in San Diego."

Kowalski became more alert. "You're goin' to San Diego? Why?"

"A mission. I don't know anything about it."

"*Shit!*" Kowalski yelled, then winced. He touched his head lightly. "Ow," he said more quietly.

Bryan laid a hand on the sergeant's bare arm.

"Please don't say 'Watch yer ass,' sir."

"I wasn't going to," Bryan said. "Just 'take care.' "

"Thank you," Kowalski grumped. "Sir?"

"Yes?"

"If you see the doc, tell him I need more painkillers. Or Southern Comfort, whatever is handier. An' I'm gonna want both if I gotta fly a lumpy troop transport a few thousand miles."

"I'll tell him," Bryan said as he left. "Rest, now."

"Right. By the way, sir. Thanks for pullin' me out."

Bryan smiled and left the room. He walked slowly so as not to aggravate his own wounds. He stepped outside the medical center, where the sky was already sunset red. That was caused by volcanic dust diffusing light toward the long end of the spectrum. The air also had a dusty taste, like an area around a campfire that had burned itself out. Bryan saw the car that had been sent. He walked toward it along the rich, neatly clipped lawn.

It had to be tough, being laid up and skipping a mission. Everyone who had volunteered for the LASER Ops did so to work. Whether it was to help people, challenge themselves, or most likely a combination of both, the team members lived to be out in the field.

The hotel lobby was thick with military personnel who were chatting about the volcano and the tsunami that hit the California coast. As he waited for the elevator, Bryan heard a snippet of conversation that intrigued him between a pair of young naval lieutenants.

"I heard that it's burning underwater," said one.

"That wouldn't surprise me. Watertight means watertight," replied the other.

"Excuse me," Bryan said. "Are you men talking about Coronado?"

"Yes, sir," said one. The young man was instantly on guard, obviously concerned that he'd said something he shouldn't have.

"What's going on there?" Bryan asked.

The elevator arrived. The three men stepped in, Bryan entering first.

"We're not sure, major," said the man. "We were talking about something we heard."

"Which is?"

"That a flattop went over and was burning underwater."

"You heard this from whom?" Bryan asked.

"My girlfriend is a radio dispatcher at the San Diego fire department, sir," said the other officer. "She said they had airborne units trying to put out a fire two miles out, in Wreck Alley. She heard it was underwater in the *Hidalgo*."

"We didn't think it was classified, sir," the other added quickly.

"It's not, don't worry," Bryan assured the sailors. "I was just curious. It's been difficult getting news out of there."

"Yes, sir," the two men said, visibly relieved.

Bryan exited and the men saluted as he left. The major bent into his own salute so he wouldn't pop the bandages around his shoulder. He didn't know for sure, but he had a feeling that LASER's destination was the overturned aircraft carrier *Hidalgo*. While there were plenty of military units trained for rescue, very few of them had top-level security clearance. Whatever NB Coronado was doing, possibly in conjunction with White Sands, it was obviously too secret to be discussed over an open line. Also, Beaudine probably wanted someone he knew he could count on.

The major didn't exactly grab his gear. He picked it up carefully so as not to aggravate his wounds. He was back downstairs in ten minutes. Military personnel of all stripes were still gathered about the lobby discussing the day's events. Many of them were collected around a TV in a corner of the lobby. Other members of the LASER team had begun to gather around a vintage player piano that was tinkling out traditional Hawaiian melodies. Bryan set his grip beside the piano bench and Cowan scooted over to make room. The operatives were openly delighted to see the major though they didn't ask how he was. That wasn't a slight; it was an unspoken military tradition. Attention made covert ops uncomfortable and a group hug was that, squared.

"I want to thank you all for hauling us out of there," Bryan said. "Though I also want to point out that while your search and rescue effort was not unwelcome, it *was* unwise." Official military policy—one of the first things they hit you with in boot camp—was that the safety of the few was not worth risking the many. Unofficially, however, from the Marines to Delta, from the SEALs to the Army Rangers, there wasn't an elite services unit in the U.S. armed forces that would fail to use everything in its arsenal to rescue a missing, injured, or captured member.

The team listened to what Bryan had to say and then was silent for several seconds. Sergeant Major Cowan finally looked at the others and said, "I *think* that means we did a bad thing. Sort of."

"No," said Lieutenant Black. "I believe the major is saying it was a good thing, just not a smart thing."

"Heck, how many smart people would do what we do for a living?" Captain Gabriel added.

Bryan made a face. "Not too many. I would have done the same thing in their position."

"I believe you did, sir, going into the mouth of an erupting volcano to try and find Kowalski," Black pointed out.

The major frowned. That was a one-off, a mission commander looking for a missing man. But he wasn't going to debate the point.

"Has the general been down?" Bryan asked, glancing around the lobby. Lieutenant Kodak, the team's recon specialist, had arrived. He was sitting off to the side on the periphery of the group.

"General Scott was here about ten minutes ago and left," Lieutenant Black said. "He went to Pearl to check on the flight arrangements."

"You would think he'd bring someone from the NASCC to do all that," Cowan suggested.

"The general likes to make sure things are done right," Bryan said. "He also doesn't like to sit still."

"Man, if I could sit on my butt all day I would *not* be looking for things to do," Cowan said.

"That's why the general is not still a sergeant major, sergeant major," Gabriel pointed out.

"The general did tell us you were going to go see Kowalski," Lieutenant Black said.

"How is he?

"Banged up but sorry that he isn't going with us," Bryan said.

"Right, sir. Though I'm guessing that 'sorry' isn't exactly the word Kowalski used," Gabriel snorted.

Bryan smiled just as the other team members arrived. Everyone looked a little shopworn from the day's events. The major hoped they would all have time to rest before they tackled whatever they had to do in San Diego.

"Sir, are you at liberty to say anything about the SOS General Scott received?" Gabriel asked Bryan.

"Captain, I don't *know* anything about it," the major told him. He did not like to repeat hearsay or speculate. "I'm not sure the general does, either."

"Into the unknown, the life and legacy of a sailor," Master Chief Petty Officer Wingate remarked. "I like that."

"I'll take my journeys with a GPS, thank you," Black replied.

General Scott returned a few minutes later. Without conversation or delay, he ushered the LASER Operatives onto a twenty-eight-seat mid bus. As soon as they were seated the general told the team that the quickest flight out was an aging Hercules C-130E operated by the 15th Airlift Wing out of Hickam. A flight had been hastily scheduled to run emergency personnel to Coronado. The Air Force was holding departure for the arrival of the LASER Ops. The transport was smaller and slower than the C-17 the group had flown to Hawaii. It would also be noisier and colder than the modern C-130K LASER had at its disposal in Corpus Christi. But Bryan didn't care. It would be quieter than the volcano, and he wouldn't mind the chill. Not now.

Since the Air Force was transporting mostly personnel instead of heavy equipment and vehicles—those were coming from naval bases north of San Diego—the seats of the Herk were arranged in rows instead of along the cabin wall. They were upholstered, not fold-down plastic with a cushion, and there were headrests.

The major fell asleep five minutes after the "E" took off.

FOUR

Over the Pacific Ocean

General Scott had made certain the bus driver brought a secure global sat-phone he could take with him on the trip. The young junior non-com was carrying the latest in the Motorola 9500 series. The unit was virtually indistinguishable from an ordinary cell phone.

As soon as the "E" was airborne, Scott found a relatively quiet section in the forward part of the aircraft. The cabin narrowed near the cockpit because of the lockers and shelves stuffed with gear; they muffled the sound of the four massive Allison T56-A-7 turboprops. After making certain that the phone wouldn't interfere with the aircraft's communications or navigational system, the general flipped down a wooden stool near the lavatory and put in a call to Will Beaudine. The brigadier general took the call immediately.

"Thanks for doing this, Ben," Beaudine said.

"All we did was get on an airplane," Scott said. "That was easy. What's the rest of it?"

"I assume you know the carrier *Hidalgo* turned over this morning."

"Yes. Pretty tough to imagine."

"The Navy and the Air Force obviously thought so. They were conducting a joint, top-secret experiment from the carrier bridge when they were hit," Beaudine told him. "A vital piece of equipment is still onboard, on the bridge. We need to try and recover it. When we ran the mi-creds you came up on top."

The mission-credentials were culled from reports that commanding officers filed with the Department of Defense. In the case of LASER, what got them burped to the top of the list were probably "underwater salvage," "top security clearance," and "on-site backup." The latter was important. LASER was larger than the average military search-and-rescue unit. If some of the members were lost, there would be others to take their place.

"We've got excavation teams down there now working hard just to get into the bridge," Beaudine went on. "What's making it especially difficult is that the waters are still very unsettled, portions of the ship are on fire, and other sections are either flooded or packed with mud."

"Do we know if there are survivors?"

"There are pockets of personnel in different parts of the ship. Rescue crews are setting up underwater rescue tubes so they can cut through and get them out. But the bridge was pretty hard-hit and most of it is still buried. We expect to have a way of ingress by the time your team arrives."

"Can you tell me what the test was about and what kind of equipment we're looking for?"

"The test was for a new kind of defense system, one which I'm not free to talk about," Beaudine said.

"Is this system still operational?"

"It is," Beaudine told him.

"Is it armed?" Scott asked. He felt a burning in his gut.

"Ben, I can't—"

"All I want to know is whether my people will be at risk," Scott said.

"Not from the target, no," Beaudine said. "The item on your mission docket is a remote-control platform. We had a backup system at Coronado but it was destroyed in the wave."

"Is there a locator beacon on the device?"

"Not as such," Beaudine told him. "There's something, Ben, but——I'm sorry. I just can't say anything more."

"I understand."

He did, too. There was the security factor, of course. Need-to-know was simply good business. Beyond that, though, there was the psychological factor. Special Ops units were trained to focus on mission parameters, to master specific skills and details. Worrying about the big picture only complicated things. The added pressure caused distractions, overcaution, mistakes.

As a commander, Scott understood. As a soldier, though, he was damn curious about what the Navy and Air Force were up to.

"As for the site itself, the engineering crews are reporting a lot of debris between themselves and the device," Beaudine went on. "Hopefully, by the time your team arrives we will have been able to clear enough of the tower base of water to give you a staging area nearer to the target."

That will leave just the mud, crushed metal, and burning compartments, Scott thought.

Beaudine said that he would e-mail blueprints of the aircraft carrier to Scott, as well as on-site photographs of the interior taken with a fiber-optic probe and streaming video of the rescue effort.

The general returned to his deeply cushioned seat in the front row—the row reserved for dignitaries like the secretary of defense when they traveled with the military—and booted his laptop. He logged onto the Herk's wireless Internet system. Most of the LASER team members were sleeping. Scott did not want to disturb them. He would save the pertinent data and review it with them before they landed.

He didn't bother looking at the blueprints. He went right to the photographs. As the images downloaded he was reminded of the newspaper and magazine pictures he had seen as a child of the Japanese attack on Pearl Harbor. Scott remembered the black-and-white photographs of the *Arizona,* the *Utah,* the *Helena.* Five of eight battleships had been sunk or badly damaged, their hulls smoking, sailors moving across them as they tried to extinguish the blazes and search for survivors. These images were less repugnant because the event was the work of nature, not an act of aggression. But they were no less humbling.

It made him heartsick to think that so many human endeavors had cataclysmic moments like these, from the *Titanic* and the *Hindenburg* through the *Apollo 1* fire and the twin space shuttle disasters. Acts of God, acts of carelessness. The cause didn't change the fact that the freedom to journey and explore was rarely free. With just a small flexing of its muscles the earth had easily overturned a modern aircraft carrier, the pride of American strength.

Or is it? he asked himself. *Is any machine that?*

The general opened the link to the streaming video. The vantage point was sea level, from a small floating rescue platform alongside the bridge. The pylon containing the satellite dish array was bent beside it, jutting from the water at an angle. Dark gray smoke filled the air behind the tower. The staccato images reminded Scott of the old nickelodeon machine he used to watch for a penny at the barbershop back in Wabash. But the people whose pixilated movements he was watching were not actors. Scott thought of the personnel sitting behind him. The LASER Ops were going to be ordered to enter this blazing hulk, risk their lives for a piece of electronic equipment. They would do so willingly, never weighing what they might lose so the nation might benefit.

That was American strength, he reminded himself.

"Sir?"

Scott glanced up. Lieutenant Kodak was standing in front of him. The powerfully built twenty-eight-year-old recon specialist seemed uneasy. The general could see the boy in the man.

"What can I do for you, Renny?"

"Sir, I was wondering if you have any way of checking the status of individuals stationed at Coronado."

"Who are we talking about?"

"My mother," he replied. "She's the civilian music librarian for the Navy Band Southwest."

"Do you know for a fact she was there?"

"Yes, sir," Kodak replied. "I called my dad from the hotel."

"He's retired navy, isn't he?"

"A captain, sir. He was based in Georgia and doesn't know anyone at Coronado. He hasn't heard from her and we're concerned because the music center is on the side of the base that got hardest hit."

"I can tell you there was a general evac of military personnel, and I believe the civilians were free to go before that," Scott said. "But I'll call the base liaison and see what I can find out. What's her name?"

"Barbara," Kodak replied.

It wasn't that Scott thought there would be a lot of "Kodaks" to search. He just wanted to know.

"Mom loves her music," the lieutenant added. "I can see her staying to batten everything down."

The lieutenant left and Scott put in a call to Beaudine. He asked the brigadier general to find out when Coronado might have a list of casualties. The request sounded cold, statistical.

"I'll try, but everyone on the base had to swipe their ID badge to exit. You can get a jump by checking the guard-post logs."

"Do you happen to have the password?" Scott asked.

"Checking now. It's JURYTRIAL."

"Thanks," Scott said.

Scott logged on to the Coronado website and accessed the restricted sector. He input the code and went to the gates log. The names were alphabetized. He looked at the screen for a moment, then turned around. The lieutenant was sitting in a window seat, staring out. General Scott set the laptop aside and went to him. There was nothing impersonal about what he was feeling now. The seat beside Kodak was empty. Scott slid into it.

"Renny—your mom exited the base at 10:33 hours," the general told him.

"Right before the waters hit," he said.

"She didn't give herself a lot of pitch and yaw space," Scott agreed. "I'm guessing the base wireless tower went down; your mother would have had a tough time getting to a land line with all the traffic and crowds. That's probably why your father hasn't heard from her."

"Thank you, sir," Kodak said, his lips pressed into a tight, trembling smile. "Thank you very, very much."

"She stayed for music," Scott said with open amazement.

"Yes, sir. Mom is the navy's top recruitment officer," the lieutenant said, still beaming.

"Oh?"

"She says that everyone becomes a soldier when they hear *Stars and Stripes Forever*."

Scott smiled. He couldn't dispute that.

Kodak thanked Scott again and the general returned to his seat. He picked up the laptop, sat down, and went back to the streaming video.

As Scott watched he noticed something odd in the top right corner of the image. He clicked on that section to enlarge it, then leaned closer to the screen. He noticed that seabirds were hovering above the wreckage. That was unusual, given the toxic nature of the smoke pouring from inside. No one on the team knew much about wildlife so Scott looked up seagulls on the Internet.

What he discovered intrigued him. He turned and motioned toward Lieutenant Kodak, who hurried over.

"Do you know anything about infrasound?"

"Not much, sir," he said. "It's very low sound, 20 Hz or less, below the range of what humans can hear."

"Birds use it to navigate to shore," Scott said. "The distinctive sound of the waves tells them which direction to go."

"I don't know about that, General. I only know that we use it in electronic recon to swallow aircraft."

"Swallow?" Scott asked.

"That's when we send up a beam that covers a wide area,"

Kodak said. "The absorption of sound by air increases with the frequency. The lower frequencies create a large, solid footprint that let us read the motion of the ailerons and flaps of an aircraft, as well as any dramatic shifts in flight path."

"Whereas radar only gives you a blip, and satellite imagery covers too narrow an area."

"Exactly, sir. Homeland security is just starting to use that as an early warning system for wide sections of border."

Scott nodded. "Thank you, Lieutenant."

Kodak went back to his seat and Scott continued looking at the laptop. He shifted to the fiber-optic images of the tower's gnarled interior. There were sharp edges, dead ends, and oil-fueled flames everywhere. Hopefully, some of those impediments would be removed before LASER arrived.

His mind returned to potential scenarios Beaudine had not wanted to discuss. Maybe the missing test control system had switched to battery power. There were also generators on the rescue platform. Perhaps engineers had managed to power up a section of the tower and turn the control device back on. If the seabirds were responding to a strong infrasound signal, the marine recovery units might be using that to try and pinpoint the missing device. Then they could create a path as close as possible for LASER to use.

The more General Scott thought about it, the more he began to imagine a possible profile of the experiment. The *Hidalgo* had gone to sea in the dark. It had sent a top-secret aircraft toward White Sands. That was what carriers did: they moved aircraft to where they were needed. The *Hidalgo* did not sail with a carrier group because they wanted to limit the number of eyeballs on the experiment. That was also why they stayed within national waters. To prevent foreign ships from getting too close.

The test plane was probably unmanned; otherwise, regaining control of it would not be such a problem. But why take it to sea? Why not launch from one of the airfields at Coronado?

The general didn't understand why the Air Force didn't simply knock the damn thing down. The aircraft hadn't been invented that could survive a sustained attack from air-and-ground-based ordnance—

He felt his brain stop short.

Or had it?

FIVE

San Diego, California

General Scott tapped Major Bryan awake an hour before landing. The major's mouth and nasal passages were desert dry. The machine-circulated air onboard these giants sucked all the humidity out of it. Bryan went forward to the first-aid kid and grabbed a bottle of nose spray and eyewash. Then he bummed a bottle of water from the flight crew. They had an ice chest in the cockpit that had containers of yogurt in addition to the water.

"Actually, I use the Yoplait when my hands get cramped," the pilot confided. He indicated the crook between his thumb and index finger. "It stays cool and doesn't drip into the mechanism the way ice cubes do."

Bryan smiled. That was a TV endorsement he'd have loved to see. Feeling somewhat refreshed, the major walked to the front row and sat beside the general. "Has there been any news?" he asked.

"The C-130 from NSCC arrived at Pendleton ten minutes ago," Scott told him. He looked up from his computer. "Other than that, I know very little. Here's a photo of what you're going in to retrieve." He uploaded an image that Beaudine had forwarded: a silver-white console that resembled a speaker's podium, with two computer keyboards mounted on top. "The brigadier general says the unit is bolted to the floor of the command center. At least, they hope it still is. They don't want the stand, just the keyboards and the computer."

"Presumably, they were also screwed in place."

"Yes."

"I'd have thought the insides of this thing would be corrupted by the salt water," Bryan said.

"Apparently the device was pretty well insulated. I'm guessing that whatever data they can pull from it is more than they have now."

"True. And we don't know what it does?" Bryan asked, studying the unimposing unit. "No clue?"

"I'm pretty sure it interfaced a test plane of some kind," Scott said. "That was reinforced when I saw this FAA notice of a lockdown at all airfields west of the Rio Grande in New Mexico through southern Arizona."

"That's along the flight path to San Diego," Bryan observed. "It could signify a return trip from White Sands."

"Exactly," Scott said. "I've been going over DoD files to try and figure out what they *might* be doing out there. The avionic technical files are eyes-only, but I do have access to the civilian personnel they've hired over the last few years. Four are pretty significant. They have Dr. Hank Hathaway and Dr. Sherrie Gati, both of whom are experts in automated flight systems. You might expect that for an airplane. But the most interesting hires were a Dr. Maxwell Blue and Dr. George Mason. Blue's specialty is hydrodynamics and Mason's specialty is nitrogen fuel conversion."

"That would be the power-generating action of water and—what? Turning air-gas into some kind of propulsion," Bryan said.

"Correct. But in the aeronautics arena, not in the sea."

"Meaning?"

"I haven't a goddamn clue," Scott replied.

Bryan looked at him. "I was hoping for something more enlightening."

"Sorry," the general said. "There's a lot of data out there but not a lot of answers. I've got photos of the site, I've printed out an equipment inventory the rescue workers are using, and I still have no idea what we're looking for—other than what it looks like." The general flicked a finger against the monitor. "Sometimes using these things is like shaking one of those Magic 8 Balls. You know the toy I mean?"

"Yes, sir. I was a kid once," Bryan said.

"My nephews used to play with them," Scott said. "Half the time the answers were wrong, and even when the answers were right they still didn't tell you a damn thing. I never understood their appeal."

"You weren't seven years old, sir."

"No," Scott agreed. "I've been shaking this bastard for hours and getting nowhere." The general folded the computer away. "Hopefully, we'll have answers soon enough." He looked at his watch. "We should be landing in about twenty minutes. Do you have any preferences for the A and B teams?" He took a roster list from the laptop's carrying case.

"No, sir." Bryan smiled. "I'm betting you didn't play very much as a kid."

"Why do you say that?"

"Because you're awkward when you try and relax. Like a flat-footed dancer at the prom."

"I played baseball," Scott said defensively. "And there was the occasional picture show, as my granddad called it."

"But that wasn't really 'play,'" the major replied. "Not unless you went home and threw a blanket over a piano bench and pretended to be Hopalong Cassidy or the Lone Ranger."

"I didn't do that, no," Scott said. "There wasn't time. Or a piano bench. We had chores or schoolwork."

"My point exactly. That's all you do. Hell, sir. I'll bet you don't even carry some of those old movies to watch on your laptop."

"No, Major."

"You should. You don't even have to call it play," Bryan said. "You can call it downtime, like most people."

Scott grinned. "Point taken. Recommendations?"

"Yes, sir. When this mission is completed I think we should play baseball. All of us. You manage one squad, I'll manage the other."

"I'd kill you."

"You'd try, sir, I know that. I think it would be good for morale. And a helluva lot more fun than dodging lava rock."

"You've got a deal," Scott said.

"Good. Choose your A and B Teams for this mission. Those will also be the teams we field back home."

"I'll pick the teams, you choose the one you want to manage."

"Very fair, sir," Bryan replied.

The general chose his squads with care, distributing power and agility, cunning and aggressiveness equally. Major Bryan almost managed to forget, for a few minutes, that the assignments had nothing to do with baseball. The personnel had to be equally well-balanced. B Team would be responsible for completing the carrier mission if anything should happen to A Team.

Most aircraft plip-plopped to a landing. The Hercules did not. The C-130J landed hard, all 120,000 pounds of it. The landing was more like a gentle collision than a touchdown as two massive objects met, the ground and the aircraft. And the aircraft was flying ultralight, no cargo, in order to achieve its maximum 2,200-mile range to complete the 2,100 mile trip.

The LASER team was met by a pair of Hueys. The team from Corpus Christi was already onboard one of the helicopters. General Scott had spoken to them while they were en route. They were fully briefed on what had happened in Hawaii and what they were expected to do in San Diego. Both helicopters were also carrying the equipment the LASER squad might need for the mission, including scuba gear.

General Scott went to the cockpit and Bryan crouched

among the bags, backpacks, and cases. He looked around. Gabriel squatted beside him while the other LASER members took seats along the fuselage. They were slipping on the wetsuits and equipment belts. "They assume we know how to use this stuff," Gabriel remarked as the chopper lifted off.

"Our qualifications are on file," Bryan said. "I'm not seeing anything here that scares me."

Gabriel picked up a yellow plastic case and popped it open. He removed a device that looked like a big gold tuning fork with a garden hose nozzle at the end. Beside it was a red cylinder that resembled a flashlight.

"I'm guessing this is an underwater cutting torch and igniter," Gabriel said as he examined the tool.

"It's a Paramount Model R," Ensign Galvez said from his seat. "You can distinguish it from the Model P by the shroud behind the nozzle."

"No, *you* can. What's the big deal about the shroud?"

"It prevents backflashing up the fuel line."

"Okay, that's something we'd want," Gabriel said.

"Safe and state-of-the-art," Lieutenant Black said from her seat.

"Cutting edge," Galvez added with a wink.

"I guess we know our stuff," Gabriel said.

General Scott rejoined the group. He was wearing a headset that connected him with the loudspeaker in the other Huey.

"NB Coronado has narrowed the target area to a site fifty feet from the surface," Scott said. "You will be entering a section of the carrier bridge that slopes down at a thirty degree angle. There is a fire on top, which is being fueled by ruptured fuel tanks on the flight deck, just below the neck of the bridge. That neck is now on top of the inverted command center. Under the bridge, in the Pri-Fly level, is mud that was pushed into the tower structure from below. I'm told it's like quicksand. The device you want is located between them."

"Does Coronado have any suggestions?" Bryan asked.

Scott repeated the question for the other chopper. "They

do not. They haven't been able to get anyone inside yet. Just images from a fiber-optic lens."

"Do they have power on-site, sir?" Lieutenant Black asked.

"Yes."

"Hoses?"

"Three-inch polyester, rubber lined," the general replied. "But the emergency crews haven't been able to get the ammonium polyphosphate drums through to the fire."

"We won't need chemical retardant, general," Lieutenant Black said as the helicopter reached the carrier.

"What will you need?" the general asked.

"Just the hoses, a T-connector, and a way in," she replied.

SIX

Wreck Alley, California

The helicopters landed on floating platforms just forward the target area. The teams got out with the gear. Using the general's squad list as a guide, Major Bryan gave out the mission assignments. He would be taking the first team in with Lieutenant Black as his second. Captain Gabriel would be in charge of the B Team. The captain wasn't happy to be held in reserve, though there was a great deal his squad would need to do on the surface.

Ensign Galvez, on B Team, was busy talking to emergency rescue personnel about the hoses A Team would need.

As the LASER Ops prepared, General Scott walked around the Huey. He stood with his legs spread wide on the gently rocking platform. As motorized dinghies arrived to transport the team Scott took a moment to look out at the overturned aircraft carrier. It was not like the pictures from Pearl Harbor or the webcam images. It had scope that filled his vision and his senses. He could hear the small voices of the rescue workers and the hiss of the hoses, the noise of the generators and the gentle under-sounds of the ocean and air. It was disturbing to see the thousand-foot-long flight deck with seawater splashing against its surface, smoke pumping from cracks in the hull and from the exposed anchor well.

The 22,000-pound anchor was lying along the side, partly deployed. Rescue workers had used it as a place to hook their lines so they could rappel into holes cut into the flight decks.

An emergency worker on the platform told the general that only a hundred or so seamen had been rescued thus far. "We've recovered nearly two hundred fatalities," he added.

Scott forced himself to turn away. The spectacle was overwhelming and disturbing. Yet he didn't see it as a Tower of Babel. It was a big, heaving setback, but it wasn't a mandate against human aspiration. He was willing to bet that the people working over and around the fallen carcass, hurrying like ants in the African veldt, could devise a way to defeat the sea. A flying carrier. Inflatable rapid deployment pontoons. Sonic cannon to break up the waves.

Something.

Back on the Huey, after reviewing photographs on General Scott's laptop, it had taken Lieutenant Black just a few seconds to come up with a plan to get into the carrier's bridge. Scott believed there was no obstacle the human mind and spirit could not overcome. He went over to the A Team. The unit would be out of voice communication until they reached the bridge. However, Lieutenant Kodak would be wearing a hood-mounted videocamera. The general would watch their progress on a palm-sized remote monitor. If the team became distressed or disabled, the B Team would be dispatched to help.

As soon as they were suited up and armed with the tools they would need, Bryan's group set out. Scott stood beside Navy Lieutenant Vic Greenville.

"How is the NURT operation going?" Scott asked the navy liaison.

"They've got about ten minutes to go, sir," he replied.

The Navy's underwater recovery team was twenty feet down, finishing their work in the bridge near the command center. They did not yet have video access to that sector; debris and fire blocked the way. Rather than waste time trying to reconnoiter, they were in the process of installing a means of ingress. The team was using a backpack-carried tactical cutting system, a heavy-duty torch that could slice through ten feet of one-inch-thick steel in ten minutes. The problem was not cutting a four-foot-diameter hole in the metal. It was preventing additional flooding that might compromise sealed chambers or cause the oil-fed fire to spread. To do that, the six engineers had to fill each cut with a foam barrier. When they were finished, they would attach a PUG, a portable underwater gangway. This was a squat hatch with an airlock. The base was inserted directly into the waterproof foam. The first person inside would have to remove the metal plate that had been cut in the bridge. Ordinarily, that would have been structural engineer Kowalski. In his absence, Sergeant Major Tony Cowan would do the honors. He was an experienced diver who also had experience with PUGs.

Scott switched to watching the hood-mounted video. The twelve team members sat on the slip-proof plastic benches of the black rubber rafts. Scott watched as the LASER Ops checked their air tanks, masks, and regulators. They were wearing hard-soled neoprene boots instead of flippers, since they did not expect to be doing much swimming. When everything had been okayed, the members slipped on their warm water gloves. The palms were textured poly-vinyl. This was an environment where the diver wanted his grip to be secure.

Scott looked out across the water as the NURTs emerged. They climbed onto one of the generator platforms beside the bridge and gave the LASER Ops a go-ahead. He saw Sergeant Major Cowan go over the side. Lieutenant Kodak followed him down to relay images of his progress. The general returned to the monitor, sharing it with Lieutenant Greenville. Major Bryan had one as well so he could keep track of the advance team's progress.

The image was difficult to follow at first, since Kodak was bobbing and turning to get to the PUG. Though both men were wearing shoulder-mounted flashlights, it was difficult to make anything out at first. The water was unusually murky due to the silt the tsunami and seaquakes had stirred. The video became clearer when they reached the white hatch of the PUG. Cowan opened the outer door. The two men entered; it was extremely cramped but they managed to shut the door behind them. The sergeant major activated the pump that flushed the water inside. Cowan removed a hammer and chisel from his equipment belt. He tapped along the edge of the circle cut by the NURTs. When it fell inside, Scott could imagine the heavy clang it must have made. Cowan leaned into the opening. He slipped the flashlight from its holder and shined it around inside. Kodak moved in closer to transmit the images.

Apparently, the day was going to end as it had begun.

SEVEN

Wreck Alley, California

"Déjà vu," Ensign Galvez said.

There was more flaming mud. Major Bryan wondered if hell had it in for the LASER Ops.

"At least we have oxygen tanks this time," Moses Houston added. The medic would not be going down with the unit but would remain in the raft in the event anyone were injured.

Major Bryan was sitting in the center of the raft holding his video monitor. Except for Lieutenant Black and Corporal Marc Wright—an Army Special Forces electronics expert who had been aboard the Corpus Christi flight—the other A Team members were gathered around watching the feed. The video image showed a hilly carpet of mud inside the bridge. It was covered with burning oil. Visibility was extremely poor, even though the smoke was being drawn through the bridge like a flue rather than spilling into the PUG.

Bryan looked out at the generator platform as the dinghy pulled alongside. Black and Wright had hopped aboard and were unfolding the hoses that had been brought out to execute her plan.

"Let's get this operation on its feet," Bryan said.

The members of the unit left the rubber raft one at a time,

joining Black and Wright on the forty-by-forty-foot platform. The surface was a high-strength steel and aluminum alloy covered with studded rubber panels. It rested on a pair of pontoons that kept the surface of the platform just above the water.

Black and Wright had attached two hoses with a T-connector, a joint with an adjustable mouth that could be attached to the fan exhaust of the generator. Black knelt at the edge of the water and held one end in. Wright held the other end over the side. They had a Navy technician turn the fan on. Water was sucked through Black's end and came out the other.

Black raised a fist and shook it triumphantly as the siphon worked. She indicated for the technician to cut the engine.

"We're ready, sir!" she shouted to Major Bryan.

"Well done!" Bryan said. He handed one of the Navy technicians the video monitor. "When I give you a thumbs-up, turn on the generator."

"Yes, sir," the young man replied smartly. "One thing you should know, Major."

"Yes?"

"This area is structurally and geologically unstable," the seaman remarked. "Our guys had to withdraw a number of times to keep from being trapped by shifting water and buckling walls."

"Thank you. We've got a torch and we'll keep a foot in the door."

"Sir?" Black shouted.

"What is it?" Bryan asked impatiently.

"When the generator starts, tell them to evac the platform," the lieutenant said. "Some of the fire may get through."

Bryan regarded the technician. "You heard the lieutenant."

"I did, sir."

Bryan thanked him and joined Woodstock Black. Ensign Galvez was right behind him carrying the small Model R torch. The ensign had measured the diameter of the hose nozzle. He felt it should take no more than three minutes to cut a same-size opening in the bridge. Behind him, Air Force Captain Ron Reno, a ballistics man also out of Corpus Christi, was carrying a tank that looked like a fire extinguisher. It was filled with the same foam sealant the NURTs had used to secure the PUG. The plan was to feed one end of the hose into the bridge and then seal it before too much leakage had occurred. The rest would be up to Lieutenant Black. Behind Reno, Coast Guard Commander Jacinto Sierra carried two lengths of hose and a waterproof bag for transporting the device.

Bryan winced as he took a broad step up onto the platform; one of the burns on his back had reminded him it was still there. He stopped suddenly, withdrew, and took a slow breath.

"Are you all right, sir?" Galvez asked.

"I'm fine," Bryan replied. "Just pulled a muscle." He directed the ensign to take the rest of the A Team ahead. The major was annoyed. He didn't like to show weakness or indecision to the squad. He didn't look over at General Scott. He was afraid the CO would call him back. Fortunately, the tight wetsuit was helping to hold the bandages in place.

While he waited for the pain to subside, Bryan noticed something unusual about the color of the water. He knew at once what it was: crude oil. This plan was going to be riskier than he had anticipated.

Bryan resumed the crossing. He stopped beside Woodstock Black. "Lieutenant, did you notice the crude oil on the water?"

"Yes, sir. Probably from the stricken tanker."

"Thoughts?"

"Well, there are cleanup crews about two miles out, mopping up the major spill. I asked one of the Navy team, who told me it will take about an hour for them to pack up and come in."

"We can't afford to wait that long," Bryan said.

"No, sir. I've alerted Lieutenant Wright. He'll be careful

where he points the hose." The lieutenant studied the major for a moment. "Sir, are you sure you're up for this?"

"Why?"

"You're standing a little lopsided."

"I'm fine," Bryan said. "Besides, I'm just going for a swim. You guys are doing all the heavy lifting."

The rest of the team reached the platform. With Master Chief Petty Officer Gunther Wingate assisting Wright on the hose, and Commissioned Warrant Officer Jason Foote, a Navy electronics technician, assigned to Lieutenant Black, the team went into the water. The LASER Ops were just twenty feet from the bridge. The moved quickly to the PUG. After looking at the video it had been decided to place the hose on the right bottom side of the entrance, the point farthest from the flames. The mud would be able to flow down to that point.

Major Bryan was the last team member in the water. He joined the others as they waited to enter the PUG. Cowan and Kodak had joined them outside, sending video to General Scott. As soon as Black got the siphon working, the team would go back inside two at a time. If everything worked the way it was supposed to, the mud would flow from the bridge and exit the hose on Wright's end. That would give the team room to maneuver.

Ensign Galvez completed his work quickly. The nozzle was inserted and sealed and Bryan used the video camera to send a thumbs-up signal to the surface. A moment later they heard the distant chug of the engine. A few seconds later the flat hose began to fill. Major Bryan gave Sergeant Major Cowan the go-ahead to re-enter the PUG. The rest of the team stood back so they wouldn't be caught in the wash from the airlock. There was both a red and a green light on the outside: when the green light came on, the next group of two would enter.

The water felt good. Bryan was standing on a concrete block, part of the artificial reef, moving his arms slowly in the murky sea. The buoyancy of the water, and the therapeutic caress of the current, made his aches and stings much less oppressive. Launching himself forward, the major cut in line.

Lieutenant Black had left Commissioned Warrant Officer Foote in charge of the siphon. She made a face and shrugged a "what gives?" as he swam in front of her. He pointed to the PUG. When the green light came on he entered with her, bumping Captain Reno to the end of the rotation.

The two squeezed into the small opening, bent over with their backs against opposite walls. Black shut the door and pushed the big red button that activated the drain. The water was noisily expelled from the short tunnel.

It had been decided that the crew would continue to wear their masks and use their oxygen tanks when they were inside the bridge. It would be difficult communicating and maneuvering through the wreckage, and tiring to carry them out of the water. But the fires made that imperative. Hopefully, Black's siphon would extinguish the flames by drawing away the oil.

When the tube was dry, a green light beside the inner door came on. Lieutenant Black pulled the latch on the right side. An accordion door folded to the left and allowed them to enter the bridge. The radios built into the hoods and throat sections of the suits would work in here.

The crater of the volcano had been intimidating, but that was about latent force. A big punch and it was over for anyone in or around the mountain. The feeling inside the tower was different. The death blow had been delivered. The danger now was in the tics and spasms of the corpse.

Bryan and Black moved in to make room for the next two. They were standing on the forward wall, which sloped toward shore at a thirty-degree angle. Silty mud was piled against what used to be the corner of the portside wall and the ceiling. It was starting to slip away thanks to Black's hose. A few puddles of fire were burning on oil-covered muck that had collected in the other corners. The black smoke they produced was heavy and sinuous.

The map printout that General Scott had given to Cowan

was useless; the room they were in was so bent and crushed, with smoke cloaking the corners, it was unrecognizable. Bryan walked over to Cowan and Kodak and removed his mouthpiece.

"We're somewhere in the base of the tower!" he said. "We need to go where the fire is!" The men nodded. Bryan went back on the oxygen. The air was pungent and choking with the smell of burning wires, plastic, and whatever protective coating had been sprayed in the vessel to protect it from the corrosive effects of seawater. Two or three gulps of that and a man would be unconscious.

The LASER Ops waited until the mud had been drawn off to a point where it was no deeper than their boots. Some of the fires slid along with it, being extinguished by the silt as it moved. All of the team members were in the tower by then. Bryan organized them into groups of two. Two pairs, A-Team Up, were sent to try and find a way out that did not involve the PUG. Though the LASER Ops could get out by way of the sea, Bryan liked having an alternate route in case that exit became blocked. The two teams climbed up the sloping floor with the help of ropes and hooks. They marked the way with flares and remained in touch with Bryan via radio. The other eight LASER Ops, A-Team Down, went deeper into the tower. Despite the shallowness of the mud the suction was significant. The team was forced to slide along the wall rather than step.

There was a long, jagged, diagonal break in the ceiling just ahead. There were no protruding edges, just the split; the ends of the room had simply pulled away from the center when the tower struck the seabed. The team members were able to step through at the widest point. They entered a level where the mud was thicker. It had obviously oozed through the Pri-Fly deck, which was now the lowest point of the tower. The mud down there was apparently what kept the sea from pouring in. Before the team could go further, the mud would have to be removed.

Lieutenant Black and Commander Sierra went back to

the hose and added the extension. While they snaked the added section of hose into the next room, Bryan contacted General Scott.

"It's difficult to breathe, so I'll make this brief," the major said. "I'm not sure what section of the tower we've entered. I've sent four men to try and find a dry way out. They're following the smoke and water from the fire hoses. We're draining mud from the chamber above the PUG access and should be able to enter in about five minutes. If the device isn't in one of the next three or four rooms, and the fires are still burning, we're going to have to come out for more air."

"I'm having additional tanks sent to the platform," Scott said.

"Do you recognize anything you're seeing on the monitor?"

"Nothing that looks like the 'before' pictures," Scott replied.

As the mud began to drain, Bryan saw a section of inverted wall that looked passable. "I'm going to see if I can get a peek at the next room," he said. "Maybe that will tell us exactly where we are."

The major motioned for Ensign Galvez to follow him, then walked along the bottom of what used to be a shelf of some kind, possibly for equipment. It was welded to the wall and the V-shaped juncture provided a sturdy bridge. The opposite wall, which was above him, had been bent down far enough that Bryan could push up against it to help steady himself. Extending his arms also stretched the bandages, but that couldn't be helped.

The next room was accessible through a severely lopsided doorway. Bryan put both hands against the frame and leaned through. There were no fires inside so the room was dark. The major removed a small flashlight from his equipment belt and shined it ahead. The room sparkled like a mythical treasure cave.

Particles of glass, he thought.

Window glass.

He turned the light around the room. Mud had filled more

than two-thirds of the right side, preventing seawater from entering, but he could make out communications consoles along the walls above him and several broken stands that once had held swivel chairs. Then he noticed something else. Bunched fabric poking here and there from the mud. Fingers and hands protruding from the dark, silky surface.

The door had been opened from the inside. People were trying to get out. Holding on to the jamb to which the hinges were attached, Bryan leaned in and examined it. The door was pressed to the wall by mud. Any distinctive markings were buried. Then he noticed the edge of a manual sticking from the mud. He handed Galvez the flashlight and indicated where to point it. Bryan squatted on the jamb and reached in. He grasped the tip of the book and worked it free. There was a chain on the buried end, but he was able to read the cover: *Daily Codes*. Only the radio operator on the bridge would possess that.

Bryan pulled out his mouthpiece. He told Galvez to bring Lieutenant Kodak over, then switched on the radio. "General? I think we've reached the bridge. The room is full of mud but we can't risk using the siphon here. The windows have been shattered and the only thing keeping the sea out is mud that looks like it was pressed in from the sea floor."

"Major, if that's the only way to find the device we may have no choice."

"I'm going to send you pictures. Maybe the brigadier general can give us a clue where to look."

"All right," Scott said.

Kodak arrived and Bryan stood shoulder-to-shoulder with him in the slanted doorway. The major helped to steady the lieutenant, who leaned forward to video as much of the room as he could. Suddenly, they heard a soft banging sound. At first, Bryan thought it was the carrier shifting. But nothing had moved. He listened and the sound came again, to the left. Three distinct raps. He shined his light in that direction. Bryan saw nothing. He moved the light up toward the ceiling—what used to be the aft wall. It looked like the entrance to a corridor of some kind.

"Is anyone up there?" he shouted.

There was another very faint knock.

Bryan handed Galvez his radio, then looked around for a handhold. He saw equipment brackets about two yards away. He told Kodak to brace himself against the jamb and give him a push up. The lieutenant put his back to the open doorway, which left him lying at an angle of fifty-odd degrees. He put his hands against his chest and with the help of Ensign Galvez Bryan stepped on Kodak's palms. Working together, the men pushed him up. The major grabbed the brackets and pulled himself higher. He made his way up the wall another ten feet by grabbing pipes and rents, anything he could hold on to. When Bryan reached the area where the sound had originated he shined the light inside. It was the lookout's post. The glass here was intact.

The small, phone booth–size cubicle was not empty. A man was lying against the wall. A captain. He was pinned there by the floor, which had been crushed down from above. The struts that had pushed through it were lying across the man's legs. His eyes were open and blinking. His left arm was free; he had used his knuckles to rap on the wall. Bryan turned back toward the team. "We've got a survivor here!" he yelled. "I need the cutting torch and hands! And drinking water! Have someone from B Team bring it."

"Coming, sir!" Galvez called up.

"And contact A Team Up. I need a dry way out of here ASAP."

"Yes, sir!"

Bryan crawled over to the man. His face was greasy with perspiration and smoke. He was lucky there had not been a fire in here. He obviously had enough air to sustain him.

"We're going to get you out," Bryan said.

"Link," the man rasped weakly.

"Is that your name?"

The man shook his head. Then he shut his eyes.

"You rest, Captain," Bryan said.

The major had a look at the man's name tag—it read "Captain Flynn"—then shined the flashlight around his chest, looking for blood. He saw none on the man's clothing, then checked his mouth, ears, and nose. The officer probably didn't have internal injuries; there was nothing around that could have caused them. He was pinned at the right thigh and left shin. It shouldn't be difficult to get him free.

Galvez squirreled his way to the cubicle and stuck his head in. "You want me to do the cutting, sir?"

"All right."

Bryan lay down and slid back so that Galvez could creep in.

"Sir, A Team Up reports they've got a way to the hull," Galvez said as he edged by. "The NURTs are cutting through to them now. One pair is coming back to collect the survivor."

"Excellent."

"Moses has water and a stretcher ready. And here," Galvez said, handing him the radio. "General Scott wants to know who we have."

Bryan took the radio and finished backing out.

He would tell the general they'd found a captain named Flynn and that the first and only word out of his mouth had been "link."

As in "missing."

EIGHT

Wreck Alley, California

While awaiting the arrival of Captain Flynn, General Scott called Brigadier General Beaudine with news of the find. He had already forwarded Kodak's video showing the condition of the bridge. Beaudine had not commented on that, but he was excited to learn about the discovery of Captain Flynn.

"Did Flynn say anything?" Beaudine asked.

"He said 'link,'" Scott told him.

"Nothing else?"

"No, but he was very weak. What does that mean, 'link'?"

"That's the device," Beaudine told him. "That's what we're looking for. Captain Flynn was the on-site project officer. Whatever he knows, I need to know."

"I understand. Look, they're coming out now. The raft will be here in a few minutes. I'll find out what I can and call you back."

"Ben—"

"I know. It's important. I'll tell the medic to do what he can to bring your man around."

"He knows to report anything Flynn says," Beaudine said. "And he won't give you a hard time about waking the captain if he's unconscious?"

"Yes to both, but the doc will do what he has to," Scott replied.

"I appreciate that, Ben," Beaudine said. "In the meantime, I need your people to continue searching for the device. They may find it before Captain Flynn can tell you anything."

"Bill, you saw the videos," Scott replied. "That environment is extremely unstable."

"I know. And I wouldn't ask if it weren't damned important."

Scott knew that. He said he would have his people continue to search. He relayed the message to Tom Bryan. The major said that they were moving the hose into the bridge but that they were going to proceed with caution.

"As I said before, I'm concerned that the mud is the only thing holding the ocean back," Bryan told him. "The consistency is extremely loose, more so than in the other sections of the tower. It's as if water is already percolating through."

"Do what you can," Scott said. He bit off the part about how vital this was. Bryan knew that or they wouldn't be here.

It was twilight. The sun was a burning wick on its own waxy, elongated reflection. The winds were growing insistent, the waters a little choppier than before. Scott picked up his binoculars and watched as Captain Flynn was lowered from the hull in a stretcher that Moses had sent up.

The B Team was standing, sitting, and, in the case of Captain Gabriel, pacing on the other side of the platform. Scott had given Army Corporal Emens the video monitor. Several of the team members were gathered around him, watching the broadcast and commenting on the destruction.

Scott wished he knew more about this damn project, whatever it was. The military had two kinds of emergencies: real ones and cover-your-ass ones. The latter were alarmingly common, like putting a dictator in power, having him turn on you, then coming up with a moral lie that would justify having soldiers die to take him out. Or using friendly fire or a dangerous mission to take out a rival or informer—known as

'U-Turn,' named after Uriah, the Old Testament soldier sent to the front by King David so the king could be with the man's wife, Bathsheba. Scott would hate to put his people in an extreme high-risk situation to clean up a CYA disaster.

Captain Flynn was loaded onboard the raft. While Moses checked him for external injuries and prepared an IV, a seaman guided the raft toward the platform. One of the Hueys would airlift him to Pendleton.

After I interrogate him, the general thought unhappily. And that was exactly what this would be. Information extracted without consideration for the well-being of the bearer.

Captains Gabriel and Puckett went to the raft as it pulled alongside the platform. The men lifted the stretcher onboard as Houston held the IV bag in place. Scott walked over.

"Set him down," the general ordered.

The two captains did as instructed.

Still holding the bag, Houston bent with them. He looked up. "Sir, this man is dehydrated, hypothermic and—"

"Keep him wet and warm," the general interrupted.

"Sir—"

"We need this information, and we need it now," Scott barked. He knelt beside the officer. Flynn's eyes were shut, but his tongue was moving across his lips. "Captain Flynn, can you hear me?"

The officer nodded once. He hacked fitfully; Houston used a handkerchief to wipe his mouth.

"Captain, what happened to the control device? The link?" Scott asked.

Flynn shook his head.

"You don't know?" Scott asked.

Houston gave Flynn a few drops of water from a plastic bottle. He swallowed and opened his eyes. They were bloodshot from the smoke and seawater.

"Gone," he said.

"Gone where?"

"Burdo . . . Hart," he whispered.

"Are they crew members? Did they take it somewhere?"

"They were . . . crushed. Tanker. Wave . . . knocked me back."

"You're saying the tanker that was struck collided with you," Scott said. "Is that it?"

Flynn nodded with great effort.

"But the water washed you into the lookout corner where they found you," Scott said.

"Don't remember," Flynn said. He shut his eyes again. "Last thing . . . I saw. Captain and Hart at link. Shattered. Pieces . . . everywhere."

"Are you sure the link was destroyed?"

Flynn nodded. "Washed away . . . parts lost."

Scott got on the radio. "Major Bryan?"

"Sir?"

"Hold all activities."

"Freezing activities. Yes, sir."

The general turned behind him. He motioned to the Huey pilot with a vertical rotation of his hand, signalling him to start the rotors turning. Then he bent back over Flynn. "We're going to airlift you to the hospital, Captain. Before you go, is there anything else you can tell me?"

"Couldn't fix," he said.

"You couldn't fix what? The link?"

He nodded, then opened his eyes suddenly. "What about Coronado?"

"Hit by the wave," Scott told him. "The link there was lost as well."

Flynn closed his eyes. He seemed to deflate. "No hope," he said in a low, low whisper. "No hope."

NINE

Wreck Alley, California

"What's the hold about, major?" Lieutenant Black asked.

"I don't know," Bryan replied.

The major and the rest of the A Team were standing in the second chamber, just outside the bridge. A Team Up had just returned from bringing Captain Flynn to the surface. They reported that the climb was relatively easy, though they had not had a chance to explore the hanger deck they had crossed, or the adjoining elevators.

Thanks to Black's improvised vacuum the room was nearly free of mud. Seven bodies had been recovered and were collected in a corner of the room. The remains were laid shoulder-to-shoulder on the sloping wall, their heads facing up, arms at their sides. There was nothing with which to cover them and not enough water to clean them. There was no blood. Mud crept along their skin and uniforms giving them the illusion of movement; water that separated from the silt looked like perspiration. The poor souls looked alive. But they were not. There was an unnatural droop to the lip of one, a careless twist to a wrist or finger or foot of another, the stillness of the chest and eyes to all. The blessing of Bryan's business was that there was rarely time to contemplate the dead. Whatever had killed them was usually still in the neighborhood, still a threat.

The tower had obviously struck the seabed and the mud had come through the bridge into the lower chambers—which were now above it. Bryan suspected that the Pri-Fly section had become detached when the carrier went over and the tower hit the ocean floor. Bryan looked behind him, toward the raised base of the tower. "There's no point waiting around here," he said to the crew. "Let's go to the hanger deck and look for survivors." Everyone moved with speed that suggested unanimous agreement. While they exited, Bryan stayed behind to radio Scott. He told him what they were going to do and suggested that B Team be added to the search party.

"I was just about to radio," Scott said. "I'll send them at once."

"Have them come in through the PUG for practice," Bryan said. "A Team is busy stringing rope ladders for the ascent."

Scott gave the order to Captain Gabriel, then got back on the radio. "They're on their way."

"Thank you, sir. Any luck with Captain Flynn?" Bryan asked. His voice echoed deep into the mudless room, which was empty now except for the bodies. Death in war was something with which he was familiar. It had a distinct personality, a post-climactic sense of despair laced with relief and guilt at having survived. Death in peace was just flat.

"He said the link device was destroyed," Scott said. "I informed Beaudine, who said he would contact Coronado for further instructions."

"Do you think he'll want us to search the bridge?"

"He may want us to, but I'm not sure I'll go along with that. Not if it's as unstable as you say," Scott said. "In any case, he got off the phone quickly when I told him what Captain Flynn said. He no longer seemed interested in the bridge."

"So that could be it for us."

"Apart from helping with the cleanup, it would appear so," Scott said. "Though I have to say, it still doesn't make sense."

"Bringing us all this way to do something the SEALs could have handled?" Bryan asked.

"Exactly."

Bryan told the general about the bodies they had recovered, then went to join the team on the hanger deck. It didn't hurt as much to climb the rope ladder as it had to move through the tower. The bandages on his back had come free, so there was no tugging. He refused to worry about it. Not as he left seven dead seamen lying on a sloping wall behind him.

The Navy was still bringing lights and mobile cranes into the hanger deck. The scale of the destruction could only be measured by what Bryan saw in pockets of light. It was numbing. Aircraft had tumbled one onto the other, creating a shattered, haphazard pile of wings, fuselages, wheels, and glass. There were wide streaks of oil and smaller skidmarks of what Bryan assumed was blood. The starboard hull was intact so there had been no major flooding—just the drip from water that had washed in from the rents in the port side. Elevator shafts had been ripped open as though they were made of aluminum foil. If the destruction outside the light was anything like this, the scale would be impossible to grasp.

Bryan swung onto a rope bridge that his team had slung between the top of the rope ladder and the exit that had been cut in the port side hull by the rescue workers. He planned to find whoever was in charge of the operation and see where LASER could be be utilized.

Heavy rope hung all along the vertical deck like vines in a rain forest. Scaffolding had been strung between many of the lines. They were being used for lights and as launching pads for crews and smaller equipment such as generators. The larger pieces of machinery were being lowered from the hull by crane. The air was clear in here and the major removed his mouthpiece. Smoke, thinner than below, was still filtering through the exterior hole. There had been fires in here as well. Though they were extinguished Bryan could smell the distinctive odor of burned rubber and plastic. Two of the LASER Ops came back along the bridge. They were carrying fire extinguishers to put out the few blazes clinging to life in the tower.

Two ensigns came by with a stretcher. A stack of body bags was folded neatly on top. Bryan stopped them to ask where he could find the director of rescue operations. They told him that Lieutenant Greenville was on a floating platform near the stern. It was marked with a red flag. Bryan thanked them and pushed himself upward along the rope bridge. He was grateful for the full-gear runs they took once each week. The seventy pounds he carried across the beaches of Corpus Christi took the edge off this climb with oxygen tanks.

The closer Bryan came to the opening in the hull of the *Hidalgo,* the more he heard of all the topside activity. Helicopters were arriving and departing, welding torches were burning through metal plates, rescuers were shouting for medics as survivors were found. It was inspiring. LASER's training was about squeezing into places and pulling people out. It was not about shoring up or clearing out whatever system had failed. It was easy to get tunnel vision doing what LASER did, to forget the size, dedication, and resourcefulness of the military machine that was ready to move in behind them. A machine that was dedicated to life, not destruction. While regretting the circumstances that had brought them here, Major Bryan was glad to be reminded of that.

"Major?" General Scott's voice crackled over the radio. Bryan snatched it from his equipment belt.

"Here, sir."

"I need you at the staging area ASAP."

"I'm almost at the opening in the hull," Bryan said. "I can be there in about five minutes."

"Never mind," Scott said. "We'll come and get you."

"We, general?"

"Huey and me," General Scott replied. "We're taking a short trip."

"Where, sir?"

He replied, "The Naval Warfare Assessment Division, outside of San Diego."

PART THREE

Earth

ONE

Tucumcari, New Mexico

For over a decade, sixty-eight-year-old Arnie Walters had been more than just the announcer at the annual Tucumcari Airshow. He had been its ambassador, its heart, and its chief cook and bottle-washer—literally. A Korean war fighter pilot and former commercial pilot for Pan Am, Walters retired when the airline folded and opened the Pilot Bread at the Tucumcari Municipal Airport. Everyone from professional pilots to hobbyists to police air patrols stopped in for breakfast or lunch.

As a commercial pilot, Walters had always enjoyed providing entertaining radio reports to passengers. After opening his restaurant, he enjoyed chatting up the customers. When the airshow was started by the local Rotary Club and they needed someone knowledgeable to call the flyovers and provide color, the Texas native was a natural choice. Crowds loved his slow, dry, funny delivery.

Walters had been looking forward to this year's show, the first evening event in the history of the attraction. After a sunset demonstration of precision flying by the Air Force Thunderbirds, there were going to be spotlights, flares, fireworks, and even a flight by a full-scale amateur re-creation of the rumored Air Force LRV from the 1960s, the Lenticular

Reentry Vehicle or "flying disc." This one had been coated with glow-in-the-dark paint to simulate a UFO landing. Of course, people with motor homes would be able to stay the night for a price. That was a big consideration behind the scheduling of the event.

Right now, however, the normally good-natured announcer was in a provocative mood. The Thunderbirds had been grounded at Holloman Air Force Base in Alamogordo for unspecified reasons, and flights throughout the entire southwest were being cancelled—commercial, private, military. Only a few emergency military flights were given clearance, and only outside a certain perimeter. Even balloons and hang gliders were ordered to keep out of the skies. The FAA announcement issued only two hours before said there was an unspecified military "action" taking place in the region. Though lockdowns were not unprecedented they were usually not so comprehensive. Tests of missile systems or experimental aircraft often required portions of the state's air lanes to be closed for brief periods. Some of that was due to the safety of the nonmilitary traffic, some for security concerns. The military did not want outsiders spying on their operations. But the operative word was usually "brief": *this* order was open-ended and would last a minimum of six hours.

The Rotarians had gathered quickly in their command trailer at the base of the control tower. The dozen men were all veterans, many decorated, of three wars. They felt that military restrictions did not apply to them. The FAA order was intended for those other guys, the recreational and commercial pilots who had never dodged flak or live ammunition, who would gawk at an unexpected streak in the sky instead of saluting it and moving on.

Walters poked his head in from time to time to see what was going on. The inclination seemed to be to let the show proceed in a modified version. For one thing, this airfield was on the northeast fringe of the lockdown area. For another, there was some question about whether the FAA restrictions applied to aircraft that remained below a certain altitude.

Only "flights" were expressly banned. There was no mention of takeoffs and landings. Two of the day's participants, a reconstructed Sopwith Camel and German Fokker triplane, would be engaging in a simulated dogfight just a few hundred feet up. That was lower than most hang gliders. The thinking was to dance around the FAA order and present a show with most of the aircraft that were already at the field. Whatever the military was testing probably wouldn't last more than the six hours, and almost certainly wouldn't be impacted by a few low-flying planes and a mock flying saucer. The airshow organizers felt they could stall with the smaller events until they got an all-clear for the bigger ones. They might even be able to persuade the Thunderbirds to make a dramatic entrance at the end of the show.

The manager of the airfield, Jolly Hyatt, was concerned about losing his license. But he was equally concerned about the movers and shakers of Quay County, Rotarians all, shifting their shipping operations, private planes, and future airshows to Clovis International, which was new and up-and-coming and looking for tenants.

While the go, no-go call was debated and stalled—the FAA might yet rescind the order—people continued to arrive. The Rotary Club did not make any announcements about a possible postponement, cancellation, or scaling-down of the airshow. That would have ended up on local radio stations and people would not have driven out. Those who were already there would have left. This was the year's biggest fund-raiser and the Rotarians hoped to sell at least a break-even supply of baseball caps, T-shirts, banners, and programs. Walters needed to sell virtually all of the extra food he'd bought.

As the sun dropped lower and word of the FAA ruling spread through the crowd, dissension grew among the thousands of attendees. People came to the control tower and Rotary trailer for news, horns were tooted impatiently, and pilots who were standing by their aircraft drew questions and even jeers from crowds that had come to look at the

World War I fighter planes, the Yak 54 Russian Thunder stunt plane, the P-51 Mustang, and the F-86 Sabre. The LRV was inside one of the hangers and would not be revealed until the climax of the airshow. The Rotarians ordered it to be rolled out prematurely to keep people from leaving. The show was a half-hour late and there was no further word from the FAA.

Finally, Walters decided to get on the mike. People were not sure whether to stay or to go and they were definitely not spending money on beer, chicken, tri-tips, and fries. The issue had to be pushed one way or the other.

"Folks, I just don't know what to tell y'all," he drawled. "I see all these wonderful aircraft just sittin' on the ground. Pilots, lemme ask ya: why are your airplanes still tail-down on terra firma?"

Here and there, the crowd cheered.

"I'm thinkin' our beloved Eddie Rickenbacker didn't let fire from a twelve-pounder keep him on the ground," Walters went on. "Are we gonna let some paper do that? *Paper* from a bunch of paper tigers in Washington?" He was starting to make himself indignant. This time the crowd howled its support.

Ahead, a full moon was showing itself above the flat horizon.

"The Man in the Moon is wonderin' the same thing," Walters continued. "Who's gonna turn somethin' on? Anything?"

As the crowd began to chant "Fly, fly, fly!" Walter noticed a light moving horizontally above the moon. It was in the no-fly region to the southwest. The object was flying too slowly to be a shooting star or a missile, and not traveling along any of the established flight lanes. It could have been an aircraft, though the light did not flash the way beacons did on regular aircraft. There was also no contrail; the moon would have illuminated the exhaust from behind. And there was no sound. Even distant planes made some noise. It was just five or six miles up, too low to be a satellite. In any case, it was headed away from the airfield. Whatever it was, the flying object would soon be out of sight. And that meant the curfew would be lifted.

Walters radioed his suspicion to the Rotarians and suggested that, at the very least, they send up some fireworks.

They agreed. Meanwhile, they asked Jolly Hyatt to contact the FAA and explain the situation, perhaps ask for an exemption.

Walters told the crowd to watch the skies. As soon as the fireworks started, retired engineer Jackson Goddard—builder and pilot of the LRV—put on his silvery flight suit and domed helmet, slipped into the flying disc cockpit from below, and fired up the disc. The showgoers cheered their approval.

"Let's crank it up for the Man from Moxie," Walters gushed as a ring of flashing red, white, and blue lights came on around the saucer. "For those of you too young to remember, that means the guy's got pluck." He glanced at his crib sheet. "Our hero Jackson Goddard, the Tucumcari John Glenn, is going to ascend to the forbidden skies on twin counter-rotating coaxial propellers powered by two 44 hp/4000 rpm, four-cylinder, opposed, two-cycle Nelson H-59 engines."

The crowd, psyched now, cheered for the engines.

The phone beeped in the booth. Walters clicked off the microphone and answered.

Errol Calmus, the president of the Rotary Club, said, "Arnie, we did not clear the flight."

"You want me to announce that?" Walters said. "Should I tell him to shut 'er down?"

"I don't see that we have a choice."

There was a sputtering from the airfield. Lit by fireworks, the two World War I fighters were just starting up. The mechanics gave each of the propellers a spin-start. As the men backed away they removed the wheel blocks that held the planes in place. The pilots obviously intended to join the flying disc in the air, which was just rising slowly from the tarmac some fifty yards away.

"Is that a Bentley BR.1 I hear?" Walters said into the microphone. "And a Mercedes D-III? Let's hear it for Dar Norton and Andre Grives, the Dogfight Duo, who will be taxiing to theater right." The announcer turned off the loudspeaker and said into the phone, "Errol, we've got one attraction on the way up and two more ready to go. What do you want me to do?"

"For one thing, stop revving the crowd," Calmus instructed. "Then tell Norton and Grives to stay where they are. Hyatt is still on the phone with the FAA asking for clarification of the order. As soon as he's done we'll make a determination about where to go with this."

"Have him ask them something else," Walters said. "Why I'm seeing something in the sky."

"What?"

"A plane, I think. Going slow and steady about thirty thousand feet up. Right in the middle of the you-shouldn't-be-here zone."

"That could be a military plane."

"It could be," Walters agreed. "It could also mean the ban is over."

"Where is it?"

"A hundred, hundred and fifty miles off. You know, if that's some kinda test and we're supposed to stay away, we're *already* pretty far away."

Calmus was quiet as the biplanes began to turn from the hangar toward the airstrip. The flying disc was now twenty feet up and rising. Camera flashes gleamed off its white exterior.

"Ladies, gentlemen, and ETs, time has been folded for your viewing enjoyment," Walters said over the microphone. "We are privileged to bring you the beginning and the future of flight."

The two vintage aircraft began to taxi side-by-side along the floodlit tarmac. The fireworks had been halted for now. Something attracted Walters' eye. It was the distant plane. The light was growing larger. He looked down at the runway. The two World War I aircraft were just leaving the ground.

"Hyatt just got off the phone with the FAA," Calmus told him. "The order stands. All airworthy devices are to remain on the ground. Arnie, I don't see that we have a choice."

"Okay."

"Hyatt is contacting Jackson to land the disc."

Walters flicked on the microphone as he kept his eyes on the spot of light. It was now twice the size that it had been before. "Pilots, ladies, and gentlemen—I'm sorry to have to say this, but we have just received word from the great and powerful Federal Aviation Administration. For the moment, the Tucumcari Airshow cannot go on. We have not been given a reason, only this directive: nothing can leave the ground." He watched as the two aircraft banked north and south and rose. They would have to come around in order to land. "We hope this order will be lifted soon, but for the moment I repeat: pilots, return to the field."

The spot of light was now a bright cone screaming in their direction. The flying disc was just a few feet from the ground. The fans on the undercarriages were blasting dust in all directions as it returned to earth. The two vintage aircraft were circling for a landing. They had to take extremely wide turns to the east and west to avoid the dust cloud.

"Looks like we have an FAA hall monitor coming in from the southwest," Walters said. He gave the crowd a moment to turn and look. "Those of you who bought your banners—let's show these boys what we think of detention."

Thirty or forty banners were thrust skyward and waved vigorously as the light approached.

"Take that, cyclops-eye."

The flying disc set down, sinking low as it settled on its four hydraulically operated legs. The two older aircraft completed their turn back toward the field and were leveling for a landing. They were less than two hundred feet up. Ground-based spotlights followed them as they flew nearly wingtip to wingtip, their machine guns firing blanks as they came in. The spotlights were shut and the sharp backflash of the guns was visible against the dark sky.

So was the light in the distance. It was definitely closer and appeared to be lower than before.

The machine guns went silent as the planes touched down. The two aircraft bounced from wheel to wheel as they landed, screeching dramatically toward the crowd. The plans veered and braked at the last moment, forming a dramatic V in the center of the landing strip.

"No hits and no errors, a dogfight fought to a standstill for your observing pleasure," Walters said. "Tucumcari Airshow and I want you all to stay where you are. Don't go taxiing off. We're going to keep after those aerocrats in Washington and get the rest of our show going just as soon as we can."

As Walters finished the announcement, the white light in the sky gave birth. He fell silent as he watched it spawn hundreds of smaller lights. The sight reminded him of a meteorite breaking up in the atmosphere, but this was definitely not a chunk of rock. The object had changed course and was moving in a controlled descent. Directly at them. So were all the little lights.

Members of the crowd who had watched the landings were beginning to notice the offshoots of the white light. There was a lot of pointing, and those who were near the open hangar that housed the flying disc moved inside. For once in his life Walters didn't know what to say. The streaks dimmed and went black. They had obviously been lit by the glow of the skylight. But what the hell were they?

Walters went to the door of the booth, opened it, and stepped onto the small, windswept deck that stood two stories above the airfield. He listened. Walters had very good hearing. It came from years of piloting, from listening for whines and pings that were different from the usual myriad sounds. He thought he could hear a high-pitched whistling—perhaps it was many smaller whistles together. It became louder as the seconds passed. The spotlight was still small but it continued to grow. It was about twenty thousand feet up and now Walters could hear a very faint hum coming from that direction.

Suddenly, the whistling became a shriek. The spotlights at the airfield picked up the incoming objects; there were more of them than Walters could have imagined. Each streak was comprised of dozens, perhaps hundreds of small oval beads. They had long tails, like white thread pulled taut at the top, spreading into a conical shape toward the end. They looked to him like severely elongated shuttlecocks. They had to be traveling at near-supersonic speed.

It took the projectiles roughly a second to pass the field lights. Then they vanished again, though not for long.

Piñatas.

That was Walters's first thought as he watched the two taxiing planes come apart. The fabric wings were chopped to confetti and flew everywhere. The wood spars and ribs beneath them were punched to sawdust and splinters and simply dropped to the tarmac. The flight wires were severed and whipped in all directions before dying. The landing gear and tailwheel were still turning, still carrying the fuselage forward, as they were blasted to flat, jagged shards. The propeller turned even as the wooden blades were chewed apart. The fragments were flung from the plane in a clockwise spiral, the direction in which the propeller had been turning.

The pilots never knew any of this was happening. They jerked and spasmed in the initial salvo as though they'd been hit by gunfire from a passing plane. Little fountains of blood erupted from skull to feet—no portion of their bodies escaped the attack. They did not break the way the plane did. They simply dropped to the tarmac as the cockpit around them disintegrated.

It took a moment longer for the LRV to be destroyed as a second wave of "beads" struck from another angle. The light above had moved swiftly behind the announcer's booth to make that possible. Walters knew it was a new cascade of the beads because he saw the streaks reappear briefly as they passed under the lights of the hanger before hitting the flying disc. That ruled out one of his thoughts, that the initial streak was a breakup of some kind, possibly a satellite or test plane. This was a targeted maneuver. There was no explosion and very little ancillary damage. A few people were hurt by flying debris but only the pilots, still in the cockpit, were fatalities. The edges of the shattered bubble cockpit were streaked with blood.

The maelstrom was finished in an instant, yet every phase of the assault had registered on Walters. One thing was perhaps most amazing of all, however. As he watched the last of the aircraft snow down in multicolored pieces, Walters saw no marks on the tarmac. Bullets would have continued through the flimsy aircraft and dotted the asphalt with pips.

Whispers and movement broke the horrified silence that followed the attack.

Walters looked up. The light was gone. He went back inside and called 911 to report injuries and was informed that the incident had already been phoned in. Probably by Errol Calmus. Walters could already hear sirens in the distance.

He got back on the loudspeaker. People were starting to hurry away, some of them running back toward their cars.

"Ladies and gentlemen, it would appear whatever this incident was, it is over. Help is on its way. I urge you to remain where you are, to not crowd the roads until the police, fire, and emergency medical personnel have made their way onto the airfield. I would also ask individuals who took pictures or video of the incident to give it to the authorities to review. Your contribution could be the key to preventing an event like this in the future."

People did not appear to be listening. And if they did hear, the "not me" rule appeared to be in effect, the idea that laws, restrictions, and requests for cooperation applied to everyone else.

Walters felt like shouting at them but knew it would be useless. Errol Calmus called, wanting Walters to stay around. Walters said he would, of course.

"Arnie, what the hell was that?" Calmus asked. "No one here has ever seen anything like that. It looked like hail."

"I don't know what it was, Errol," Walters told him. "But it took down everything that flew. Not only took it down but caused very little collateral destruction." He was still numb, still trying to process what he had just witnessed.

"This had to be why the FAA didn't want us flying," Calmus said. "Maybe a freak meteorological condition."

"I don't think so. There was also that bright light," Walters said. "That was a part of it."

"A part of what, though?" Calmus asked. "What did the FAA know that they didn't tell us?"

"Probably not much," Walters said. He watched as members of the crowd fought the exodus to get to the hangar. Souvenir seekers or doctors? Both, probably. It always astonished him that the same disaster could bring out the best and the worst in people, the heroes and the survivalists, the saints and the exploiters.

"God help us," Calmus said anxiously. "We shouldn't have been so flip. This has to be why they wanted us to stay out of the air."

"So some gun-happy kid in a hot new hunk of flying machine wouldn't shoot down biplanes or a flying disc that didn't get much higher than the hangar?" Walters declared. "That's ridiculous."

"Obviously not," Calmus fretted. "We're dead, Arnie. Dead as the LRV. We knew about the restriction and we disobeyed it. We lost pilots and property and we have injured showgoers. This is it for us."

Walter didn't bother responding to that. They were guilty as charged and they would have to deal with that. Tomfoolery and hotdogging had cost fighter pilots their lives in Korea, too. It did bother him, though. They had broken the lockdown and sent planes up—playfully, teasingly—yet that didn't change one key fact.

The planes were *out* of the air when they were hit.

TWO

Norco, California

During the 1920s and 1930s, the building that now houses the Naval Warfare Assessment Division was the Rex Clark Resort. It was a hideout for Hollywood celebrities ranging from Walt Disney to Bob Hope. It was close enough to Hollywood to provide access but far enough to forget about the industry for a while. With the shadow of war falling over the Pacific, the Navy bought the facility—which was a short flight from San Diego—and turned it into a hospital that specialized in rehabilitation. As the needs of the Navy expanded, and the technology of late– and post–World War II combat became increasingly more sophisticated, the Department of Defense expanded and transformed the cloistered facility into a missile research and development center. It had both the capacity and mandate to conduct and analyze ballistics from ordnance designed in other "wire-works," as they dubbed the newest forms of hi-tech warfare.

Today, in addition to being a center of electronic warfare research, the NWAD also houses the Defense Logistics Agency, which teaches advanced, all-services courses in military logistics, research, and systems planning.

This was where the GAP was born.

Tom Bryan had never heard of the place, let alone imagined

that the military would have a super-top-secret center that looked like a college campus sitting amidst an agricultural swath of Riverside County right off Interstate 15. General Scott said he had been here once, back in the early 1980s, to review early plans for President Reagan's space-based Strategic Defense Initiative. That was before there was a freeway. If you didn't fly, you took lumpy dirt roads. In that respect, the location probably made sense. No one was going to just drop in and spy on you. Now, of course, the place was secured by fences, guards, and surveillance equipment. Not that they were necessary. The freeway was usually so congested that it would be difficult for a spy to get anywhere in a hurry. The sentries would probably be able to stroll out and nab him.

Right now, the major and the general were following I-15 north toward the NWAD. They were riding the Huey that had brought them to San Diego, where they had picked up two men: Rear Admiral Edward Parks and Dr. Hank Hathaway. Bryan and Scott had remained in the chopper; except for introductions the two new arrivals had said nothing.

Because it was dark, it had been difficult for Bryan to comprehend the scope of what had happened in San Diego and the NB Coronado. The chopper was noisy, so the quiet at the base was not noticeable. There were worklights on, many of them makeshift illumination suspended from cranes, but that did not seem extraordinary. What made it so were the expressions of the men. Their eyes and the turn of their mouths painted a portrait of despondency and gloom unlike any Bryan had ever seen. Faces in warfare were often twisted in shock or horror. This was different. There was something miserably helpless about these two, about their silence, about the way they just looked off at the dark walls of the Huey.

Then, too, it had been a helluva long day. For all of them.

The chopper landed next to the stark Warfare Assessment Laboratory. Armed guards allowed the passengers out in turn, after first checking handheld PSISs—photo security information systems—which contained not only mug-shot style photographs of the individuals taken from their top-security files, but also a question that came from the dossier. These had to be answered on the screen in their own hand-writing—the analysis of which was the third proof of identity. For Bryan, this month's question was, "How did you break your leg in the fourth grade?" The answer was "Ice-skating." The sentry cleared the officer with a salute and passed him to the guard who would take them inside. As the major stood awaiting the others, he noticed a deep, ripe, very pervasive smell in the air.

"Corporal, what is that odor?" he asked the second guard.

"Horse exhaust, sir."

"Pardon?"

"It's manure, sir," the corporal replied. "The rest of the county smells of car fumes. The locals all have horses. They call this smell their horse exhaust."

"I see," Bryan replied. "Do you get used to it?"

"Only if you breathe through your mouth, sir," the corporal replied.

The other three men joined Bryan. The two corporals brought them into the WAL, one man walking in front and the other behind. They were serious about their duties. Bryan found it odd that neither of them said anything about Coronado. The men knew from the IDs of Parks and Hathaway, possibly from past encounters, that the men had probably come from there.

I guess high security means high security, Bryan thought. No one talked business with anyone, not even to say, "Glad to see you're all right, sir."

The men walked them through a keypad-entry doorway in the side of a bare stucco wall. There were no windows on this side of the building, which faced the freeway and the mountains beyond. A shoulder or nearby foothill would be a good vantage point from which to peek into rooms, to read lips or even the vibration of windowpanes. Conversations could be reconstructed by transforming those oscillations into graphs and then back into speech.

A young lieutenant met them inside and took them to a conference room a short walk down the corridor. She was sharp and efficient and also not conversational, except to ask if they would like food or beverages. The men from Coronado asked for sandwiches and coffee. Scott and Bryan said the sandwiches sounded good but they would rather have a Coke.

Different caffeine delivery systems for different overly tired folk, Bryan thought. The air-conditioned room was on the chilly side; Parks lowered the thermostat slightly. A circular table was set in the middle of the small room under banks of fluorescent lights. It was strange to see a man as bronzed as Rear Admiral Parks look so strangely worn and unhealthy.

A built-in TV was tuned to CNN. There were pictures from earlier in the day, showing the destruction in San Diego. Neither Parks nor Hathaway watched. The lieutenant said that the computer on the table was booted and only needed the rear admiral's password to be operational.

"Rear Admiral," the lieutenant said before leaving, "we've been notified that an eyes-only message came in several minutes ago."

Parks thanked the lieutenant and she shut the door. The men sat in the four leather swivel chairs that surrounded the table. Parks and Hathaway sat heavily. Parks input his password and read the message.

"Sweet Jesus," the naval officer said.

The rear admiral swung the monitor toward Hathaway. The scientist winced but said nothing.

Parks looked at the other two men. "General Scott, Major Bryan, forgive me. It's been a bad day."

"Worse for some," Scott observed.

"That's very true," Parks agreed. "To begin with, I want to thank you for all that you and your team did today." He regarded the major. "I understand you went from fire to fire."

"Yes, sir," Bryan said. "I'm sorry our expedition to the *Hidalgo* didn't work out better."

"You saved the life of Captain Flynn. As the general just reminded us, that is very significant," Parks said "Unfortunately, the good news is far outweighed by the bad." He poked a thumb toward the monitor. "That was the start, I'm afraid, of the bad. From Brigadier General Beaudine at White Sands. He said that three aircraft were destroyed at a local airshow. The MO sounds like our Angel."

Scott leaned forward. "Rear Admiral, perhaps we'd better scroll this back. We have not been briefed at all about what has gone wrong."

"I know," Parks said. "Only a handful of individuals know anything about this project, and fewer know that it has slipped out of control."

There was a knock at the door. Bryan admitted a corporal who was pushing a cart from the commissary.

"Just leave everything," Parks said.

"I added a few cookies, sirs," the corporal said, saluting before he quickly set out the styrofoam containers. "Everyone always forgets to ask for them but is always glad they're here."

"Thank you," the rear admiral said. "We appreciate the backstop."

"My job, sir," the corporal smiled.

The young man left. Hathaway passed out the sandwiches—they were all turkey club—as Parks continued.

"Eleven years ago, before we even had a department of Homeland Security, the military started looking into the idea of using high-altitude endurance unmanned aerial vehicles for more than just reconnaissance over hostile territory and the surgical elimination of enemy factions," Parks said. "We started working on modifications at this facility, using the Global Hawk UAV as a springboard. Dr. Hathaway was the point man in the design and construction of a new type of defensive-offensive drone. We called the program the Guardian Angel Project."

While he spoke, Parks peeled the lid from a container of coffee. He drank it black. Bryan noticed that his hand was trembling.

"You recall that after the attacks on the World Trade Center and the Pentagon, the major problem in maintaining aerial patrols over American cities was pilot fatigue," Parks went on. "The GAP was conceived as a means of placing dozens of aircraft in our skies, flying at altitudes well above commercial and private flight lanes. They were designed to target hijacked or illegal aircraft and to remain aloft indefinitely, propelled by nitrogen-powered engines and armed with a gun that draws water vapor from the air and compresses it into a friction-free superfluid helium shell."

"There's a virtually limitless supply of these ingredients in our atmosphere," Hathaway added.

"A perpetual-motion aircraft with a self-stocking arsenal," Scott said.

Parks nodded. "These guns fire a spray of pellets that disintegrate on impact, thanks to the thinness of the shell," he said. "Until that point, the pellets travel at seven thousand feet a second. That's forty percent greater than the velocity of a projectile from a high-powered rifle."

"But the water-helium ordnance only impacts what the Angel has targeted," Hathaway added. "There is very little collateral damage."

"Except for whatever is beneath the targeted aircraft," Bryan observed through a bite of turkey.

"An unavoidable casualty of the system," Hathaway allowed.

"The system with no off switch," Bryan added.

"I take it the device we were seeking controls a test version of the Angel," Scott said, firing a "stow it" look at Bryan.

"This is more than just a prototype," Parks told him. "It's the first production-line model."

"What's the difference?" Scott asked.

"If all went well—and it did, the test was successful—the aircraft was designed to stay aloft," Parks replied.

"And if it didn't?" Scott asked.

"We would have brought her back to the *Hidalgo*," the rear admiral told him. "Unfortunately, that became impossible. And now—" Parks looked at the computer monitor again, this time with sadness. "Now the bird is up there doing its job."

"Running off onboard programming," Scott said.

Parks nodded. "The Angel was designed to hit three targets at the White Sands Missile Range. After that, the aircraft was to go into operational mode. We had planned to send it patrol coordinates as well as potential targets, whenever they appeared within its monitor grid."

"An enemy fighter or a hijacked airliner," Scott said.

"Right. Hank, maybe you'd better explain how that was going to work," Parks said.

Bryan did not like the words "going to."

Hathaway took a bite of sandwich. He thought as he chewed. "The Angel is programmed to spot aircraft," the scientist told them. "Fixed wing, motorized, gliders, hanggliders, vertical takeoff, missiles, even balloons. It's designed to watch anything that doesn't flap. This data was programmed to be received and read at Coronado for now, ultimately in Washington, D.C., with Coronado as a backup."

"At Andrews Air Force Base," Parks added. "This was going to remain a military operation, though we didn't expect to keep the Guardian Angel Project secret for much longer. We wanted it to be a very public, very visible deterrent. We also wanted it to be foolproof. Invincible, if you will. There's no point having a security system if it can be compromised."

"And that's where we got our ears pinned back, I'm guessing," Scott said.

"Absent a specific signal, the Angel is hardwired to destroy any incoming object," Hathaway told him. "Aircraft, missile, disintegrating space debris that crosses its path— anything. It is also hardwired to protect the nation in the event of a catastrophic first strike."

"For example, if Andrews were shut down by an electro-magnetic pulse attack the Guardian Angel would have been free to retaliate," Parks said.

"Against?" Scott asked.

"Any aircraft not listed in the no-kill database," Parks replied.

"In other words, it would have let our military aircraft take off but nothing else," Hathaway said. "Everything else in the zone would have been grounded. The problem is, the Angel that's aloft is still in its trial mode. We were attempting to send it a recall—which apparently got through—and then a blanket no-kill instruction when we lost contact from both links."

"In its present command configuration we believe the Angel will head back for Wreck Alley, where it was launched," Park said. "It will search for the link but without any restraints."

"With no conscience," Hathaway said.

Scott pointed to the back of the computer monitor. "It shot down additional aircraft, didn't it?" he asked. "That's what you were reading."

Parks nodded and explained about the airshow.

"Shooting them down is not quite accurate," Hathaway pointed out. "Those aircraft *had* been aloft. The Angel had locked on them and pursued them to the tarmac."

"Like a hit man," Bryan observed. "Once the contract's in, it's in."

"An apt comparison," Hathaway said.

"If this was an airshow, I assume reporters were in attendance," the major said.

"Yes, though fortunately there were no live broadcasts" Parks told him. "We are in the process of gathering all the pictures and home video shot at the site. We had to stretch the letter of the Homeland Security mandate, but we can't afford to have enemies analyzing the images until the fleet is fielded. We are in the process of drafting a statement acknowledging that there was a weapons test in progress, though we can't say any more at present. The organizers of the airshow have admitted ignoring an FAA order grounding all aircraft."

"Just so I understand," Scott said, "if those aircraft had taxied but not taken off, would the Angel have targeted them?"

"No, General," Hathaway replied. "The Angel works off a complex vector of velocity, configuration, geographical location, and shadow-to-source transition—that is, the change in the silhouette of the target aircraft relative to the constant position of the Angel."

"We gave it everything except what we need now," Parks said. "A one-button self-destruct system."

"We couldn't afford to," Hathaway said. "If you give someone a way in, a software program, they will find a way to use it against you. Everything is hackable."

"We'll hold the postmortems for another time," Parks said. "The FAA has grounded all aircraft in the Angel's projected flight path. We have a little time, at least."

"To do what" Scott asked. "What happens when it gets to Wreck Alley?"

"We don't know," Hathaway admitted.

"How many possible options are there?" Bryan asked.

"More than I would like to see," Hathaway told him. "We came out to NWAD to run simulations. The Angel won't 'see' the flight deck of the *Hidalgo,* so it will probably remain aloft."

"On patrol," Scott said.

"Yes," Hathaway said.

"In just that area of the California coast?" Bryan asked. He did not think the answer would cheer him and he was right.

"I don't think so," Hathaway replied.

Parks added quickly that the patrol zone of the Angel was not their current concern. Stopping it was. The rear admiral offered that too quickly to suggest ignorance, Bryan thought. The men probably knew exactly where the Angel would go and what it would do.

"I assume you have some thoughts about how to stop your rogue Angel?" Scott said.

"We're looking into that," the rear admiral told him, "which is why we wanted you here. We are hoping there may be a way to get a man up to it."

"Praying, would be more like it," Hathaway said.

"That, too," Parks admitted. He looked at Major Bryan. "What I need to know, Major, is whether you or anyone on your team might be willing to undertake such a mission."

"The fact that you're looking at me and not the general suggests a plan that has the name 'Bryan' where it says fill in the blank."

"We are working on one," Parks agreed. "Your dossier showed you highly rated for solo passengership."

"Solo passengership on what? *For* what?" Bryan asked.

"The sailplane into Brackettville," Scott said with a voice that carried the hint of a moan. "Rear Admiral, I gave the major that red-flag commendation because it was a helluva a flight for a nonpilot."

"You did that, sir?" Bryan asked.

"Exactly," Parks replied. "The major is a natural."

"Maybe. We don't know that."

Parks's eyes shifted to Scott. "General, we don't have a lot of options or a lot of time.

"I understand that, but we do have a pilot on our team—"

"Captain Puckett, who is an experienced helicopter pilot. That's not going to help us at fifty thousand feet," Parks said. "I looked for someone who was in the vicinity, who was not tied up with other duties, and who had been on a multihour one-man Lindbergh. Major Bryan is the only one who has flown a fixed-wing aircraft *and* who has shown the ability to improvise in difficult situations." Parks regarded Bryan. "You did an exceptional job on the Tempest rescue."

"That was a group effort," Bryan replied. He was still surprised and flattered that General Scott had noted the glider flight to Brackettville. The major had undertaken a high-risk training scenario. Though he hadn't mastered the art of sailplaning, the top brass wouldn't know that when it came time to consider Bryan for promotion. A HiRTS would help to get him his colonelcy.

"Any team has a commander, and you were that man," Parks said. "Major, we can't send a team and we don't want a hotdogger going up. We need a steady hand, one who has been crisis-tested. If we can work out a realistic abort scenario, will you be part of it?"

Bryan glanced at Scott, who didn't look happy. But there was resignation in his eyes and in the tips of his fingers, which he raised in deference or submission—Bryan wasn't sure which.

"Of course I will be part of your operation," Bryan replied.

The rear admiral thanked him and asked if the men would prefer to be taken to quarters or to sit with them while they worked on the problem. Bryan said he would like to rest. Scott said he wanted to stay.

Pity poor Parks and Hathaway, Bryan thought. This was where Scott did due diligence to make sure everything possible would be done to safeguard the major. The general could get pretty rough in these situations.

Parks phoned the lieutenant, who came back to escort Bryan to the subbasement guest quarters. He grabbed his sandwich and left with her. As they took the elevator below, Bryan learned that the third level down was known as the Rex Clark Memorial Resort.

"No windows, no hot springs, but no wait." She smiled pleasantly. She added that all the rooms down here were no smoking. Bryan said that wasn't a problem.

The major did not doubt the correctness of his decision. He had joined the Army to protect his nation and its Constitution. He had also been looking forward to challenges. Bryan had gotten those. He had also learned something at a relatively early age that a lot of young men didn't: that they weren't invincible. That it was all right to acknowledge fears and weaknesses as long as you didn't let them stop you. That was growth he wanted to continue to experience.

Bryan entered the small guest cubicle. The cinder-block walls had been painted a fawn color. Photographs of vintage naval vessels adorned the walls. They were preferable to the generic art that decorated most hotel rooms.

The lieutenant turned on the nightstand lamp and left, telling him to punch 1015 on the phone if he needed anything. There was a TV in the corner with basic cable, though he assured her he wouldn't be needing that. He was whipped.

Bryan unlaced his boots and showered in the tiny bathroom. Wrapped in the towel, he sat on a corner of the twin bed and ate his sandwich as he stared at the cream-colored carpet. He wondered at what point did overriding one's fears become complete, self-sacrificial stupidity?

When it was impulsive, like road rage, and not worthwhile, like safeguarding the nation, Bryan decided. Besides, if he made it through another HiRTS he would be that much closer to a promotion. *A big rise or a big, fifty-thousand-foot fall.*

He finished eating, lay back on the bed, and switched off the light. Whether it was wooziness or exhaustion-induced clarity talking, Bryan was a little unnerved to think back over a day and realize how much it had been like life itself. A violent, eruptive start followed by bumpy journeys—the C-130J, the Huey, the *Hidalgo,* and another Huey. Now he was in a small, quiet, underground box.

As he fell asleep, he was grateful for one thing. If that was really what life was about, he was glad his journeys had been exciting ones.

THREE

Shanghai, China

The People's Liberation Army Naval Flight Unit at the Shanghai Dachang Airbase was considered a poor brother to the Shanghai Jiangwan facility. Twenty-nine-year-old Lieutenant Commander Bruce Chan knew that probably had nothing to do with geography, since the two airfields were close enough that pilots taking off from one could see gestures made by pilots on the ground in the other. Usually, those gestures were friendly. Competition among Chinese pilots was intense, but camaraderie and nationalism was greater.

No, the growth of Jiangwan was probably the result of old family ties between this member of government and that commander, ancient dynastic loyalties—or rivalries—that went back centuries. Also, Dachang was used as a staging area by the PLANFU. Jiangwan was primarily used by the People's Liberation Army Air Force. PLA Central Command reasoned that the air force should have the most modern air facilities. At least PLACC was consistent: PLAAF ships that were used to recover jettisoned pilots or participate in war games were restricted to a single shed and run-down dock down the coast at Ningbo.

Ironically, the best fliers were stationed where the technical

and logistical facilities were the weakest, at Dachang instead
of Jiangwan. That also kept Chan and his Dachang comrades
away from the best and newest fighters, like the JF-17 Fierce
Dragon with its mighty Kunlun II engines, sophisticated
navigational equipment, and an inflight-refueling probe; and
the J-13 Hidden Dragon with its stealth capabilities. Chan
and the other pilots in his Soaring Hawk team had trained in
them, since one day they were supposed to replace the aging
MiGs at Dachang. But until that time arrived, Chan was assigned to a MiG-21.

Not that he was complaining. As much as Chan loved the
newer planes and yearned for a chance to shake a few of
them down, he had joined the PLANFU in order to fly. He
had been doing that for two years now. The Russian-made
MiGs were not known for their electronics. Even the late-
model 21 had limited ability to acquire and target enemy aircraft, to use or avoid radar, to navigate with great finesse, or
to carry overwhelming force into battle. It was renowned, in
fact, for just two things: the simplicity of its design and
responsive handling. But those were qualities that made it a
pilot's aircraft. Like the biplanes of the early twentieth century, the MiG was flown by a man, not by a program. It
could also be built quickly and cheaply. It was an ideal plane
for an air force that wanted to throw overwhelming numbers
at an enemy. That had been the Russian and Chinese mind-
set for centuries. The MiG-21 was an aerial expression of
that tactic. Chan was reminded of that every time he slid
into the cockpit. One of his flight instructors had once described the cabin as the inside of a toolbox and he was right.
Wires, switches, structural supports, and gauges were everywhere. The cockpit was neither aesthetic nor symmetrical.
But the parts worked, Chan knew where everything was, and
not many men got to sit here. As he prepared to take off into
an overcast morning, he did what he did every morning:
cherished his good fortune.

Chan had paid his dues with a year of service onboard a
decommissioned Ukranian aircraft carrier. A Macao-based

travel agency had bought it to use as a floating entertainment complex. Before its makeover, Chinese naval officers studied the vessel from aft to prow and bridge to keel, seeing what was right and wrong and figuring out how to best construct a fleet of modern Chinese warships. Chan's job was to help collect and organize data gathered by the engineers and military advisers. When that assignment was finished he was finally enrolled in the East Side Fleet flight academy. Chan had spent all of his downtime onboard reading the manuals and finished in two years of training at the top of his class. He made landings on his old carrier stomping grounds. He graduated with the rank of lieutenant and was quickly promoted to lieutenant commander. Chan's patrol sector was Zone Eleven. That took him northwest over Luodian and then due east over the Yellow Sea, south into the East China Sea, then west to Yuhuan before turning north and returning to base. It was about a thirteen-hundred-kilometer round-trip, three hundred kilometers within the MiG's maximum range. If he faced an engagement of some kind near the end of his patrol, he would be able to meet it and still return to base.

These patrols were extremely important. China did not have the satellite capabilities of the United States, Russia, or their allies. They hacked these on a rotating basis to observe foreign territory. To watch their own territory they relied on airborne observation. The patrols were also different from day to day. The air currents changed depending on the hour or the time of year, which affected the performance of the aircraft. The lighting on the land and on the interior of the cockpit were also different. Most significantly, the political circumstances were ever-changing. Tension with South Korea, Vietnam, Japan, Taiwan, and the United States always played out in the air or upon the sea. That put young navy men like Chan on the front line of their nation's defense. He was always watchful and alert, in a defensive mode. Encounters with foreign forces were usually cautious or marginally provocative. If there were pre-existing tension inside or outside

China's territorial waters, Chan patrolled with what the PLANFU pilots called "ready thrust." Outwardly nothing changed. Not speed, not altitude, not flight path. Inside, however, the pilot was different. His heart rate, respiration, eye movements; everything was battle-ready.

Today Chan had two additional missions. One was unofficial. His sister, Dr. Christine Chan of the Academia Sinica's Institute of Earth Sciences, had called and asked him to watch the sea for unusually tall or active waves or signs of unusual migration. He would only be able to see big schools or the larger creatures from his cruising altitude of fifty thousand feet, but he told her he'd keep a lookout. The other mission was an official one. The Civilian Air Control Bureau in Beijing had received a notice from the Federal Aviation Administration in Washington, D.C., that all aircraft were to avoid the southwestern region of the United States. The PLANFU Intelligence Division based in Jiangwan received all commercial airline notifications and found this one unusual. Short-duration bans near American missile sites and air bases were not unusual. Even closures across a wide region were not unprecedented. That happened along the flight path of the space shuttle whenever it returned from orbit. But there was no announced space mission. Nor was there a stated time of completion for the closure. That made it unprecedented. PLANFU-ID wanted Chan to watch the skies to the east for any unusual flashes or aircraft.

Aerial phenomena to the east, oceanic phenomena below, Chan thought as his MiG charged from the airfield. The g-forces from acceleration pushed him back against the seat. He took off from the south and banked gently to the west as he rose through the early morning clouds that hung low over the field. He passed from dreary gray to blinding sunshine within moments. He flipped down the tinted helmet visor and the world turned a pleasant amber, free of glaring ultraviolet rays.

As he pushed the fighter into a steep climb, Chan received a message from tower command at the base. He was told to divert immediately to Jiangwan. He was not told why.

"Report to Base Commander Shin upon your arrival," was the only additional information the pilot was given.

At once, his mind raced through a checklist: there was something wrong with his aircraft; he had done something to offend a superior officer that morning; or there was an emergency. He couldn't see how it was any of those. He had done a walk-around inspection of the MiG before takeoff and everything had checked out fine. His instruments were showing no anomalies. It was early in the morning and he had barely spoken to anyone, superior or subordinate. He couldn't imagine having upset anyone. Finally, on takeoff, the MiG was on an open channel with other MiGs in the squadron. His was the only plane that had been ordered to land. If this were an emergency, the entire group would have been recalled. And to Dachang, not to Jiangwan.

Perhaps something had happened to a member of his family, he thought suddenly. The lieutenant commander was very close to his parents and sister. That was not something a base commander would need to tell him, yet the fear stuck in his chest and filled it.

Chan's hands perspired beneath his leather gloves as he guided the aircraft in a big, arcing loop toward Jiangwan. He dropped back through the thin blanket of clouds and visually sighted the air base. The control tower picked him up and told him he was cleared for an immediate landing on runway seven.

The g-forces pressed Chan into his seat once again. They were slightly less assertive than during takeoff because the rate of descent was less than the rate of climb. The air currents gave the wings gentle taps to this side and that as Chan guided the MiG in. Ten minutes later, helmet in hand, the pilot was jogging toward the Jiangwan command center.

FOUR

Shanghai, China

Senior Captain Peter Shin, Jiangwan base commander, was an imposing man. He was short but stout, with a bald scalp that shined. He had lively eyes and a fixed smile that was probably misleading. Chan could not imagine that a man with the senior captain's responsibilities—both here and to PLAN leadership—would be perpetually happy. Chan noticed there were no laugh lines around the officer's eyes, which reinforced his initial conclusion.

His helmet still under his arm, Lieutenant Commander Chan entered the second-floor office. It was located on the far eastern side of the base. The Yangtze River was visible below. The senior captain was seated behind his desk, an aide standing on either side. He appeared to be reviewing nautical charts. The other men gathered them up and left when Chan arrived. The lieutenant commander saluted quickly, then snapped his arm back to his side. He stood at stiff attention. Shin rose and came around front. He stood eye to eye with the pilot.

"Are you well rested, Lieutenant Commander?" Shin asked. The senior captain had an unusually high, melodious voice. It seemed to complement his smile.

"Sir, I am." Chan always slept well. The barracks at

Dachang were far from the roaring flight paths of departing and arriving aircraft.

Shin nodded his acknowledgment. "Your records indicate that you are rated for the JF-17," the base commander went on. "You are also uniquely qualified for a mission we wish airborne within the hour. It is outside your current patrol zone. Do you feel comfortable with that?"

"Sir, I do," Chan replied enthusiastically. This was becoming very interesting. It was the first time since earning his wings that the lieutenant commander had been asked to do anything other than patrol his sector. The pilot's hands were sweating again, this time from excitement.

Shin had not broken eye contact since walking over. He seemed to be measuring the pilot's worth, or at least his concentration. After a long moment of silence, the senior captain returned to his desk.

"You are aware, from the briefing this morning, of the no-fly region established over a portion of the American west coast?" Shin asked.

"Sir, yes."

"We received word less than thirty minutes ago that three amateur fliers at the very edge of that perimeter were shot down. We want to know more about what is in the air in that region of the country, whether there is a new kind of aircraft or weapons system being used."

This was too exciting. Chan had difficulty standing at attention. "You will fly due east, at thirty-five degrees latitude and a ceiling of sixty thousand feet," the PLAAF commander went on. "We want you to have the widest radar range possible. An H6-U will refuel you over the North Pacific, just west of the international date line. After that, you will fly to the coast of California and head south—or inland, if possible, across San Diego. The defense capabilities there have apparently been compromised by the tsunami. You may be able to penetrate a considerable distance before you are intercepted. Throughout the mission you will take extensive radar readings. When you are finished, you will turn southwest and land on the Brazilian carrier *São Paulo* to refuel. They are in the Pacific to help Colombia track drug shipments to Asia. We have a military observer onboard. He will let you know whether you are to continue your reconnaissance or return home. Are there questions?"

"Sir, I am honored by your trust," Chan said. "I would like to know why I was selected."

"You are one of the few JF-17–rated fliers who has served on a carrier. You are the only one who could be in my office this morning. The other pilots are inland. Is there anything else?"

"Sir, no."

Though Chan had no other questions his brain was stumbling over the magnitude of this briefing. The lieutenant commander had never been a political creature. His family, his commission, and his nation were the only things that mattered to him. That, plus ceremonial masks. From the time Chan was four years old he had helped his father sell them in Tungkang. Some days his own sales were higher than those of his father. He had mastered the art of being cute. By the time he was seven he was carving them. Making and vending masks had never been what Chan wanted to do for a living, but he could never pass one in a market or shop without attempting to identify the god or demon and evaluating the craftsmanship.

It had been a big jump, going from selling masks on a bench to piloting jet aircraft. Yet that had been a gradual change. In just a few minutes Chan had gone from looking after a single domestic sector to becoming the only reconnaissance officer in an international security operation.

"I want you to understand, Lieutenant Commander, that my decision will be scrutinized by the Ministry of the Bilateral Air Command," Shin said. "They will want to know why I reached out to another air base. I am putting a great deal of responsibility on your shoulders."

"Sir, I do understand," Chan said. "I will do credit to the faith you have placed in me."

MoBAC was the three-man panel that oversaw all PLAAF and PLAN flight operations. The board made certain that any rivalries that existed between the divisions were minimized. Pilot competition was healthy and encouraged, as long as it did not compromise the good of the nation.

Apparently convinced of Chan's sincerity, the senior captain smiled warmly for the first time, then called one of the men back into the room. The aide was told to take Chan to the ready room, which was located in the Flight Dispatch Center, a high-security facility which handled all schedules, routes, and communications with PLAAF aircraft. The ready room consisted of ten rows of fold-down chairs, a blackboard, and several computer stations. Those served as data bases as well as flight simulators, where pilots got to look at digital video images of terrain they might have to navigate.

A senior flight instructor gave Chan a quick instruction-manual refresher course on the aircraft, in particular the in-flight refueling process. He also reviewed those aspects of piloting that required computer assistance, such as high-speed turns and the approach to the aircraft carrier. The lieutenant commander felt confident with the controls and the electronic interface. Flying wasn't only Chan's vocation, it was his hobby. He'd made it a point to know all the planes he might be asked to pilot.

When the FI was convinced that the pilot was all his record said he was, he signed the flight order. He motioned over Shin's aide, who had remained nearby—no doubt to report to the senior captain. The aide escorted Chan to the airfield. The lightweight fighter jet was sitting on its three slender landing gears, its fuselage gleaming golden yellow under the breaking cloud cover. The stubby wings were set well back, almost to the tail fin, to provide room for the two forward-set A-6 engines with their wide V-shaped air intakes. The sight of the aircraft literally caused Chan to lose a breath. It was not just a beautiful machine, it was *his* machine.

Mechanics were hurrying to ready the aircraft for flight.

They were not rushing; they were moving with quick precision. Most of these men knew the planes as well as the pilots did, sometimes better. Back at Dachang, Chief Engine Mechanic Benny Hong—who had learned his trade in the late 1950s, under Mao's Great Leap Forward industrialization program—swore that he could sense when something wasn't right. Chan didn't doubt it. He had actually seen the veteran engineer sniff an engine to determine its condition.

Chan borrowed a flashlight and walked around the aircraft, checking the engines and wheel wells himself. As he once joked with Hong, sometimes it was necessary to use your eyes as well. Everything looked fine. Chan returned the flashlight, then swapped helmets with the on-field quartermaster. The avionics in the JF-17 included a heads-up display that would only work with a customized helmet. When they had adjusted the fit, Chan went to the roll-over ladder and climbed to the cockpit. He put his hands on the sides of the shallow cockpit and stepped in.

The lieutenant commander liked the fit. Very much. He smiled as he immediately began running an equipment check, moving from communication to electrical to navigational to mechanical and finally to avionics—radar and proximity alerts key among them—in that order. His radio contact at the Flight Dispatch Center was Captain Mok Chung, who was hard-core PLAAF. Chan knew that at once: the subordinate addressed him as "PLAN Lieutenant Commander Chan," which was technically correct but also a way of differentiating the two services. Chan didn't mind. He was the one at the controls of the JF-17.

Chan manually released the latches and pushed a button to lower the cockpit canopy. Captain Chung informed Chan that he had clearance for immediate takeoff on runway three. The pilot acknowledged—without calling his liaison "PLAAF Captain Chung"—and waited until the chief of the ground crew gave him the all clear sign. Chan's only regret was that he was not carrying the four wing-mounted PL-5E antiaircraft missiles. Without their weight or drag he would be able to wring extra distance from his craft. Still, it would have completed the dramatic symmetry of the fighter to have them there.

After listening to his headset for several moments, the CGC crossed his upraised arms, indicating that all the workers were now clear of the aircraft. The CGC then saluted the pilot and ran off. He was replaced by a deputy field flight director, a specialist who wore a red jumpsuit and would use lighted batons to direct Chan from the Flight Dispatch Center to runway three.

Chan removed his glove to input his pilot code number into the keypad beside the ignition console. That six-digit number had already been sent to the aircraft from the tower. It prevented unauthorized personnel from attempting to use the plane. He typed 552103. A green light came on to the right of the pad. That meant he could fire up the engines.

The lieutenant commander punched the turbofan on, starboard first and then the port side. That was the pilot's choice. Chan did it that way out of old habit. Whenever he used to carve a ceremonial mask, he'd start with the right side. His father usually sat to his left; if he made a mistake, he didn't want his father to see. A wise man did not change something that worked for him. The engines hummed smoothly, producing a cottony roar that was deeper yet quieter than the full-bodied scream of the MiG's single Tumansky R-11F-300.

Chan watched the gauges as they climbed to 25 percent of full takeoff thrust. He checked the flaps a second time. Everything was functioning properly. Holding the wheel with his right hand, the lieutenant commander released the wheel locks with his left. Chan felt himself become part of the aircraft as the power of the engines flowed into his hand, along his arm, and into his skull and chest. The union was as intimate and empowering as lovemaking, and it was one reason many good pilots had trouble ejecting when their aircraft ran into trouble. The other reason was that no pilot wanted to return to base without his wings. Survival was honorable and it was sensible. It was also scrutinized closely and often harshly. The PLAN and PLAAF had far more pilots than it did aircraft.

Chan slapped down his visor, attached the heads-up-display as he turned the sharp nose of the JF-17 onto the runway. After a final systems check he revved the engines to half and began rolling along the strip. He raised the throttle to full takeoff as he accelerated. The G-forces were no different than they were in the MiG, though the fuller, more detailed contour of the seat gave his legs and arms more support and thus relief from the pressure. The angle of the windshield was slightly lower in the JF-17, lowering the drag created by the canopy and also cutting a bit of the view from the bottom. The T-shaped avionics panel also cut into his view. It supported three small computer panels, one at each of the uppermost points of the crossbar. The first was a map display with superimposed grid markings, the second was a magnified view from any point of the aircraft, and the third offered thermal or night-vision views. The panel also provided the helmet with its heads-up display, superimposing any of these readings on the silver-tinted visor. Even though the straight-ahead view was impaired slightly, the sides of the canopy were closer to the pilot and tapered inward slightly. That gave him a cleaner view of what was below the cockpit.

Achieving maximum thrust, Chan nosed the jet skyward. The response of the wheel and stick were more sensitive than the MiG. It reacted to what pilots described as "tickle" instead of "pull." The application of an entire hand was not needed to move the wheel or throttle, just a finger. The control was mostly in the index finger, with the rest of the hand used primarily for support. It was the way Chan had learned to control a carving knife, and he liked it.

The plane rose gracefully, and Chan was through the clouds in moments. The sun warmed the cockpit quickly but the automatic thermostat responded instantly, cooling the air and the pilot. Captain Chung gave Chan the go-ahead to climb to cruising altitude and wished him a safe journey.

"Thank you, Captain," Chan replied.

He shot toward the sun, his spirit lifted even higher by the pride he felt. He could not imagine a finer day or a richer moment.

Or a greater challenge.

FIVE

Norco, California

"It's going to be a challenge reeling her in," Captain Parks said.

The two officers were still sitting at the small conference table. The sandwiches and beverages were finished, though General Scott didn't remember having eaten his. Everything was a blur. Everything except the data, and that would not go away.

". . . the size of a 737 . . . stealth profile and components . . . out-of-communication. . . ."

"Challenge" was not the word General Scott would have used to describe the situation they were facing, or the solution. "Ordeal," "Long shot," and "Hail Mary" were the words that came to mind.

While Hathaway joined engineers in another part of NWAD working on a scenario that Parks had not yet discussed, Scott and the rear admiral sat in the conference room discussing the rest of the hows and whys that brought them to the point of having this rogue Angel on their hands—and, worse, some of what the aircraft was capable of doing. Parks was just describing an aspect of the Angel that had helped to give the plane its name.

"The wings are not fixed as in most aircraft," the naval

officer told him. "They are completely aeroelastic—pliable plastic filled with EMG, electroimpulse morphing gel, a putty-like substance that shifts instantaneously in response to electrical impulses from the cockpit."

"It sounds like one of those snaking toys you squeeze but have trouble holding on to," Scott said.

Parks smiled slightly. "That's where Hathaway got the idea, in fact," the rear admiral told him. "In shearflexing mode the wings can flap, allowing the craft to hover. They can alter the leading and trailing edge surfaces to turn suddenly at speeds of Mach 3 and higher. They can expand outward, allowing the Angel to ride the thinner air of the mid to upper stratosphere. They can even be withdrawn to turn the Angel into a guided missile. In short, they can assume any flight pattern necessary for every atmospheric or assault condition imaginable."

"In addition to possessing unlimited armaments and fuel," Scott said.

"That, too."

"What about stopping it with an air-exploded nuclear or electromagnetic pulse bomb?"

"We considered that, but those devices require a delivery system," the rear admiral replied. "The Angel would see either of them coming and shoot it down or get out of the way."

"You wouldn't do any damage?"

Parks shook his head.

General Scott was stunned by the magnitude of this. He was also surprised that DoNDEM/VAL-D had let the project go ahead with just two recall options—one, really, a primary and a single redundancy. But then, many test planes, missiles, and ordnance delivery systems didn't have even that. There was an abort button to blow up errant projectiles or drones and not even that for aircraft. Those were allowed to crash, hopefully into the desert. Besides, as Parks and Hathaway had explained it, in the absence of commands the Angel was supposed to return to the carrier. They hadn't expected the carrier itself to be MIA.

"Can you tell me anything about what they're talking about down the hall?" Scott asked.

"I'd rather not," the rear admiral replied.

"May I ask why?"

"Because I don't know you well enough."

"Helluva thing to say when we're already under the covers," Scott said. "And at *your* request."

"That isn't what I mean, General," Parks told him. "I'm looking out for your man. If this mission isn't feasible I don't even want to float it."

"I'm confused—"

"This is the kind of mission any good officer would want to undertake," Parks said. "If I were to tell you what it is, and you told Major Bryan, he might want to take this thing by the horns. I wouldn't blame him. You probably have the DoD connections to make it happen, but that's not how I want this to go down."

"I won't tell him," Scott said.

"I've met him," Parks replied. "I watched him watch you, and us. Major Bryan will intuit enough to figure out the rest."

"And you think he'll pressure me to do whatever is necessary so he can climb in the saddle."

"Wouldn't he?"

Scott didn't answer.

"General, do you know about the poll NASA took of its astronauts after the *Columbia* disaster?"

Scott shook his head. He hoped this wasn't one of those statistical reductions that had nothing to do with what people did in a real-life crisis. Too many armchair officers from defense secretaries down used them to determine future policy. They were always too conservative or too liberal, discounting the contagious nature of both adrenaline and fear.

"One of our aerospace guys heard about it, very low profile," Park said. "The reason it was low profile is the results would have been embarrassing to the brass. The agency talked to everyone in the astronaut corps, wanted to know who would have gone up to try and rescue the crew or repair the shuttle if NASA had known the extent of the damage. It would have been an insanely risky operation: close proximity flight, unrehearsed space walks, a big question mark about the ability of astronauts to function with that kind of stress in that kind of environment for that length of time. You know where this is going."

"Everyone would have volunteered."

"One hundred percent of the corps, trainees included," Parks replied. "Two-hundred-odd pilots and mission specialists in all. Do you know what kind of position that foreknowledge would have put NASA in? Had they known about the shuttle's damaged wing, they would have had no choice but to roll the double-or-nothing dice. That's the situation we are in, General. Brigadier General Beaudine briefed me about your team and about you, General. This kind of mission is what you people do. You break tough horses. Well, we've already got a lethal situation here. I don't want to throw nonreplaceable assets at it, either human or technological, unless I'm sure we have at least a fair chance of succeeding."

Scott sat back. He nodded once and gave Parks his tight-lipped "fair enough" look. The general understood the rear admiral's concerns. He also knew that the rear admiral had unspoken territorial interests at stake. Whether by carelessness or due to an act of God, this crisis had occurred on the Navy's watch. If a make-it-right mission were authorized, Parks would want that to come from the Navy. It was called bookending a mission. The top DoD brass expected tests to go wrong from time to time. They also expected that if you screwed it up you would clean it up.

"What's your backup plan if we don't do this?" Scott asked.

"We don't have one," Parks admitted. "How do you stop a perpetual motion machine when you can't get near it? The best we can hope is that it returns to the carrier and stays in that area."

"Do you think that will happen?"

"We don't know," Parks said. "We certainly can't count on it."

The room was very quiet for a moment.

"We really thought we had all the contingencies covered," Parks said finally. "We worked as hard to protect the Angel from enemy signals as we did from enemy weapons. We made her damn near invincible, a big leap in homeland security. We never imagined we'd have to protect ourselves from her."

Most armies were usually prepared to deal with the enemy. What hurt them was the soldier who snapped and rolled a hand grenade into his own tent or the friendly fire miscalculation. Those cost lives and, perhaps just as important, they took a big toll on morale.

"You ever have a situation get away from you, General?" Parks asked.

"Once," he replied. "There were no lives at risk, just my career."

"What happened?" Parks asked. "If you don't mind my asking."

"I don't mind you asking," Scott told him. "It's talking about it I hate."

"I'm sorry. I shouldn't have—"

"No, it's okay," Scott assured him. "I had a half-dozen mandatory sessions with the base shrink after the incident. He said it's good for me to talk about it. Let's see if he's right. I was in line for a post at NATO. I was going to head the intelligence operations of the NATO-Russia Permanent Joint Council. I heard from a friend in the RAF that the French didn't trust the U.S. to have that much power, so I went to talk one of their heavy hitters, General Augustine Dupre. Figured I'd get out in front of the problem. Instead, I walked right into a trap."

"How so?"

"Dupre told me that wasn't really the reason. He said that because my wife had been married before, they needed to background check her, make sure she didn't marry me to get access to secret information."

"Come the hell on."

"I'm serious," Scott said. "Those bastards knew just how to play me. They couldn't attack my record so they attacked my wife. We got nose-to-nose over it and I threatened to bust him one. I didn't, but he said I did. That was both the start and end of my career as an intelligence officer. I stayed on with the National Emergency Airborne Command at the Pentagon until LASER came along. I got to build something from the ground level, so it worked out okay."

"Any missteps along the way?" Parks asked.

"There are always missteps," Scott told him. "The key is how we apply what we've learned."

"I've learned to put my doomsday weapons in outer space," Parks said as Hathaway returned. "If they malfunction you simply rocket them into the sun." He regarded the scientist. "What have you got, Hank? Please make it good news."

"Simulations give the Seraph a sixty-forty chance of reaching the target," Hathaway told him.

Parks and Scott exchanged glances. "It's better than fifty-fifty," Scott said.

"What about the beacon?" Parks asked.

"That's the big question," Hathaway said. "We think we can match the flight pattern. Where the odds go down is whether the Angel would accept the signal."

"Back up," Scott said. "What are we talking about here? What is the Seraph and what needs to be done?"

Parks regarded Scott. The rear admiral's eyes had caught fire—just a little, but it was good to see.

"The Seraph is the prototype aircraft we built before constructing the Angel," Parks told him. "It's the same size and configuration, but without all the bells and whistles. It has the same outgoing signal as the Angel and may be the only aircraft our rogue will allow to get close."

"And if we can accomplish that much," Hathaway said, "then we might be able to interact with the Angel."

"Through someone onboard the Seraph," Scott said.

"That's right," Hathaway said.

"I take it the Seraph is large enough to hold only one passenger?"

"Well, not yet," Hathaway replied. "But it will be."

SIX

Norco, California

"I've got a question for you," General Scott asked Parks.

The two men were following Hathaway down a corridor. They exited inside the NWAD complex. The largest research lab at the facility was located in a windowless, hangar-style structure across a small courtyard.

"Why don't you just put the Seraph beacon inside an F-18 and knock the Angel out of the sky?" Scott asked.

"Because the Angel also reads aircraft configuration," Parks said. The rear admiral and Scott waited while Hathaway swiped his access card. It was strange. Hathaway seemed more anxious than before while Parks felt a little more hopeful. That was probably because it would be Hathaway's job to get the Seraph up in the air with a man onboard. Hathaway was not a soldier. The scientist was accustomed to risking hardware, not lives. "We made this thing as airtight as possible. We didn't want someone replicating the beacon and getting close."

"What makes you think it will let the Seraph near?" Scott asked as they entered the hangar.

"The Angel series was designed to patrol in tandem with other Angels," Parks replied. "We did not remove that RAC from its program." RAC was recognize and cooperate, a term that was coined for Internet communications but now included all manner of hardware and software.

"What makes you think there will be a problem?" Scott asked as Hathaway turned on the lights.

"The Angel may read the added weight and life-support systems inside the prototype," Parks told him. "These planes were designed to be one hundred percent mechanical."

That put a frown on the general's face. It disappeared when he saw the Seraph floodlit in the center of the hangar. Workers had already moved scaffolds into place around the forward section of the aircraft; now men and women in lab coats and masks were hurrying into the hangar from the opposite side, grabbing tool kits from shelves, rolling over heavier equipment, making things happen. But most of the Seraph was still visible.

"Shit," Scott said succinctly as he took it in.

The Seraph wasn't as clean as the Angel. The lines weren't as sleek, the wings were mech-morphs—the reconfigurations were accomplished mechanically, not by gel—and the aircraft was still marked with lines and numbers where engineers had made structural changes. Some of the panels were missing where the electronics had been studied, refined, and retested. But it was still an impressive aircraft, unlike anything else in the skies.

The men walked toward it.

The plane was silver. It looked like lightning when it flashed through the sky. It sat on three wheels that looked like black soccer balls: once the plane was airborne it did not need the added weight; the wheels deflated and were drawn inside. The Seraph was designed to remain aloft for ten years. The wings were nearly as long as the fuselage. They were slender and swept back dramatically, like a boomerang that had been bisected by the fuselage. The two ailerons on each wing were angled, their outer edges pointing in toward the fuselage. That gave the wing a slightly scalloped, bat-like appearance. The extended leading edge helped the aircraft make especially sharp turns. There was no cockpit: the nose of the plane came to a sharp, highly aerodynamic pencil-point. At the other end, the tail structure had a very low-lying fin that could be raised or lowered; the tail wings were each shaped like half a crescent moon. There was a long, straight, narrow funnel on the outer edge of each wing. The air that passed over and under the main wings hit the funnels and was cooked by small internal engines to give the plane afterburner capability.

Parks explained all of this to Scott as they walked toward the aircraft. The general did not take his eyes off the plane the entire time.

"I feel the way I did the first time I saw a stealth aircraft," Scott told him. "This is a quantum jump. Look at that design."

"The Angel is even more impressive," Parks replied.

"I don't doubt it." They stopped when they reached the tip of the starboard wing. "What's inside this aircraft?"

"Components," Hathaway told him. "The crews are going to get inside and start moving things around, making room for life support and a passenger."

"Rear Admiral, this is damned impressive," Scott said. "But we have a problem. You said something before about Major Bryan having flown a fixed-wing aircraft. He's had exactly one flight in a sailplane, and all that had were two pedals and a stick. What makes you think he's qualified to pilot—?"

Hathaway raised a finger to interrupt. "Actually, General, he wouldn't be piloting the Seraph," the scientist said.

"Excuse me?"

"We'd be flying the aircraft from here," Parks told him.

Scott was silent for a moment. "Spam in a can."

"Sorry?" Parks said.

"That's what the Mercury astronauts called themselves," Scott said. "They were meat stuffed inside a tiny capsule over which they had no control."

"Well, seeing as how Major Bryan's not a pilot, that's probably for the best," Hathaway observed.

"Yes, but I don't like the idea—nor will he—that if the

Angel decides it doesn't like him, there's nothing he can do."

"General, don't forget. It wouldn't make any difference if the major were at the controls of a B-1 or lying inside the Seraph," Parks said. "The Angel is designed to recognize or destroy airborne objects. If it decides on destruction, it will hunt an enemy to the ground."

"And right now there isn't an aircraft flying that has a friendly beacon other than this one," Hathaway said.

Scott shook his head. "Those odds that Dr. Hathaway quoted a few minutes ago—they don't excite me so much anymore. You said that Major Bryan would be lying inside—"

"On his back, near the center of the aircraft," Hathaway said, pointing. "Engineers are dotting the i's on a high-alt pressure suit. They've installed a Mylar lining. The idea is to cut down his thermal output so the Angel doesn't see him."

"The pressure suit will automatically regulate his body temperature as the Seraph climbs to keep him from freezing," Parks added. "The interior of the Seraph has no climate controls or oxygen, which is why he'll carry several tanks. That will also allow him to egress when he reaches his destination."

"The exit is the first thing they're going to work out," Hathaway said. "The Angel was designed to be entered through the starboard wheel well—one less opening to put in the craft, more usable interior space. The thinking is to have the major lying on his back inside the Seraph and come at the Angel from below, exiting through a sort of manhole cover—"

"Which will obviate the need for a docking port that would create a major alteration of the aircraft's profile."

"Making it a certain target."

"Correct. It also saves prep time," Parks added.

"If we had more time, would that change the odds in the major's favor?" Scott asked.

"I don't believe so," Hathaway stated.

"A docking port would require very specific maneuvering when the Seraph gets in close," Parks added. "That would be extremely difficult to accomplish from the ground and we don't have the time to add pilot controls to the Seraph."

"We're talking about a man's life," Scott reminded him.

"We don't believe the open-air transfer adds much risk factor to the mission," Hathaway stated. "Getting that close is the only problem. It's the reason we can't use the two hatches located topside. There would be no way for the Seraph to get Major Bryan close enough."

"This thing has doors?" Scott said, surprised.

"For engineers to use when the Angel is on the ground," Parks said. "The aircraft was not designed to be entered from the air. They're located forward the two solar panels, but he would still have to approach the Angel from below and then make his way to the latches."

"General, believe me. This is the safest approach," Hathaway assured him.

The rear admiral was growing impatient. He was concerned enough about the mission. If Scott had doubts they would have a negative impact on the team. "Like a conscientious objector in a war zone," as his Uncle Dick Breen used to say whenever he hit a wall on anything.

"General, you're still uneasy," Parks said.

Scott looked back at the aircraft. His silence was answer enough.

"I understand that," Parks went on. "But you know what's at stake."

"That doesn't make this easier, only necessary," Scott said. "It's like leaving a soldier behind to cover your retreating ass and knowing you'll be writing a letter to his mother."

"I wish there were some other way to deal with the danger posed by the rogue Angel."

"I get that. I'm just having to accept that you want to add my team leader and friend to your bottom line."

"Hopefully, the major will succeed and, in the process, prevent anyone else from getting hurt," Parks said. "Is what we're proposing so much more dangerous than your last mission?"

"Let's just say your scenario has fewer options going in or getting out," Scott told him. "There were several ways to enter the Weddell Sea and there was also an abort button. If something went wrong the team could have surfaced."

"Would they have?"

Scott was silent for a moment. Parks watched as the general's doubts took on some steel.

"I didn't think so," Parks said. He turned his back to the plane and faced the general. "The next few hours are going to be difficult for everyone. I need to know that you're both fully committed to this."

"You know the major will be," Scott replied. "He doesn't have much of a choice once he takes off, does he?"

"No."

"As for my doubts, they don't leave this hangar. That will have to be enough."

"I understand," Parks said sincerely. "Will the major pick up on your conditional approval?"

"He might," Scott admitted. "If he does, we'll talk it out. It won't affect his performance." He took another moment to study the aircraft and the crew working on it.

Parks was proud of his team, of their skill and their dedication. He had come here several days a week during the construction of both planes and knew them all by name. They were smart, dedicated, passionate people. They were not bureaucrats. If something wasn't right, they would let him know.

These men and women would not ignore the fact that a life depended upon the work they were doing.

The life of their nation.

SEVEN

Miramar, California

The 115-foot-tall air traffic control tower at Marine Corps Air Station Miramar resembled a cubistic lighthouse. It was a rectangular column capped with a hexagonal command center that was wider at the top than at the bottom. The outward-sloping windows provided a commanding 360-degree view of the woods and hills. The job of the full-time staff was far more difficult than that of civilian air traffic controllers. The military personnel had to monitor not just AMMOs—airborne military maneuvers and operations—conducted by the seventeen squadrons based at Miramar, but all such activities within the Southern California region as well as the movement of civilian air traffic throughout the region. The Marines did not want to be conducting a live air-to-surface missile drill at Pendleton or over the ocean or Inland Empire desert and have a commuter plane buzz into the attack zone.

Thirty-one-year-old Tower Supervisor Sergeant Sandra Ocean was a six-year veteran of the flight control center. During her eight-hour shift—plus the unofficial hour or two she tacked onto each end—the five-foot-tall Georgia native watched her command like a Catholic school nun at nap time, as one of the staff sergeants put it when he didn't think she was listening.

The staff sergeant was right. To Ocean, this was not just a job. It was a responsibility. It was a privilege.

It was her life.

Her father had lost his eyesight in Vietnam. But he had not lost his sense of duty or patriotism. He became an attorney working for other veterans. She saw her own work as a way of continuing his, of supporting and validating what he had sacrificed. It was also a way to plug into everything that was given, and experienced, by every soldier who ever took up arms for the flag. There was not just safety in numbers. There was also strength.

And on days like today, when the local military had been hard-hit by an act of God, those qualities were more keenly felt. Aircraft with backup personnel and equipment had been moving through the region without letup. The smooth operation of this facility was a key component to the recovery.

As usual, Ocean walked rather than sat. That kept her in the 'now.' The views, the stimuli, the data were constantly changing. It enabled her to keep an eye on everything, including her staff. The sergeant was strict about protocol and operations, from the creases in their cammies to the dust collecting on computer screens and radar grids. During each pass of each station she looked down at the monitors, glanced out the windows, made sure her people were on their game. There were six others in the tower at all times. She could tell from the way they sat, from the way their eyes wandered or didn't, whether they were paying full attention to their jobs. The set of every mouth told her whether an individual was too tense or too relaxed. She was pleased that no one's demeanor changed whenever base commander Captain Jack Mann came by. They were professional whether the chief was watching or not.

"Sergeant Ocean?"

The blue-eyed woman fired a look to her right, to the pale, freckled face of her radio operator, Lance Corporal Eric Velk. He was already removing a second headset from a hook at his station and extending it toward her. She walked over.

"Code red from White Sands," Velk said.

It was not unusual for Miramar to talk to air command at the missile range. White Sands operations occasionally extended into her airspace. It was unusual, however, to get a code red call from the missile base. She presumed the emergency notification had something to do with the lockdown in New Mexico and California. Perhaps it was being lifted.

"This is Sergeant Ocean," she said as she adjusted the headset.

"Sergeant, this is Brigadier General Will Beaudine at WSMB. You are to ground all military aircraft immediately, no exceptions. You are to issue orders to all civilian aircraft within range to set down under emergency operations procedures. Nothing flies, not even traffic copters. Is that clear?"

"It is, sir." It was clear, but confusing.

"This order is being E-mailed under my signature to you and to all military commanders at Unified Pacific Services HQ in Long Beach. It covers all of Southern California and offshore concerns. This is an open-ended restriction that is to be rescinded only by direct contact from myself or from Rear Admiral Edward Parks. Are there any questions, Sergeant?"

"None, sir."

"Thank you. Please see to it."

The general hung up and Sergeant Ocean picked up the intercom that allowed her to talk to the entire tower, including the offices and rest quarters below. She repeated the general's instructions in a very firm voice, a talent unique to the military: orders had to be issued with conviction even when the officer or non-com giving them had no idea why they were being given and, for the sake of credibility, had to conceal that ignorance from the curious, questioning glances of subordinates.

But as Sergeant Ocean watched her team go into action, scanning radar and contacting aircraft individually, she could not help but wonder what could have caused an alert of this scope. The tsunami, undoubtedly, but how and why?

Even during the terrorist attacks of September 2001, military and police aircraft were not grounded. Whatever this was and whatever concerns she had, Sergeant Ocean was excited and challenged to be a part of it. As the first planes started to come into Miramar, she was also unafraid. From the sound of it, this was a vast operation in which countless shoulders would be sharing the burden. Hundreds of thousands of dedicated Americans were standing shoulder-to-shoulder, attacking a crisis.

This thing was as good as licked.

EIGHT

Norco, California

Thomas Bryan awoke to the pop of distant guns. At least, that's how his sleeping ears interpreted the sound. His eyes opened slowly; it took him a moment to remember where he was.

He wasn't on a battlefield. That was the only part of his dream he remembered. The shots came again. Only now they were knocks on the door.

"Coming," he shouted.

Bryan swung his legs from the cot and sat there for a moment. He didn't often have combat dreams, but then he wasn't usually around so much brass in a lather. Corpus Christi was a relatively stable environment. This was a little disorienting. He swallowed the pasty taste of sleep from his mouth and took a moment to press his temples. There was a dull throbbing behind his eyes, the result of too much activity and not enough rest. He glanced at his watch, then rose slowly and went to the door. General Scott was standing there looking the way Bryan felt. His features were creased, and though his shoulders were back, the general's arms hung limply at his sides.

"Did you come for me or the cot, sir?" Bryan asked.

Scott grinned. "Do I look that bad?"

"Commanders *always* look bad during an operation,"

Bryan reminded him. "Are you coming in or am I coming out, sir?"

"I'm coming in," he said. "We'll talk, then we'll go."

Bryan moved aside to let the general enter. He shut the door as the general sat in the room's only chair, a straight-back wooden seat that looked like it came from a high school. Bryan dropped onto the edge of the bed.

"You look off, sir," Bryan said.

" 'Off'?"

"In the wild blue. What's wrong?"

Scott shook his head. "So much for promises."

"Sorry?"

"Something I said to the rear admiral," Scott said. "Not important now. Major, did you ever have to fight panic when you were in combat?"

"Never, sir. I was too busy surviving."

" 'I ain't got time to bleed.' "

"Something like that," Bryan agreed.

"I was just thinking, most of us do that at the front. Behind the lines, though, when you've got troops out there following your game plan—that's a different animal. I think grunts feel they can stay lucky for two, three, maybe four battles. The odds of surviving are with them. Commanders don't have that. They know that one day they are going to make a wrong call because of faulty judgment or bad information."

"Goes with being human. May I ask, sir, what brought this on?"

Scott pointed at the door. "The short walk to this room. Damned bad idea, walking alone anywhere. It gives you time to second-guess yourself."

"I take it you're referring to the game plan of the NWAD brain trust?"

"Here's the deal. They've got a solid plan. They need one person to go up in a robot prototype and chase the Angel. Once the pilot is there he's supposed to climb inside the wheel well, worm his way to the control center, and input the changes Hathaway is going to provide."

"I assume that one person is still me?"

Scott nodded again.

"Odds?"

"Better than average, once you've made the initial approach," Scott told him. "Hathaway is pretty confident the Angel will recognize the prototype's signal and let it belly up to the undercarriage. But he can't guarantee that, of course. All of this will be happening at sixty-one thousand feet, which adds its own flavor."

"So I should pack a sweater."

Scott smiled. "Not necessary. They've got that covered. In Mylar."

"Comfy. So when do we go?"

"They've got a couple of hours of prep work left," Scott told him. "I let you sleep until they said they absolutely had to start giving you a crash course in reprogramming the Angel."

"Great. Just let me wash my face and I'm ready to go," Bryan said.

"Take your time."

Bryan rose and looked down at him. "General, in case you've got any doubts about this, don't. I *want* to do it."

"I know. And I signed off on it."

"But you had that think-walk," Bryan said.

"Which is nothing I wouldn't have done back in Hawaii or on any drill," Scott said. "You have a second and you start reviewing the what-ifs."

"Which is a pointless exercise, sir, because you know that nothing ever goes as planned and you can't anticipate more than a few of the what-ifs. We've got a situation here and our team is as qualified as any to address it. I'm psyched."

Scott shook his head. "I was supposed to be the cheerleader, not you."

"I'm just the grunt dodging bullets on this one," Bryan said. "You're the man who made the call."

Scott rose and clapped a hand on the major's shoulder. "Go wash your face. I'll see you back in the conference room. That's where they're assembling the materials on the Angel."

"I'll be there in five." Bryan frowned. "You know, sir, something just occurred to me."

"What?"

"If this operation doesn't work and Parks needs to come up with a plan B, we won't be able to fly LASER over," Bryan said. "It might be a good idea to get the team out here and briefed, just in case."

"Already in the works," Scott replied. "I made that call before coming to see you. The squad is being brought out here by bus and should be arriving in about two hours, just in time to see their leader off." The general grinned. "If nothing else, I wanted to see Puckett's face when he gets a look at the prototype."

"Is my girl that sweet?"

"I don't know if that's the word I'd use to describe the Seraph," Scott told him.

"Is that what they called it? The Seraph?"

Scott nodded. "One of the first order of angels. It's impressive, and I know Captain Puckett will think so. For me it was a little off-putting, like a statue with dead eyes. Something so powerful should have a soul calling the shots."

"With luck, that will be me."

Scott smiled. "A good soul at that."

"Thank you, sir. It's kind of weird, when you think about it, though."

"What is?"

"Using a soul to take out an angel," Bryan said.

Scott nodded, then left the room. Bryan went to the washroom. He scrubbed away the last of the sleep, then sat on the cot and put on his boots. They were cool and damp inside, from the sweat of a long day.

"And probably a dash of seawater," Bryan said. He had put the boots on immediately after getting out of the wetsuit. His foot scraped over some fine lumps. He removed the boot and shook it out over the trash can. There were a few particles of gray rock, probably from the volcano.

A mix of elements, mementos of a busy day, he thought

as he put the boot back on. Bryan left the room, passing the lieutenant in the corridor and thanking her for her hospitality. As he headed toward the conference room, he wondered what else he would collect before the day was done.

Probably one or two more elements—perhaps ice, cloud vapor, and whatever else lurked in the lower stratosphere. And maybe something more important. A lesson or two.

NINE

Norco, California

General Scott was correct. The Seraph was frightening to see, but in a much more sinister way than Bryan had imagined. It reminded the major of the Frankenstein Monster: something that resembled what it was supposed to, but with a strange and disturbing geometry. The Seraph looked like an aircraft, but not one that was designed to carry passengers or cargo. Perhaps the name was more appropriate than the creators had realized. This thing had everything but a flaming sword.

Bryan had met Parks and Scott in the conference room, then was taken to see the aircraft. The rear admiral gave him a tour of the Seraph. What impressed him from a distance were the lines. What struck him up close was how heavily armed the aircraft was, from the undercarriage guns in the rear to the undercarriage guns in the nose to the rotating turrets underneath the wings and the wide, flat vapor intake between the wings. That was where the icy projectiles were formed. Incredibly, each white steel muzzle had a rotating plug about four inches in diameter. Each of these had fourteen holes around its perimeter. That made eight barrels, one hundred and twelve separate openings, ten projectiles per opening per second—well over one thousand "bullets" each second, which could be directed at a single target or spread over multiple ones.

No sword of flame but guns of ice, Bryan thought as he finished the tour.

When that was over, Parks, Hathaway, and Scott took Bryan back to the conference room. They sat at the table and watched digital video recordings of the Angel itself. Scott and Bryan took notes—which, they were informed, could not leave the conference room. Most of the images showed the interior of the aircraft, where the major would be spending most of his time. It was a long tube, no flat surfaces, and nowhere to stand. The space looked like the inside of a flashlight, except it was entirely white and emptied of batteries. There were narrow grates along the side walls, top, bottom, and center, and at the far end of the floor and ceiling.

"The interior is made of a very soft, light plastic to reduce the weight of the aircraft," Hathaway told him. "It's held in place by twelve titanium ribs forward, center, and aft. The entire structure allows a great deal of give during turbulence, to prevent anything from being dislodged or disabled."

"But it *will* hold the weight of a man?" Bryan asked.

"Absolutely," Hathaway said. "The only reason the conduit is there is to allow the installation and eventual replacement of parts."

"You have to be lying down," Scott observed. "There obviously isn't room for you to stand."

"Not here," Hathaway said. "The conduit occupies the core of the fuselage, about a meter wide, or one-fifth of its diameter."

"I assume those mesh screens are access ports of some kind?" Bryan said.

"Yes, although this is the only one that concerns us," Hathaway said. He clicked on the grate located in the ceiling of the forward section. Six schematics appeared on the screen, each showing the inside of the area from different angles. "The section we need you to fix is located in module 1102." He

placed the cursor on that section and magnified it. Another
six-angle view appeared. "It's an override juncture for hardwired command systems pertaining to aircraft recognition."

"You're saying that when I reprogram the box, Angel becomes a big flying puppy dog."

"Not tamed but muzzled. It will not attack other aircraft,"
Hathaway said. "That will allow us to put teams aloft that
will be able to harness the aircraft and bring it down. But before we do that, you have to do one thing more." He went
back to the previous screen and clicked on another section
of the forward ceiling. "This is module 1017. That controls
the flight path of the Angel. We're going to need you to descend her and change her course so that she stays in American airspace."

"We have the commands you'll need to input," Parks told
him. "They will all be on storage discs that you plug directly
into the system."

"The discs will bring up screens and we'll radio instructions on what to do when you access those," Hathaway added.

"If the radios fail?" Bryan asked.

"They shouldn't—"

"Your track record with electronics is spotty," the major
pointed out.

"Touché," Hathaway replied. "The screens pretty much
walk you through the operations. If for whatever reason
we're out of touch, all you have to do is back up until you
find the correct command-and-control screens. All of those
have a CAC logo in the top left. But the radios won't fail,"
Hathaway added confidently. "We bought them from the
private sector."

"Are you certain Angel won't read the radio waves and
interpret them as hostile?" Bryan asked.

"Absolutely. Part of Angel's hack-proof system includes
ignoring incoming messages," Hathaway told him.

"That's one reason we're in this fix," Parks reminded them.

"Excuse me," General Scott said. "You said you want
Major Bryan to drop the Angel to a lower height."

"That's right," Parks said.

"What happens to the Seraph?"

"Once the major is onboard Angel we'll move the prototype away."

"Effectively stranding him."

"He'll have a parachute if everything goes to hell," Parks said. "It's a special high-altitude cockpit design that minimizes pilot encumbrance. The canopy pack extends from the shoulders to just above the knees. The entire system is just two-point-five inches thick."

"That's still an iffy out at that speed and height," Scott said.

"We'll also be tracking the Angel closely," Parks added. "When the major puts her into a descent we will lower the Seraph right along with him. Ideally, his ride home will never be more than a minute or two away." Parks looked at Bryan. "Major?"

"Not the best emergency escape plan I've ever heard," he said. "But if that's how this has to be played, then that's how we play it."

"Thank you," Parks said.

"Although I am curious," Bryan went on. "And I hope you'll forgive me for asking something a little off the wall, Dr. Hathaway—"

"Not a bit."

"Are we talking about some kind of AI here? The Angel isn't going to attack me for trying to shut it down?"

"That is well beyond anything science is capable of producing," Hathaway assured him. "The Angel can't learn. It has no sense of self-preservation other than what we gave it."

"Getting back to the game plan, you said you want to keep the Angel over U.S. airspace," Scott said, consulting his notes. "If it doesn't stop when it reaches the *Hidalgo*, what will it do?"

"We aren't entirely sure," Parks replied.

"Our programmers have been running simulations," Hathaway said. "They have three likely scenarios. The first is that it will remain in the area, following a criss-crossing search pattern. The second is that it will kick itself back to 'start' and repeat the White Sands run. The third is one we don't want to consider."

"And that is?" Scott pressed.

"Something we don't want to consider," Parks repeated firmly.

TEN

Kure Atoll, North Pacific

The refueling of the JF-17 was a unique experience for Lieutenant Commander Chan. For one thing, the *Lin* class tanker was enormous, with a 130-foot wingspan and four very powerful, very loud 21,634-pound engines. It covered Chan's field of view and its bellow was all the pilot heard for the half hour the refueling was underway. For another, the air currents created by the tanker caused Chan to pilot in the moment. He had to pay very close attention to what he was doing.

The refueling tube was located on the right side of the forward fuselage. It was covered with a flush-door rather than a blister-door, which helped to cut down drag. When the connector was extended, it was raised to an angle of sixty degrees to receive the probe from the tanker. The long, narrow tube extended from the back of the tanker undercarriage. It was a careful mating process that Chan thoroughly enjoyed. The Fierce Dragon used a bent probe that forced all the fuel back. Some of the earlier inflight probes were vertical, which caused leakage, which allowed fuel to be sucked through the engine intake, causing the aircraft to explode.

Chan's aircraft didn't explode.

It was strange to feel the JF-17 fully fueled again. The

lieutenant commander had felt the aircraft lightening, handling more fluidly as he ate up kilometers. With full tanks there was a palpable tail-heaviness. Not that one situation was better than the other; the pilot simply had to compensate with flaps and thrusters to retain his same-speed progress.

Personally, Chan preferred the full-tank status. It was empowering. It meant that he could continue to stay aloft.

Here he was, north of the Midway Islands, and a little more than halfway to his destination. Thus far, the only novelty besides refueling had been the modern "water packs" for urination. Chan was accustomed to having two sixteen-ounce bottles in the cockpit of his MiG. The JF-17 had three twenty-ounce bags with plastic zipper tops. There was a spout at the top for easy access. They sat in the lap much more conveniently than the rigid bottles.

The hours passed quickly, as rich, blue skies became purple with sunset and then dark in very quick succession. The stars at this altitude were sharp and plentiful, the blurry swath of the Milky Way visible directly overhead. It was strange that they did not seem any closer than they did from the ground, only clearer. Except for the howl of the engines, Chan felt as though he could be lying with his sister on the shore of the lake just outside of Tungkang. They had done so often when they were young, Bruce saying that he wanted to fly to them and Christine deciding that she would rather understand how they were made and why they burned. It was gratifying to think that they had both realized their ambitions.

The radio hissed and Captain Chung from the Flight Dispatch Center got on. "Lieutenant commander, Beijing Civilian Air Control Bureau has just received an update from the American Federal Aviation Administration," Chung said. "The lockdown area has been extended west to include the southern region of California."

"Are we changing my flight plan?" Chan asked. He hoped not. He wanted to fly to the American coast.

"To the contrary," Chung replied. "American news reports

say that aircraft, both civilian and military, appear to be landing throughout the region. We suspect you may not be challenged by military aircraft."

"They do not say why this lockdown has occurred?"

"The news media suggests it may be related to the tsunami," Chung replied. "We believe that to be true. The Americans would not want flights over military installations when they cannot protect them."

"They can still shoot down enemy aircraft."

"Perhaps not," Chung said. "We are detecting very little radio traffic other than local talk, which suggests a major disruption to the communications and command structure. Unedited videotape from local news centers to stations around the United States shows aircraft and personnel being flown inland before this latest lockdown. We believe that key individuals are being relocated not for safety but to try and reorganize.

Senior Captain Shin would like you to adjust your flight path to take you over the United States Marine Corps Base Pendleton. The coordinates are being sent to your navigation system. You are to fly a low-level pass, at twenty thousand feet, and record the recognition signals. They will most likely warn you off by radio. You will forward the message for translation but you will not reply. We will send you instructions. If you detect thermal signatures consistent with a missile ignition you are to leave at your own discretion. Our best intelligence is that the Sparrow missiles are deployed at the base. It will take twenty seconds for a surface-to-air launch to reach your position. That is sufficient time to release a jamming array and escape its radar guidance. Do you understand the emergency procedure?"

"I do," Chan replied. It was a simple deployment: fine particles of aluminum were fed into the exhaust stream. The metal caused thousands of false readings on missile radar, effectively shielding the aircraft from recognition.

"The senior captain wishes all reconnaissance systems operational during your sweep," Chung went on. "If you are not challenged and have sufficient fuel to reach the aircraft carrier, the senior captain wants you to make a second pass over the base at ten thousand feet."

"I will do so," Chan replied. The lieutenant commander nearly choked when he said that. He was barely able to rein in his excitement. Short of combat, this was the kind of mission in the kind of aircraft that every pilot coveted.

Captain Chung signed off. The lieutenant commander was still many hours from his target. But the time would not be counted off in seconds but by his quickening heartbeat. His vision would sharpen the closer to the target he came, not just defensively but also to complete the mission, to reconnoiter, to discover. Yet for Chan, that was not the most important aspect of this flight. Technologically, the Chinese military was decades behind that of the United States. They did not have the satellites, the sophisticated listening devices, the hi-tech aircraft. But the Chinese had one asset that was second to none: China had the best and bravest pilots in the world.

Chan would prove that by carrying a PLA flagship to their shores and back.

ELEVEN

Norco, California

The bus from Coronado passed through the NWAD main gate and stopped in the spotlit courtyard. The LASER team emerged, looking as though they had done a long tour in a war zone. They were wrinkled, dirty, and slope-shoulder tired. There was barely a boot that didn't drag as they stepped from the bus.

General Scott came out to welcome the group. He was accompanied by the two corporals who were in charge of main gate security. They had been instructed to take the LASER ops to the guest quarters for cleanup. After that, they would be taken to the hangar. Scott had spoken with Rear Admiral Parks about involving the rest of the team in the Seraph project, even though they did not possess that level of security clearance; but then, neither did Major Bryan. Scott was insistent. He did not want Bryan going aloft without sympathetic eyes and ears on the situation: observers who could best represent the interests of a teammate in a dangerous situation.

Scott also felt that the people of LASER represented an invaluable cross section of experience. If things went wrong with the Seraph plan, Puckett or Black or one of the others might have insights on how to salvage it or what to do next.

The rear admiral could not refuse. It made tactical sense. More important, it made psychological sense. A drum major was much less effective than one who had drummers marching behind him. The boost could prove decisive. Parks could not dispute any of that. Besides, as Scott also pointed out, this operation would become part of the LASER mission log. The team would have access to the major's report.

The group had barely an hour for cleanup and a light dinner before Scott came back to bring them to the hangar. Major Bryan was standing under the fuselage with Dr. Hathaway and Rear Admiral Parks. A roll-up staircase sat beside them. A technician stood on top, his upper half inside the aircraft.

"Please tell me what I'm looking at," the Tennessee-born Captain Puckett said as the group walked toward the Seraph.

"What would you guess?" Scott asked.

"It looks like an update of the JB-2," Puckett said.

"Which was what?" Captain Gabriel asked.

"The U.S. version of the German V-1, the pilotless flying bomb," Puckett replied.

"A 'buzz bomb,'" Gabriel said.

Puckett nodded.

"That's a good guess, Captain Puckett," Scott said. He told the team what the Seraph was and what this mission was about.

Puckett was openly impressed. "The major is going to be the first passenger on a perpetual motion aircraft," the captain said. "He's going to make aviation history *and* save the world. How freakin' great is that?"

"You're not jealous?" Lieutenant Black asked.

"Green as a pickle," Puckett replied as they neared the starboard wingtip. "But I'm proud of the major and also whoever invented these birds." His eyebrows raised like little wings as he gushed, "I'm happy just to be a part of it."

"Even though the 'bird' that's already up there could end aviation as we know it," Captain Gabriel observed.

"That's not going to happen," Puckett told him.

"How can you be sure?" Gabriel asked.

"'Cause there isn't a problem Americans can't lick if they apply themselves. Especially these Americans." He made an all-encompassing circle with his finger. "We've got the best minds and the best soldiers in the world."

"No argument," Black said. "It would also stand to reason that we'd make the toughest Frankenstein Monster on the planet."

"I was just thinking that," Ensign Galvez remarked. "We made the H-bomb and we still haven't figured out how to shut that down."

"Sure we did," Gabriel said. He pointed ahead. "With this baby. An enemy bomber takes off or a nuke fires up—Frankenplane sniffs 'em out and buries that bone."

Rear Admiral Parks walked over. Hathaway and Bryan were engrossed in a laptop that the scientist was holding. Engineers moved about the men like fish around a coral reef. "You ought to work for our public affairs office, Captain," Parks told Puckett. "I like your sense of spin."

"I fly helicopters," Puckett replied. "What do you expect?"

"He wasn't spinning anything, sir," Lieutenant Black told the rear admiral. "The captain believes in what he says."

"Glad to hear someone is an unapologetic optimist." Parks smiled. He himself looked anxious. He introduced himself to the captain and the group.

"How's our topkick doing?" Gabriel asked. He spoke loud enough for the major to hear.

"He's cramming," Scott answered when the major didn't react.

"What time is takeoff?" Black asked.

"Just under ninety minutes," Scott replied.

"Not a lot of time," Puckett said with the slow head shake of one who knows the playing field. "Where is this Angel now?"

"She's closing in on San Diego," Rear Admiral Parks replied. "That will be our first milestone, when we find out what the Angel's next move is."

"I can tell you that now, sir," Puckett said.

"Oh?"

"From what the general told us she's going to bolt."

"Bolt?" Parks looked at him quizzically.

"She's gonna continue west," Puckett said. "She has two directives. One is to return home and the other is to shoot down aircraft. It sounds like she already chose to ignore directive one when she tagged the three aircraft at Tucumcari. There's no reason to think she won't do that again."

"Those aircraft in New Mexico were up illegally," Parks pointed out. "We've grounded everything in the Angel's search zone."

"That doesn't mean you won't have some reporter hijack a traffic copter looking for a scoop," Black said. "Something that'll get them national attention."

"Calls are being placed to every media center, hospital, and law enforcement that under no circumstances is any aircraft to fly," Parks assured her.

"Respectfully, I still think that's all beside the point," Puckett replied. "The Angel showed her nature by putting one instinct above another. I know we're talking about a machine here, sir, but I have worked with machines since before I was potty trained. It's like when I go hang gliding—the wind and my wings tell me where I'm going. I just hold the base bar and offer suggestions. What you just said only makes me more convinced that the plane will do what it did before. It will look for a new target. And it won't look where it's already been."

"We're not convinced of that," Parks told him.

Gabriel nudged Puckett in the ribs. "Say good-bye to that job in public affairs, Tyler."

Puckett shrugged. "I hope I'm wrong. I just got a feel for aircraft."

"Too bad rank has privileges," Gabriel said, nodding toward Bryan.

"The major'll do this right," Puckett said.

"Why do you say that?" Parks asked.

"I know flying machines but I've seen the major operate

in tripwire situations," Puckett said. He nodded up. "He's the man you need there."

"You just got your job back," Gabriel teased.

"Personally, I don't understand why we just don't send him up with C-4 and a timer and let him blow the thing to hell," Black said.

"We'd like to get our aircraft back—" Parks told her.

"He can pack it as an 'if all else fails' option," she interrupted.

"—plus the electrostatic field generated by the Angel's instrumentation make detonators unreliable," he went on. "We're afraid they could blow prematurely, not only injuring the major but causing damage before he could finish lining the interior with explosives."

"Ah," Black said.

"As you can see, the situation on all fronts is very fluid," Scott said. "The reason I brought you all out here is because the major will require backup. I wanted you to see the plane, to understand the situation, and to give us the benefit of your own experience as Captain Puckett has done. Hopefully, we'll be able to anticipate any surprises that might be waiting for the major."

"Question," Black said. "If the Angel decides it doesn't want the Seraph to approach, does the major have a way out?"

"Parachute," Scott said. "He'll already be carrying oxygen to survive inside the Angel and he'll have a beacon to help us locate him. All he has to do is get to the exit and bail."

"A parachute is a flying object," Black said. "What makes you think the Angel will let it get away?"

"Parachutes are the only airborne devices hardwired into the Angel's 'ignore' program," Parks said. "She would have IDed the craft that carried the chutists as friend or enemy. Anything more would have been overkill."

To Scott, that seemed like an arbitrary limitation to have given a machine with the capacity to destroy everything that flew. Still, it was a limitation the general accepted gratefully.

Parks excused himself and returned to the Seraph. The LASER team stood there looking on.

"However qualified the major is for this mission, it's going to be a tough one," Gabriel said.

"I was just thinking that," Lieutenant Kodak remarked. "Are you sure there isn't room for two or three in there? It's a big aircraft."

"I'm told the weight affects the air displacement, which has to remain consistent with what the Angel knows the Seraph to be," Scott said. "Besides, there's barely room for one. The Seraph and the Angel are both loaded with instrumentation."

"Except for the Lassie Come Home switch we really need," Galvez said.

"General, you said the major will require backup," Black said. "What were you referring to? Some kind of tech support, or did you just want to have friendly, familiar voices on the radio?"

"I need ideas!" Scott told her. He stepped in closer, made it more of a huddle and lowered his voice. He wanted to sound eager, not desperate. "Maybe everything will go perfectly up there. Maybe the major will reach the Angel without a problem, fix the program, and come back safely. But if he doesn't, I don't want to be looking at my lap wishing we had an hour or two instead of minutes to think of a way to help him or shut down the rogue aircraft."

"What kind of help are we getting from those guys?" Gabriel asked, looking over at the NWAD engineers.

"You mean the ones who created this mess?" Galvez asked.

"New plane, new sets of challenges," Puckett pointed out. "There's never been a test aircraft that didn't have problems."

"At least those had eject buttons," Gabriel said.

"Which means what, exactly?" Puckett asked. "When I was growing up Air Force Captain Iven Kincheloe was my hero. I had a book about him. I read it so much the binding fell apart. Back in 1956 Captain Kincheloe flew a Bell X-2 right to the edge of space. The man was actually weightless for fifty-six seconds. That was before there were any astro-nauts, before there was such a thing as an artificial satellite. Two years later he took up a new F-104. He had an ejection seat. When his plane died under him he bailed. He landed in the wreckage and was burned to death. You can't anticipate everything. You just can't."

There was a short silence. Kodak broke it.

"As you said before, General, this is a fluid situation. We understand the broad parameters. Is there something you want us to do specifically?"

"Right now I need you to stay alert," Scott told him. "Whatever else we may think, this is an unprecedented situation. Watch what's going on and if you have any sugges-tions I want to hear them, however outlandish they seem."

"One thing we should do, sir, is contact foreign govern-ments," Black said.

"To warn them?"

"No, sir," she said. "To see if they were spying on this project. If they were, they may have thoughts on an anti-Angel offensive system."

"I see a world of diplomatic hurt in that idea," Kodak said. "Washington isn't going to admit to foreign govern-ments that we have an out-of-control killer plane patrolling the skies."

"They're going to have to acknowledge that eventually," Black pointed out, "especially if the Angel does what Captain Puckett suggests and goes looking to acquire new targets."

"That's a clever response but it's going to require State Department and CIA involvement," Scott said.

"How much do you think *they've* been told by DoD?" Ko-dak asked.

"Not much," Gabriel replied. "Brass probably came up with a cover story for the lockdown and a promise to clean this up ASAP."

"Which is why we're here," Scott reminded them. "Lieu-tenant Black, I don't want to discourage out-of-the-box think-ing. You've got a good idea but it will take time to execute—"

"Unlike the spies, which is why no one would fess up to having that intel," Gabriel said.

Major Bryan would have told the captain to curb the asides. Scott just rolled over them. "I want to concentrate on what we can bring to this situation given the manpower on hand and the available hardware," Scott continued. "As long as we don't interrupt anyone or bump into electronics, the rear admiral has given us permission to observe activities here, use selected computer files in the conference room, or brainstorm in the guest quarters. Any questions?"

"Just one, General" Puckett said. "We've seen a string of nasty geologic events today. This is Southern California. What precautions have these boys taken to make sure they don't lose control of the Seraph in case Norco is shut down by an earthquake or wildfire?"

Scott stared at the pilot, dumbfounded. He had absolutely no idea. Worse, despite everything that had happened this morning, the question had never occurred to him. Scott went over to Parks—fortunately, it had occurred to the NWAD engineers. Major Bryan would be carrying software to link the Seraph to backups at White Sands and at Naval Air Station Key West—which had a complimentary system, originally developed for tracking the space shuttle—in the event of a communications breakdown.

Scott was glad to hear that and informed his team. But it demonstrated how one could be so close to a project that obvious problems were overlooked. It also dramatically illustrated the adage about learning from history lest it be repeated. Scott still felt foolish but he was glad Parks had it covered.

The LASER group had remained under the wingtip, not saying much. Scott dispersed them and went back to the undercarriage of the Seraph. Major Bryan was now inside, communicating with Hathaway and Parks via headset. Above them, mechanics were installing the egress hatch.

Scott thought back to what Captain Puckett had said before about the early days of high-performance aircraft. He remembered how Chuck Yeager had to use ten inches of sawed-off broom handle to close the hatch of the X-1, the plane he had used to break the sound barrier.

Maybe this is the way it's supposed to be, Scott reflected. Problems solved and progress made by instinct and improvisation rather than with playbooks. It is what Americans did best. More importantly, it seemed to work.

There was just over an hour until the Seraph sailed skyward with Major Bryan inside. Scott was tired but didn't want to leave the hangar. Even if the men didn't speak, the general wanted Bryan to know he was there, watching his back. It was a cosmetic gesture at best, and both men knew it. Once the Seraph took off, the major was on his own.

TWELVE

Norco, California

Major Bryan couldn't remember when time had skated by so quickly. He also couldn't remember a lot of what he had heard during that time. It was a smeary mass of detail, like a Roller-blader racing by in the park. The major knew from years of cramming for drills and missions that a lot of the information was floating on the top of his head, accessible if he needed it. He didn't know how that worked but was glad that it did. If the Bryan memory system failed, Dr. Hathaway would be in constant radio contact to jumpstart it. Right now Bryan was simply trying to remember the basics, such as how to operate the hatches of the two planes and what to stick inside where when he got onboard the Angel.

During the overlapping tutorials from Hathaway and system-specific engineers, Bryan had noticed the arrival of the LASER team, but he didn't want to break concentration to greet them. He knew they would understand. From the quick glimpses he got of the crew, they seemed awed or intense or both. General Scott, on the other hand, seemed jumpy and concerned, much more so than on previous operations. Bryan knew the general wasn't keeping any bad news from him; that wasn't Scott's way. More likely it was the fact

that this was Parks's operation, not his. The general was un-
accustomed to taking a secondary role.

Or being responsible for saving the world, Bryan thought.
That provided its own set of pressures.

But Tom Bryan could not concern himself with the psy-
che of Benjamin Scott. Every detail of the mission might
have been difficult to retain, but not so the implications of
failure. The Angel would have dominion over the skies until
a beacon could be constructed to allow another plane to get
close to it. That would take at least three months. During that
time there was no telling where Angel would roam.

*Or what a nation would do when its military aircraft were
struck in their own airspace,* Bryan thought.

The Seraph was tractored to the airstrip, a fifteen-minute
process. Bryan took the opportunity to go to the hangar rest-
room. A few of the LASER team members were standing
around the hangar, talking to engineers, and he didn't want
to see them. When a team was going into battle everyone
was juiced. There was an organic sense of purpose and a
contagious spike in courage. That "gung-ho Joe" mentality
did not exist among squad members who had to sit on the
bench. Guided by reason and not adrenaline, they were the
ones who typically showed fear, who expressed silent concern for their teammates. Bryan didn't want to look into
their eyes. He didn't want to see any doubts they might have.
That could be contagious, too.

The major went to the small cubicle and shut the door. He
felt protected in this small space, safe from exposure to un-
wanted attention. Twenty minutes from now he would be in
another small space feeling something far different. A fitting
capstone to a day of opposites. Bryan washed his face, took
a few sips from the faucet, then walked around the room
shaking out his hands, breathing deeply, touching his toes,
doing everything he could to relax.

There was a knock at the door.

"Major?"

"Yes?"

"It's Puckett. I wanted to make sure you were okay."

"I'm fine, thanks."

"You sure?"

"Yes, positive. Be out in a minute."

Bryan did not hear the telltale scrape of boot sole on concrete. The captain was still standing there.

The major decided there was probably nothing that would distract him in Puckett's eyes. The pilot was the team stoic. Feeling as loose as he expected he'd get, Bryan opened the door. Puckett's expression was uncharacteristically relaxed. He had grease on his forehead and hands. He saw that Bryan had noticed.

"I was helping the mechs check your engines, sir," Puckett said. "Hope you don't mind."

"Of course not. How do they look?"

"There are no obstructions, but that's about all *I* could tell," Puckett informed him. "I've never seen anything like them before. They're beauties."

Bryan smiled. That's why Puckett looked so content. The captain had enjoyed what pilots, helmsmen, tank commanders, and other transportation officers called "technoporn," a new machine that was supermodel-sweet.

"Sir? I wanted to tell you something else," Puckett said. "You're going to kick some rump up there."

"I hope so."

"You will. I know it. That's the way it works."

"The way what works?" Bryan asked.

"Flying a test plane," Puckett said. "See, every hot dog who ever did what you're about to do will be in the aircraft with you. They've got this kind of spiritual 'neighborhood watch' thing going that's real tough to explain. It's like what LASER has, only you can't see the guys who are watching your tail. You'll feel it, though, Major—if that makes sense."

Puckett spoke with conviction. Bryan told him he understood and appreciated the heads-up. The major wasn't sure he believed it, but hope, even faint hope, was better than a void.

It was time to go. Bryan gave Captain Puckett a handshake

and a half smile. As he did, the major saw Lieutenant Black walking over. Bryan started walking quickly toward the hangar door. He didn't want this to become a group hug. Warm wishes could be as deadly as fear. They were always tinged with the unsettling sense that "this could be good-bye."

Puckett kept up with Bryan. "The general teamed us up to check out the Seraph," the captain explained as Black approached. "The lieutenant—she wanted to say something, too."

Bryan slowed but did not stop. Lieutenant Black fell in beside them.

"How are you, sir?"

"Fine, Lieutenant," Bryan, said with a little nod.

"I wanted you to know there's nothing in the engines that'll explode," she assured the major.

"Thanks," Bryan replied. There was no fear in Lieutenant Black's eyes, either. Just pride.

She saluted and he returned it. To his surprise, it wasn't a farewell salute. There was a snap at the end of it, more like "Off you go into the wild blue yonder." Perhaps he had underestimated the team.

Puckett and Black had a reason to brief the major. The other LASER members did not. They continued whatever they were doing as Bryan stepped out into the cool night. General Scott was there watching as the Seraph was detached from the tractor. Together, the men headed toward the undercarriage. Hathaway and Parks were there with the engineers, who were busy reopening the hatch.

"How do you feel?" Scott asked.

"Ready," Bryan told him. "By the way, sir—did you ask the team to give me space?"

"No. I think you did that by hanging back in there. Why? Did you want them to give you a send-off?"

"Not at all. I was just curious."

Scott stopped and faced Bryan. "Major, even if it's a mission of one, these people take their lead from the commander. When they first got here, your team hit the rear admiral with a LASER-brand reality check. Twenty megatons coming from all directions with just one purpose: they wanted to make sure they could trust your life in NWAD's hands."

"That shouldn't have surprised me," Bryan said.

"But it did. Major, these aren't grunts. They're professional soldiers. Don't lose sight of that."

Bryan turned back toward the hangar. The LASER Ops were beginning to gather in the doorway to watch the take-off. The major took a moment to salute them as they looked on. Captain Gabriel was there and he shouted the team to attention. The missing members hurried over. They stood in a line and saluted back on the captain's command. Bryan couldn't see their eyes. If he could, he knew it would not be fear he saw there but respect.

A soldier had four phases: action, recreation, sleep, and time to think. The last was something a warrior wanted to avoid. That was the staging area for doubt. Maybe the fear didn't go any farther than what Bryan himself had carried into the lavatory. Hopefully, it had stayed there.

He did not feel bad for having insulated himself. He had needed to keep his eye on the prize. But he had misjudged LASER—or himself. Maybe they saw him as tougher than he saw himself. The officer who had saved the crew of the submarine *Tempest D* was the man to tame the Angel.

Bryan turned to the Seraph. The hatch had been opened and the staircase was being locked into position. Bryan saluted the general. Here the major saw a trace of something that was less than fear; it was concern that wrinkled the corners of the general's eyes and dipped his brow. That was to be expected. But there was a "go get 'em" smile, too, tugging at the sides of Scott's mouth.

After one of the engineers helped him on with his oxygen tanks and parachute, Bryan made his way into the belly of the prototype. The additional tanks were already onboard. Bryan checked them himself. They were full. As long as this operation took less than eight hours, he wouldn't suffocate.

Bryan crawled onto a reclining seat that had been pulled

from an F-16 and bolted beneath the hatch. It wasn't elegant but it would keep him from rolling around the fuselage. He strapped himself inside with the top of his head facing forward, put on the headset, and tested the communications. It was working fine. There was nothing else to do, nothing to look at. The only light was the flashlight hooked on the cabin wall to his right. He wouldn't be needing that until Parks told him he had reached his destination.

The hatch was shut beyond Bryan's feet. It was dark and that was good. He didn't want to be inside a porous plane.

With nothing to look at, Bryan just lay there and listened. There were the predictable whirs and shouts, clanks and hums. His heart was tapping pretty loudly as well. At least the engines were quiet. Until he started to taxi, Bryan did not realize the engines had been started. The soccer-ball wheels provided a very smooth ride, though it was a little unnerving to think that this thing was being flown by a man in a tower with a joystick. He felt the aircraft turn and stop, then both felt and heard the engines rev. The aircraft eased forward, accelerating rapidly. He had never gone into the air head-first. It was a strange feeling as the Seraph became airborne. There was very little vibration and the aircraft itself still generated very little noise. The rush of air was louder than the throaty hiss of the engines.

Parks was busy monitoring the takeoff, and the radio silence gave Bryan a few moments to reflect. He didn't think about the mission but about his team. The major didn't know about that spiritual fraternity of test pilots. But he was happy to know this much: whether on the ground or sending good thoughts his way, his own team would be doing their damnedest to help him.

THIRTEEN

San Diego, California

Chan was still seventy-five miles from the American coast when his radar picked up a blip on the very edge of its range. The seven-inch monochrome multifunction display showed an aircraft moving southwest at approximately 700 kilometers an hour. It was traveling through the lockdown zone at a forty-two degree angle to his own flight plan. The other plane was not on an intercept course.

Lieutenant Commander Chan radioed the information to Captain Mok Chung in Jiangwan.

"You have had no communication from the Americans?" Chung asked.

"None, sir."

"That is surprising. If these jets are on your radar, you are surely on theirs," the captain observed.

Chung told him to stay on course. Flight Control would advise him whether to alter his route to reconnoiter.

Less than two minutes later Chan picked up a second blip. This one was moving due west. It appeared to be on a course and at the right speed to link up with the first aircraft. The pilot passed the update to Jiangwan.

"Captain, do you think the lockdown is due to the tsunami, or could it be some kind of military test?" Chan asked. "I've been trying to think of what else would cause an entire region to be closed—"

"We have been doing the same," Chung said. "We now believe that a lockdown of this magnitude is counterproductive to rescue efforts. If it were a test, one would have expected it to be postponed after what happened this morning. Whatever this is, it was either very secretive or very sudden. An ally in the office of Taiwan's Minister of Defense informs us that Taipei's request for an explanation has gone unanswered. They made the call over an hour ago using the recently installed hotline, suggesting some urgency on the part of the minister."

Chan felt privileged to have that information shared with him.

Chung stopped broadcasting to take a call. A moment later he was back on the radio. "Lieutenant Commander, I have just heard from Senior Captain Shin. You are to alter course and identify the aircraft that are defying the lockdown," Chung said. "Based on the coordinates you provided, you should be able to complete that mission and still reach the carrier."

"That is my assessment as well," Chan said. The pilot was busy changing his heading as they spoke. "At least both aircraft are heading toward the coast. That will bring them closer to me, allowing me to conserve fuel and lower the risk of an intercept once I cross into American airspace."

"You will have a nearly full moon and night vision," Chung went on. "You are to use your own judgment about the proximity of your approach."

"Yes, sir."

"You are also instructed to put through any communications you may receive from the Americans," Chung went on. "Their coastal radar systems may have been compromised but inland systems or those aircraft will pick you up. We have English speakers who will explain that you are in the region to survey the damage and assess the kind of support our government might be willing to offer."

That is very clever, Chan thought. The lieutenant commander had a flash of being a child again, making fierce masks to hide timidity or carving peaceful masks to hide aspects of war. In this case, diplomacy was a mask being used to hide intelligence-gathering. Even if the Americans could shoot him down they wouldn't use it as a first resort. And however long it would take them to say "no, thank you," that time could be used to pursue the mission.

The communication from America came through moments after Captain Chung had broken off contact. It was a full-band broadcast, covering all radio frequencies with a sharp squawking "alert." That was designed to get the pilot's attention. The message itself would follow. Chan punched a dual-channel button that would make the JF-17 a conduit for the signal.

The pilot listened as the chatter began, a drawling speech that was answered with a more clipped form of that speech. He had no idea what either side was saying, though voices were calm throughout. The only word he was able to pick out was the one that concluded each broadcast from America, probably the name of the person or place that was responding: "Miramarover."

FOURTEEN

Miramar, California

Sergeant Sandra Ocean stood behind Lance Corporal Velk as he spoke to the bogey. Her arms were tightly crossed as she listened to the conversation on a second set of headphones.

The tower supervisor was not having a very good evening. A half hour before, radar at Marine Corps Air Station Miramar had picked up an unidentified aircraft moving into California airspace. She ordered Velk to try and contact it. He failed. Ocean relayed the information to Captain Oaks at Unified Pacific Services Headquarters in Long Beach. UPSH/LB was the next step in the DeCoIn ladder: Detect, Contact, Intercept. If an unidentified aircraft refused to speak with them, or did not respond to instructions, it was up to Long Beach to order a takedown. Captain Oaks was the liaison between local air control operations and activities within the entire Pacific region.

Oaks told Sergeant Ocean to ignore the blip.

Five minutes later their radar picked up a second blip moving in the same general direction. UPSH/LB told them to ignore that one, too.

Now, what appeared by its radar profile to be a Chinese JF-17, the so-called Fierce Dragon, was racing toward American airspace. The aircraft was midair refuelable and was probably on a test run. The DoD had known the planes were being fielded but, so far, none had left the Far East. The aircraft had maintained radio silence until it was within thirty-five miles, at which point Velk was put through to Lieutenant Commander Wei at a Flight Dispatch Center in Shanghai. At least this aircraft—or, at least, its home base—was talking to them. Velk had just informed the FDC that their pilot did not have clearance to enter American airspace.

"Our aircraft does not have hostile intentions," Wei replied in adequate English. "We wish to offer help to those who were afflicted by the tsunami. We cannot do that unless we know the extent of the damage."

"You do not have clearance to enter American airspace for any reason," Velk replied firmly. "Your pilot is twenty miles from American territorial waters. We demand that he turn around."

Velk was reciting orders from the playbook. Absent a countermand from Ocean, he would continue to do so. She was disinclined to interfere until the last moment. It was just one plane and they could still intercept it, if the no-fly order was lifted for this emergency. She believed it would be useful to know how far the PLAAF would go in a game of chicken.

"We believe that the extraordinary events of this day have obligated us to see firsthand where we may be most useful," the Chinese spokesman replied. "If you wish to escort our unarmed pilot, we would welcome that."

"Your pilot does not have permission to enter our airspace," Velk repeated. "We demand that he turn back."

There was no response. The problem was now above Sergeant Ocean's pay grade. She jumped to the internal communications station beside Velk's post and told Corporal Kavli to put her through to Captain Oaks.

Oaks told her that UPSH/LB was just picking up the intruder now. He said that they would take over communications with Shanghai.

"Should we have fighters ready to scramble?" Sergeant

Ocean asked. She was already accessing the duty roster on the computer at the IC station.

"Negative," Oaks replied.

"*Will* fighters be scrambled?" she pressed.

"I cannot answer that," Oaks informed her.

As a radio systems supervisor, Sergeant Ocean was very good at reading voices. Oaks's tone was not the stonewalling "ears-only" she was accustomed to hearing in top-clearance situations. It was the voice of ignorance. The captain couldn't answer because he didn't know.

Ocean suddenly felt extremely helpless. Worse, she felt vulnerable.

The sergeant waited until they heard the Long Beach communications officer cut in, then instructed Velk to break off contact.

"Sergeant, this is very bizarre," Velk said. "Do you have any idea what's going on?"

"The Chinese are obviously testing our response capabilities in light of what happened this morning," Ocean replied. "What I don't understand is why we aren't responding. We obviously have the aircraft in the region."

"You mean those first two blips."

"The Chinese jet is heading right toward them," said Corporal Bryant, the radar operator.

"Maybe Long Beach knew he was coming," Velk suggested. "Maybe that's why we have the lockdown."

"You think there'll be a shooting match?" Bryant asked.

"I can't believe that," Ocean said.

"They'll probably force them down," Velk said. "It would be sweet to get a next gen PLAAF aircraft."

"Draw them out with a lockdown, then take them to ground," Bryant said, nodding. "Clever."

Ocean still didn't believe that. She thought the lockdown was probably tsunami-related and the Chinese were simply taking advantage of that. But that didn't explain why the two American planes came up as "unknown" on the radar screen's data overlay readout. The tower computers were programmed to recognize every known model of aircraft, military and civilian.

Unfortunately, the matter was out of their hands. All they could do was watch the radar screen as three navy blue marks converged on a relief map. Sergeant Ocean made sure that everyone was watching their screens and listening to the airwaves, making sure that the Chinese plane was a lone eagle and that no other nation decided this was an opportune time to go sightseeing over the United States or its bases.

FIFTEEN

Norco, California

After the Seraph was airborne, General Scott and Rear Admiral Parks joined Dr. Hathaway in the communications center. The radio room was an undistinguished bunker located a few paces from the hangar. Until the late 1980s it had been an observation room for tests of new engines, warheads, and occasional test aircraft. NWAD was not, as a rule, a nexus for contact with or tracking of aircraft of any kind. The Seraph radio system had been put together with elements salvaged from Coronado and from an existing uplink that was already in the bunker. Swivel chairs were brought over from the conference room. The jury-rigged radio setup, secure phones, and laptops were arrayed on gunmetal desks that had already been in the room. The computers were linked to radar systems and data bases in other locales.

The joystick pilot running the craft, Captain Fred Mudd, was in the small control tower at the eastern end of the facility. His display was linked to one of the laptops in the communications center as well as to Major Bryan's wireless radio set.

No sooner had the two officers settled in than the rear admiral received a call from Captain Townsend Oaks. NWAD had sent UPSH/LB a top-secret communique regarding an "in-progress" test that was responsible for the lockdown. Parks wanted to be notified at once if anything occurred that compromised the integrity of the region.

The JF-17 qualified.

Oaks informed Parks that Shanghai was adamant about not turning the jet around. The captain wanted to know if there was anything they could field to change the PLAAF's mind.

"No," Parks replied.

Scott sat beside him, listening in on his headphones. Hathaway continued to keep an open channel to the Seraph. This was another of those possibilities that should have been obvious and hadn't been.

"What about the two aircraft that are already moving southwest?" Oaks said. "They are off transponders, obviously covert military—"

"They're unavailable," Parks replied.

Oaks hesitated. "Can you elaborate, sir?"

"I cannot," Parks told him.

Scott did not like this. Oaks was going to need to cover his ass. They were going into lose-lose territory.

"With respect, sir, SOP in this situation is clear, as are my responsibilities," Oaks went on. "We alert the intruder, we field intercept craft, and if it doesn't respond we disable the aircraft using any means at our disposal."

"I know the protocol," Parks snapped.

"No disrespect intended, sir."

"We can't shoot it down," Parks said. "The aircraft is unarmed."

"So the Chinese say."

"If they say so and we clip its wings, and there are no armaments in the wreckage, we lose," Parks said. "Big-time."

"If we don't respond to an enemy aircraft when it enters our airspace, we lose more than a diplomatic edge," Oaks replied. "It may be reading our radar for future incursions, testing our reaction in a crisis—or it could be the vanguard for a larger force. We cannot discount any of these possibilities."

Oaks had a point. It was an overly dramatic one, but then so was Pearl Harbor and the September 11 attacks.

"In any event, sir, response protocol does not distinguish between armed or unarmed intruders," he went on. "For all we know the aircraft itself is the projectile. The pilot could reach a target, 'run out of fuel,' and eject before the plane goes down. Into the San Onofre nuclear facility, perhaps."

"Captain, this is General Benjamin Scott. Let us handle this situation. We have an option I'm not free to discuss."

"General, the security of this region is my responsibil-ity—" Oaks said.

"We're relieving you of that responsibility," Scott replied.

"Sir?"

"The rear admiral will put that in writing and e-mail it to you within two minutes," Scott told him.

"I'll look forward to that," Oaks replied curtly.

"Have the JF-17 radio link put through to us," Scott added.

"It's coming through now, General. Long Beach out."

Parks clicked off. He regarded Scott. "What's on your mind?"

Scott punched on the headset intercom and looked at Hathaway. "I need to talk to Major Bryan," he said.

"I'll let him know," the scientist said.

The general looked back at the rear admiral. "Please write the stand-down orders for Captain Oaks. I don't want him thinking about this too much and deciding to do an end run. He or the DoD may decide that surface-to-air missiles are the correct response after all."

"The problem is, it might be," Parks said.

That surprised Scott. "Why?"

"Because if this guy hesitates for another hundred and fifty miles, the Angel is going to get a whiff of him," Parks replied. "When it does, it's going to go after him. That will take it off course from the *Hidalgo*. It may not return."

"Why not? It got back on track after diverting to the air show."

"The Angel has two modes: free range within its patrol zone, and homecoming. Once an Angel is in the final approach corridor it's locked in—unless it gets distracted. That wouldn't happen under ordinary circumstances since the FAC is designed to lie in the zone of another Angel. If the Angel is pulled away, either by directive or in an emergency, it has to be recalibrated manually."

"Which we can't do," Scott said.

"Correct," Parks said. He pointed toward the radar link on one of the laptops. "The JF-17 is heading directly toward the Angel's final approach corridor. If we don't take him down and the Angel IDs him as hostile—which it will—she'll be on her own. There's no telling where it could end up."

"The third option," Scott said.

"Pardon?"

"The third option—the one you said you didn't want to have to consider," Scott told him. "The idea that the Angel could do just what the Chinese pilot is doing, fly into the airspace of another country."

Parks nodded. "Except that our baby is armed."

Hathaway told Scott that Bryan was on the radio, green line. "The Shanghai control tower is also coming through, red line."

Scott punched the green button and got on.

"Major, how are you doing?" Scott asked.

"Little light-headed from the oxygen so I fixed the mix," he said. "Otherwise, fine. Why?"

"I need you to do something," Scott said.

"If it involves lying down in a cigar tube, I'm yours."

"All you have to do is tell someone who you are and what you did," the general told him.

"I don't understand—"

"Just hang on a moment and I'll explain," Scott replied as he punched the red button.

SIXTEEN

Corona, California

Major Bryan was annoyed.

He had been airborne less than fifteen minutes when the game plan was altered. That in itself wasn't what bothered him. It was not uncommon for a mission to get on its feet and have people or hardware perform differently than expected. What troubled Bryan was that this had nothing to do with improving the scenario. It was to keep things from getting worse.

As contact with the Angel neared—seven minutes till it saw him and, assuming he survived, ten till he reached the underbelly—Bryan had been reviewing his emergency escape procedures. He remembered it all, the timing, the functions, the exit process—everything. He was supposed to be at the hatch at the seven-minute mark in case the Angel turned on him. NWAD engineers had installed a pair of explosive bolts that would blow the manhole-size door up and away. The two charge mechanisms had been pulled from a spare-parts bin they kept for test planes. The scientists had cribbed gunpowder from shells in a 9mm clip. In theory, the bolts would work. All Bryan had to do was flip down the plastic lids, press the buttons, turn around, grab the forward edge of the hatchway, and push himself out headfirst—toward the tail.

As soon as the hatch blew, the joystick pilot at NWAD would put the Seraph into a dive. The force of the wind would blow Bryan away from the aircraft. It was a risky maneuver but it beat raining to earth in ice-blasted particles.

Bryan wondered if any of the scientists saw the humor in the fact that the Angel "iced" its prey. He did. If the Angel decided not to recognize him an American soldier, he could well become a victim. That would be ironic, too. But he didn't feel anxious about that. One of the Mercury astronauts—he believed it was Gus Grissom, the second American up—said he wasn't afraid of being blown up, only of screwing up. That was how Bryan felt.

If the Angel allowed the Seraph to approach, Bryan would open the hatch using the pair of latches at opposite ends of the rim. There was a handle in the center so he could pull the door in. He would set the steel disc on a hook provided for that purpose. Engineers had calculated that with the Angel flying a few feet above, only a minimal amount of airflow would race through the open hatch into the cabin of the Seraph. The joystick pilot did not anticipate much trouble from that. If the calculations were wrong and the Seraph drifted off, Bryan still had the parachute. If he succeeded in reprogramming the Angel and NWAD regained control, he might even get a ride back to Norco.

If.

That had suddenly become a much bigger word.

Just three minutes ago, Hathaway had told Bryan that everything was on time and on course for the rendezvous. The Angel was just soaring over Red Mountain, California, which was northeast of Bryan's position. The converging flight paths represented exactly thirteen minutes of flying time. Now, General Scott was calling to tell the major that he had something else to do, something that could save a life and prevent the Angel from changing course. He had to convince a Chinese flight dispatcher to pull a fighter jet from American airspace.

"Shouldn't that be a Pacific Command motivational speech?" Bryan asked.

"They tried."

"Did they try it in Mandarin?"

"We're thinking that you may have some credibility with them," Scott said, ignoring the quip. "You're the officer who pulled eight Chinese sailors from their wrecked submarine."

"What makes you think they'll believe I'm that guy?"

"It's not the kind of deception we'd keep in our active file unless it were true," Scott pointed out.

"And if I can't convince him? What's the 'or else?'" Bryan asked.

"Tell them the fighter will be shot down."

"They'll like that," Bryan said. "Do I tell them how? If this pilot has surveillance equipment, and I'm sure he has, they'll find out soon enough—"

"If the Chinese pilot turns back he won't know anything else about them. I want to try and keep it that way," Parks cut in.

The order was direct. Though the rear admiral hadn't struck Bryan as much of a leader, he was used to making command decisions—even if they had to do with budgets and deadlines instead of lives.

"I assume there's a translator," Bryan said.

"On and waiting," Parks said.

"Put me through," Bryan told him.

A moment later Hathaway said, "Major Bryan, you're on with Captain Chung and his translator in China."

"Captain Chung, this is Major Thomas Bryan. I was the officer who rescued eight of your seamen from the *Song* class submarine in the Weddell Sea."

Bryan listened as the translator spoke. The major could tell that the pace of this exchange was going to be frustrating. On the other hand, the delay did give him a few moments to think of what he was going to say next. Diplomacy had never been his strong suit.

"Thank you, Major," Chung replied.

That was all the Chinese captain said. This was going to be a long, hard slog.

"Captain, your pilot is in imminent danger," Bryan told him. "There are two aircraft headed toward him. Their orders are not to escort him to safety but to shoot him down. He must withdraw from American airspace."

Bryan had a feeling that was not going to go over any better than the previous requests.

"Our pilot tells us he is experiencing mechanical difficulties," Chung reported. "It may be necessary for him to land."

Captain Chung was trying to buy surveillance time. The Chinese would never land their newest aircraft on U.S. soil.

"Captain, I risked my life to save your sailors," Bryan said. "You *must* believe that I have your pilot's best interests at heart."

"Over those of your country?" Chung asked. "If that is true, allow him to attend to his problems and leave."

"That is out of my hands," Bryan said. "He has less than two minutes to turn around. That is not a negotiable deadline."

Bryan looked at his watch while the translator spoke. The Chinese pilot had less than two minutes until the Angel saw him; Bryan had about the same. He knew from his briefing that if the Angel had two aircraft in its patrol zone it would destroy the nearest one first, then turn and deal with the other.

"We will discuss with our pilot the condition of his aircraft," Chung said through the interpreter.

Another stall.

"I repeat, sir, the condition of your aircraft will be extremely grave if the pilot maintains his current heading," Bryan replied. "Find another way to test your new aircraft. Don't sacrifice it *and* the pilot for an extra minute of surveillance. It will cost you everything."

The translator passed the suggestion along. There was a brief silence. Bryan couldn't imagine what there was to think about.

"Your concern sounds now like a threat," Chung said. "Can you tell me why aircraft are flying in a lockdown zone?"

"Is *that* what this is about?" Bryan asked.

Parks cut in again. "Tell him they're enforcing the no-fly order." The rear admiral sounded more urgent than before.

Bryan repeated what Parks had said. The major knew exactly what was coming next.

"That does not explain why the area is closed to air traffic, or why the boundaries keep changing," Chung said.

"Captain, an explanation will be forthcoming, I assure you." He looked at his watch. The Angel would see them both in about thirty seconds. "Please. Secure the safety of your aircraft first. A minute from now it will be too late."

"You are in one of the two aircraft, are you not?" Chung asked.

Bryan hadn't expected *that*. "What do you mean?"

"Your voice sounds hollow," Chung continued. "I suspect you are breathing through a mask with a vocal attachment."

"Okay. Do you think that gives me some control over the situation? Because it doesn't."

"It makes me wonder, Major. If you are the man who saved our seamen, why are you willing to shoot this one down?"

"It isn't a matter of 'willing,' Captain. That's just the way things are. Look, I really hate to say it but you've got about thirty seconds before your man and his jet are taken down. I hope you'll do the smart thing. Over."

The major unbuckled the cross-your-heart-harness. "Sorry, Rear Admiral, but that's all I've got time for," Bryan said.

"Unfortunate, but completely understood," Parks replied.

"And predictable. The guys in the field always take one for the team," Bryan replied. The major put his gloved hands on the floor and raised his butt. He carefully slid himself over the hump at the base of the chair. He crab-walked through the narrow compartment to the hatch. It was awkward because of the Mylar lining. There wasn't a part of him that didn't get scraped. But better him than the parachute.

The wireless radio continued to connect him to NWAD. So far, Chung hadn't responded. The major lay on his back and reached up. He flipped down the green plastic covers of the explosive bolts and waited.

"We're at fifteen seconds to Angel patrol zone," Hathaway said.

"How far is the Chinese plane?"

"Ten seconds. Major, you're going to feel a jolt. We're increasing your speed," Hathaway said. "We have to get you into the zone first. The other plane may draw Angel away and make it impossible to catch."

Bryan felt the bump. It knocked his legs and spine toward his head; only the backpack prevented him from sliding away.

"Doc, you'll have to give me a countdown," Bryan said. "I need to be ready in case I have to eject."

"You're on an even clock with the JF-17 at seven seconds, six—"

Bryan's heart was slamming in all directions. He reached up and placed his thumbs on the red buttons.

"—you gained a second on him. In at three, two—"

Bryan could literally feel his blood flowing. But this is what he lived for: the crunch moment. It was better than sex.

"—one."

The air whooshed, the Seraph hummed, and nothing blew up.

"You did it," Hathaway said, his voice catching. "Angel bought you."

Bryan's heart slowed as the climax fled. "What about the intruder?"

"He's still coming," Hathaway replied. "And the Angel is turning to meet him."

SEVENTEEN

Norco, California

"Change Seraph course to shadow Angel!" Parks said into the mouthpiece.

The room was chilly but Rear Admiral Parks was perspiring. He watched the radar as, at his command, the Seraph was moved in a new direction with its twin. The blips were nearly merged. He hoped the joystick pilot was as good as the Angel's auto controls. The Chinese aircraft was still moving inland.

"With the JF-17 and the Angel moving toward one another, the encounter will take place in less than two minutes," Hathaway said.

The men watched the radar in silence.

"I'm going to call the Navy secretary," Parks said quietly. "He has to inform the president."

Hathaway switched back to Seraph communication. "Major, you'll be go for transfer in three minutes."

"Roger. I'm skewing to port side inside here. Did the Seraph just change direction?"

"Yes," Hathaway said. "The Angel's chasing the Chinese jet. We're pacing her to get you aboard."

"Pilot, are you okay with that?" Bryan asked.

The joystick pilot, who was plugged into the major's headset, replied with a clipped, "Yessir."

"Great. Let me ask you something, Doc," Bryan said. "The Angel's patrol zone—it isn't set, is it?"

"No. If it were this would be a lot easier. We could just keep everything outside that box."

"What about the Angel's controls? Acceleration and thrust—are they locked?"

"Yes," Hathaway said. "Why?"

"I'm thinking that maybe we can use the Seraph as a kind of booster. Crank her up and push Angel in a totally different direction from the Chinese jet."

There was a short silence. Hathaway and Parks exchanged glances. Hathaway seemed intrigued.

"In theory, yes. But as long as the jet is anywhere in the zone parameters, the Angel will turn and seek it out," Hathaway told him.

"That means we'd just have to keep pushing the Angel until it's out of range," Bryan replied.

Parks was still looking at Hathaway. "Could it work?"

"It could. Keep in mind, though, that this will push Angel farther from *Hidalgo*. If we had any hope that she'd return to that area and stick around, this will make it even less likely."

"Hopefully, Angel will be responding to our signals in an hour or two and we can land her wherever we want," Parks said. "Major, I'm willing to try this but I won't authorize the maneuver until you're onboard the Angel. Contact between the aircraft could damage both of them. We can't risk losing the Seraph *and* having you chute to safety. There would be no way to get back to the Angel."

"I understand," Bryan replied.

"Question," Scott said. "What if this succeeds and the Chinese jet changes course, continues to follow the Angel?"

"I'll lean out the wheel well and spit at the dumb bastard myself," Bryan said. "At least we'll have tried to save him."

"I like your style, Major," Parks said. "Dr. Hathaway, make it happen."

Hathaway nodded. "Meanwhile, Major, you have one minute, ten seconds to transfer. Did you reshroud the explosive bolts?"

"I did."

"Is there any ice on the egress latches?"

"No condensation, no freezing, not even a breeze coming in. The engineers made a tight hatch seal. Should be a smooth half-turn."

"Very good," Hathaway said. "Time to transfer—mark, one minute."

Bryan acknowledged and the scientist conferred with the joystick pilot about the upcoming redirection.

While they spoke, Parks slid his chair over to one of the secure phones. It was time to update the Secretary of the Navy, Marcus Whittle. Whittle was not a micromanager. He trusted his field commanders to make decisions consistent with administration policy. But this situation was unique: a natural disaster releasing a rogue drone aircraft followed by a foreign fighter moving into American airspace. It was unique in the elements and unique in the fact that there was nothing anyone could do to control them. If the Seraph nudge didn't redirect the Angel, the Chinese pilot would be dead within minutes.

To Parks's surprise, Whittle was unavailable.

Well, shit, Parks thought. Captain Oaks must have updated the secretary first. Whittle knew about the rogue Angel and had approved the lockdown with the president's knowledge. The rear admiral would not have had that kind of authority. The secretary's unavailability now was probably a case of plausible deniability: if anything happened to the Chinese jet, the buck stopped on Parks's desk. Since the Guardian Angel project was under his command, he would endure the political fallout for having shot down the Fierce Dragon.

He returned to the console table.

"The aircraft are aligned," Hathaway said tensely. "The major is removing the hatch."

Scott was sitting absolutely still beside him, his shoulders slumped. Parks had stopped sweating; he was cold now. Very cold.

"Anything from Shanghai?" Parks asked.

Hathaway shook his head. The rear admiral wasn't surprised. The question had been posed to break the silence more than anything else. If the Chinese had replied, Hathaway would have said something. Parks looked at the radar screen. The JF-17 blip was still on a direct course to the Angel.

"Stupid bastard," Parks muttered.

The men were anxious to ask Bryan how it was going. They didn't. If the major had anything to say he would have said it.

The voice they finally heard was not the one they wanted to hear. It was the joystick pilot.

"Sir, new telemetry from the Seraph—the coordinates are giving us degrade-level downdraft from the Angel."

"In layman, please!"

"The wind is pushing the Seraph down," the pilot replied. "We have to throttle up now or pull away."

"You can't!" Bryan shouted.

"Major, what's wrong?" Scott said. He shot upright in his seat.

"I'm outside the Seraph." His voice was a barely audible blur in the rush of the wind.

"What's wrong?" Hathaway asked.

"The Angel tire didn't fully retract!" he yelled. "I can't get inside!"

EIGHTEEN

California City, California

If there were such a thing as a worst case scenario for transferring from one vehicle to another, it was being stuck between the two with no easy way backward or forward.

Bryan knew the Seraph was being hit hard by the downdraft. It was wobbling underneath him. He was standing just behind the open hatch holding on to the rectangular wheel well of the Angel. The pilot had done a remarkable virtual job of getting him this close. But the wheel had not entirely deflated and the major couldn't push the huge, heavy rubber mass aside. Unfortunately, if he let go to try and climb back inside the Seraph there was no guarantee that he wouldn't be blown from the back of the aircraft. The transfer was supposed to have been quick, up through one opening into the other. He wasn't supposed to be standing here like Atlas.

To make things worse, the Angel was going to open fire on the Chinese jet in a few minutes. That was surely going to cause the aircraft to vibrate. It would make holding on even more difficult.

Unless the rear guns take you out, in which case that won't be an issue, Bryan thought. He had to get off here. He looked up, around, and down for inspiration. All he saw was airplane and wind.

And then something occurred to him.

"I see something that may fix this," Bryan said into the mouthpiece. "I need the Seraph up about two feet."

"Major," Parks said, "you heard what the pilot—"

"Raise the plane or we abort. I've got a good grip on the Angel's wheel well. If I lose my footing I'll be okay. I've got my chute if I have to bail."

"Adjusting," the pilot said.

Bryan heard the Seraph's hum become a grumble as the aircraft started to rise. Some of that was echo from the undercarriage of the Angel. The two craft were shifting relative to each other so the ascent didn't feel dramatically different, except for the fact that the Seraph hatch was coming closer.

Holding on to the edge of the wheel well with his left hand, Bryan reached down with his right.

"I need another foot or so!" the major said.

The Seraph continued to edge upward. If it got too high he could always drop into the hatch: the opening was close enough now so that he could probably drop clean through.

The wings of the Seraph were moving up and down, shifted by the winds and the downdraft from the Angel. Now and then the fuselage itself rolled, like a dinghy on a wave at sea. He could hear tapping above the scream of the winds, imagined the Seraph knocking gently against the Angel here and there. The major didn't dare take his eyes off what he was doing to check. Besides, he had a feeling he would know if there were any serious damage: one or the other of the aircraft would suddenly drop from the sky. He wished he had a free hand to keep on the ripcord.

Bryan continued to stretch his gloved hand downward. A few more inches and he would have what he was after: one of the explosive bolts.

His fingertips reached the top of the bolt on the starboard side. Both bolts were held in place with a snap-lock: the locks would release when the charge detonated, making sure that any residual powder, burning or inert, did not drop into the cabin. Bryan was able to free the bolt.

"Hold present position!" Bryan yelled into the mouthpiece.

"Holding," the pilot replied.

Bryan stood and tucked the four-inch-long unit under the tire. He placed it as deep inside as he could reach. He didn't want to blow himself up in the process of deflating the tire. The only drawback, and there was no getting around it, was that he had to have his hand beside the bolt in order to press the button. Hopefully, he would be able to slip it out in time.

There was something we forgot to pack, Bryan thought as he flipped the protective cover back. *A first-aid kit.* All these geniuses, all this battlefield experience between himself and General Scott, and they had all overlooked something else that should have been obvious.

He bent his back slightly to give his arm a straight shot out of the wheel well. He pressed the button and snapped his arm back so fast he nearly lost his balance. He thrust it back, held the rim of the well with both hands, and ducked as a resounding bang and a sound like a breaching whale rolled through the belly of the Angel. Bryan felt a gush of air from above and looked up as the tire collapsed. It seemed to suck in on itself in slow motion. As it did the major shifted his hands so they were on perpendicular sides. He pulled himself up and rolled toward the stern, away from the tire. He didn't want it to fall on him and push him back out.

"I'm in!" he shouted, panting as he got on his knees. He just sat there, trying to catch his breath and get on top of a nasty headache caused by the drumming winds.

"How'd you do it?" Scott asked.

"Used an explosive bolt to deflate the tire," Bryan said.

"Good thinking," Scott said.

"I don't suppose there's a pump and a patch kit aboard," Bryan asked.

"Already on the list for the next trip," Parks joked.

"One thing you can definitely put on the list is a first-aid kit," Bryan said. "I could use a few Ace bandages and a couple of aspirin. I felt like a friggin' wind sock out there. My head's still ringing."

"Noted," Parks replied.

"Brace yourself, Major!" the pilot said. "I'm boosting Seraph to try and change Angel's course."

Bryan didn't have time to get the flashlight from his equipment belt. There was light coming from the open wheel well; the only thing he saw nearby to hold on to was a narrow conduit on the port side. He wrapped his hands around it. His fingers were cold and tired and his ankles were sore from pushing his feet down on the back of the Seraph. But he was happy to be here. It was relatively warm and definitely quieter inside the Angel.

"I'm braced," Bryan said.

There was a nudge from below. The Angel began to shake as Bryan heard the Seraph engine revving up. It reminded him of something from his Philadelphia childhood: the sound of a snowblower roaring up through his earmuffs as he cleared the driveway. He remembered how powerful he felt slashing his way through deep snow with that beefy little five-horsepower engine.

The Angel tilted up slightly, then angled toward the starboard side. It felt like any airliner banking. Then the Seraph powered up again. There was a harder bump and this time the portside rose to at least thirty degrees. The major was literally leaning on the conduit. "How are we doing?" Bryan yelled.

"The Angel is being overpowered," Parks said. After a minute or so he said, "Your heading has changed and the JF-17 is out of range. We're going to pull the Seraph away and see what happens."

"Sounds good," Bryan said.

Bryan felt, then heard, the Seraph back off. The vibrating stopped and the scream of the engines receded. The Angel leveled off. If the two aircraft had kissed each other it didn't seem to do them any harm.

"It just got a whole lot quieter up here," Bryan said.

"That's what it was supposed to do," Parks said.

"Radar has you looking good," Hathaway added.

Bryan used the downtime to retrieve his flashlight. He slipped the small, powerful penlight from its loop and shined it ahead. The Angel looked just like it had in the computer simulations, except that it was longer. It was shameful that some of the video games he'd seen Corporal Wright play were in 3-D while cutting-edge NWAD technology was not.

Maybe a merger is the answer, Bryan thought. *Ninten-DoD was not without a certain pizzazz.*

Or maybe his brain wasn't getting enough blood. High altitude could do that. The headache was still there, behind his eyes. At the moment, the pain was his firmest tie to reality. Tired of waiting, the major got to his feet. Knees bent, head bowed so he could stand in the cabin, he started moving forward. He held the conduit for support as he made his way along the narrow path between the cabin wall and the tire well that still had a tire. Maybe it was his light head talking, but it was reassuring to know that both tires had failed to fully deflate. It meant that the Angel was built wrong, right; there was a design flaw and not a mechanical flaw. With luck, the rest of the aircraft would function the way it was supposed to.

"You still with us, Major?" Scott asked.

"Most of me," he replied. "I was feeling a little light-headed so I decided to head for—"

"Shit!" Parks said suddenly.

Bryan stopped just forward the tire well.

"What's wrong?" Scott asked.

"Obviously, our warnings didn't impress Shanghai," Parks said. "The JF-17 is back in range."

Bryan felt the Angel simultaneously swing down and bank sharply to the starboard side.

"And we're gunning for her," he said. "Crap! I hope Shanghai wasn't listening to that—"

"No. I switched you off," Parks said.

"Good. I don't want them to think this is personal," Bryan said. He heard a sound in the front and back of the aircraft. It was a loud but high-pitched whir. "The Angel's doing something," he said.

"Did you just hear something?" Hathaway asked.

"Yeah. Sounded like a dentist's drill."

"The Angel's arming itself," Hathaway told him. "She's using condensers to pull water vapor from the atmosphere, forming projectiles."

"Is there some way I can stop them?"

"No."

"Why not? Give me *something* to try—"

"You couldn't get to all the systems in time, and the barrels themselves are outside the craft," Hathaway said.

"Our warnings may not have had an impact, but this sure as hell will," Parks said ruefully.

Bryan felt helpless as the Angel got ready to shred the Chinese fighter. It was like watching a mugging from a rooftop. There wasn't a damn thing you could do. True, the pilot shouldn't have been in this neighborhood. But it wasn't his call. He was following bad orders from smug superiors.

"If anyone has any ideas, this would be the time to throw them out," Hathaway said. His voice sounded like Bryan felt.

There was a heavy silence. And then General Scott broke it.

"I've got one," he said. "We give them the Road Not Taken."

NINETEEN

Norco, California

The Road Not Taken was a code name coined during the Truman administration. It referred to the option, offered and urged by pacifists close to the president, to detonate the first nuclear bomb over the ocean instead of in the heart of Hiroshima. Ultimately, Truman decided that road would not demonstrate the power of the bomb as effectively as its use against a city.

General Scott's idea was a little less dramatic than burning off a few cubic tons of sea water. But the principle was identical.

"Why don't we try and maneuver the Seraph between them?" Scott said after mentioning the Road Not Taken to the others. "Let it take the hit. When the pilot sees that he'll have to turn back."

"Along with, we presume, up-close images of the Angel in action," Parks said unhappily.

"One way or another we're about to get busted," Scott said. "Shanghai will see the recon sent by the 17 and they'll definitely see what takes him out. Suppose we let them have a look, but save the pilot and his jet."

"At the cost of the Seraph," Hathaway pointed out.

"At the cost of an unmanned drone," Scott countered.

"General Scott, they are in *our* airspace, spying on *our* military bases, and have refused our demand to turn back," Parks said. "I'm not entirely clear why I owe them the destruction of a billion-dollar aircraft."

"Whatever we do, we've got about ninety seconds to decide," Hathaway said.

"The JF-17 is almost in range of the Angel's weapons."

"I could say it's the right thing to do, but you already know that so here's a different take," Scott said. "If that plane is shot down the Chinese won't believe we couldn't prevent it."

"Who cares what they think?" Parks snapped. *"They're* intruders. They've been warned."

"Dammit, this is a game that goes on all the time!" Scott said. "We fly over China; now they have the capacity to fly over us, so they're doing it, swinging their dicks around. But *we* know this situation's different."

Parks was silent for a moment. He didn't seem like someone who had just seconds to decide whether a man lived or perished. "Hank?"

"I'm sorry, but I say we let the Angel do what it was designed to do," Hathaway said, "secure the homeland."

"Sacrificing the Seraph *does* that," Scott insisted. "It shows Shanghai what the Angel can do *and* it does one thing more. It gives you the high road. That's going to matter." Scott didn't have to elaborate. He could tell by the way Parks's expression softened that the rear admiral understood. The DoD and the Congressional Armed Services Committee were going to be all over this debacle, from the morning launch to the eventual resolution. Restraint in the face of a crisis tended to play well with Congress, especially when potential international showdowns were avoided.

"Pilot, do it," Parks said. "Put the Seraph between them."

"Yes, sir."

"Do we talk to China?" Hathaway asked.

"No. Screw them." Parks regarded Scott. "Are you onboard with that?"

"Not talking to them again or your plan?" Scott asked.

"Both."

"One is pointless, the other is necessary."

Parks nodded. "And for what? I feel as if I'm betraying my uniform. Our job is to protect the nation, not coddle its enemies."

"This enemy is leaving," Scott said. "Shooting him down serves no purpose."

"It would save my Seraph," Hathaway said.

"The Seraph is dying a hero's death," Scott said. "Be proud of that."

"I'm not. I'm angry," the scientist said. "This is happening because someone in Shanghai fielded an aircraft that had no business being where it was."

Scott fixed his eyes on the scientist. "Then I guess I should be angry, too. Major Bryan is at risk because someone in San Diego did the same thing."

Hathaway had the look of a man who had taken a bullet in the forehead. The general didn't care. Sometimes you took another road to avoid an exchange. And sometimes you dropped a bomb to clear the way.

In a room that suddenly seemed less like a command center and more like a bunker,

Scott looked back at the radar to await the intervention.

TWENTY

Lancaster, California

One morning when Bruce Chan was a boy, about three or four years old, he walked outside the family's small hut and saw a collection of cricket legs on the ground beside an old oak tree. It was an odd sight, to be sure, and he couldn't figure out how they got there. How did legs go anywhere without a body?

He decided to watch the spot for a while and, with a bowl of porridge, planted himself on a nearby boulder to observe. Soon, he saw sparrows fly to a limb of the oak. They had crickets in their beaks. As they ate the meaty bodies in lunging bites, the insect legs fell to the ground.

It was at that moment Chan realized the advantage birds had over all living things. He could hold a porridge spoon in his hand; that was his reward for living on the ground. But a bird could fly with its "hands," and all it sacrificed were cricket legs. That seemed a good exchange. Only years later did Chan realize that he could have it both ways. He could have hands *and* be an airborne predator.

He was finally getting his wish. According to his radar, he was moments away from making visual contact with two American aircraft. Captain Chung had ascertained that they were military planes: he had spoken with an officer who was onboard one of them, a Major Bryan. Chung was very keen to know what kind of planes they were and why they were defying the lockdown. Chan would be able to answer at least one of those questions for him.

"They may try to force you down," Captain Chung told the lieutenant commander. "If they do, turn back to sea. The Americans will not shoot an aircraft that is withdrawing." Chung was careful not to refer to it as a retreat. That was not something a Chinese warrior did.

While he flew toward a rendezvous with the two craft, Chan kept a very careful eye on his fuel gauge. He only had twelve minutes more of pure reconnaissance time before he had to turn around and head for the Brazilian aircraft carrier. Even then, he would only have enough fuel for one pass at the flight deck. That should be enough to put the JF-17 down; it would have to be enough. He had used his onboard computer to plot a return that would take him along a slightly different route, one that would allow him to pass over Edwards Air Force Base, due east of his position. Captain Chung had approved the course change.

As the blips on the radar screen neared overlap, Chan peered out at the horizon. The jets would be about thirty kilometers away and he would have visual within seconds. The identity of the aircraft was a mystery. The computer didn't recognize it. The speed and size suggested a commercial plane like the 737. Yet the military would surely have fielded a fighter to enforce a no-fly mandate.

The answer was just moments away and the anticipation made Chan feel electrified. The lieutenant commander would have a look, take pictures, then turn and head toward the *São Paulo*.

The night was rich with stars. The overhead smear of the Milky Way broke the sky into two distinct halves. The sky was different than it was in China, the constellations and the planets different from what he was accustomed to seeing.

A pair of sharp lights at eleven o'clock grabbed the pilot's attention. One was approximately forty meters below the other. They quickly grew from brilliant star-like spots to beacons. Chan changed direction so that he could come at the aircraft from the side. The digital cameras would have a difficult time shooting accurate images with their infrared lenses as long as the brilliant light was shining at them.

Chan was surprised when the two aircraft changed direction as he did. The upper one shifted almost at once, the lower craft a moment later. Typical first encounters were fly-bys. These planes seemed more interested in a collision. Perhaps this was their way of what was called a silent encounter, a means of communicating intent without radios. Their intent was to knock him from the sky.

He held his position. The planes were still not close enough for the cameras to get good images. Chan wouldn't return to Shanghai without them. Because he was heading directly toward the two planes, their relative speed was tremendous. They would meet in less than thirty seconds. Chan had no intention of allowing a collision to take place. Once he had his photographs, he would veer off.

The gunfire was an even bigger surprise. Chan saw what appeared to be a stream of tracer bullets streak from four points of the upper aircraft. He threw the JF-17 into a power dive, heard a fearsome series of splats against his tail section, then saw the cockpit light up as the beacon turned down on him. He had never seen a fixed-wing aircraft execute a turn like that. He was in its sights again. Looking up at the on-coming spotlights, Chan was about to report his situation to Shanghai when he was hit with the biggest surprise yet. The lower of the two aircraft, which had not fired on him, suddenly swung from a dive to a horizontal slam, as the PLAN pilots called it—a sudden right-angle turn that knocked the pilot back with so much force that it was known to crack ribs. The plane was putting itself between him and the attacker.

The Chinese pilot continued to dive as looked up through the cockpit. Backlit by the attacker, the second plane took salvo after salvo. He was only able to grab a quick look at the silhouette of the aircraft as it literally disintegrated: it did not look like any configuration he had ever seen, a cross between an American space shuttle and a B-1 bomber. It was magnificent. As particles of grain-size debris fell from the skies he realized something else.

It was gone.

Chan hit the afterburners and headed west. He did not get the boost he was expecting. He was also having trouble maintaining horizontal stability. He hit the diagnostic button to try and determine the extent of the damage. The pilot had turned off his radio; the frequency of the open line could have been used to target him. Now it didn't matter. He checked his radar. The remaining aircraft was still there. It was not firing; perhaps it was out of range. With his diminished speed, it would not be out of range for very long.

"Shanghai, I've been hit. The attacker is still in pursuit."

"How severe is the damage?" Chung asked.

"I'm running the diagnostic now. The initial scan shows perforations in the rear flaps and tail fin. Stabilization has been compromised. Sir, I don't know if the images came out but I've never seen an aircraft or weapons like this."

"They're dark. We're working on them."

"It was like a spray," Chan said. In case he did not survive or the images couldn't be enhanced, he wanted to try and impart as much information as possible. "It was twice the size of a typical fighter and made high-speed ninety-degree maneuvers. It destroyed one of its own when the aircraft got between us."

"An accident—"

"I don't believe so," Chan said.

"Ridiculous and unimportant," Chung replied sharply. "Will you be able to reach the carrier?"

"Possibly, though not if the attacker continues its pursuit," Chan said.

"We'll talk to the Americans. Continue on course. You've done well, Lieutenant Commander."

"Thank you, sir," Chan answered smartly. The compliment had an echo of finality about it.

Chan continued to watch the radar. The American aircraft had been seven kilometers away when it first opened fire. It was twelve kilometers distant and closing. Chan decided to dive to a lower altitude. The gravity-assist would give him additional speed relative to the pursuit plane. He pushed the JF-17 into a sixty-degree descent. It was as steep as he dared with the damaged tail section.

Despite the gravity of this situation Chan couldn't get over what he had witnessed. He envied the pilot, though it was odd: he hadn't seen one eject from the plane that was destroyed. Perhaps Captain Chung was correct and the attack was an accident. There may have been a miscommunication about where the second plane was to move. Tandem fighters occasionally crossed one another's line of fire, especially in the confusion of combat.

Not that this was combat. The JF-17 was unarmed. And now it was crippled and unarmed.

The g-forces pressed Chan hard against the seat. He didn't feel like he was flying so much as plunging. He hoped no other damage would show up now that the plane was in a dive. The diagnostics program was still running. It did not suggest any other problems.

And then he saw one on the radar: the pursuit plane had thrown itself into a vertical dive. Though the hypotenuse course of the JF-17 was shorter, the speed of the descending American jet was faster. If it executed another right-angle turn, leveling out below Chan, his own course would put him directly in the sights of the attacker.

Chan rolled to starboard and changed the direction of his dive without altering the angle. The pursuit plane tracked his movement, drifting north as it plummeted. The American jet was below him now and had started to come out of its dive. It was less than nine kilometers away and still closing on him. Even in a healthy plane, Chan didn't see how he could get away from this juggernaut.

He leveled off and accelerated as he reached his right hand to the computer. He touched the screen to bring up the

overview map. Then he touched the blinking light that signi-
fied the aircraft carrier. He pushed the menu option that offered to put the jet on the most direct route.

The selection took just moments, but in that time the
American aircraft had once again closed to within firing
range. Chan had seen how quickly the other plane had been
obliterated; the instant he heard the distinctive reverberation
against his tail section, he knew what he had to do.

On his left was a red lever. He released a catch from the
top and pulled it down.

The clear canopy of the JF-17 blew off. Behind the lever,
exposed by pulling it down, was a glowing white button.
Chan punched it. An instant later he was blown skyward by
the underseat rocket. His spine felt as if it had been com-
pressed to half its length as he was kicked free of the confetti
that used to be a state-of-the-art PLAAF jet.

TWENTY-ONE

Norco, California

"Major, are you all right?"

General Scott had watched the scene as it played out silently on the radar screen. Bryan's report, had he made one, wouldn't have been of much value. He was inside a wildly flying aircraft, with no windows, probably trying to keep from getting hurt or tossed out the open wheel well. Now that there was just one blip on the radar screen Scott felt the communication wouldn't distract Bryan.

"I'm okay," he said. "I heard a lot of shooting—"

"The plan didn't work exactly the way we had hoped," Scott said.

"I was afraid of that. Our last dive was for a kill." Bryan was huffing as he spoke. He was probably making his way through the aircraft.

"We believe the pilot may have left the craft successfully," Scott told him. "There was a blip that conformed to an ejection profile."

"I didn't hear additional firing after the target was destroyed," Bryan said.

"Remember, parachutes wouldn't trigger an attack."

"I was thinking of the ejection seat, sir," Bryan said. "Obviously, we would want to capture enemy pilots intact."

Scott hadn't considered that. He looked at Parks. The rear admiral nodded.

"Good get," Scott said. "Edwards has dispatched ground personnel to try and find him."

Bryan snickered between grunts. "The Air Force is on the ground and the Navy's in the air. It's a strange world, sir."

"It's a *new* one, I'll grant you—"

"Shanghai wants to talk," Hathaway interrupted. He still looked and sounded numb.

"I heard, sir," Bryan said. "I'm almost in the nose section. I'll keep you in the loop."

"Good luck," Scott said as he switched to the second line. There was a great deal of strong speech on the Chinese end.

"This is an act of historic criminality," the translator said in a softer tone. "There will be grave repercussions."

"I would remind the captain again that your aircraft was illegally intruding on American airspace during a lockdown situation, and that it refused numerous orders to depart," Parks replied.

Scott noted that Parks did not "respectfully" remind the captain. He had been in enough sessions with Asian military leaders to understand the significance of that. No doubt Parks did as well. The absence of the one word suggested that the fault was Shanghai's and that the rear admiral did not consider this a friendly conversation.

"We were on a mission of aid, not aggression," the captain replied. "Our pilot was withdrawing from his mercy flight when he was fired upon."

"Your pilot was violating our sovereign airspace."

"Sovereign or secretive? What did he see that concerned you?" the Chinese officer demanded.

Still pushing for information, Scott thought.

Hathaway hit the mute transmission button on his console. "Rear Admiral, we have a new problem. The Angel is not returning to its previous heading. That bump we gave her pushed the plane in a new direction."

Parks nodded. He thought for a moment. "Captain Chung, we sacrificed one of our own aircraft in an effort to protect your pilot. That effort failed. However, we believe it bought your pilot time to eject safely. We are attempting to find him now."

"There would have been no need to eject if you had allowed him to complete his turnaround," Chung said.

"Captain, you are not the wounded party. There is nothing more to discuss. If you stay on the line we will report the status of your pilot as soon as possible."

Hathaway was still on mute. "You might want to tell him a little about what we're dealing with," the scientist said.

Parks hit his own mute button. "Why?"

"Because he may find out on his own."

"How?" Parks asked.

"I've projected the Angel's current course," Hathaway said. "If the major can't stop it, this bird is going all the way to China."

Parks didn't seem surprised.

The Chinese captain was talking about the leaders in Beijing drafting a military response. When he was finished, Parks told him that the PLAAF would be notified, through channels, on the disposition of their pilot. Then he terminated the communication and regarded Hathaway.

"I'm not authorized to discuss eyes-only research with anyone," Parks said. "I'll brief the secretary and he can take this up with the president."

"When you do, tell him that the Angel could conceivably be in Chinese airspace before noon tomorrow."

"I will," Parks said. "Hopefully, Major Bryan will be able to turn her around before then." He regarded Scott. "Did the major have anything else to report?"

"He said he'd reached the control sector and would brief us on his progress," Scott replied.

Parks sat motionless for a moment. "Hank—give a shout at the hanger. I want to get all our people together."

"What are you thinking?" Scott asked.

"I'm praying for Major Bryan but I want to find out if anyone has any other ideas," Parks said.

"I see. Does that include LASER?"

"Of course," Parks said.

"Then talk to their CO before you give any orders," Scott said.

Parks appeared surprised. "I'm sorry, General. I didn't mean to grab the baton. I was suggesting an informal think-tank session—"

"My group doesn't do 'informal' when they're on duty," Scott replied. "That gets people killed."

Parks rubbed his eyes. "You're right. As I said, no offense intended. I think we're all stressed, tired, and a little scared."

"That's why we need structure wherever we can find it," Scott said. "Something to hold on to."

Parks regarded him. "We were understaffed on this, General. What government R&D isn't? But we did the best we could. Whatever you may think, no one on *my* team was informal."

"I never thought that," Scott told him. "Let's go see the troops."

Parks nodded and half-turned. "Hank—"

"I'll stay and monitor."

"Thanks." Rising, Parks removed his headset and took a point-to-point radio from the table. "Holler if anything happens." General Scott rose as well. It wasn't an optimistic next step but it was a practical one.

Scott silently prayed for Bryan, too; not just for his success, but for his life.

PART FOUR

Air

ONE

Gorman, California

As Bryan made his journey forward he thought of the story of Jonah stuck inside the whale. Bryan didn't remember much from Sunday school, but he remembered that the prophet was being punished for some infraction or other and was spit up after a couple of days to be given a second chance. The story had stuck in his six-year-old mind because it seemed more like an adventure than a parable. Twenty-eight years later it still did. Whether it was Jonah or Pinocchio inside a whale or Bryan in the Angel, it was all about a little man in the belly of a great beast. If there were a moral, it was probably to keep your feet on familiar ground.

The major's progress had been slowed by the changing slope of the aircraft. The walls were smooth and there weren't many projections to hold on to. Moving ahead was a matter of leaning forward or back, and side to side, to maintain balance. It was a lot like surfing but without the spray or sunshine. It had the surf-like noise, though. The sound inside the Angel wasn't the same as in a conventional aircraft. Instead of having engines that sounded like muted vacuum cleaners, these turbines were more like muffled clarinets, generating a low whistle that permeated the cabin.

Oddly enough, the guns were relatively quiet. They had

released their projectiles with a fluid but harmless-sounding *phut-phut-phut*.

The cabin narrowed like an hourglass at the wings, then widened again before a C-shaped section with an extremely narrow passage on the port side. The access way reminded Bryan of the corridor outside a sleeper car on a train. Instead of cabins, however, the starboard side of the aircraft was comprised of twenty sealed compartments standing şide by side. They resembled fat high-school lockers with horizontal computer ports instead of doors. The electronics for the weapons systems were stored in these steel cabinets. The engineers had told Bryan that they were difficult to shut down on-site because the vapor intake was tied into the aircraft's fuel intake. The designers had never imagined it would be necessary to get inside and actually turn off the weapons.

Beyond the compartments was the nose section, which contained the avionics and ground links. It was about the general shape of an airplane lavatory, with sloping walls and a low ceiling, but about ten times the size. Still bent at the shoulders, Bryan wormed through the narrow passageway beside the compartments. He stopped at the end and shined his flashlight around. The virtual tour the engineers had given him did not do it justice. It was like being inside a hi-tech beehive, only instead of drones moving about there were lights. They surrounded whirring disc drives, slots filled with modular hardware, and bundles of wires. What was disturbing was that this was not a place designed for human occupancy: there were no monitors, no seats, no cup holders. It was the inside of a machine brain, one designed to communicate directly with man-operated machines on earth.

Or to function entirely on its own if need be.

"I'm at the avionics core," Bryan said into the microphone.

"Do you see your objective?" Hathaway asked.

"Not yet." He was supposed to find drawer three in module 13F. The "F" designation meant it was forward. He moved ahead. The lights were not for illumination: they

were to trigger electronic sensors in sections on opposite
sides of the nose section. The equipment was designed this
way to keep from having to string cables throughout the
cabin. That kept the weight of the Angel down considerably.
Bryan had to make certain he stayed out of the way of the
uppermost lights: the starboard-side equipment read the atmospheric conditions and fed data to the Angel's wing controls on the port side. Without that link the wings would not
change shape to adapt to new conditions.

Bryan ducked lower as he moved through the nose section.
He thought again about Jonah and his trials in the belly of the
beast. Bryan was in even deeper, prowling about the brain of
the beast. He didn't know whether it was hubris, stupidity, or
both that made him think he could just pop in and pop out
again. Fortunately, his own brain was too full of those
moment-to-moment details to worry about the big picture.
Besides, that was counterproductive. Unknowns like this were
inevitable and had a way of making plans irrelevant.

The depot numbers were painted in black on the white
surfaces. They were clearly marked and he had no trouble
finding 13F. He moved closer and spent a moment examin-
ing it. The data depot, as it was called, was about the size and
shape of a safe-deposit box. Bryan looked for the release
switch, a latch at the bottom of the face of the depot. He
found it and frowned. His finger wouldn't fit in the slot. Not
with his glove on. His suit wasn't pressurized, but that
wasn't the problem; taking the glove off would mean setting
the flashlight on the ground and risk having it roll away if
the aircraft changed course.

"Got a little delay here," he said into the microphone. He
knew how frustrating the sound of just heavy breathing
could be.

"What's the problem?" Hathaway asked.

"My glove won't fit in the release. I'm going to use a
screwdriver."

"What's the temperature up there?" Hathaway asked.

The major checked the gauge on his multipurpose wrist-watch. "Twenty-seven degrees Fahrenheit," he said. He un-zipped the equipment pouch on his waist and fished out a small slotted screwdriver. He carefully placed the edge against the latch. Once he popped it, the entire depot was supposed to slide out like a big CD dish. The contents were collected vertically, about two dozen discs arranged like rec-ords in a jukebox. Each slot was numbered. The major was supposed to replace disc 23. That would reprogram the An-gel to accept commands issued from the Seraph console.

"Wait!" Hathaway shouted. "Don't open the hatch!"

Bryan stopped. "What's wrong?"

"That cabin is below freezing," Hathaway said. "The bloody circuits weren't designed for direct exposure to that extreme."

Bryan slumped. "You've *got* to be kidding."

"No," Hathaway assured him. "We didn't count on the open wheel well. I'll talk to the engineers. Be back with you as soon as possible."

"I'm not going anywhere," Bryan replied.

Tired of crouching, the major put away the screwdriver, zipped the bag, and sat in the center of the nose section to wait. The floor was cold. He could feel it through the seat of the flight suit. Flying west, as he was doing, would keep the Angel in night for several hours more. At this altitude, with the wheel well open and the deflated tire allowing air to en-ter, it would get even colder. He doubted that sunrise would bring the cabin temperature above freezing.

He looked around. There was nothing to use as insula-tion, and he wasn't keen on sacrificing his parachute for the cause. If the reprogramming didn't work he would be stuck on the Angel.

This is the kind of downtime a soldier doesn't want, Bryan thought. Time with nothing to do but think, that dreary, confidence-sapping *we're-on-the-boats-to-Normandy* time. He tried to think of ways to raise the temperature. The tire was too large for him to move, so plugging the well wasn't going to work. He glanced back at the narrow passage that led from avionics. Maybe he could erect a door of some kind, something to keep the heat in the brain center.

Maybe you should just let the scientists work on this, he decided.

Hathaway returned after fifteen minutes. "Major, I think we've got something to solve the temperature problem."

"I'm listening," he said.

The scientist told him what the solution was. When he finished, the major felt perspiration warming his cool flesh.

"That sounds like one helluva maneuver," Bryan said. "What were the specs at Tucumcari?"

"Not quite the same as these," Hathaway told him. "In theory, though, the Angel should be able to handle it."

"Should? Are we talking fifty-fifty?"

"Major, I'll be frank. We're talking 'it's all we've got.' The rear admiral is already in contact with the DoD. We need to stop this bird."

There was something uneasy, almost sad in the scientist's voice. Bryan had a good idea what it was. If the plan itself didn't work, the very act of executing it might well destroy the Angel.

TWO

Norco, California

Meeting with the engineers and LASER operatives was a short and unproductive exercise for Rear Admiral Parks. He wasn't sure how much he had needed to talk to them and how much he just needed to get out of the comm shack for a few minutes. Either way, it didn't help.

The two groups were tired and confrontational. Ensign Galvez suggested having Major Bryan bail out and then launching a barrage of Tomahawk or Patriot missiles loaded with electromagnetic pulse bombs to shut down the Angel. One of the aeronautic engineers scoffed and said that the missiles would not get close enough to discharge their warheads and, besides, the first missile to blow would neutralize the others. One of the project engineers recommended having Major Bryan go outside and try to disable the guns.

"Just take a stroll on the fuselage, huh?" Captain Gabriel said. "Using what for a tether?"

"The straps from his parachute pack," the engineer suggested.

"Leaving him with no way down," Gabriel replied angrily.

Scott ordered Gabriel to back down.

Other suggestions ranged from jamming the plane with satellite signals to having Major Bryan just start pulling wires.

Parks pointed out that the Angel was insulated from outside electronics, and that the aircraft systems were piggybacked to save space and weight. Without a team of engineers beside him, and several hours to work, Bryan would not be able to do the kind of complex surgery necessary to turn the aircraft off.

"I don't understand," Gabriel said. "He couldn't just spit on a bunch of microchips and short them out?"

"Sure he could," one of the electronics engineers said. "But the cascade effect of the integrated circuits would be unpredictable. It could cause the guns to turn on permanently without stopping the plane. Or it could open the antenna to anybody with a ham radio."

"This is not a vehicle we want to start suddenly responding to commands from a foreign power," Parks said.

The rear admiral was about to pair LASER ops with engineers, mix and match for hopefully better results, when he received a call from Hathaway that they had a new problem. At that moment, the idea of yanking out circuits didn't seem like such a bad idea. Parks excused himself and, with Scott trailing behind, headed back toward the radio shack. The rear admiral punched in the navy secretary's direct line on his secure cell phone. An aide said the secretary was unavailable.

"*Make* him available," Parks said.

His tone did not leave roar for debate. The aide put him through.

"That's not what I was hoping to hear," Whittle said when Parks had finished his update. It wasn't a condemnation, just a sigh with words.

"I'm sorry, Mr. Secretary."

"What do you need to fix it?"

"Permission to launch a QUAV from Miramar," Parks said. "We believe that will do it." The QUAV was the Q-series of Unmanned Aerial Vehicle.

" 'Believe' or 'hope'?" Whittle asked.

"Some of both," Parks acknowledged.

"Won't your Angel knock it down?" Whittle asked.

"That's what we want, Mr. Secretary," Parks told him.

"You lost me."

"The QUAV will be directed to fly at ten thousand feet within the Angel's strike zone. The Angel will descend and attack. At that height we calculate the temperature in the cabin will be raised to above freezing."

"Do we know that the Angel will survive a descent like that?"

"No, sir," Parks admitted.

" 'Believe,' 'hope,' and now 'calculate.' Rear Admiral, you boys don't seem to know very much for sure."

"Mr. Secretary, considering that our key people and most of our equipment are under a brand-new coastline, we're doing the best we can."

"Fair enough," Whittle said. "I'll send the authorization to Miramar. You'll call the plays."

"Thank you, Mr. Secretary. I'll get them the rendezvous point. If we make it north of the Angel we can swing her up the coast, keep her in our airspace."

"An act of international diplomacy or security?" Whittle asked.

"Both, Mr. Secretary," Parks said.

He hung up just as they reached the radio shack. Scott looked at him.

"You look a little roughed up," Scott said.

"He was just covering his ass. All that matters is, we got our QUAV."

"Down to ten thousand feet," the general said. "That's an aggressive descent."

"Close to test parameters."

" 'Close to,' " Scott said. "We don't know for certain whether the Angel will survive?"

"No," Parks admitted. "Say, maybe you ought to get in line behind Whittle."

Scott said nothing.

"Sorry," Parks said. "I'm just looking for some optimism somewhere."

"Like you said, there's a new coastline. Everything's been relocated."

"I know." Parks turned his attention back to the mission. He had to. "We'll have to reposition the major near the open wheel well, tell him what to watch out for."

"A plane coming apart around him in a Mach 2 dive?"

"There will be sounds to listen for, stress points that will surrender before the rest of the aircraft." Parks regarded the officer. "Don't worry, General. We'll watch out for him."

"We *all* will," Scott said.

The men started down the steps into the bunker. Scott said nothing more. Like Whittle, he didn't have to.

It would take about twenty minutes to fuel and prep the drone, and fifteen minutes, concurrent, to program her. In a half hour the QUAV would be airborne. Parks entered the shack, asked Hathaway for the Angel's zone parameters a half hour hence, and called the commander at Miramar, Captain Jack Mann. The two men knew each passingly.

Mann did not know about the Angel program and had not been told the reason for the lockdown. As Hathaway marked a computer map for Parks, the rear admiral informed Mann that the QUAV—a Predator drone, the same kind used in the Afghan and Iraq wars—was to fly on a heading that would put it over Santa Barbara in forty-five minutes. The coastal city was dead-center in the zone Hathaway had provided. Five minutes after that it would be over international waters. Mann said he would have the QUAV there. He did not press for additional information. He was too professional for that.

Scott took his seat and slipped on his headphones. Parks did the same. Hathaway was doing calculations on his computer.

"Major, how are we doing there?" Scott asked.

"Sitting in the brain center of the Angel, freezing my butt," Bryan replied. "Literally."

"You won't be there very long. We have a go on the QUAV maneuver," Parks said.

"Good. I guess."

"What's wrong?" Parks asked.

"I've been thinking about the dive," Bryan said. "I'm not a pilot, but this bird will be pulling some serious Gs. Are you sure she'll hang together?"

"Major, we simulated dives like these with computer and 3-D models," Hathaway assured him. "We scored well above expected parameters."

"How well?" Bryan asked.

"Ninety-four percent survival rate," Hathaway said. "That's higher than commercial airlines are required to score in their hazard tests."

"How does my added weight and the air drag from the open well affect that?" Bryan asked.

"I've been working on that," Hathaway told him. "Your weight shouldn't impact the descent at all. The weight of the deflated tire shifting around might cause very minor acceleration, but the drag caused by the open well should actually mitigate that. What we're going to need you to do is lie flat on the floor to keep you stabilized. There's a section just forward the open well where you can do that. Go there and I'll talk you into position."

"As long as I don't have to lie on my backside, fine," Bryan joked.

Scott slapped the mute button. "Which of the mock-ups failed during the dive simulations?" he demanded.

"PA-4 and CA-22," Hathaway replied. "One of the small-scale prototypes and a full-scale computer simulation."

"Did you solve the problem?"

"Figured it out, worked it out, and put it all together in this Angel," Hathaway told him.

"But still not tested."

"No."

"We wouldn't have fielded a billion-dollar aircraft if we weren't confident," Parks added with a touch of annoyance.

Scott gave him a long, critical look that seemed to say, *But you sent up an aircraft you couldn't control.* Or maybe that was Parks's own feeling of self-recrimination talking.

The situations weren't the same, of course. One was a narrow margin for error that came from a careful process, the other was an act of God. Parks didn't bother to explain the difference; General Scott knew it. But Scott was also on the sidelines and was worried about his team leader. He had every right to be, and there was no one else he could express that to.

Parks listened while Hathaway used a computer schematic to talk Bryan into position. Scott was sitting deep in the swivel chair, slumped and very still, listening and watching intently. He seemed to be looking for any lapse, any reason to order Bryan to bail out. Parks couldn't blame the general for that, either. The rear admiral was actually glad to have an extra set of eyes and ears turned on this situation, reporting to someone who was keyed to just one aspect of the mission. That was a luxury the rear admiral couldn't afford. Even as Hathaway spoke Parks was watching the clock on his own computer screen, counting down the minutes until the QUAV was aloft. Part of his brain was also on the next phase, the aerial encounter. Armchair generals got a bad rap because they gave orders from places of safety. He envied the men with one goal: survival. This kind of multitasking was a slower, more painful killer. The worst part was you could rarely make a clean call. Whatever you decided, someone usually got hurt, and you had to live with that.

In less than ten minutes Major Bryan had retraced his route to the wheel well. He braced himself between rib F-40 in the fuselage and the steamer trunk–size metal housing that held the tire retraction motor and also anchored the tire retraction arm. The arm was bent back, like a chicken wing, four feet above and nearly parallel to the cabin floor. That gave Bryan something to hold while he lay on his side, pushing his feet against the exposed rib and his shoulder against the casing. If the aircraft started to break up it would most likely happen at the nose section, which was taking the bulk of what the engineers called the maximum stress or GAFF point—the g-force and forward friction. Bryan was told that the indicators of an imminent breakup would be unmistakable: a loud crack, like a snapping tree branch, followed by a knife-edge of wind. If that happened, probably along a forward seam, the major would have about five seconds to swing aft around the tire retraction hub and drop out the open well. It would be challenging because the slope of the plane would force him to climb up. That was why Hathaway had positioned the major with his feet facing forward, so he would be able to dig in his rubber soles and climb.

The men sat in silence as they waited for word from the Miramar tower that the QUAV was airborne. When that call came, right on schedule, Parks told the others and Hathaway switched the monitor to radar.

Scott turned off the mute button and informed Bryan.

"I kind of figured that," Bryan replied.

"Why?"

"Because this baby just came alive."

THREE

Santa Barbara, California

Banks of computer hard drives had began to turn in the avionics section, generating piccolo-high sounds, like a flock of nesting meadowlarks. These were followed by much louder sounds from the sides of the fuselage. It reminded Bryan of the *whooshing* sound of an oil burner turning on as the mercury-filled bladders in the wings began to shift, changing their shape. Beneath all the electronic and mechanical noises was the roar of the wind just outside the tire well. The howling was so full it had body and heft, more like a subwoofer than sound.

Moments after the wings had reformed the Angel nosed down. It held that position for a moment then dove like a roller-coaster car plunging over a steep incline with one difference: this drop didn't stop. And, once begun, there was no terminating it until the Angel had reached its destination.

Or come apart, Bryan thought.

The major's belly tickled painfully from the dive and his ankle started to cramp as he pushed against the rib of the aircraft. Virtually everything from his heartbeat to his eyeblinks came faster due to the g-forces. The one exception was the flow of blood to the brain, which slowed. If it slowed enough it could cause unconsciousness. Bryan coughed every few seconds to stimulate the flow of blood upward through his throat. It wasn't working as well as he'd hoped.

The sounds of the aircraft were drowned by the whistle from outside as the Angel screamed toward earth. Then he heard a new sound. And it wasn't coming from the nose section.

"I've got a screech at two o'clock, portside!" the major shouted into the microphone. "It's not like a tree limb snapping. It's like a violin."

"Inside the fuselage?" Hathaway asked.

Bryan turned his head so he could see the cabin wall. The ribs and skin were fine. "Negative. It's outside!"

"Outside?" Hathaway repeated. "The wing is behind you—"

"Forward the wing!" Bryan said. He had a horrible thought. "FYI: that was one of the spots where the fuselage of the Seraph may have bumped against the undercarriage of the Angel!"

There was a long silence. Bryan spent it trying to "ride his own heartbeat," as the high-performance flyboys called it, breathing deeply to try and relax his body. The trick was to slow the palpitations without hyperventilating.

The screeching became grinding. It continued for a few seconds longer and then stopped. Bryan reported it all to NWAD.

"You're sure it's gone?" Hathaway asked.

"Yeah," he said, still listening. "My ears are singing soprano but nothing else. Any thoughts about what it was?"

"We're working on it," Hathaway replied.

Bryan swallowed hard to try and clear the sounds from his head. Beneath the ringing his ears were thumping with the sound of his hardworking pulse and his vision was starting to flash, a result of decreased oxygen flow.

"Major, we have a possible ID on the sound," Hathaway said in a slow, low monotone.

"I'm guessing it's not good news," Bryan said.

"We're concerned that one of the turrets may be turned toward the Angel," the scientist told him.

"How turned?" he asked. It took all his concentration to focus on what they were saying.

"Our sims show that the Seraph may have struck it and the subsequent firing may have loosened it," Hathaway informed him. "The good news is the Angel may fatally wound itself."

"Odds?" Bryan asked. He glanced around. The idea of ice bullets tearing through one of the cabin walls did not please him.

"To hell with the odds," Scott said. "I want you out of there now. You only have a few seconds until the Angel fires on the QUAV."

"Understood. But if the Angel doesn't blast itself we have no way of reprogramming it," Bryan pointed out. "No repro, no recovery team. No recovery team, it goes where it wants."

"Major, we don't have time for this," Scott snapped. "I'm ordering you out of there. Acknowledge!"

"Out of here, sir," Bryan said. He didn't agree but that didn't matter. He moved around the tire housing and slid on his belly toward the open well. The wind was rushing hard along the undercarriage toward the tail. That was the direction Bryan would be swept when he wormed out. He reached across the sloping floor, grabbed the edge of the well, and pulled himself toward the opening. The major could feel the force of the rushing air blast past the tips of his gloves. He moved his head toward the well. The Angel's small white exterior lights were the only illumination. Bryan saw nothing but darkness beyond, no sign of land or clouds.

"Ten seconds until the QUAV is in range," Hathaway said.

"Your status, Major?" Scott demanded.

"Leaving, sir."

He was trying to, anyway. The major's vision was clouded with swirling red and black circles. The exertion had been greater than he had anticipated. It was also difficult to think. His mind was swimming in both internal and external sounds; it was easier to simply do what he was told.

"Five seconds," Hathaway said.

Wriggling forward, the major hunched his head into his shoulders to give it support when he dropped into the ferocious wind. Without hesitation Bryan hurled himself into the void headfirst, facedown. He hugged his arms straight against his sides and turned himself into a human missile that would fall in a direct, streamlined course to the ground. He rotated onto his back as he fell away. He looked between his feet and saw the faint spark of the Angel's guns as the sharply angled aircraft bore down on its target. He heard the faint chatter from the four turrets.

The major saw the aircraft become lost in the night.

He did not see it come apart.

FOUR

Norco, California

There was a tense silence as the men watched the radar screen. The Predator drone disappeared. The Angel did not.

"Still holding its old course," Hathaway reported.

"So she's probably not damaged," Parks said.

"I'm not sure," Hathaway said. "There appears to be a slight wobble."

General Scott was more interested in Major Bryan. Just a few minutes earlier, the search party from Edwards had radioed to say that they had found the Chinese pilot on a hillside and were taking him back to base in the truck that had brought the all-terrain vehicles to the site. The pilot was conscious, he appeared unhurt, and he did not struggle. When Parks called back to tell the air force base about a second jumper closer to Santa Barbara, a fresh set of ATVs was sent to look for him. Parks told the dispatcher that this search would be easier since the major would not be coming down stealth but trailing red smoke from a flare that had been packed in the chute. The time-released signal, with magnesium powder for illumination, would be visible for five miles.

Though it would have been easier if the search unit could

have used helicopters, Scott was confident that the team would find Bryan. The man had survival training in tropical jungles and polar regions; he would be able to make it through a night in Southern California. Scott was also confident in the call he had made for Bryan to abandon the Angel. He had made it based on very little information, just one overriding thought: that he would rather be sitting here wondering, again, how to stop the Angel rather than mourning the major's death.

The other two men in the radio room were clearly not as comfortable with that decision. While Parks spoke with Edwards AFB, Hathaway studied an enhanced replay of the radar image, looking for any sudden change in the Angel's course, something that might indicate it had been hit.

He found something else.

"I was right," Hathaway said when Parks hung up the phone. "Angel's having trouble holding course and I think I found out why."

The other men leaned forward. Hathaway used a pencil eraser to point out a small blip moving vertically from the flight path.

"See this?" Hathaway asked. "I think she may have lost one of the guns."

"That would be consistent with the screeching Major Bryan apparently heard," Parks remarked.

The "apparently" rankled Scott. His man was more reliable than these two put together.

"What could have caused it, though?" Parks asked. "Detonating the explosive bolt?"

"More likely the untested dive," Scott said angrily. That was the second oblique knock at Bryan. Even if it were unintentional, he didn't like it.

"I think it's more consistent with those love taps the Seraph gave the Angel," Hathaway said thoughtfully. "If the turret were jarred, even slightly, the alignment of the vapor condensers would be off. After the attack on the JF-17, vapor would have collected in the gears and frozen. When the guns turned to target the drone the entire mechanism could have been knocked off track. If this gun attempted to fire, the impact might have booted it off."

"How does this help us?" Scott asked.

"I'm not sure it does," Hathaway said. "It doesn't give us a blind spot for a second assault. The Angel seems to have compensated for the loss of stability. She's flying steady now and will still attack anything in its patrol zone, though with twenty-five percent less firepower."

"The remaining turrets will still knock anything from the sky," Parks said. He picked up the phone. "I'd better let the search team know they're looking for hardware as well as a jumper."

"Maybe we should be targeting those guns somehow," Scott said when Parks finished his call.

"If you have any ideas, I'm listening," Parks replied.

Scott removed the headphones. He heard he wind rush past the bunker. For the first time since arriving the general could hear the distant traffic on the interstate, the sound of life going on as it should. Momentary problems supplanted by each new one. People had to know that crises were happening all the time, some moderate, some grave. The general didn't envy them their comfortable ignorance. He liked being in a position where he could do something about the dangers facing his nation.

So do something about this, dammit.

That was the challenge and the reward. This was not a job where a man could afford to bat anything less than a thousand. And it wasn't even his field. Scott excused himself and went outside. He was going to tell his team about Major Bryan's changed status.

To his surprise Lieutenant Black was out there with her partner, one of the engineers, chuckling. She stopped and introduced inorganic chemist Dr. Marlon Mill. The morphing wings of the Angel were his design. The stout, red-cheeked man did not look much more than thirty years old. He was wearing the hint of a smile.

"Did I interrupt something?" Scott asked.

"No, sir. How is it going in there?" Black asked.

"Not well," the general said, and updated them. "Thinking back, I don't understand why we didn't just open that drawer and let the cold air give the aircraft a lobotomy."

"That may not have worked, General," Mill said. "You may have short-circuited the wrong control sector while leaving everything else intact. That could have ruined any chance we have of recovering the plane."

"I'm not sure that would have been much worse than our present situation," Scott replied.

"We didn't bring it down but we wounded it, sir," Black pointed out. "That's something."

"Unfortunately, it took our best shot to get that much," Scott said.

"With respect, sir, that wasn't our best shot," Mill said.

"Oh? Explain."

"Our best shot is the one that's going to work," Mill explained. "At least, that's how we think in the lab."

"The power of positive thinking?" Scott asked.

"Not exactly," Mill replied. "The prospect of being able to sleep again. For a scientist an unsolved problem is like an itch you can't reach, a 24/7 nightmare. It never leaves you alone."

"I see," Scott said. For a soldier, the slide to failure was not a reversible process but a moment of weakness or confidence. Scott would prefer the constant pinch of a problem to the finality of a loss, or death. "So what are your thoughts about the Angel? What's the look and feel of our best shot?"

Black snickered but recovered quickly. "Sorry, sir."

"I *am* missing something," Scott said.

"It's nothing. Really," Black said.

"No. 'Nothing' is what I came out here with. Let's have it, Lieutenant."

"Well, sir, it's just that before you got here we were talking about how the ideal solution would be a very big gun and a human cannonball."

"Which was something we came upon after considering an idea that was a little more practical, a blast from the NIF to try and knock the Angel down," Mill told the general.

"What is the NIF?" Scott asked.

"Oh, sorry. That's the National Ignition Facility," Mill told him. "It's located north of here in Livermore, home of a laser that can put out 500 trillion watts in a single burst, about a thousand times the power generated by the entire United States. And it can decimate a target the size of a shirt button. I know. I saw the test. The problem is, the Angel is shielded with the same material as the barrel of the laser."

"The beam is not presently mobile, and we thought of trying to put it through the open hatch, but there would be nothing in there to destroy," Black said. "It would only have struck the ceiling and bounced back."

"In a very straight and destructive line," Mill added. "Then the lieutenant said, 'Too bad we can't use that to launch a human cannonball,' and we were off on that." There was an embarrassed little twist to the scientist's mouth, as though he were ashamed that for a moment he'd gotten silly.

"Well, I respect noncausal response thinking," Scott assured them. "Something that comes at a problem from a totally unexpected direction. That's how Moe Berg happened."

"Now it's my turn, General," Mill said. "Who?"

"An American baseball player who was invited to Japan in the 1930s," Scott said. "Someone in the government thought it would be prudent to have up-close-and-personal pictures of Japan, just in case. That was good decision number one. Good decision number two was to recruit Berg. The government had him get a hotel room with a view of Tokyo and take movies and still pictures of military installations. Jimmy Doolittle used those images to plan his bombing raids of Japan."

"Ingenious," Mill said.

Scott looked up at the sky. It was getting close to morning and only the brightest celestial objects were visible. There was a faint, feathery flash as a shooting star blazed across the freeway.

No, he thought. *Not across. That's only our perception of it. . . .*

"Well, I think we'd better go back and see what the others have come up with," Black said. "Now that the Angel is at a lower altitude, maybe we can send up a pelican with C-4—"

"Not 'up,' " Scott said.

"Sir?"

"Down," the general told him. "The next approach at the Angel has to come from above."

"That won't make a difference," Mill said. "She sees in all directions."

"Even so, what could you hit her with?" Black asked. "She'll ID an incoming missile and tear it apart."

"I'm not thinking about a missile," Scott said.

"What, then, sir?" Black asked.

The general didn't answer. He was still trying to pull the elements together. It was going to be difficult to do with the supersonic Angel heading away from California. But difficult wasn't impossible.

"Are you thinking of hitting her from space?" Mill asked. "If you are, one of the engineers talked about dropping a satellite on the rogue Angel. Even if NASA could realign a booster, the fluidity of the atmosphere would make precise navigation virtually impossible."

"That's not exactly what I have in mind," Scott said.

"What could we possibly have up there that could hurt this bird?" Black asked, chucking her forehead toward the sky.

"Probably nothing, but you're still thinking as if the Angel were fifty-odd thousand feet up." Scott turned and headed toward the bunker. "Lieutenant, ask Captain Puckett to come and see me."

"Yes, sir."

"You come with him. I may need punch as well as lift."

"Yes, sir."

General Scott still wasn't sure how all of this could come together, but he had a feeling he was on to something—thanks to Bryan, a human cannonball, and a shooting star.

FIVE

Santa Barbara, California

Time seemed to slow and space seemed to expand—or
maybe it was Chan who shrank—when the pilot ejected from
the cockpit of his stricken JF-17.

It wasn't like the rocket sled drills at the Chendu airstrip
in the Sichuan province. Those were crushing, vertical rides
that lasted just fifteen seconds. It wasn't like the underwater
centrifuge that disoriented a pilot in an exposed seat that
turned like a pinwheel. The reality was a combination of
those physical stresses with a powerful psychological component, an awareness that there was not necessarily going to
be a soft landing or helping hands whenever and wherever
the ride ended. The terminal point might be a high tree or a
cliff that could shatter limbs, or a body of water where a
man could drown beneath his shroud. Just testing for all of
that might have caused casualties and still failed to take into
account other variables. Perhaps the flight physicians had
simply wanted to make sure the body was strong enough to
survive the hammering. The rest was up to the pilot.

The initial blast of the rocket seat crammed Chan's head
into his shoulders with such force that had it gone forward
his neck might have snapped. That was the advantage to the
high shoulder harness and contour seat. His spine was shoved

into his pelvis and his toes were crushed earthward. Simultaneously, his sense of up and down vanished; there was just
the immediate vicinity. The comforting hum of the jet was
replaced by the wild scream of the air, so loud it caused his
helmet to vibrate and generate its own buzzing tone. After
the launch the parachute deployed, pulling the harness with
it and allowing the chair to drop away. As it did, peace en-
veloped Lieutenant Commander Chan and an odd and inde-
pendent thought slipped into his head: that this was how a
molecule of boiling water must feel right before it's taken
off the flame. Intense activity in which you are a passive par-
ticipant, then release from captivity.

The momentary gratitude Chan felt about being alive, and
apparently intact, was blackened by the realization that he
had lost his aircraft. And not just any plane, but the JF-17.
He had been given this assignment because he had experience landing on an aircraft carrier. And he had managed to
let the jet be shot from around him before making it back to
sea. He knew that the flight center would understand. He did
not know whether they would forgive.

Chan spotted lights here and there as he drifted earthward. For someone who had never been away from China, it
was both exciting and frightening to be dropping to earth in
the United States. At night, nothing seemed distinctive about
it. He did not see the lights of high buildings or great arenas
or bridges. Perhaps this part of the country did not have
those things.

You will find out very soon, he told himself.

The lights seem to spread as Chan descended. He saw
smaller lights, automobiles moving along twisting roads.
Chan maneuvered the parachute toward the darker patches
below. He would prefer to come down in a field or on a hill
instead of on a main road. He did not expect to hide when
he touched down, but he did not wish to be hit by a truck,
either.

Chan had done two nighttime jumps, both onto airfields.
This was new and challenging; unlike the ejection it was

something over which he had some control. As such, there was an element of exhilaration to it.

The lights began to vanish behind big black contours in the terrain. Chan knew he was close and made sure his knees were slightly bent. He didn't want to hit the ground stiff-legged.

And then he was down. It happened fast, with an upward bump that was nowhere near as sharp as the ejection jolt but still got the attention of his ankles, backbone, and skull. He was on a gentle slope and fell back as the parachute was blown in that direction. He popped the release so he wouldn't be dragged along, then turned quickly to grab the shroud lines. He pulled the parachute in and bundled it to him, sat on it, then pulled off his helmet. The cool night air felt refreshing on his perspiring scalp. It felt strange to be on ground that did not move, not even slightly. To have changing sounds instead of the steady hum of the engine. He took off his gloves, bent his fingers back against the ground. After flying for so long they tended to become locked in a 'grip' position, even at rest. The soil beneath him was dry, yet there were grasses blowing around him. He remembered a farmer in the village telling him once that the strongest bushes and oldest trees were those that were not watered. Dryness forced the roots to dig deep for water, enabling the foliage to endure strong winds. He pushed his fingers into the soil. What made him strong? The freedom of flight?

No. The home that had nurtured the dream of flight. The family that had helped him appreciate birds and wind and sky. A family very much like the birds he admired. Masks had been their work but creating a nest had been their life. Even now they would help him, even here. He would do nothing that failed to make them proud and safe, in that order.

Chan drew his fingers from the earth, then hugged his knees as he sat there deciding exactly what *to* do. He had two options: stay here and wait to be found, or head toward one of the roads he had seen. The pilot opted to stay: if the United States Air Force had tracked his descent and did a quadrant search, they would have a better chance of finding a stationary target. Finding him, they would put him in touch with someone who spoke his language, who could inform Shanghai that he was all right. That was all he wanted right now.

The wait was not long.

Chan heard the growl of engines to his left. Moments later he saw an arc of white light rise behind a slope. Six headlights burned through the glow, too brilliant for him to make out whatever was behind them. He had no idea what kind of reception he would receive and put his hands on his head to show his intention to cooperate. Only one thing surprised Chan: that they hadn't searched for him with helicopters. Perhaps the lockdown pertained to low-flying military aircraft as well. If so, the reach of that jet he had seen must be enormous. Not to mention thorough. His craft had not just been destroyed, it had been erased.

Soldiers with flashlights and guns surrounded him in a tight circle. They shouted instructions that sounded like dogs barking. He didn't move until someone came over, tapped him hard on the shoulder, and motioned for him to get up. He stood with his hands still on his head, not showing fear but cooperation. It was the only means he had of communicating with these people. He was not sure what he would have done had they attempted to put hand-restraints on him. He wanted to be treated as an unwilling guest, not as a captive.

The men formed ranks around him, two in front, two behind, two on the side as they marched him to the waiting vehicles. They were like Jeeps only smaller and chunkier. They put him in one and turned around. He was not manacled here, either. Obviously, they felt that if he didn't want to be found he would have tried to hide in the hills where he had landed.

The ride through the darkness did not take long, perhaps a half hour. Their destination was a military base, where Chan suffered his first indignity: he was forced to wear black, wraparound sunglasses when they entered. He agreed to do that because it was not a blindfold. That would have been degrading.

Chan was taken to a room, not to a cell; after his sunglasses were removed the door was locked. There were no windows in the room. He could hear more of that dog-talk outside the door, suggesting that there was a guard. That was all right. He wasn't going anywhere.

He looked around. There was a desk, a pen, and a yellow pad. Someone had provided a pitcher of water, a glass, and a small selection of fruit and crackers. There was a television, which he had no desire to turn on. When he was home Chan watched very little. He preferred to read about aviation and play cards with his fellow pilots and mechanics. In bars and on several bases—where it was viewed clandestinely—he had caught glimpses of gaudy game shows and lurid variety programs made in Hong Kong and could not imagine the experience here would be much different. There was also a telephone but Chan did not pick it up. What would he say, and to whom? For all he knew it was an intercom with no outside access. Anyway, who would understand him?

Chan used the closet-size lavatory, caught a glimpse of his face in the mirror, and for a moment didn't recognize himself. He was pale and drawn, his eyes bloodshot. Though he had bitten off the pieces one at a time—the long flight, the daring penetration of American airspace, the surveillance, the loss of the JF-17, and the ejection—it had been a long, long day. He washed his face in water that had an unusual smell, then lay on the bed to rest.

Before he could shut his eyes there was a knock on the door. A man entered. He was a young blond fellow with a strong jaw; he wore a uniform and carried a medical case. After motioning for Chan to sit on the edge of the bed he proceeded to give the pilot a general examination. There was a gentleness about the man as he checked the pilot's eyes and ears, his throat, his chest, his temperature, and his pulse. He left pills on the night table, beside the phone. He indicated the first bottle, touched his own head and grimaced, and said they were *ah-spah-reen*. For headaches, Chan surmised. The man touched the second bottle, then pressed his hands together and lay his head on the back of one hand. *To sleep,* he called them.

When the doctor left Chan shut the bedside lamp and lay back down. He noticed a white disc on the ceiling. There was a green light in the corner, and vents. It must be a spy system, he suspected. That was fine with him. The lieutenant commander had nothing to hide.

The next thing Chan knew something was ringing. The phone. He swung his legs from the bed and answered it.

"Lieutenant Commander Chan?"

"Yes."

"Good morning. I am Zhong Jian, deputy consul general of the PRC in the city of Los Angeles," said the caller.

"Good morning," Chan said. "What time is it?"

"Five past five A.M. You have been a guest of the United States Air Force for two hours. Have they been treating you well?"

"Quite."

"You were not handled roughly?"

"No."

"Have you seen a doctor?"

"Yes."

"Has anyone asked questions about your mission?"

"No," Chan said. "At least, nothing that I understand."

"Our understanding from the PLAAF is that your mission of charity was aborted and you were in the process of vacating American airspace when your jet was attacked and destroyed without provocation."

Chan didn't know how to respond to that. He was not on a mission of charity, and the provocation was entering American airspace.

"Lieutenant Commander, have I accurately described happened?" the official pressed.

"Sir, I am not at liberty to discuss my mission," Chan answered truthfully. "As to provocation, my aircraft carried no weapons." He was very satisfied with that answer. It was worthy of a senior captain.

"I respect your fealty to your command structure," the official said, though it didn't sound sincere. It sounded annoyed. Perhaps the Americans were eavesdropping and Zhong Jian wanted them to hear something different. "I will be arriving at the base in approximately two hours. It seems I must drive rather than helicopter to see you. Do you know anything about why that is?"

"Not with certainty," Chan replied. "But I can tell you this. The aircraft that drove my plane from the sky would make very quick work of a helicopter."

"I see. Lieutenant Commander, we are going to do our best to bring you home as quickly as possible."

"Sir, am I a prisoner?" Chan asked.

"Our position is that you are not free to leave. Therefore, you are a prisoner," Jian replied.

"What about my family? Have they been told that I am all right?"

"They are being notified by a representative from the flight dispatch center," Jian told him.

"Thank you," Chan said.

Jian told the pilot to refrain from discussing his activities with anyone until he arrived. When he hung up Chan lay back down. He didn't feel like a prisoner but he supposed he was; he hadn't felt like a spy, either. He was still Bruce Chan, aviator, son, and brother. He didn't know whether that made him naive or strong. When he figured that out he would add it to the list.

He sat there thinking not about his situation but about that aircraft he had seen, and the way it had shot down its companion jet.

Why? It seemed to have been an accident. Why else would they sacrifice another obviously new aircraft? It had to be a very expensive way to show what the jet could do. Though what the plane could do was impressive, from its speed to its maneuverability to its destructive power.

China had nothing like it. Technologically, the PLAN and PLAAF were decades behind the American air force. In Chan's mind, that fact justified the incursion he had made. His commanders had to know what they were facing or how could they prepare for it? And even though he had not learned much, perhaps something he had seen would point more experienced intelligence operatives in new and significant directions. As he had been taught since enlisting, every pilot, every seaman, every soldier was an important part of the national defense.

He went to the desk and ate some of the fruit, then drank water from one of the plastic bottles. The banana he had gave him a flash of being a boy and eating a lunch his mother had packed. Meat and water tasted different from province to province, but he suspected that fruit was the same everywhere. When Chan was finished he decided to use the pen and paper to try and write down the details of the aircraft he had seen and the events as they had happened. With the surveillance cameras on the JF-17 destroyed, the pilot's recollections would be the only intelligence the PLAN had about the aircraft. Even if the Americans confiscated the paper, writing his thoughts there would help write it in his memory.

Chan shut his eyes to help visualize the encounter. He imagined himself back in the cockpit of his fighter, looking at the radar screen, then actually seeing the plane approaching from above. He heard the voice of Captain Chung giving him orders. With a slow, involuntary movement his right hand curled around the throttle. For a moment he felt he *was* back in the air.

A moment after that he fell asleep in the chair, nothing written but everything remembered.

SIX

Catalina Island, California

Kingsbury Hall was tired of waiting.

His yacht, the 175-foot *Prince Idaho*—named for his home state, where he'd made a fortune in lumber and real estate—had been at anchor for over a day. He had come to Catalina for dinner, not to sit in his yacht and worry. He had come to have dinner with Barbara Holmes, the wife of a business associate. Dinner in a restaurant noted for discretion. Barbara, too, was on the yacht. She was supposed to be home from visiting her sister in Carmel. Hall had to get her there.

The Coast Guard was planted in the Santa Barbara Channel, not letting anyone come or go because of the still-turbulent waters and the fears of an aftershock from the initial quake. Even dinghies were forbidden from plying the sea. There was no word about when the sailing ban would be lifted.

Captain Raphael, who ran the yacht for Hall, had worked for the billionaire for twelve years on three different vessels. They had been around the world together. The sailor knew his boss and he knew the capabilities of the Coast Guard. He did not recommend trying to break the blockade.

"What I think, though, is that the United States Coast

Guard would not dare shoot down a helicopter making a low, quick run to shore," Raphael said as the two men stood on deck in the darkness. "Especially a helicopter that is registered to Mr. Kingsbury Hall." Raphael was correct. The aerial lockdown also applied to the Coast Guard. And if all USCG and police patrol craft were grounded, who would there be to prevent the sea-level dash to return Barbara to shore, to her Jaguar? Hall's philosophy, in business and in life, had always been to ask for forgiveness, not permission. He believed that would serve him well when the authorities came calling. *If* he were still in United States territorial waters.

Hall told the captain to arrange the trip. The first mate of *Prince Idaho* was also the pilot, one who would do whatever he was told. He would enjoy this assignment. He used to fly tourist helicopters around Tasmania until his license was suspended for flying under the influence of a controlled substance. The authorities didn't believe that the pot was secondhand from a passenger. Hall got him a license in the United States, with the provision that he come work for him.

The gold Eurocopter AS-365N3 sat on the helipad, which was located aft in an area otherwise used for sunbathing. Usually, the lights were turned on for takeoffs and landings. Raphael made sure they remained off. They would be illuminated only for his return. Barbara Holmes was brought on deck, took a good-bye hug from her lover, and slid into the passenger's seat. Her side-slit red gown blew like a commoner's rags in the backwash, and her long hair twisted like seaweed; it made the young woman seem so much less appealing to Hall at that moment. Not because of her unsettled appearance but because of her sudden fragility.

Hall stood with Raphael on the terrace outside the bridge. Raphael had popped a fuse on the radio so no one could contact them with a protest. The helicopter was relatively silent because of the expensive sound mufflers he'd installed. The men watched as the dark shape rose, blotting the lights of downtown Santa Barbara and, in a few moments, the lights of the houses scattered through the Santa Ynez Mountains.

The wind from the rotor mixed it up with the steady sea breeze, creating a tempest reminiscent of this morning. They had gotten the winds but not much of the water. Hall believed the rest of this was all an overreaction, something federal attorneys had ordered to limit the inevitable liability suits.

The chopper took off toward the open sea so it would clear the bridges of boats docked to the east of the *Prince Idaho*. When it cleared the marina the helicopter swung back, its lights dark, and headed toward the shore.

Beyond it, Hall saw a bright light in the sky. He nudged Raphael and pointed toward it.

"Obviously, not everyone is obeying the lockdown," Hall remarked smugly.

The light grew larger and sharper. Suddenly, there appeared to be spots like pepper spread across the face of the beam.

"Mr. Hall, do you see—"

"Yes," Hall said. "Glasses, please."

Raphael reached into the bridge for binoculars. He handed them to Hall, who swung them toward the light. As he did, two things happened. First, he saw a titanic fireball off the port side. Second, his forehead blew open.

Hall's body dropped to the polished wood of the terrace as ice bullets tore through the sky. The helicopter had exploded when fire from the Angel ripped through its rotor and sent still-spinning shards into the fuel tank. The heat of the gears ignited the fuel, which blew what was left of the helicopter to singed-gold fragments. Projectiles from the Angel continued to fire through the raining debris, much of it hitting the anchored yacht. Raphael fell a moment after his employer, his torso ripped by pellets. There was screaming across the deck of the *Prince Idaho* and below as the attack continued. Only when there was no longer any part of the helicopter aloft did the attack stop.

But the yacht had been set ablaze by flaming pieces of the Eurocopter. A boatwide alarm sounded, which was wired to a central fire bell at the marina. Other boat owners woke and came on deck to see what was happening. Unfortunately, the fire on the yacht had reached its own fuel tank. The *Prince Idaho* exploded with a riotous pop that sent flames, metal, and glass flying in all directions. Several yachtsmen tried to cut anchor and leave the marina but, with smoke and darkness obscuring visibility, that created a bottleneck, which enabled the fire to jump easily from vessel to vessel. Firefighters who rushed in from Santa Barbara arrived just as a massive set of explosions took out the clustered yachts, the dock, and finally set fire to the marina itself.

Ironically, an aftershock far at sea sent sizable waves rolling well north of San Diego, knocking the flaming hulks one into the other and punching holes in the hulls that allowed them to sink. While the firefighters concentrated on containing the blaze at the marina, the sea took care of its own.

No one paid attention to the beam above that turned from the devastation and joined the other small lights in the nighttime sky.

SEVEN

Washington, D.C.

It had been a horrific day for the Navy. And after meeting with the president and the joint chiefs of staff, Secretary Whittle knew that against all odds it had the potential to become much worse.

The new crisis was referred to as an AAS, an advanced accident situation. Technically, it was pronounced "Oz," but most people called it "ass," mostly because when you had one, somebody's ass was on the line.

In this case, there were two careers at risk, those of Rear Admiral Edward Parks and Navy Secretary Whittle. Though the sixty-three-year-old secretary was worried about that, he was more concerned with the prospect of the United States losing a valuable new tool for homeland security. A Louisiana native, the honorable Marcus Whittle had moved from service on a battle group in the South Pacific to naval intelligence at the Pentagon to serving as director of the CIA's Department of Asian Maritime Intelligence. While there, his team uncovered a plot by Malaysian extremists to blow up airliners using gunpowder smuggled onboard inside innocuous-looking packets of hotel coffee. His reward was a promotion to Under Secretary of the Navy. A new administration bumped him to the top spot with offices at the

Pentagon and at the White House, not far from the under-ground situation room.

Whittle was in the underground situation room now, alone, the president, vice-president, and joint chiefs having left. He was waiting for a call to be put through to Rear Admiral Parks. He was enjoying the moment of quiet and relative darkness in the wood-paneled room. Except for the glow from computer monitors at each station, the room was unlit.

It had been a terrible day and a long one, beginning with the sinking of the *Hidalgo*, the effective loss of operations in the San Diego region, and the deaths of at least three hundred seamen. Now there was the failed attempt to bring down the rogue Angel. Word of that "missed objective," as Parks had called it, came as the men were just settling in for their meeting. The rear admiral mentioned the loss of the turret, but admitted that this was a "three-legged dog that still had a lot of bite and unimpacted mobility." Before Whittle had been able to tell the group that NWAD was still trying to come up with alternative responses to the AAS, the president received a videocall from the American embassy in Beijing. Ambassador Velma Morrison informed him that the premier was demanding an immediate apology and full explanation, access to the crash site, and the return of their pilot.

"And, of course, restitution for the lost aircraft," she said.

"What did you tell them?" the president asked.

"I told them they had entered our airspace illegally, that the pilot was given several opportunities to turn around or land, and that we consider the downing of any foreign military aircraft in our airspace to be a justifiable act of self-defense."

"Their response?" the president asked.

"They repeated their demands and said that, in the in-terim, an immediate personal apology from you would demonstrate the sincere regrets of our headstrong military," Ambassador Morrison said.

"The burglar wants an apology because the guard dog bit him," the president said.

"That's not going to happen."

"It shouldn't, sir," Morrison said.

The meeting had been interrupted when Whittle received a call from Rear Admiral Parks at NWAD. The news was not what the secretary wanted to hear. Not only was the Angel still airborne, but it had destroyed a helicopter that had taken off in Catalina Island—along with the yacht from which it had launched. There was an explosion and fire, but that was not the worst of it. The Angel had changed direction. Again. It was now headed west on a course that would take it into Chinese airspace in less than fourteen hours.

Whittle briefed the others. When the secretary was finished, the room was silent save for the leather seats, which groaned and squeaked as their occupants moved forward or slumped back. Then the hawkish chairman of the joint chiefs of staff, General Paul Ponce, spoke.

"If the Angel does go all the way, will it chew through anything the Chinese send at it?"

Whittle nodded.

The president had sunk slightly into his chair. Ponce's question brought him back up. "Why do you ask, general?"

"Because as I think about it, I'm not seeing that as such a bad thing," Ponce told him.

"Excuse me, but what part of this can you possibly regard as good news?" Whittle asked. He was almost afraid to hear the answer.

"Rear Admiral, the joint chiefs have been wondering how to unveil the Angel; providence may have given us the answer," Ponce replied. "Her debut in Chinese airspace will take some of the steam out of their teakettle when it comes to demands, not just now but in the future. It will also put us in a favorable position with others who see the aircraft and what it can do."

"The Road Not Taken," Parks muttered.

"Excuse me?" Ponce asked.

Parks explained the reference as Scott had explained it to him. The joint chiefs smiled.

Whittle wondered if Truman had men like these at his elbow.

"General, are you actually suggesting that we leave this aircraft aloft?" the president asked.

"We may not have a choice," Ponce replied.

"We could send up another drone and try to turn the Angel around," Whittle suggested.

"To what end, Mr. Secretary? So we can have the Angel crisscrossing American skies, grounding our own air force?" Ponce asked.

"Temporarily, perhaps," Whittle said. "This *is* a problem that we created."

"An act of God created it," Ponce said.

"I'm with the general on one point," the president said. "Putting aside for a moment the precipitating factors, we can't let this situation debilitate us. What do we do if the Chinese decide to lob missiles at two points just beyond the range of the Angel in retaliation for the JF-17 hit?"

"Seattle and Phoenix are on just such a war-sim strike list," Ponce said. "There's double jeopardy—the flawed Angel can't protect both cities. And if it's turned inland we'll still have our planes on the ground."

"That won't happen," Whittle assured him. "I know the Chinese. They'll work for a psychological win, not risk a military escalation." He regarded Ponce. "Unless, of course, we allow the Angel to continue toward their shores."

"Mr. President, we have no intelligence on Chinese activities since the attack and, with respect to Secretary Whittle, he has been out of that arena for several years," General Ponce said. "I recommend that we keep any other options under our hats for a while. We can spin this as a deployment in response to the Chinese incursion, not as a preexisting AAS. We say that we were testing the aircraft and sent it to stop the invader. The air show planes unfortunately got in the way, but defending our territory must remain a priority."

"General Ponce, do you understand that we have zero

control over this bird?" Whittle asked. "The Angel will shoot down any military *or* commercial aircraft it encounters."

Ponce shrugged. "We'll give them ample warning. If they disobey they pay the price."

Disobey.

The word stuck in Whittle's head for the few minutes that remained in the meeting. When it broke up, he stayed behind and poured himself water from a cut-glass pitcher in the center of the oval conference table. It tasted thick, tart. Or maybe it was just the bile in his own throat. No one understood better than Whittle the importance of defending the homeland. But the key word was defending, not bullying. Especially a nation as proud as China.

The president had instructed Whittle to continue searching for alternative responses but did not commit to using them. The commander-in-chief had never worn a uniform and Ponce was the go-to guy when it came to saber rattling. He was persuasive in that department, a no-nonsense Vietnam veteran who had been awarded both a Bronze and a Silver Star and was the head of U.S. unified special operations forces during Desert Storm.

Nearly half the time it was solicited, the president took Ponce's advice. That was a good batting average for the job. Whittle hoped this was not one of those times. The cover story Ponce had suggested might explain the next few hours of the Angel's flight. But what happened when the Angel had cut its way across China and headed to Europe or Africa? Or what if it were turned around in the pursuit of PLAAF aircraft or commercial planes and doubled back toward the United States?

Whittle had plenty of questions and no answers when Rear Admiral Parks got back on the phone. The navy secretary briefed him and asked for suggestions.

"About the plane or the Chinese?" Parks asked.

"Both," the secretary replied.

"General Scott is talking to his team about a possible re-approach, provided we can get everything we need."

The rear admiral told him what they had in mind and what they needed to pull it off. He was hopeful that between NWAD and Miramar, they could access all the necessary components. "And if that fails, we do have one additional asset," Parks said.

"What's that?"

The rear admiral told him. Whittle smiled a tired smile. In all the activity of the past hour he forgot that they had their own "go-to" guy. The only man who would have any kind of a chance convincing the Chinese that the United States had not begun a tactical air war against them.

EIGHT

Santa Barbara, California

Major Bryan wanted to punch something. Not because the order to leave the Angel was a bad call; it wasn't. It was just the wrong one.

Bryan arrived at Edwards Air Force Base just as the sun was spreading light above the horizon. It didn't seem like morning, just sun up. The night had been made up of so many parts in so many places that it could have been a week, not a day. Hawaii seemed very far away. Unfortunately, the Angel seemed very, very close. So close he felt he could reach back and rewind his life to the point where he jumped. Even as he drifted to earth Bryan had kicked the air in an awkward—and dangerously destabilizing—expression of frustration. Second-guessing those decisions was usually an empty activity. Still, retreat under fire was understandable; retreat anticipating fire was eating at Bryan, even though the decision had not been his.

Not exactly. He knew he shouldn't have bailed. His gut had told him that when he was still onboard. But the ride was too wild for him to think clearly, and his commanding officer had given him an order.

Now he needed to go back. He *would* go back.

Bryan had landed on a mountain peak well east of the ocean, not far from Painted Cave Road, some four thousand feet above sea level. A sherif's deputy had seen him come down and drove out to see what that was about. Though hang-gliders and parasailers often jumped up here, they didn't do it at night leaking blood-colored smoke. Deputy McCauley called in their location and the rescue party found him with no problem, their ATVs descending like a pack of boars. An airman first class gave Bryan a bottle of water and a thin, silver, emergency thermal blanket.

It was strange to be at an Air Force base and hear nothing but the wind. It was nearly as strange not to have General Scott here to meet him. The craggy officer had been a fixture of every coming and going over the past ten months. Bryan felt vaguely detached. And there was something else here, too. No one felt it, no one but Bryan knew about it. The odor of failure. He didn't blame himself for what happened up there, but he knew that he hadn't been able to rewrite the program. He also suspected that the Angel hadn't self-destructed. Despite the scream of the wind, he would have heard and certainly seen an explosion.

General Scott was on the phone for him, however. When they reached the gate Bryan was taken to a small security trailer just inside the main gate. There were two other men inside, a lieutenant and a sergeant. They left when Bryan arrived. Their salutes felt good; he felt anything but officer-like. Having jumped from danger, he felt anything but soldier-like.

"How are you, Major?" Scott asked.

"Sore, raw, and pissed-off."

"I want you to visit the infirmary," Scott insisted.

"I will, sir. What's happening with the Angel?"

"Nothing fatal," the general replied. "That turret dropped off when it fired. That didn't stop it from kicking the crap out of the QUAV."

"Did we get her altitude down?"

"We did. That part worked exactly as planned," Scott told him.

"That's something," Bryan said. "What about the Chinese pilot?"

"Recovered and tucked somewhere at Edwards," Scott said.

"Glad to hear that. So, has the brain trust figured out a way to get me back onboard the Angel? The medics aren't going to find anything wrong with me—"

"Major—"

"General, sir, you know how I feel about finishing a job I've started," Bryan said. He hesitated before deciding not to add, "*And I would have done it if you hadn't ordered me off the Angel.*"

"I know you want to go back. But this is about the Angel, not about Tom Bryan," the general replied. "Let's not lose sight of that."

"Yes, sir," Bryan replied.

Unlike Bryan, when Scott had something to say he said it. While the general could be unmercifully frank, it was rarely without good reason. It was also true that when Scott was blunt or critical, "the shit passed quickly," as Gabriel once put it. Because he spoke his mind, the general didn't stay cranky. Bryan also had to assume Scott was a little frustrated with himself for making the wrong call to abort the mission. There was some of that disgust in his voice, too.

"Now, we've been talking about getting back on track with a HAP assault," Scott told him.

"High-altitude parachutes?" Bryan said. "Why do we need those if the Angel is lower now?"

"Because an aircraft has to be far enough—and high enough—to be off the Angel's radar," Scott said. "In order to deploy LASER Ops, the team has to came at the target from above."

"I see," Bryan said. "At that distance the Angel doesn't seem as though it'll present much of a target."

"No."

"What if our guys miss?"

"We'll have Navy recovery ships in the area," the general told him. "A couple of patrol boats that survived the tsunami have already set out. Barring severe aftershocks, they'll circle the coordinates calculated by Hathaway. He'll also be flying the jump plane."

"Hathaway?"

"He's rated for the aircraft we hope to be using," Scott said. "He also knows the Angel, just in case there are any surprises."

Now *there* was a joke. Bryan was ground-bound and Hathaway was headed into action. "So the cleanup looks good, and everything works out on Hathaway's computer," Bryan said. "But it's still going to be quite a race, sir. The Angel has a helluva head start."

"It's over the Pacific and heading west. Miramar radar is watching to make sure it doesn't get turned around again. They are preparing to fire SAMs at anything headed into its sector."

"Do you have the gear you need?"

"We dug up four more PHAOS like the one you had and high-altitude jump surplus from Vietnam."

"Where are you leaving from?"

"Miramar, just as soon as the Angel is further out. That's where they keep the aircraft we'll be needing."

"Then I'd better get moving, sir. It'll take me at least three hours to get down there by land—"

"Don't worry about that, Major," Scott said.

"What do you mean?"

"After you get checked out I need you to sit tight."

The order shot up his back and stiffened his neck. "Excuse me, sir?"

"Major, I know you want to get back in there. But I need you on the ground at Edwards."

"To do what?"

"Parks told me that the Secretary of the Navy may need you to talk to the Chinese about their pilot," Scott said.

"Why?" Bryan asked. "Or rather, why me? There are far more senior officers at this base."

"The way it was explained to me, the Chinese are big on continuity. It has to do with taking personal responsibility, finishing what you started."

"But I didn't start this," Bryan pointed out.

"You were there. In the eyes of the Chinese that's the same thing," Scott told the major. "Secretary Whittle used to work in the Asian theater. He would know what's needed."

"So I just sit tight," Bryan said, repeating what the general had told him.

"For now."

"Dammit, General, it's killing me to have been so close to an objective and not be able to bag it."

"I know what that's like," Scott said pointedly. "Otherwise, I'd be running the intelligence operation of the NATO-Russia Permanent Joint Council and you and I wouldn't be having this conversation."

With those words, Bryan felt the anger leave him. He also felt somewhat ashamed. What he had just experienced was upsetting, but not nearly as much as Scott having his career stopped dead due to politics. If the general could recover from that, Bryan would survive this.

"Now, we've got a team to field," Scott went on. "I'll talk to you after you've gone to the infirmary. And don't worry, Tom. When you're not working for Secretary Whittle, I'll make sure you're plugged into the operation."

"Thank you, sir. If I'm still getting probed and poked at H-Hour, give the team my best."

"I will," Scott said.

The general hung up and Tom Bryan sat there. He felt deflated, the heat gone out, the venting finished. He also felt somewhat ashamed for having bitched to the general about his own situation. There were much larger issues on the table, such as stopping the Angel and preventing a military showdown with China. He should feel privileged just to be a part of the process, to be part of a team. Not just the LASER Ops, but a team charged with defending America.

It had taken a bit of wrestling, both inside and out, but this much had been accomplished.

Tom Bryan felt like a soldier again.

NINE

Edwards Air Force Base, California

Chan did not know how long he had sat there, asleep. He woke when his head suddenly fell forward. He had been half-thinking, half-dreaming about a girl he used to fancy—Mei Mui, her name was. She was a friend of his sister's. Mei had gleaming ebony hair that smelled of fresh morning air and hung to her delicate, white jaw. She had narrow brown eyes, though they seemed to widen slightly whenever they spoke. Her voice was strong and sounded older than her years. Her mother was a secretary for the local magistrate and her father was a constable. They had considerable influence in the village, and Mei's parents were always helping the Chan family with permits and with extensions when they were late with tax payments.

Chan learned to respect power, in people as well as in birds, though he never coveted the kind of access the Muis possessed. He wanted to know that people liked him for himself, not for what he could do for them.

Chan liked Mei for herself, but he was not socially acceptable to the family. He knew that because, as the years passed, his mother quietly discouraged him from seeing Mei except when she was with Christine. Eventually, she married a provincial magistrate and became an influential figure in relaxing the restrictions on how many children married couples could have.

Deputy Consul General Zhong Jian had power. *Real* power. A good word from him could probably protect Chan from any repercussions that came with losing his aircraft.

Chan wondered how he should present himself to the official. Humble, of course, but many military officers preferred humility with strength. It was a difficult balance, like when his father used to carve masks of gods who were strong but not disapproving. Chan would find a way to give Jian that.

The official and an aide arrived with a two-man Air Force escort. Jian was not quite what Chan was expecting. He was a very elderly, very short, and portly gentleman with short white hair and a scar that ran diagonally across his forehead. He wore a gray business suit and had thick, fair hands. He walked with a slight limp. His aide was more what Chan had imagined Jian to be: thin, with a black buzz cut, sharp and precise movements, and a set, humorless expression. He carried a slender briefcase.

"Lieutenant Commander Chan," Jian said in a surprisingly deep voice. "I am delighted to meet you." His narrow eyes fixed on those of the pilot. "Is there anything you need?"

"For myself, nothing, sir," Chan replied.

The aide took the chair from the desk as Jian entered. The door was shut behind him. He sat heavily. The aide stood beside him.

"You would think, after such a long ride, I would wish to stand," Jian said. He patted his left leg. "I would wish to, but my leg has other ideas. I was wounded during the Long March with Mao. I was a boy but the artillery shell did not care." He gestured grandely. "I am here because of the clement weather. Our nation honors those who serve it."

Chan went to the desk and picked up the pad. He started drawing pictures and making notes. He wrote, "*I have been writing down what I saw. Do you think this room is bugged?*"

"Probably," Jian said. "But it doesn't matter. Nothing you and I have to say is a secret. My only concerns are your well-being and quick release."

"Is there a problem with that?"

"Whenever I go someplace or receive someone, it is to solve a problem," Jian said. "The Americans believe that you were engaged in espionage. Whether you were or were not is ultimately irrelevant. They say yes, we say no, and eventually we will reach an agreement."

Deputy Consul Jian was *definitely* not what Chan was expecting. He was not like a smoldering fire. He was more like fog. The pilot placed the pad back on the desk. "What can I do?"

"The problem is not you, Lieutenant Commander, but your aircraft," Jian went on. "It was destroyed. We will not simply absorb that loss, and you are the hostage the Americans will use to try and persuade us otherwise."

"How long will that take?" Chan asked.

"Diplomacy is not like a flight where you can plot the points from here to there," Jian told him, punctuating his remark with slow, successive stabs of a thick middle finger. "This is a very different kind of journey, one that requires low energy, not high, patience instead of adrenaline."

Chan didn't know what to say. This kind of thinking, this kind of competition, was beyond his experience.

A light on the top of the briefcase flashed and the aide quickly set it on the bed. He popped the latches. There was a telephone inside. The aide handed it to Jian. It was obviously a secure line of some kind. Jian listened but did not speak. Chan tried to interpret his expression. He couldn't. Jian covered the mouthpiece and regarded Chan. "You saw the aircraft that attacked you?"

"I did, sir."

"Can you say how large it was?"

"Nearly three times the size of my own aircraft, sir."

Jian repeated what Chan had told him. Then he hung up. He rose. "Russian radar on Sakhalin has detected an aircraft moving from this region out across the Pacific," Jian said. "According to the PLAAF, its flight path and speed strongly suggest that it is the same aircraft that shot you down. Your estimation of its size confirms that." He looked at his aide and nodded toward the door. Jian's manner was somewhat more serious now. "I am going to have a talk with your hosts. Is there anything you would like me to get for you?"

"I would like to speak with my family."

"A reasonable request, and I will make it. It is a compassionate gesture that I'm sure the Americans will be eager to make. And then announce to the press." He pointed to the briefcase. "This, unfortunately, needs a matching connection. Is one great or small when he can speak to some of the most powerful men on earth yet not call for dinner reservations? I don't know."

Chan wasn't sure he understood. All he knew was that he felt helpless. "Sir, isn't there anything I can do?"

Jian nodded toward the notepad. Chan understood. He should finish writing whatever he remembered. The pilot was gratified that he had at least been doing something right.

The aide closed the briefcase and rapped on the door. One of the airmen opened it. The deputy consul smiled at Chan and left, followed by his aide. Chan felt strangely more isolated than he had before the men arrived. Suddenly, there were layers of Americans he didn't know, with agendas he could not imagine, standing between himself and freedom. That was really why he had asked to talk to his family. It was strange. He never felt trapped when he was inside a tiny cockpit. Here, even though he could move about, he felt cornered.

Maybe what bothered Chan was that he had just seen his own future. Or at least, a possible future. Obviously, Deputy Consul Jian had lived a very full, active, and dangerous life. Now the official preferred to live comfortably while he fought the battles of state inside his mind.

From childhood, Chan had been outside doing things, exploring nature and the world. He could not imagine a life that was internal. And this room was a taste of that.

With a sense of duty and a hint of desperation, he returned to the desk alert and determined, and began writing about the attack.

TEN

Edwards Air Force Base, California

Out of my element.

Despite the many dangerous places Bryan had been, those words had never taken a spin through his head. Not when he was at the bottom of the South Polar seas or sailplaning over a Texas plain or walking around the mouth of a volcano. He had always seized a challenge and throttled it.

Not this one.

As Scott had strongly suggested, Secretary Whittle called Bryan and asked him to join base commander General Victor Backer for an important conference with Deputy Consul General Zhong Jian of the Chinese consulate in Los Angeles. They would be meeting in the general's ready room. Both an American and a Chinese translator would be present. The American was a professor from the University of California, Santa Barbara. Bryan passed him as he waited in the hall. He was of Asian descent. Bryan didn't know why, but he expected the translator to be Caucasian or Black. Our side, their side. It was ridiculous, he realized and he felt stupid.

Bryan knew nothing about General Backer. He knew nothing about the Chinese diplomat. Maybe that was why he felt so uncomfortable. There was no mission profile, no equipment analyses, no weather reports and maps. *And* he had no experience in this arena.

A young staff sergeant came to escort Bryan to the general's office. Bryan was told they would not have much time to talk before the Chinese official arrived. The general was a giant of a man, around six-foot-seven, with a shaved head and thick, graying eyebrows. He dominated the desk he was behind. Another staff sergeant was reviewing papers with him when Bryan arrived. The sergeant hurried off. Bryan saluted. The general returned the salute without looking up. Bryan was good at reading "snaps." It was sharp and dismissive.

This wasn't going to be good.

"Leave it to the United States Navy to screw things up for the Air Force," the general grumped as he reviewed the printout. He dropped the open folder on the desk and slapped it with both hands. "This is a short history of the Guardian Angel Project. You know how it reads to me, Major? Tell no one about it, then ask someone else to fix it when it breaks."

"I'm Army, sir."

Backer looked at him. "Did I ask what you were, Major?"

"No, sir." Bryan shut up tight. General Backer was one of *those,* an angry son-of-a-bitch commander who enjoyed being angry and in charge whether it helped get things done or not. The major had come to accept that every now and then he would run into a prick like this. It didn't thrill him but it didn't faze him, either. The drill was to say nothing unless you were asked, then to answer truthfully. Once they had you in line they tended to soften. Besides, sometimes they served a purpose, especially when dealing with a bastard on the other side.

"Mr. Whittle seems to think you can help us," the general went on. "How? Can you get my planes back in the air?"

"No, sir."

"The Navy has turned us from eagles to ostriches," Backer snapped. "And from what Mr. Whittle tells me your day hasn't gone much better. You went up there to fix this goddamn plane and ended up standing by while the Angel brought the Chinese aircraft down."

"I tried to get him to turn around, sir."

"And failed, so they give you another shot." Backer looked back at the folder, shaking his head. "That's the Army. It says you have another connection with the Chinese. Saved some of their sailors from a submarine, another Navy snafu. How does that help me?"

"It's supposed to prove that we don't want to hurt them—"

"An American officer rescuing a couple of Chinese sailors does not define United States policy. We'd love if the Chinese became court eunuchs and did nothing but make toys and clothes and Christ knows what else for ten cents an hour. And Beijing knows it." The general studied the folder for a moment. "The reason I wanted you here, Major, is in case I need someone to help me bullshit through this chat with the Chinese representative—not that I'll be telling him much about the aircraft. What can you tell me about this 'Guardian Angel' that's not in this joint chiefs overview, which doesn't give me much more than sunshine-up-the-ass projections bookended by wingspan, speed, and test results?"

"It turns an aircraft to powder in seconds, sir."

"So it says here, with 'ice bullets.' Do you know how they work?"

"As I recall from my briefing, sir, each projectile has an exit mass of six-point-seven grams, of which twenty-odd percent melts during delivery, depending on external conditions. But leaving enough mass, traveling at sufficient speed, to penetrate steel," Bryan said.

Backer raised his eyes without raising his head. For the first time he didn't look as if he wanted to tear off someone's head and spit in the neck. "You remember all that from your preflight briefing?"

"Yes, sir."

"You didn't have to write any of it on your wrist or palm like some of these yahoos?"

"No, sir."

"Impressive." The phone beeped and the general drove a large finger into the speaker button. "Go, Sergeant!"

"Sir, the Chinese delegation has been delayed."

"Why?"

"They haven't said, sir."

"What do you mean?"

"They're back in their van and refuse to talk to us, sir."

"Knock on the goddamn window," Backer said. He looked at Bryan. "Is a diplomatic car considered sovereign foreign territory?"

"I don't know, sir," the sergeant replied. "But the deputy consul does have immunity, sir. We have no authority to force him to do anything."

"He's still on *my* base—"

"Hold on, sir," the sergeant said. "General, security says the Chinese contingent is coming in."

"Smart move. What the hell is it with these boys?" the general asked.

"They probably had to call home," Bryan offered. He knew the general's remark was a declaration and not a question but he decided to answer anyway. "Also, no."

"No what?"

"The car would not be considered foreign territory. General Scott arranged for a State Department lecture in case we ever had to evac a foreign embassy. You would have the right to verify the status of all subjects in the vehicle. Anyone not a member of the diplomatic corps is subject strictly to the laws of this nation."

The general said nothing. He shut the folder and waited with his big hands folded. "You're just full of helpful insights, Major."

"I like to learn things."

"What was the name of the Chinese sub you helped?"

"*Destiny,* sir."

"What did you learn from your experience with *Destiny*?"

"The Chinese think way different than we do, sir," Bryan said. "I learned to keep a wide open mind."

There was no further conversation until the sergeant informed them that the Chinese were in his office. Backer told him to send in the UCSB translator first, then the men from the consulate.

"Make them wait while a flunky enters," Backer said. "Show them what it's like to idle your jets. The Chinese won't like that, right?"

"I believe they will perceive that as an insult, waiting on someone of lesser rank," Bryan agreed.

"Good."

The translator entered alone and the general gestured toward an armchair near the desk. The man sat in it. Bryan remained standing. Backer waited about half a minute, then asked the sergeant to bring in the "Chinese visitors." From what Bryan had learned in the submarine rescue, even the use of their nationality was a pejorative: it meant they were not welcome as people, merely as representatives. Whether intentional or not, it was a significant distinction.

The deputy consul entered, followed by the translator. Even if the latter were not carrying a small tape recorder, the deputy consul was recognizable by the proud elevation of his chin. He wasn't about to surrender his dignity to his host.

Backer rose. He did not offer his hand. When the deputy consul bowed slightly, the general did the same. He seemed more amused than respectful.

"Have a seat," the general said, gesturing toward a leather couch along the inner wall.

"Not at present," the official replied.

The American translator told the general what the deputy consul had said. When the general spoke it was the Chinese translator who interpreted for the Chinese representative. The American also had a tape recorder, carried discreetly inside his jacket with a microphone clipped to his lapel.

The deputy consul ignored both Bryan and the American translator. The major was neither surprised nor wounded. That was the Chinese official's way of establishing his rank.

Jian folded his hands on his lap. "General, I have just received a disturbing report from my superiors in Beijing. The aircraft that shot down our pilot in an unprovoked and aggressive act is now flying over international waters. I am informed that on its current course it is headed toward our republic."

"I don't know about the aircraft's location or where it may be headed," Backer replied. "If, as you say, it's in international airspace, then your government has no grounds to complain."

"I was expressing a concern, not registering a complaint," the official corrected deferentially. "I will inform you, however, as will my government to your superiors, that we are fielding a squadron to intercept and destroy the aircraft should it venture into Chinese airspace."

"You mean, the way your fighter jet did ours."

"Our jet was on a mission of charity, a fact that was clearly expressed to your personnel on the ground," the deputy consul corrected him again. "Your aircraft has shown a much different personality."

"With respect, Mr. Deputy Consul, your aircraft was spying. It was *repeatedly* asked to leave our airspace by the gentleman standing behind you, Major Thomas Bryan. I can play the tapes of their conversation if you like. Major Bryan is the officer who rescued several of your seamen from the stricken submarine *Destiny,* and he had every hope your pilot would depart."

"Our pilot was in the process of leaving your stricken territory when he was shot down." The official turned toward Bryan. "I believe you were informed, *repeatedly,* that his aircraft carried no armaments. That fact must also have been apparent to an experienced observer."

Bryan had hoped to stay out of this back-and-forth, particularly since the Chinese diplomat wouldn't have asked him a question if he didn't already know what the answer would be. Besides, he was too concerned about what the diplomat had just said, that the PLAAF was prepared to respond to the approach of the Angel.

"Sir, we never expressed a concern about being attacked, only about surveillance," Bryan replied.

"You had evidence of recording devices onboard?"

"Don't insult me, sir," the general said, with open impatience that bordered on disgust.

"That is not why I have come here," the diplomat replied overly graciously, once again regarding the general. "I have come to express my country's unhappiness with the imprisonment of our pilot—"

"We *rescued* him."

"—and the heading of an aircraft that has already shot down one of our aircraft."

"Your concerns have been noted by this command," Backer replied. "I can do no more than that."

"Your Air Force has nothing to say about this aircraft?"

"This command does not speak for the Air Force, Mr. Deputy Consul."

The diplomat turned back to Bryan. "I am familiar with what you did for the crew of the *Destiny.* Your actions do you honor."

"Thank you."

"May I ask how you came to be involved in this current situation?"

"You may ask but he will not answer," General Backer said. He rose. "Sir, I believe this audience is concluded."

"General, permission to address the deputy consul on another matter."

Backer's thick brows nudged one another. "What matter?"

"The PLAAF action," Bryan replied.

His voice just a whisper, the Chinese interpreter leaned close to the deputy consul, translating. The American officers were silent for a moment.

"Go ahead," the general told him, "as long as the major understands that there are issues which should not be addressed and the deputy consul understands that you are only speaking for Major Thomas Bryan."

"I think we both understand my limitations, sir," Bryan said with an edge of resentment. He couldn't tell whether the general had caught it, though he didn't imagine his tone would faze the officer. Backer could turn him off with a word, which was all that mattered to a man like him.

The major walked around to where the deputy consul could see him without turning. Bryan had no proof that the gesture would show respect, but reasoned it couldn't hurt. The official fixed his eyes on Bryan as soon as he came within view. The official's expression was neutral, as it had been since he entered the room.

"Mr. Deputy Consul, what happened today was not an act of war," Bryan told him. "Please don't turn it into one. In the South Pole and again today I have worked hard to see that innocent people are not hurt. It was bad luck that destroyed your aircraft, nothing more."

"Major Bryan, your efforts and sincerity are commendable, and I believe they are honorable. Your nation is less so. The United States believes it can go where it wishes, when it wishes. If, as you say, this aircraft is not on a mission of war, then it will not find war. But it has left American airspace and we will fly wherever it flies, as is our right *and* our responsibility."

Bryan couldn't tell him that to do so would cause exactly the kind of disaster everyone was trying to avoid.

"You are silent," the deputy consul remarked.

"There's nothing else to say," Bryan replied. He didn't try to conceal the helplessness he felt.

The official held Bryan's eyes a moment longer, as though encouraging him to speak. The major did not. He didn't know at what point national security ceded priority to common sense; if LASER couldn't bring down the Angel, the Chinese would learn about its capabilities soon enough. But that wasn't his call to make.

The deputy consul shifted his gaze to the general. "Since you are unable to tell us more about the attack on our retreating aircraft, we will go."

Backer rose. So did Bryan. The general tugged the hem of his jacket and stood with his arms stiffly at his side.

"It's been every bit as enlightening for me, Mr. Deputy Consul," the general declared.

"Beijing will continue to pursue the release of our unlawfully held pilot through diplomatic efforts and the defense of our nation through military means," the diplomat informed him.

"Your pilot was here unlawfully. He is being lawfully billeted," the general replied. The entire audience was like listening to a midlevel game of tennis doubles. Cautious play, a few dramatic rallies, and then everyone left the court. In the end, it appeared as though nothing had been accomplished save for the play itself.

The Chinese official bowed at the neck and the general dipped his head as slightly as he felt he could get away with. The entire meeting had been a disheartening display of diplomacy, the art—and it *was* an art—of neither advancing nor retreating from a stalemate.

When the Chinese had left the room the general told the American interpreter he wanted a transcript of the meeting e-mailed to Secretary Whittle.

"Are we finished here, sir?" Bryan asked.

"Apparently." He looked over. "Why? I hope you're not going to make another run at the deputy consul."

"I was considering it, sir. Perhaps in a less official setting."

"Denied."

"Sir, if the Chinese launch fighters and they meet with the Angel—" "They will be blown from the air, Major. I know that. I also know there is a contingent in our government which may want exactly that."

"They want a war?"

"No. They want to prevent one. Not being able to stop the Angel may be a blessing. If the Chinese see what that bird is capable of, they will have a long think before penetrating our airspace again."

Bryan stood still for a moment. He didn't realize until Backer glanced down that his hands had formed tight fists. He relaxed them.

"Would you like transportation back to NWAD?" the general asked.

"Perhaps later, sir? I'd like to rest a while longer."

"You earned that much," the general said, then asked the sergeant to put in a call to General Ponce in Washington.

The major saluted smartly and left; it was more anger than respect that made his hand rigid. He understood the concept of deterrents and how they didn't work unless the other guy knew you had them. He and General Scott had often talked about President Truman and the Road Not Taken. But there had to be other ways of making this particular point.

Hell, the point was already made, Bryan thought. *We popped the pilot's ride from under him.*

He stopped in the corridor outside the staff sergeant's small office. He walked slowly. General Ponce, the Chairman of the Joint Chiefs, was a tough old warhound. Bryan would not put it past him to call off the LASER mission and let the Angel continue flying west.

And NWAD takes the hit for failing, Bryan thought.

He needed to talk to General Scott about what had happened. But first, there was something else he had to do. He hadn't mentioned it to General Backer for fear of being shot down. The major waited until the UCSB professor emerged from the general's office.

"I need you to do me a favor," Bryan said as he walked briskly alongside the interpreter.

"I'm kind of in a hurry," the young man said.

"You heard what happened in there," Bryan said. "This is important."

The translator asked what it was. Bryan told him. The young man looked back at the general's office. "That won't make him happy."

"Not part of my job description," Bryan replied.

The translator thought for a moment, then grinned. "I'm with you," he said.

Bryan thanked him, then led the way down the corridor.

ELEVEN

Norco, California

General Scott watched his four-person team board the camouflage-painted bus to Miramar. As he did, he reflected that this was a very different world from the one for which he was trained.

Hell, Scott thought. *It's different from the world for which this unit was trained.* His LASER team was about to go into battle armed not with bullets but with software.

Against an American target, no less.

Scott had selected Captain Gabriel, Lieutenant Black, Ensign Galvez, and Sergeant Major Cowan for the mission. In addition to the software they hoped to install, Black and Galvez were carrying C-4. If they couldn't recapture the Angel's attention, they were going to have to destroy it.

Provided they can get to it, Scott thought. He stood by the door and the team saluted as they boarded. Hathaway was the last to arrive. Scott followed him through the doors and the bus departed. The general would follow the team's progress from the control tower at Miramar; that was as close as he'd be able to get and he intended to be there.

The bus started out as the general took a seat beside Hathaway, in the front behind the driver. The scientist was sitting by the window but he did not look out. He was even more reserved than before.

"Are you going to be all right?" Scott asked.

"You mean, can I do this?" Hathaway smiled. "Yes." He nodded confidently. "I was eggshell before I was egghead," he told the general, referring to the smooth off-white helmet worn by many test pilots. The name was a reference not just to the color but to the fact that if something went wrong, chances were good the helmet wasn't going to be much help. "I'm one of the few aeronautical engineers who has worked both sides of the desk."

"I thought there was more to you than crunching data."

"Why?"

"I've worked with research and development people before," Scott said. "They tend to focus on their own areas. I watched you. Despite a few emotional upticks you listened to everyone, even when it had nothing to do with you. I figured either you had been in combat or handled a vehicle of some sort."

"Only someone who had been there would notice," Hathaway remarked.

"Why'd you give it up?"

"My commission? I liked flying test planes but I absolutely could not deal with the prairie apples," Hathaway told him. "It distracted me up there." He snapped his eyes up and back. "The pork barrel politics, hundreds of millions of dollars going to the wrong project because it happened to be in the home state of a powerful senator. I went into the private sector, hoping to work on a hyperplane project. Passengers board at JFK or LAX, take off on a suborbital airplane flight, arrive in Tokyo three hours later. So what happened? The company I worked for was sold to a major military contractor. The hyperplane got backburnered and I was put on the Angel." He shrugged. "At least this one was properly funded and I got to do a lot more science than selling."

"When was the last time you flew?"

"About two months ago," Hathaway told him. "I took an F-16 and a Hawker 400XP up as targets during an unarmed run of the Angel. This one, in fact. We needed the extra room for instruments."

"How did you do?" Scott asked.

"Good and bad," Hathaway replied. "Captain Hathaway got torched but Dr. Hathaway was a triumph."

Scott grinned as the bus accelerated onto Interstate 15. "Then what's on your mind?"

"What do you mean?"

"Your expression," Scott told him. "It's what my grandmother used to call 'a prune face.' Not because it was wrinkled, but because of what would fix it."

"My grandmother would've smacked me with a wooden spoon and told me to stop moping," Hathaway said. "In a very heavy Irish accent that would have scared me even without the spoon." He was silent for a moment. "This is my 'what if this doesn't work' face."

"Maybe you shouldn't be thinking ahead of the mission," Scott cautioned. "My people are going with you."

"I'll be okay when we hit the tarmac," he said. "This is something I've got to think about while I've got the downtime."

"I'll leave you alone, then."

"That's all right," he said. "Conversation is good. It distracts the conscious mind, lets the subconscious do the heavy lifting."

"Is that true?"

"So the studies about problem solving say," Hathaway replied. "More than half the scientists and mathematicians surveyed said that solutions to real posers came to them during exercise, sleep, or sex."

"Funny how Grandma's solution was way off," Scott said.

"Maybe she just couldn't tell you what worked for her," Hathaway said. He pointed at his face and shook his head slowly. "The damn thing is, what you see here is frustration.

The bird itself is working exactly the way it's supposed to, and better than I could have hoped."

"We'll bring this one down and fix it. Or if not this one, the next one. This program is too important for it to die. As you said, it works."

"You've got to wonder, though," Hathaway said. "We created the atom bomb to end the Second World War. It did, but it spawned fears of radiological weapons that have civilization looking over its shoulder for every zealot with a suitcase full of cash and access to disgruntled Ukranian generals or underpaid Russian scientists. Each new cure seems to create the next generation of problems."

"And the only ones with a conscience are the guys who thought them up," Scott said. "I don't know what the answer is."

"What's scary is we keep getting better at creating the problems. We're doing damage to ourselves before the bad guys can."

"Maybe, but I realized a long time ago that nothing is clean," Scott said. "I had one cleric tell me back in the seventies that penicillin was a bad thing because it encouraged promiscuity."

"Maybe, but think of what that did for problem solving," Hathaway remarked.

Scott chuckled at that.

The men talked a little about their experiences in the military. There was nothing surprising in Hathaway's background, though it did bring the men closer. Familiar types, similar situations; a shared frame of reference bonded them in a way this crisis hadn't, perhaps because they had come at the Angel from two different perspectives. Scott had regarded Hathaway as a man who had let the genie out of the bottle, and now LASER had to put it back. In fact, the scientist was just a grunt with a PhD, someone who was every bit as rattled and concerned—and patriotic, his head in the stars *and* stripes—as the general.

Shortly before the hour-long ride ended, Hathaway went on-line to make sure the Angel was still on course. It was. The aircraft was five hundred and ten miles west of the airbase.

The team exited. They were greeted by members of the quartermasters corps and were taken to a hangar where their gear had been collected. They were shown how to use it. No one had any difficulty with the breathing apparatus or with the sample chute that had been brought over for demonstration. Scott thought he noticed an unusual deference on the part of the q-corps personnel. He had seen that once on a tour of Cape Canaveral, a palpable respect for the souls who were about to hurl themselves into space. The general found it surprisingly affecting.

Parks radioed that a Cyclone class coastal patrol boat, the USS *Phoenix,* was departing for the recovery zone.

When the equip-briefing was finished and everything was in place, the team gathered on the windy airfield to review the attack one last time. It was only the second time LASER had been briefed by Parks and Hathaway before boarding the bus. Scott wasn't overly concerned by that. The beauty about LASER was what Corporal Emens, the radio operator, had dubbed its "oxymoronic drill structure." He even wrote to the DoD to have ODS included in the Pentagon's acronym-base. They agreed. It referred to practicing improvisation: what to do when things went wrong, or new elements appeared. Major Bryan's awareness of the temperature in the Angel was a result of ODS. An operation was not just about execution, it was about a symbiotic relationship between the elements. LASER had to be the glue.

As the team walked toward the sleek white jet, General Scott reflected on his chat with Dr. Hathaway. Invention, like exploration, was an inevitable aspect of human nature. The tragedy was not that devices like the Angel were invented.

The tragedy was that the bad guys didn't give you much choice.

TWELVE

Shanghai, China

Late in 2002, the Chinese military underwent a far-reaching change in leadership as a result of Party Congress elections at the 16th National Congress of the Communist Party of China. The CPC brought younger, more aggressive men to the chiefs of the Military Commission of the People's Liberation Army, specifically the Nanjing Military Area Command; the PLA Military Department; the PLA Logistics Department; and the Armaments Department. Relatively young men, in their fifties—twenty years the junior of the men they replaced—were elected vice-chairmen of the Central Military Commission. Several of these men were also members of the Politburo of the Chinese Communist Party's Central Committee, giving them extraordinary powers in matters military and political.

News of the meeting between Deputy Consul Jian and Air Force General Backer was not well-received by the members of the Military Commission. They met in emergency session in Beijing and decided that the warning Jian had delivered must be acted upon. The accidental confrontation between U.S. and Chinese submarines in the Weddell Sea had dramatically underscored the fact that new American technology could not be met with stealth. It had to be met with the one thing China had: overwhelming numbers and a willingness to use them.

The CMC had authorized Jian to use the threat of military action to gauge the American response. As they had expected, that response was arrogant. The American ambassador in Beijing had echoed the sentiments of the commander at the air force base: the Chinese pilot had been a spy and would be released after the Chinese acknowledged that, and agreed never again to intrude on American airspace.

Privately, the Chinese considered their flyover to be self-defense. The only criminal act was the American overreaction. Beijing would not apologize or explain their actions. Moreover, the Americans had yet to explain the nature of the air lockdown or identify the aircraft headed out over the Pacific.

American technological imperialism had to be confronted now, before it pervaded every aspect of global life. Though the Chinese were behind in science, they did not lack courage, as Lieutenant Commander Chan had demonstrated. As Beijing would demonstrate, they also did not lack resolve.

The mission order was given to Senior Captain Peter Shin, Jiangwan base commander. He was to send the Liberator Squadron to meet the American aircraft. The squadron would be anchored by two Nanchang Q-5C attack aircraft armed with 100 rounds standard for each of the two 23mm cannons as well as C-801 AShMs rockets. These would be described as "purely defensive" armaments. Each aircraft would have extra fuel tanks to complete a round-trip to an interception point somewhere near what was presently calculated as the Hawaiian Islands. The squadron also consisted of a pair of Xian JH-7 attack aircraft, which were less maneuverable than the smaller jets and would fly in support of any attack.

The Chinese were not equipped to fight a foreign war, or a highly technological one. But that would change over the coming years, and that was a point the new administration wanted to make. Among the pilots there was also another agenda, one that no one addressed but everyone felt.

They wanted to avenge the shooting down of the JF-17.

They wanted to take down an airplane of the United States Air Force.

THIRTEEN

Edwards Air Force Base, California

A guard instructed Lieutenant Commander Chan to pick up the telephone. The number of his parents' home was input for him elsewhere on the base. The landline made the conversation seem more private, and certainly more personal. It was absurd to think that the Americans weren't listening. But the translucent wire gave a sense of intimacy, of solid warmth to his parents' voices. Chan was grateful for that. Their vivid expressions of thanksgiving enabled him to see their faces, to look in their eyes. Hearing them was also the first time he had been really afraid: while Chan lived the encounter in the JF-17, the events were moment to moment. Now he was getting it all in one relieved outpouring. If the Americans were listening, perhaps they would understand that the person they had in captivity was a man who was caring and cared for, not a menace to their infrastructure.

Chan was particularly happy to talk to his sister, who had gone to the house to be with their parents.

"This is all my fault, you know," Christine said.

"What do you mean?" her brother asked.

"I was the one who reported the seismic event that caused the tsunami," the young geologist replied.

"We need to find a less dangerous field for you."

"Marriage and children, Mother keeps saying."

"She would." Her brother laughed. "I don't suppose she wants me to find you a nice young pilot."

"Not anymore," Christine assured him, a laugh in her voice.

Let American intelligence scramble to figure out if *that* conversation had any relevance to national security.

The call was barely ended when the corporal came to take the telephone away. Chan was neither surprised nor offended. He had gotten to call home, and that was all he cared about.

The door was not quite closed when the lieutenant commander heard the now-familiar sounds of sluggish, syrupy English. Two men entered after a loud exchange. One of them shut the door. He was a tall, visibly irritated man. He said something and the other translated. The interpreter spoke in a neutral voice. It didn't match the conviction of the original speaker.

"Mr. Chan, I'm Major Thomas Bryan. I was the one who spoke with you from the other plane. We need to talk."

Chan wasn't sure how to respond. This man seemed earnest, but the pilot had no experience in the methods of interrogation. His sincerity could be some kind of ploy. Then again, Chan did not see what there was to lose: after all, he did not have much to hide.

"Would you care to sit?" Chan said, extending a hand toward the desk chair. He felt a flash of horror as he noticed his notes on the desk. Perhaps the major couldn't read the writing but he might recognize the sketches of the aircraft. Chan was relieved when the officer declined.

"Lieutenant Commander," Bryan said, "I just ordered your guard to let me in. That countermands the instructions of the base commander. I may not have much time to speak."

The major seemed impatient as the interpreter spoke. After the words had been translated, Chan understood why. "I'm listening," he said concisely.

"Your government is sending aircraft to intercept our plane," Bryan said. "If we can't turn it around those aircraft will be destroyed just as yours was."

"Can't?" Chan said.

"That's right," Bryan said. "The destruction of a PLAAF squadron is not going to help either nation. You must speak with them. Convince them that what you saw is not an ordinary aircraft."

"What is it?" Chan asked. "And why can't you bring it back?"

"I can't tell you that," Bryan said.

"Then I'm sorry, but I can't help you," Chan said. He was surprised by his own boldness.

Bryan approached the pilot. "I wish I could tell you more. I came here myself because I hoped I had some credibility with you, with your government. All I can tell you is that the tidal wave has caused an experiment to backfire. We're trying to fix it. If we can't, the squadron will be destroyed. That is not a threat, airman. That is just the awful truth."

There was a commotion in the hall. People were coming. The American stepped closer. "I have nothing to gain from this, and, frankly, nothing to lose," he said. "I am here to save lives but I need your help."

"And I need something to convince my government that you are telling the truth," Chan said. He, too, was sincere. And concerned. "You must give me information, a way to convince them."

"They're coming to drag me out of here," Bryan told him. "That should convince you."

"That could be a performance," Chan replied.

Bryan's mouth tightened. He thought for a moment. "I can't tell you more than that. But let me ask you: what do *you* think you saw?" The major snapped a thumb toward the notepad on the desk.

Chan shook his head. "An aircraft the likes of which I've never seen."

The door opened again. An officer stepped in, along with four servicemen. The big, balding officer did not seem pleased. He was gesturing toward the door and shouted the same phrase repeatedly: "Get off my base."

Major Bryan walked toward the door where the servicemen were standing. He paused and looked back at Chan. "If your fellow pilots intercept before we do, they will die. Save them," he said, the interpreter translating before he, too, was ordered from the room.

The door shut. The room seemed much quieter than it had before.

Chan sat in the chair and looked at his notes. He wasn't sure he believed the major. Perhaps the PLAAF *could* shoot the jet down. That would be a reason to lie. The American jet might only be effective against one aircraft at a time. The Air Force might need time to bring it back, time a Chinese attack wouldn't provide. It was likely, in any case, that the aircraft was a test plane that the Americans didn't want anyone to see. That would explain the widespread lockdown. They might not want anyone else to observe the plane the way he had.

Or there was another possibility. Major Bryan might be telling the truth. Chinese pilots could die.

Happily, choosing the right one was not Chan's responsibility. He knocked on the door and the guard opened it partway. Using his hand to signify a telephone, Chan asked if he could use it again. The guard held up a finger and slipped the radio from his equipment belt. Hopefully, the translator would return and ask who would be receiving the call. Chan would tell Deputy Consul Jian exactly what the officer had told him, as well as the circumstances surrounding his visit.

Hopefully, Beijing would know what to do. But Chan also wanted to form an opinion about the right course of action. This, too, was surveillance and intelligence analysis. This, too, was a part of Chan's job. It reminded him that something he had thought just a few minutes ago worked both ways: *Let American intelligence scramble to figure out if* that *conversation had any relevance to national security.*

FOURTEEN

Miramar, California

The jet screamed skyward. Miramar tower informed Dr. Hathaway that they were two horizontal miles and just over two vertical miles outside the range of the Angel. The pilot informed the tower that he would maintain the vertical and angular differential beyond the reach of the Angel's radar. Since the Hawker could not fly much higher than the Angel's current altitude, the plan was to drop the LASER operatives in such a way as to ride the winds toward the target.

The radio communications were piped into the headsets all the passengers were wearing. Before takeoff, Hathaway had told the crew that if there were some new development he wanted their input immediately. He was a problem solver who, as he put it, "works with data, not instinct."

Typically, Lieutenant Woodstock Black's instincts were among the most reliable on the team, and she was as gung ho as every other LASER operative before a drill or mission. Every time out, her enthusiasm was only tempered by her specialty. Working with explosives had taught her that technique was often more valuable than muscle. LASER had gone into the Weddell Sea with bravado hardened by training. Fortunately, while courage got them to the collision site, it was the skills of select team members that saved lives.

In this situation, skill and fortitude would both be compromised by a high percentage of variables. Against the best efforts of the FAA, an aircraft might enter the ever-changing no-fly area. The winds might carry them off course, a real possibility with a high-altitude drop into a small target area that just happened to be moving. Then there were the problems of maneuvering outside the Angel itself. They would be using a buddy system, like mountain climbers. After landing on the aircraft, they would tether themselves together. The idea came to Major Cowan based on something he had seen during survival training in the Australian outback: a bolo being thrown around a high branch to carry a line up a tree. The two weighted ends made for a very secure base. In theory, the operatives could take a similar approach to the Angel by moving along opposite sides of the fuselage.

None of which would concern Black greatly if her team were experienced jumpers. They were not. Gabriel insisted that after navigating the thermal currents rising from the volcano, this would be relatively easy. Just longer. Black was not so sure, but the only alternative she could think of was to drop a radio-activated proximity bomb from the Hawker. The explosive would have to be a powerful one to take out an aircraft that size and Rear Admiral Parks was concerned that it might only damage the Angel, or be carried off by winds.

The Hawker climbed to its cruising altitude of fifteen thousand feet, flying at nearly 530 miles an hour. It would take almost two hours to overtake the Angel, staying out of its way and catching the currents they needed for the jump. The currents would actually lift them up before taking them down, which was something that hadn't happened over Hawaii.

Like the rest of the LASER Ops, Black used the time to rest. Being in a rapid-deployment unit meant a soldier could be sent anywhere at anytime, including the middle of the night. That meant learning to power nap. Otherwise a team member could be foggy, which endangered themselves, their comrades, and the mission. Black turned down the volume on the headset, leaned back in the leather seat—which was far more comfortable than the fold-down chairs, benches, and slings in which they usually rode—and quickly fell asleep. Conversely, the lieutenant was instantly alert when Gabriel announced an equipment check ten minutes prior to the jump; RDU soldiers also learned to wake up fast.

Black's concerns were banished as she focused on the checklist and the mission. The parachutes were ready, the breathing apparatus was working, the headsets came off and the helmets went on. The team went to the hatch, crouching beneath the low, curving ceiling. Thirty seconds before the jump Hathaway would put the Hawker on autopilot so he could work the door.

Gabriel did his onward-and-upward best to motivate the other three team members. It was more his positive tone than anything he actually said or did. If anyone had the "cred" for that job it was Gabriel. He had pulled several asses from the ice water during their last mission, using little more than willpower to do it.

Black was second-to-last in the jump order; Gabriel was first. The jump time was calculated with the help of up-to-the-second reports from Naval Pacific Oceanography and Meteorology Center in Pearl Harbor. The weather-watchers were using three types of SPAZIs—satellite pan-and-zoom images—to chart the wind patterns: visible images, infrared images, and water-vapor images. When combined, the pictures provided what was called a MR. SID composite: a multiresolution satellite image display showing detailed wind patterns at present and over the next hour. It incorporated the movement of clouds, airborne particles that showed up as blue spots in the warmer surrounding air currents, and temperature variations that could be extrapolated into upcoming changes in the wind patterns. Gabriel had been briefed on the patterns at different elevations and would be leading the other jumpers. He would be using a wrist-worn computer linked to the Pearl's meteorological systems computer. The MSC would tell him whether he was too high, too low, or off course to reach the target.

"We deploy eighty seconds after deplaning," Gabriel said. "The first ten minutes or so after that will be like a slow-motion roller coaster. There'll be ups and downs as we ride the San Carlos easterly wave to Angel intercept. All you need to do is ride the current until it's time to bail."

He made it sound easy. Which was the point of saying it.

The next few minutes passed quickly, ticked away by the lieutenant's increasingly more rapid heartbeat. When Hathaway slipped from the small cockpit to open the hatch, Black was ready. He was wearing a flight suit, an oxygen mask, and a parachute—though the last thing he wanted to do now was go tumbling out the door. Rear Admiral Parks wanted Hathaway to continue to shadow the Angel. If this didn't work, he would be in a position to intercept the Chinese fighters. Not as a combatant, but to show them what would happen to their aircraft if they continued toward the Angel. It hadn't worked with the JF-17 but it might work with them.

The LASER team had tightly buckled all the seat belts. The opening of the hatch was followed by a punch of air that made their suits flutter but caused no other disturbance in the cabin. Moments later Captain Gabriel extended an index finger and thumb and cocked them toward the hatch, like a gun. One after another the team members stepped into the sharp blue morning.

The LASER ops dropped spread eagle, making small navigational adjustments by moving one outstretched arm or the other to turn the body. Black's ROTC instructors at UC Berkeley used to say that parachute jumping was just like flying.

They were wrong. It was just like falling with a hint of lift. The truth was, a jumper did not feel like Superman slashing through the clouds. What he felt was the inexorable pull of gravity, despite the fleecy substance of the vast atmospheric cushion through which he was dropping. Black felt the added pull against her chest, which had air tanks in front and the chute in back. She felt the strain most in her neck, which was not only supporting her head but the heavy padded helmet with built-in com-link and breathing apparatus. She had to make sure she held her head as level as possible as the air rushed past, to minimize the strain. The lieutenant wondered if this was what water surfing was like, trying to read subtle changes in the waves with your body. Only in this case she was riding air currents with her head.

The rush of the air was too loud for the jumpers to hear anything through their headsets. Five seconds before he opened his chute, Captain Gabriel released a burst of red smoke. The others saw it and prepared to pull their rip cords. When Gabriel opened his chute, the others followed. Black felt the hard tug of the harness just below her armpits as the shroud deployed, turning the thick air back into its more familiar wispy state. It immediately grew quiet as well, and Gabe ran a com check. It would be at least two minutes before they had any chance of spotting the Angel. The plane would be coming at them from behind and below, and they all watched in that direction.

The descent was as undulating as Black had expected. She felt somewhat helpless with her legs hanging useless below her. Nonmilitary paragliders used seats, which no doubt mitigated that sense of vulnerability and were surely more comfortable than just a snug harness with foam padding under the legs and none around the chest.

Though the jumpers continued to drop, their track was often more horizontal than vertical as the currents moved them along. She thought of the canopies as lily pads rushing down a river; or maybe that was the high oxygen content of her life support talking. Whatever they were, Black believed that the air waves would carry them where they needed to go. Whether the team could sufficiently fine-tune the descent for any of them to get onto the aircraft was a much different matter. Black decided that she might actually enjoy doing this recreationally, without a war hanging on what they did or did not accomplish.

They drifted for several minutes before anyone spoke. The voice belonged to Sergeant Major Cowan.

"I've got it!" he said. "Nine o'clock from due north, heading west."

Black looked to the left. She saw what had been described to her: the distinctive silvery contrail of the nitrogen-burning engine and a dagger-like glint of ivory well in front. "I see her, too," Black said.

The other two also saw it. Gabe told them to tug on the shroud lines to reduce the lift of their chutes. This seemed to be an extremely imprecise way of approaching the aircraft but Black did as he ordered. She wrapped her gloved fingers around the straps swinging beside her helmet. These were attached deep V-shaped nylon suspenders that rose from the harness. The lines themselves rose from these, each one rising to one of the cells that made up the shroud. From the center, each of the fabric panels was smaller than the one before it, which gave the rectangular chute its aerodynamic shape. She pulled tentatively, as though it were a kite string. The rate of ascent quickened as the oblong paraglide canopies sagged even deeper at the edges. The lieutenant continued to pull, releasing just a little to get the feel of controlling the lines before pulling down again.

"If it looks like we're going to beat it to the rendezvous point, we'll have to let up on the lines slightly to slow down," Gabe told them. "We're going to have to eyeball the target and 'feel' our descent."

That isn't a hell of a solid instruction, Black acknowledged privately. But then she remembered something one of her instructors once said about learning about combat from classroom lectures. *"By reducing everything to sound we make it damn near meaningless."* Soldiers—all people—had to experience things before they could truly be understood.

Lieutenant Black was getting that experiential, on-the-job training now. Though a little simulator time would have been nice, a few fake jumps along a drop line strung from a

high tower to the ground or some time in a wind tunnel. This
mini-glider was not like the parachutes Black had used before. The user was not more or less a plumb, he was a pilot.
One who had to make decisions very, very quickly. And
permanently, because there was no engine to bring him
around for a second try.

The twin solar panels of the Angel sent up two beams of
reflected sunlight. The aircraft was aptly named: wings that
moved and a pair of avenging swords. She would have to ask
Hathaway which came first, the designation or the design.
Whichever it was, the Angel was getting larger, faster.

"Black, Galvez, I want you to slow till Cowan and I are
about twice the distance from you that we are now," Gabriel
said. "Then do the same to each other. Cowan and I will try
to come at the Angel from the front, you two from the rear.
Hopefully, all of us won't undershoot or overshoot her. Acknowledge."

They did.

Lieutenant Black relaxed her pull on the cords. That allowed the edges of the chute to rise slightly and carried her
with it. When the four jumpers were arrayed in a diagonal
line they returned to their original fall rate. It had been a surprisingly simple and effective maneuver. Perhaps decep-
tively simple. Black did not imagine the final approach
would be as easy.

It wasn't.

The winds, which had been so cooperative to this point,
began working against them. It didn't carry them off course,
but it did rock them from side to side, which made it difficult
to stay aligned. When they were about five or six hundred
feet above the aircraft, trying to coordinate their approach
using the contrail as a baseline, Gabe finally gave the command Black had been expecting.

"Breakout!" he cried.

It was every jumper for himself. There was no other
choice; the four LASER operatives couldn't maintain the

diagonal phalanx and also fine-tune their descent. And it wasn't just a matter of reaching the Angel. They had to make certain they didn't interfere with one another.

The aircraft seemed to be moving faster and faster, an illusion created by their mutual approach. Black found herself tugging the cords involuntarily as she tried to keep her feet lined up with the two solar panels. The dark rectangles were too far apart for her to land on, of course, but they gave the Angel breadth. There was a surface below, not just a point in space. But staying on course was just one of the challenges. The Angel did not have many projections, and it was important that they land beside one of them: an antenna, the handle to an exterior access panel, a piece of the tail section, or one of the vapor vents near the wing joint. Once there, they had to find a way to attach a tether and get to the midsection of the aircraft. There they would find handles that would allow them to open one of the two topside hatches. The latches were set in shallow wells to reduce external surfaces that might slow the plane.

Black did not allow herself to be distracted by "what comes next." First she had to hit the aircraft. With luck, two or more of them would make it and they'd be able to help each other.

There was a "commit point" in a jump like this, a point when the jumper was too close to make any serious course corrections and had to go in as-is. Black reached that point about two hundred diagonal feet from the Angel. She focused solely on her target area, a spot just between the starboard side solar panel and the wing, which was roughly ten feet in front of the panel. She had selected it based on her drift and the fact that there was a small auxiliary radar dome she could grab, about the size and shape of a child's pail. It was also well clear of the other jumpers. Gabriel and Cowan were well to the front and Galvez had drifted toward the rear. Each of the LASER Ops announced their targets as they neared.

The winds would be unforgiving up there; once the lieutenant was down and had jettisoned the glider, staying on the

Angel would depend on getting hooked up as quickly as possible.

As the fuselage grew, so did the high whistle of the Angel's engines. The aircraft was a beautiful creation, and Black was hoping it wouldn't be necessary to destroy it. All she had to do was blow one of the critical seams along either wing or the tail section and the plane would drop into the sea. Before detonating, the team would deplane using their backup chutes. These were standard shrouds, nominally maneuverable. Hathaway would circle at a safe distance until the Angel was destroyed. Then he would descend and serve as a spotter for the rescue ship.

The ivory-smooth surface of the ship was just a dozen or so yards away. The nose section passed beneath her, then the wings. Then it was just feet away. Black was pretty much on-target and stopped trying to nudge her descent. She put her right hand on the shroud release and freed her left hand. She was going to have to get a grip on the dome before releasing the paraglider; if she couldn't hold on she was to get clear of the aircraft and continue her descent.

The lieutenant hit the fuselage with a skidding twist that left her facing the tail section. Her legs stung from heel to thigh when she hit; they had stiffened in the cold air, just hanging below her with nothing to do. Her paraglider tugged her forward, which happened to be the direction she wanted to go. If the canopy had pulled her back, her plan was to try and grab the tail fin. Fortunately, that wouldn't be necessary. She hooked her elbow around the outcrop and hugged her body to it while simultaneously releasing the parachute.

The wind was yanking it toward the aft port side, so there was no chance it would hit the others if they had managed to land on the aircraft. The lines released with a very faint *pop* and the chute darted across the sky like a jellyfish.

Lieutenant Black reached into her equipment belt for the tether. It was attached to her waist by an eyehook. The other end had been fitted with a fast-bolt. It was a three-inch screw with a suction tip and a splaying arrowhead at the other end.

After the tip was applied to a surface, the user pressed a button on the other end. That ignited a small charge that drove the anchor in. Black attached herself to the skin of the Angel, not the dome, lest she damage the radar unit inside. As soon as she was secure she raised her head. Neither Gabe nor Cowan was visible, on the fuselage or on the wings.

"This is Gabe—Cowan and I missed!" the captain shouted a moment later. "Black, Galvez, are you onboard?"

"I'm secured to a small dome aft the wings," she said.

There was no answer from Galvez.

"Ensign?" Gabe said. "Report!"

"I'm fuckin' *stuck*!" Galvez complained.

Tucking her chin into her shoulder for support, Black turned her head back into the fierce, driving wind. She saw the ensign, his paraglider draped over the tail fin, the wind pressing it so tight that the structure's narrow profile was clearly visible beneath the fabric. The ensign himself was just above the sweeping wing, his feet a few inches above its scalloped surface. He was obviously trying to get a toehold so he could grab the tail fin and pull himself onboard.

"Ensign, release!" Black said.

He continued to struggle. The wind was pushing him back, making it difficult for him to remain vertical, let alone reach the plane. She could see what he could not: that his shroud was starting to tear on the cutting edge of the tail fin. If it ripped and he fell away, still attached to the lines, they could wrap around him and snarl the deployment of his backup chute.

"Release!" she shouted. "That's an order!"

He obeyed, falling away quickly. The chute continued to flutter around the tail structure, the lines blown taut behind it by the wind. Lieutenant Black turned forward again. She could see the hatch she needed to reach. It was less than fifteen feet in front of her. She reached into her equipment belt for her claws, mittens that fit over the flight suit gloves she was wearing. The underside was lined with small, pointed studs. They had been developed for the Army Rangers to facilitate rope climbing and would help her to grip the surface of the jet.

"Lieutenant Black, this is Parks. What's your situation?"

She told him. She also heard a clanking noise coming from somewhere under the aircraft.

"Can you reach the hatch?" Parks asked.

"I think so," she said.

"Lieutenant, this is General Scott. Would you feel more comfortable blowing the thing up?"

"Negative, sir. I would like to try and save her," Black replied.

"It's your call," Scott reminded her.

"Sirs, I'm hearing a noise from under the aircraft," Black said. "It could be the wheel well that Major Bryant—"

Suddenly, Lieutenant Black felt as if she were in a shooting gallery. Small pieces of metal were whizzing by, mostly irregular pieces as far as she could tell. When she realized where they were coming from and what they probably were, she just hugged the surface of the jet and covered her head with her arms.

FIFTEEN

Norco, California

"Lieutenant Black?"

Scott listened in silence as the rear admiral tried to raise her. LASER radio operator Corporal Jefferson Emens had joined the general and Parks in the bunker. The young Army technician was manually adjusting the HF transceiver's internal antenna tuner, attempting to straddle the lieutenant's frequency in the event it had strayed. He said that the Angel's own antennae could be interfering with the signal. He used a dampener to kill that one-way frequency.

That wasn't the problem.

The empty air was a miserable sound. The general was beginning to wonder if anything was going to go right in this mission. He hadn't really expected to place all four LASER Ops on the aircraft, though he had hoped to get two of them up there. That way they could help each other.

"I'm here," she said.

"What's happening?" Parks asked.

"It looks like the turret assembly!" she replied. "The wind pressure pushing more pieces off—shooting back this way."

Something else we hadn't considered, Scott thought. *One more miss added to too many misses.*

"Is it a steady barrage?" Parks asked.

"Intermittent," the officer replied. "But I'm afraid to stick my head up—they're like bullets."

"Are you secure where you are?" Scott asked.

"I'm attached to the plane, sir, if that's what you mean," she said. "And the shrapnel isn't arcing this low. But I think I have a different problem."

"What's that?" Parks asked.

"I'm checking now—"

This silence was worse than the last one.

"Sirs, I've got a hole in my backup chute pack," the lieutenant informed them.

Her tone was professional, matter-of-fact. The general felt as though he'd been clubbed on the back of the neck. His mind went flat and his chest felt as though it were a dead, solid mass. He could barely draw breath.

"I can't take off my glove to check, but it looks like it's gone all the way through to the shroud," she went on.

"Is there any way you can make it to the hatch?" Parks asked.

"Not at the moment, sir," she said.

"Hold your position," Parks said. "We'll advise." The rear admiral punched the mute button and regarded Scott.

"She's got to get to the hatch," the general said.

"How?" Parks asked.

"I don't know. But I'm not going to lose her," Scott said. He knew that hope put into words was not "a plan." And that was what they needed.

A light on the radio flashed and Emens switched to a second channel. Both officers listened. It was Miramar. They had been told to watch the area for the two Navy jets and for any intruders.

"We've picked up the Chinese aircraft," tower supervisor Sergeant Sandra Ocean informed them. "At current rate, our planes and theirs will intercept in less than two hours."

"This just keeps getting better," Parks said.

The rear admiral went back on the radio to see if Black's situation had changed. It had. It had gotten worse. When the

turret came apart, it struck other sections of the fuselage.
Wind friction was peeling those off as well, in small bullet-
size chunks. The impact had not been sufficient to damage any
of the aircraft's electronics, just the outer skin, which was designed to protect the internal workings from debris belonging
to a plane or missile that might be destroyed near to the Angel.

That has to be the most ironic thing of all, Scott thought.
The goddamn thing was working perfectly. Scott was drained
and he was out of ideas. He called Bryan on his cell phone,
hoping the major might have some thoughts.

He had more bad news.

"They've got me under guard," Bryan said. "That thing
you hoped I could do, insert myself between the Chinese and
their mission: it didn't work."

"What do you mean?"

"We met with Deputy Consul Jian," Bryan told him.
"General Backer managed to piss him off all kinds of ways.
Maybe he was getting his marching orders from the DoD, I
don't know. Anyway, when I left the meeting I decided to
see the pilot, Chan, and get the good word to him."

"Did you?"

"Yes, but Backer didn't like that. He sent me here with a
babysitter. That's what makes me think that someone in
D.C. wants this confrontation with China. Take a sad song
and make it better."

"Possibly," Scott admitted.

"What's happening on your end?"

Scott told him.

"You don't know how bad the tear is?" Bryan asked.

"Not yet."

"The chute might survive a low-level jump without rip-
ping further," Bryan suggested.

"We are fresh out of ways to get the Angel to a lower
altitude."

"The Chinese may do that for us, sir," Bryan said.

"I hope it doesn't come to that," the general told him.
Though that was ironic, too: Black would probably be safe

atop the Angel. "Do you want me to get you out of there, Major?"

"Not yet," Bryan said. "Chan may decide he wants to talk to me. If he does, I want to be here."

"Good idea."

Parks was listening to another radio channel. He interrupted to tell General Scott that the rescue boat may have spotted Gabriel and Cowan and were still searching for Galvez. That was something, at least.

"Sir, where are they exactly?" Bryan asked.

"The Angel and Lieutenant Black?"

"Yes."

He looked to his right, to the computer with the geodesic display. "They are at longitude 141 degrees, just north of the Tropic of Cancer—"

"So they're more than halfway to Hawaii."

"Above and east, but yes. Why?"

"We've got resources there, sir," Bryan said.

"To do what?" Scott asked. "Engage the Chinese before they get close to the Angel? Secretary Whittle will never allow that."

"I don't mean the Navy," Bryan said. "I mean LASER."

Scott had to think for a moment to figure out what Bryan meant. "You're talking about Kowalski?"

"He's a structural engineer, sir," Bryan said. "He's pretty creative. He may have some thoughts about that damn thing coming apart up there, maybe some ideas on how Black can protect herself."

"I'll call him now," Scott said. The general hung up and called Moses Houston. Scott wasn't convinced that the army engineer could help. But talking to him surely couldn't hurt. The medic said that he had just gotten off the phone with the hospital and that Sergeant Kowalski was doing pretty well.

"Is there a particular reason you're asking, sir?" the medic inquired.

"I've got an engineering problem," Scott replied.

The general got the room number from Houston. He called Kowalski. The sergeant was watching television.

"I'm really glad you called, sir," the sergeant said.

"Why?"

"Because I've got a feeling CNN isn't giving me the whole story about this lockdown," Kowalski replied.

"What are they saying?" Scott asked. He hadn't even considered the impact this was having outside the theater of operations.

"Word is we were testing a new weapons system and the Chinese took advantage of the big wave to have a look," Kowalski said

"That's closer to the truth than I expected," Scott told him. He explained briefly about the Angel and about Lieutenant Black's situation.

"Shit, sir," Kowalski said when he had finished.

"That's a pretty good summation," Scott agreed. "What's your gut say?"

"That until the Chinese arrive, or parts stop coming off the aircraft, it sounds as though the lieutenant is safer where she is."

"Do you think there's a chance the aircraft will stop shedding?"

"Not for a while, sir, given the damage you described," Kowalski said. "My only frame of reference are airplanes that have taken flack. There's a lot of hardware in a wing. Planes that get hit there, assuming the strike isn't fatal, can spit aileron gears, struts, wing sleeve and rivets as long as they're airborne. The wind pressure just peels 'em back like a banana skin. And the damage tends to be exponential. The more the wings shed pieces, the more of the fuselage they hit, the more junk gets knocked off."

"If that's true—"

" 'No-active is pro-active,' as one of my instructors used to say about volatile structural situations," Kowalski said. "Is there any chance the lieutenant's chute might survive a low-altitude jump?"

"We just don't know how badly her chute may be damaged," the general said. "If the hole is small there's a good chance it will get her down. The biggest danger is the rushing air tearing through and making it larger."

"I don't suppose there's any way the lieutenant can get to the gun turrets," Kowalski said.

"To disable them?"

"To jam them somehow, to stop the vapor from getting in," Kowalski said.

"I don't know," Scott said. "She would still have the problem of getting there with pieces of plane being spit out."

"True. I'm just thinking it's too bad she can't get anywhere near the turret mechanism."

"Why?"

"Because there have to be some kind of sensors onboard to change the chemical intake of the bullets depending on altitude."

"Why wouldn't one size fit all?" Scott asked.

"I imagine it does. You create a bullet that is designed to reach the farthest target against the most air friction at the hottest time of day," Kowalski said. "One that'll be just as effective against targets that are closer when there's no sun. What I mean, though, is that the higher the plane flies, the less water vapor is available and the harder it has to suck—to put it simply."

"Like a straw when you reach the bottom of the container."

"Exactly, sir. If the lieutenant could get there she could just shut off the water intake or the freezing mechanism. The guns would fire blanks or spit water, not ice projectiles."

"Heat," Scott said suddenly.

"Sir?"

"Hold on, Sergeant," Scott said. The general put Kowalski on hold and asked Emens to get Hathaway on the radio.

Parks looked over. "Did your man have an idea?"

"If we neutralize the bullets, we can stop the Angel," he said.

Hathaway came on at once. "What is it, General?"

"Dr. Hathaway, how intense would a heat source have to be to melt the Angel's projectiles?"

"At the point of discharge or over the course of—"

"As they emerge from the gun barrel."

"Roughly one hundred and fifty degrees centigrade," the scientist told him.

"What would that do to the aircraft?"

"If it were a sunburst, probably nothing. But that would only affect a short stretch of the volley."

"What are you thinking, General?" Parks asked.

"What is the heat near the surface of a volcano, Dr. Hathaway?" Scott pressed.

"About twelve hundred degrees centigrade," Hathaway said. "What is this about?"

"A game of tag," Scott admitted, "and you're 'it.'"

SIXTEEN

Edwards Air Force Base, California

After ten months and several close calls, Thomas Bryan thought he knew his teammates really well. That was especially true of his commanding officer. Within the parameters of this nonconventional team, Scott was a conservative leader. His thinking tended to be along traditional military lines, his ideas rooted in practical operations and rational logistics.

Not this time.

Scott called Bryan to join in a conference call with Parks and Hathaway. He wanted to discuss a half-formed plan that might turn the Angel away from the Chinese aircraft and buy them time. It was not only partly formed, it was the impractical notion of a tired mind.

"We can use the Hawker to draw the Angel toward Waianae," Scott said. He was speaking slowly, as though reevaluating each word as he said it. "Dr. Hathaway can draw the Angel in along a very low flight path, one that will also allow Lieutenant Black to jump with some hope of landing safely. If the approach can be timed correctly, the Hawker will come within firing range when the Angel is passing over the caldera. The heat from the volcano will melt the projectiles and Dr. Hathaway will have a chance to pull away."

"General, do you realize how many opportunities there are for that plan to go south?" Hathaway asked.

"Yes, but you said the magic word. 'Plan.' It's the only one we've got."

"I can't argue with that," Hathaway said.

The men were silent for a moment.

"There won't be any kind of wiggle room," Parks said. "And once Lieutenant Black bails, and the Chinese turn around, we still have the problem of how to stop the Angel."

"We'll also have one thing we're extremely short of right now," Scott said. "Time."

"General, I'm not even sure the Hawker can outrace the Angel," Hathaway added. "The passage over the volcano's radiant zone will give me maybe a minute. After that the projectiles will become active again."

"I'm also not so certain the Chinese will turn around until they've had a look at the bird, by which time it will be too late," Bryan contributed. "The deputy consul was determined to swing a Chinese dick around the Pacific."

There was a heavier and very unhappy silence.

"I still think there's something to this plan," Scott said defensively.

The silence returned, but Bryan ignored the discomfort that rode the dusty airwaves. He used the silence to run variations on General Scott's original idea. One of them got him thinking.

"I have a thought," Bryan said. "It's not quite as clean as what the general suggested but it may put this entire thing to bed. General, how is Sergeant Kowalski?"

"Much better."

"Why?" Parks persisted.

"We can work the general's plan to a point," Bryan said. "Dr. Hathaway draws the Angel in low, but it doesn't come out again to put him at risk. Sergeant Kowalski knows that terrain. We put him up there with a rocket launcher. When the disarmed Angel passes overhead, he takes it out."

The group became very silent again. This time, the major wasn't even sure he heard static.

"What about it, Dr. Hathaway?" Parks asked. "Could a single RPG bring the Angel down?" The rear admiral's voice sounded hopeful.

"If he hit the Angel along one of the wing seams, that would create extreme aerodynamic instability, at least," Hathaway told them. "At best, it would take the wing itself off. Either way, the plane would come down."

"Not the way we had hoped," Parks said.

"I think we're beyond that now," Scott said.

"Sir, knocking it from the sky is the only thing that's going to send the Chinese planes back to Shanghai," Bryan pointed out.

"A squadron out of Pearl could turn them around," Parks observed. "That's what the DoD will say."

"At a cost of lives," Bryan said.

"And a possible war with China, which I hope that no one in Washington is looking for," Scott added.

"If it can be made to look like Beijing's fault I'm afraid some folks there would welcome it," Parks said.

"Would you? Do we want to give it to them?" Scott asked.

Parks did not answer.

"There isn't just the large picture," Scott went on. "The major's plan would also give Lieutenant Black her best chance to get off that pony. We would let her know when the plane is at its lowest steady passage. She can jump then."

"I'm willing to give it a shot," Hathaway said. "But if we've going to do this I need to know soon. Otherwise, I'll have to set down at Pearl to refuel. That will allow the Angel to put a lot of distance between us. It will also give the Chinese a chance to reach her first and to get themselves chewed up."

More silence.

"Set it up," Parks said. "Dr. Hathaway, we'll crunch the

numbers here and let you know the exact heading and speed you'll need."

"I'll see about getting Sergeant Kowalski togged and ready," Scott said.

"There's something else we need to do, sir," Bryan said. "I'm assuming we can fly again, now that the Angel is out of range?"

"Technically we can," Parks said, "although we can't lift the lockdown yet—we don't want aircraft leaving this area and getting in our way."

"I understand. But I think we need to get Lieutenant Commander Chan and the interpreter over to NWAD as quickly as possible."

"Why?" Parks asked.

"The Chinese will go to what seems to us like unnatural lengths to save face. If we help them, we may be helping ourselves. Show a little trust. Through Chan, we can give the Chinese a close-up look at how things really work, how we're trying to defuse this thing. If for some reason we don't manage to get to the Angel before the Chinese, and they get shot all to hell, we have someone on-site who can attest to the fact that we were trying our damnedest to prevent that from happening."

"That could be useful," Parks agreed. "Good get, Major. I'll ask Secretary Whittle to have the prisoner reassigned."

Bryan didn't like the term "prisoner"—Chan wasn't a combatant and he hadn't been tried. But the major wasn't about to argue terminology, not when he had gotten what he wanted. Backer would probably spit fire but that, too, wasn't Bryan's concern. He wanted to make sure both of his teammates were as prepared as possible for what they had to do.

Lieutenant Black had to make as safe a jump as possible.

And injured Sergeant Kowalski had to make the shot of his life.

SEVENTEEN

Midway Island, the Pacific Ocean

The two light tankers that had followed the Chinese squadron turned back after the planes had been refueled. Unlike the JF-17, these planes would not land on the Brazilian aircraft carrier. They were to reconnoiter, to respond in kind if challenged, and to return to Shanghai.

Radar at Jiangwan and on a fishing vessel north of the Marshall Islands showed the two American aircraft still traveling west. The two squadrons, American and Chinese, were headed toward an encounter somewhere off the eastern coast of the Hawaiian Islands. The Chinese planes would not cross over the islands themselves and had no reason to turn around. In the event they were approached by aircraft from Pearl Harbor, their orders were clear. The plane that had shot down the JF-17 was over international waters now.

It would be pursued.

As Senior Captain Peter Shin had told his pilots when they departed, American air might was formidable, but Chinese resolve was no less heroic. Americans did things because they could; the Chinese because they were unafraid.

Lieutenant Commander Chan had begun a surveillance mission that both Shanghai and Beijing intended to finish. The nature of the aircraft Chan had seen was a mystery, but it would not remain so past this day.

Past this hour.

EIGHTEEN

Norco, California

In the military, especially in a crisis situation, the worst thing that can happen is for personnel to lack direction during the planning stage, to fumble through ideas because they are unsure or uncommitted to the goal. Life was best, morale at its strongest, when everyone had a task—however impossible the job itself might seem.

At the moment, each part of this operation—informally dubbed Clipped Wings by Major Bryan—was a separate, very difficult challenge.

The first was getting Secretary Whittle to have Chan released to NWAD. Edwards Air Force Base was not under his jurisdiction. That required the cooperation of Secretary of the Air Force Mark Adams, who had a reputation for being a hawk and a fierce individualist. Scott was glad that job had not fallen to him.

What Rear Admiral Parks had working for him was that Adams had expected, and coveted, the Joint Chairmanship that had gone to General Paul Ponce. If Ponce was for something, Adams was typically against it. That held firm in the matter of confronting the Chinese. There was also a practical aspect to that. If the Hawker launched out of Miramar resulted in the Chinese backing down, Ponce would get the credit. If the Chinese prevailed, Adams and his air force would get the blame. The secretary did not want to risk that, especially since the Angel was not his project.

He agreed to order General Backer to release Lieutenant Commander Chan to the custody of Major Tom Bryan.

Scott's own projects were less taxing diplomatically but more complex logistically. He had decided that Kowalski should not, could not, go up there alone. He was wearing a partial brace, limiting movement of his right knee. And since he had been in the hospital, under medication, he should not be responsible for taking the shot at the Angel. The general had requested a tactical unit out of Pearl. Captain "Windy" Chap-man was in charge of special operations teams and said he would pull together a 3AF/GB—an antiaircraft attack force, ground-based. Kowalski would go with them to help position the takedown. After that, it would be an all-Navy operation. Kowalski was up for the task when it was explained to him. He was more than up for it: he was eager to make up for the mishap the other morning.

"Are you sure your injuries won't get in the way?" Scott asked.

"I would tell you if I thought they would, sir. I'd ask you to leave it entirely up to Pearl."

"What about your focus?"

"My teammate's counting on me," Kowalski replied. "The goal doesn't get much sharper than that. Besides, sir. I'd go up that mountain just to get out of here."

"What kind of meds have they been giving you?" Scott asked. "Do you need to detox?"

"Sir, whatever's in this drip can be fixed right up by some black coffee. Let me do this. Please."

"You understand that you will be there in support of the Pearl team," Scott said. "You will help them with the mountain route and work as a liaison with this office."

"Yes, sir."

"You will let *me* know if you see a potential problem, if something seems wrong operationally or tactically."

"Yes, sir."

Scott was going to add, "*I mean it,*" but that was implicit in his tone. And if Kowalski didn't get that by now, he wouldn't get it at all. The general would make sure the 3AF commander understood. The competitiveness among the team members sometimes compelled them to do reckless things.

And so far to succeed at them, Scott had to admit. But the LASER Ops were typically in perfect health when they tried it.

Scott told Kowalski he would have Hudson arrange for the dismissal. When he was finished talking to the medic, Parks turned to him.

"I don't like the way the Chinese situation is shaping up," Parks said. The rear admiral was looking at the radar screen in the bunker. "They're going to be within range of the Angel before Hathaway can lure it over the volcano."

Scott looked at the radar image being transferred from Pearl. The triangular green blips were converging toward the coast of Oahu.

"They may go into our airspace again over this question of 'face,'" Scott said.

"Dare us to shoot down more of their aircraft, planes that are armed."

"Which the Angel will do, without hesitation," Parks said.

"How will the Angel react if it has dual targets? One from the north"—Scott pointed at the Chinese squadron—"and one in the south." He tapped the image of Hathaway's plane.

"It will take out the first one, then turn on the second," Parks said.

"Not whichever is nearer?"

"No," Parks told him. "The only time Angel will switch before target one is eliminated is if target two opens fire. But with multiple turrets, even with one missing, that may not be necessary. Angel can take on several targets at once."

"We need to get its attention before the Chinese planes do," Scott said.

"That means sending a jet out of Pearl or having Hathaway make himself a target before the Angel reaches the crater. Either way, one of them will be destroyed. And if those are the options, I'm leaning toward the hawks: if the Chinese want to get shot down, that's their prerogative."

"That's an ugly choice," Scott said.

"No argument, but we're not forcing them to do this—"

"We're also not giving Shanghai the data they need to make an informed decision."

"That isn't our job," Parks told him. "Their 17 entered our airspace uninvited, and refused to depart when warned. So much of what's happened has been a result of that, including the loss of an extremely costly QUAV. Now you want to sacrifice a Hawker or a fighter to pull the Angel off their radar? I consider that very 'above and beyond.'" The rear admiral shook his head slowly. Now he looked as angry as he sounded, hours of frustration being released. "They took advantage of a natural disaster. I'm not feeling sorry for them, General."

"It isn't a question of sympathy, but of containment," Scott replied. "If we lose control of this situation there are going to be a lot of conversations like this, high-level ones, where the stakes will be considerably higher."

"What do you recommend?"

"We need to tell them what the situation is and what we intend to do about it."

"Tell the Chinese about the Angel?"

"They're going to find out soon enough," Scott said.

Parks shook his head. "Whittle will never allow it."

"He'll never allow *you*," Scott corrected him.

"And he shouldn't." He was still shaking his head. "I don't like it, either. I agreed to allow the Chinese pilot to come to NWAD to add his voice to the cause if necessary. Not to add intelligence to the Chinese database."

"I'm not saying we lay it all out for them. Just enough. The Chinese pilot is on his way here. Let's add a little to what he already knows, what he already saw. Let him tell the officers in Shanghai to give us a little time. That's all we need: just a little. Then they'll see the Angel disappear from their radar, feel they've triumphed, and we avert a showdown."

"Are we pursuing the national policy of the United States or that of General Benjamin Scott?"

Scott couldn't tell whether the rear admiral's brusqueness was more frustration or a response to that suggestion in particular. "Do you know something I don't?" the general asked. "Are we pushing for a showdown?"

"I don't know."

"I'm beginning to think you do—"

"No," Parks insisted. "But I do know I don't have orders to undertake what you're describing. I also know I won't get them, either."

"Because . . . ?"

"There isn't time!" Parks shouted. He took a moment to calm himself. "I can't take this to the president. And you know that someone or other, some member of the Joint Chiefs, will filibuster until it's too late for anyone to act. They have access to the same information we do. They have to be watching this, waiting to see how it plays out."

"We know how it'll play out," Scott said. "I'm not urging you to act on your own, just to step aside and let me do this."

"That decision is way above my pay grade," Parks said.

"It's not a decision. It's indecision," Scott said. Kowalski's comment about "no-active being pro-active" came to mind. He was right. Doing nothing could force a showdown. "What you call it doesn't change the facts, General. We are being allowed to try and take out the Angel using a plan you suggested. What the Chinese do is entirely up to them." Scott looked back at the radar. "Unless something happens to turn them around, the Angel is going to scan these planes before it reads the Hawker, turn around, and shoot the squadron down in international airspace."

"I'm sure the Joint Chiefs are aware of that."

"Are you aware of who will take the fall for that? The guy who was in charge of the program. Think about it, Rear Admiral. Ponce and his allies get what they want: the Chinese get their noses bloodied by our new weapon, and they have someone to take the fall. The guy who was in charge of the project."

"You're making a big assumption, General."

"I don't believe that. And I don't think *you* believe that."

The thumping sound of a helicopter could be heard, low and rising, beyond the thick walls. That would be Bryan and Chan arriving from Edwards. The guards had orders to take Chan to the guest room as soon as they arrived and to remain outside the door.

"Who do you think is going to be hit when the hearings and investigations start?" Scott asked. He pointed at Parks. "You. Oliver North. Congress will want Whittle's head and maybe they'll get it. But the secretary will certainly give them yours. Your actions now will be your defense."

"I know my situation, General. If I bring the pilot in, that'll top the list of punishable offenses with treason."

"No one's going to hang you for saving lives. If they try I'll tell them it was my idea. Hell, I'll call Ponce now."

Scott looked at the radar screen. They had less than fifteen minutes to make this happen or the Angel would see the Chinese squadron. Over Parks's shoulder, the general saw Corporal Emens quietly scrolling through the NWAD database of broadcast frequencies. The radio operator was probably looking for the PLAAF air command in Shanghai.

Just in case.

The helicopter landed. They could feel the beating waves against the wall. Parks was looking at the radar screen.

"Rear Admiral, I have one more question for you," Scott said. "Would you be okay with the scenario that's about to play out—would anyone dare to authorize it—if we had control over the Angel?"

Parks thought for a moment. "I can't say they would."

"So if Lieutenant Black can get inside, none of this will happen."

"Probably not."

"I'm going to give her the order to try," Scott said.

Parks's eyes shifted to the general. "No. You'll kill her. Anyway, there probably isn't time."

"If the Angel turns and ascends, Lieutenant Black will probably be swept off anyway," Scott said. "At that rate of acceleration and height, a chute with a hole will be ripped to pieces. And you're right. There may not be time. But this is the only order I've got left. It's also the only chance Black and the Chinese have of surviving. If we can't take control of the Angel, I am absolutely going to contribute my only resource to follow the original mission profile. Do you remember what that was?"

"A test of hardware," Parks muttered.

"Right. Not a deployment, a *test*. A test that the man in charge has every right to abort. It's your call."

Parks shook his head slowly. "How the hell did this get so out of control?"

"Tests sometimes do, but this one isn't that bad—yet," Scott reminded him. "Don't let Ponce or the Chinese dictate the agenda."

Parks punched the intercom to the guard shack. "This is Rear Admiral Parks. Escort the three chopper passengers to the command bunker at once, please."

"Yes, sir."

Parks regarded Scott. "They *are* going to dropkick me either way. At least it'll be for something I did instead of something I didn't do."

"I like that." Scott smiled.

NINETEEN

Norco, California

The bunker was crowded with people. Lieutenant Commander Chan did not know them. From their expressions, he wasn't sure he wanted to know them. The guard who had brought them here remained outside while Chan, Major Bryan, and the translator gathered around a man who was introduced as Rear Admiral Parks. Chan was making a run of high-ranking individuals today: another officer called General Benjamin Scott was sitting to the side like an ancient feudal lord, hopeful eyes set in a tolerant expression. He was the only one who did not seem agitated.

The rear admiral pointed to the radar screen and, through the interpreter, told Chan what they were attempting to do.

"As you know, we lost contact with our test aircraft after the tsunami," Parks said. "As you saw, the targeting mechanism is not responding to our commands. We are trying to destroy the aircraft before its radar spots your aircraft. Once that happens, we will not be able to prevent an attack."

"Your pilot cannot turn it away?" Chan asked.

"He cannot," Parks replied. "But we have a problem, Lieutenant Commander. You see your squadron approaching? They will reach it before we can accomplish our goal. If that happens they will all be destroyed. Not because we want that but because we are unable to prevent it—any more than we could save your 17."

Chan understood. He wasn't sure if he believed Parks, but he believed the eyes of General Scott. Not only did they lack panic, they lacked an aura of coercion. He trusted the facts, not the force or desperation with which they were delivered.

"I am not asking for your aircraft to be withdrawn," the rear admiral continued. "I am asking them to circle, to delay their approach while we deal with this problem. It is the same thing we asked of you and you saw what happened as a result of taking too long to decide."

Chan nodded.

"It's a matter of just a few minutes," Parks said. "Would you speak with your commanders, ask them to give us just fifteen minutes?"

"I don't know that they would listen to me," Chan said.

"I know they surely won't listen to me," Parks said. "Please." He pointed to the squadron blips. "You must know some or all of these pilots. You can save their lives for them. Try and buy us a little time."

Obviously, that was a request Chan could not ignore. He agreed to relay the information. The man at the radio handed him the headset and punched in a frequency. Chan was immediately placed in contact with the PLAAF Flight Dispatch Center. He identified himself and asked to speak with Captain Mok Chung. He did not feel comfortable going directly to Senior Captain Shin.

Chan explained the situation exactly as it had been explained to him.

"Is this conversation private?" Chung asked.

"I am the only one wearing headphones," he replied. The interpreter was not saying anything.

"Do you believe them?" Chung pressed.

"I have seen what this aircraft can do. I believe it can do it again."

"Do you believe *them*, Lieutenant Commander? Do you believe that they are helpless to turn the aircraft back?"

Chan once again looked at the faces of the men in the bunker. Identifying the meaning of a mask was something he had done since childhood. Understanding the structure behind it was not so simple. He could tell the Americans were anxious but he had seen anxious faces in the flight ready rooms in China. Sometimes pilots were concerned about a mission or their equipment. And sometimes they were concerned about impressing a superior. He did not know what this was.

"I cannot say, sir," Chan said. "If we give them the time they seek, we will know for certain."

"We may also give them time to target and destroy our squadron," Chung pointed out. "First-strike capacity is the biggest part of any engagement."

"Yes, sir."

"I will take it up with the senior captain," Chung said.

"May I tell them that?"

"Yes."

"I would add just one thing, sir," Chan said. "I am told that in a few minutes there will no longer be an opportunity to hold or reverse course."

"It was foolish of them to wait so long," Chung observed. "I will notify you on this frequency when I have word."

Chan handed the headset to the radio operator. He briefed the interpreter, who informed the men in the bunker.

Their faces went from anxious to angry.

Except for General Benjamin Scott.

He looked sad.

TWENTY

Oahu, Hawaii

Lieutenant Black was arm-weary and felt as though her head were inside a blender. The only thing she could hear was the wind, which was so loud it had started to hurt. She was cold, the perspiration she'd shed in the jump and subsequent efforts to secure herself having cooled inside her the high-altitude suit.

But there was good news, too. The turret and wing sections had stopped spitting pieces of metal, rubber, and plastic.

The radio had been on but because of the wind she had been unable to hear most of what was being said at NWAD.

"Sir, can you hear me?" she yelled. "You'll have to shout if you can."

"I hear you," Parks said.

"The situation up here seems to have stabilized," Black informed him. "I'd like to make a run at the hatch."

"Hold, please, Lieutenant."

That was strange. The rear admiral said it as if she were making a phone call to a switchboard. The lieutenant decided to start moving ahead, if for no other reason than she was stiff and cramped from being in one position. She remained tethered, the line playing out automatically as she moved.

"Lieutenant, this is General Scott. You are to prepare to abort."

"Repeat, sir?" She thought she had heard correctly. She just wanted to make sure. If she had, she wanted to try and talk him out of it.

"There is a Chinese squadron bearing down. The Angel will pursue. There isn't time to load the software."

"I'd like to try, General."

"Negative. You will jump at the command of the rear admiral."

She looked ahead at the hatch. "Sir, I can do this but I don't know if I can jump. I can't assess the damage to my pack." The Lieutenant pulled herself forward against the driving winds, pressing her iron-studded palms against the softer aluminum of the aircraft. If she ended up having to jump, she could just as easily do it from ten feet ahead as from where she had been.

"There isn't time," Scott repeated. "The chute is your best option—"

"Sir, if I'm inside, won't I be safe from the Chinese?"

"We need to destroy it, Lieutenant. The more so if it destroys the squadron. This is a political situation, too. Now here is the rear admiral. You will jump on his command. Understood?"

"Jump on command, yes, sir," Black said. *But I can reach the damn hatch,* she thought as she continued toward it. Until she received a new order, she was going to follow the old one.

And then it occurred to her. There was something else she could do.

"General!" she shouted. "Hold a second."

"That's about all we have."

"Sir, from my position I can't destroy the Angel with C-4. But I *can* hit one of the solar panels. What will happen if I take that out?"

"I honestly don't know—"

"More importantly, what will the Chinese do if they see

that? Will they understand that we're trying to stop this thing?"

"I don't know that, either," Scott said. Even through the howling winds she could hear the fresh enthusiasm in his voice. "But you stay put, Lieutenant. I'm going to find out."

"Stay put. Yes, sir."

There was a "good job" hidden in his voice. Black continued moving forward. As she did, she thought she saw a pinpoint of sunlight off to the right, to the west. She looked in that direction.

There were five pinpoints of light. And if she could see them, chances were good the Angel would soon see them, too. Quickly, she crawled to the nearby panel, then reached into her equipment pouch and withdrew the waxed paper–covered brick of explosives. She removed one of the gloves to peel off the wrapper, losing it in the wind. It didn't matter. She used her fingertips to press the plastic explosive into place along one corner of the door-size panel. When she was finished, she fished a detonator from another pouch. She removed the plastic casing on the tip and set the timer for ten seconds. It was the minimum setting. Time mattered, and that was all the time she would need, she hoped, to fall away.

She was trying to decide whether to just blow the panel and jump, on her own dubious authority as site commander, when the order came from Rear Admiral Parks.

"Lieutenant, you have a go to detonate!"

Black didn't bother repeating the order. She pushed the detonator into the C-4, jabbed the red button on the side of the timer, and let herself slide off the side of the Angel, spread-eagle.

Forgetting to release the tether.

TWENTY-ONE

Oahu, Hawaii

Hank Hathaway had been listening to the exchange between Lieutenant Black and the base. The scientist was bearing down hard on the Angel, pushing the Hawker to its limit while also keeping an eye on the radar. He didn't know if he could beat the Chinese squadron to the drone but he had to try. He did have one advantage: gravity was on his side.

The Hawker was screaming down at a sharp angle when he saw a small figure go over the side and slap against the undercarriage of the aircraft.

"NWAD, Black is snagged on the Angel—"

No sooner had he said it than the explosive spewed a brilliant orange oval that was quickly consumed by a cloud of gray.

Hathaway reported what he saw to base. There was a terrible silence on the other end.

"What about the Angel?" Parks finally asked.

"Can't tell," Hathaway replied.

The cloud had spread outward in all directions for a moment, propelled by the blast, until the forward motion of the Angel dragged it backward as a slender spearhead of smoke. "It's clearing a little—I can't see the lieutenant," Hathaway reported. "There's some scarring aft the starboard solar panel but the Angel looks like it took the hit. I'm guessing the Chinese have about thirty seconds, maybe a little more, until they're in range.

"Thank you," Parks said. "Continue on plan."

He did. But he continued to look along the starboard side, hoping to see the plume of a parachute somewhere below.

He searched, but without success.

TWENTY-TWO

Norco, California

There was no time to think, and no time to think about mourning. Major Bryan turned to Chan. The translator moved nearer.

"We tried to knock the jet down. You heard the explosion. We failed to do so. We need time. You're the only one who can get it."

Bryan all but died during the seconds it took to finish the translation. Chan didn't hesitate. Whether it was his expression or the tone of his voice, the Chinese pilot got back on the radio. From the sound of *his* voice and the look on his face, he was convinced of the sincerity of the Angel team. The silence was even worse as Chan waited for a response. The pilot had been staring ahead, listening intently, then looked at Bryan. He didn't say anything. If they had any time left it was only seconds. Emens's radio was set on Hathaway's channel.

"It looks like they're veering!" the scientist shouted. "I think the Chinese planes are turning off!"

A moment later, Chan spoke. As he talked the interpreter said, "Shanghai flight command says they saw an explosion. They will give you five minutes to report the termination of this flight."

A big, fat, fucking game to the end, Bryan thought. The Chinese called it "face" but Tom Bryan called it a sausage hang, a compare-your-dick-size exercise that made him wonder how anyone could doubt that human beings evolved from chest-thumping hominids.

"They're giving you five minutes, Doctor," Parks reported to the Hawker.

"I'm on it."

"Sergeant Kowalski, did you copy that?" the rear admiral asked.

"We did, Rear Admiral sir, and the Jeep is nearly at the crater," he said. "We're pushing to get there. This is not easy terrain."

"I can delay contact a little to give you time if you need it," Hathaway informed him.

"We'll let you know, Professor. Thanks."

Then there was the inevitable question. "Have either of you seen any sign of Lieutenant Black?" Parks asked.

Obviously, they would have said something if they had. It was the kind of question meant to prolong hope in the asking, not to satisfy it in the answering. Not surprisingly, both men replied in the negative, though, as Hathaway pointed out, neither was in a position to see her in any case. Parks contacted Pearl to make sure the scout ship that had gathered the other jumpers kept a diligent watch for the lieutenant.

Bryan refused to think pessimistically. He was actually grateful, and a little at peace, that they still had a chance to end this with the crisis defused. In a day where so much had gone so wrong, that was something.

TWENTY-THREE

Oahu, Hawaii

Bernie Kowalski felt like a kid again. Which wasn't necessarily a good thing.

Growing up near an oil field outside of Dallas, where his dad was a foreman, Kowalski learned to drive a pickup when he was thirteen. The sergeant never thought he would prefer jumping from a plane to get somewhere rather than ride in a ground-based vehicle. But that was absolutely the case as the two Jeeps hurried up the uneven, unpaved trail at speeds that would discomfit even a healthy backbone. Sharp, lumpy igneous rock was not a satisfactory riding surface. Kowalski couldn't just shut his eyes and ride it out; he had to pay attention to the road and its landmarks so he could direct the driver to where they needed to be.

As bad and as limpy as the thirty-year-old felt, he kept reminding himself that there was at least one person who would probably give anything to be in his situation: Lieutenant Black. Until now, his was the worst injury any of the LASER operatives had suffered. He hoped that was still the case.

At least the coffee had worked the way he said it would. Kowalski felt alert, and he had promised Moses Hudson that he would keep bottled water handy so he wouldn't dehydrate. As though a couple of ounces of Poland Spring would make a difference when he stood next to a sea of molten lava.

Kowalski was in the front passenger seat. Two SEALs were in the back, munitions experts who would be manning the two rocket launchers that were being uncrated and assembled in the second Jeep. Though it was unforgiving work, with small parts that had to be inserted and aligned, the SEALs had no option. The weapons needed to be ready when they arrived. According to General Scott, they wouldn't get a second chance at the rogue aircraft.

Though Waianae had quieted somewhat since its initial outburst, the volcano was still active. As the men ascended they were forced to put on breathing apparatus. The smoke wasn't as thick but the particles were smaller and more toxic; the lighter ejecta had gone higher into the atmosphere and the pieces that weren't carried away were taking longer to fall. They had to signal by hand. Now Kowalski really felt like he was back in the fields of Tulsa Holdings, with foul-smelling mist in the air—soot, not oil droplets—where you didn't open your mouth for fear of sucking any of that stuff in.

The ground was relatively quiet, though every now and then they got a good shaking that stirred things up on the roadside. There were no significant boulders here but there were large fields of rocks higher up. He hoped that none of those decided to come loose and block their passage.

All of this, and the mission, was on Kowalski's mind as they ascended. Though he had kept one of the radio earpieces in place for emergency messages from NWAD, all he could hear was his own breathing, the throaty cough of the engine, and the occasional rumble from somewhere below.

And then he heard something else. A faraway whine. He raised his left arm and motioned for the drivers to stop. Even that hurt, the sudden movement pulling on the bandages around his waist, bandages that were designed to restrict his movement, dislodge the medicated gauze on his butt, and help him heal. The guys on the oil fields used to use torn pieces of flannel shirt for that.

The whine was still there. It wasn't caused by a rock spit

from the volcano whizzing by. The sergeant sucked in a long breath, pulled off his mouthpiece, and swung around the microphone. "Rear Admiral, we can't see anything upstairs but I'm hearing something."

"I was just about to radio. That sound is Hathaway," Parks told him. "He's just flown into range of the Angel."

"Sir, I thought we were getting more time—"

"Hathaway doesn't have more time," Parks told him. "The Hawker's fuel situation is critical."

"How long does that give us?"

"The Angel should be overhead in approximately eight minutes."

Kowalski turned to the driver. "We've got to move it out, double-time!" he shouted.

The sergeant pulled the mask back over his face and was thrown back against the seat. They had to get above the thickest areas of smoke or they wouldn't be able to see the target. The only possible window of opportunity was along the caldera rim, where the smoke chugged upward and the heat of the lava kept the air rising, carrying the particulate matter with it.

Kowalski got back on the microphone for a moment. "Sir, are the Hawker and Angel subsonic?"

"Yes. Why?"

"I was hoping for a sonic boom. Thank you. Out."

The sergeant wasn't happy to hear that. He was hoping to hear something big as either aircraft neared, something to tell them that a drop-dead moment was upon them, that they had to fire upward and hope they hit something.

The ride got even worse over the wounded earth, but that seemed to matter less. Kowalski was listening to the oncoming Hawker. Because the Angel would be coming from behind, chances were good the Hawker would out-scream it. If they didn't see the drone they absolutely wouldn't know it was coming until too late. He looked back at the men with the M-72s LAWs, light antitank weapons. The grenade launchers were comprised of two tubes, one inside the other.

The outer tube housed the trigger, the arming handle, the front and rear sights, and the back-end cover to protect the man firing the weapon. The inner tube, which telescoped out in back, contained the firing pin assembly and detent lever— a device beneath the trigger assembly that locked the inner tube in the extended position and also cocked the weapon. When fired, the rocket would carry the 66mm warhead forward with insignificant recoil. As the warhead emerged, fins would pop from the base to stabilize the trajectory. Though the grenade was designed to use against grouped personnel, bunkers, and light armor, it would pack sufficient punch to crack the Angel's wing seam.

Provided we can see the bastard.

The Hawker was extremely loud now and the minicaravan was still only halfway to its destination nearly a mile above sea level. Kowalski was beginning to fear they wouldn't make the altitude or reach the window in time. General Scott had told him that the Angel had a nose light, but that wasn't going to help them target the wing seam from three or four thousand feet. These guys were good but not *that* good. They still had to eye-ball the target.

Kowalski pulled away his mouthpiece again. "Dr. Hathaway, this is the ground team—can you hear me?"

"Yes."

"Help. You know air inversion, the kind that forms a mushroom cloud in atom bomb tests?"

"A Fourier inversion?"

"If you say so, Doc. Can we create one of those in the volcanic smoke?"

"Possibly. If you detonate a high-explosive device in the air—"

"Yes or no. Will an RPG do it?" Kowalski asked.

"Yes, but there are variables," Hathaway told him. "You need to estimate the thickness of the smoke and multiply that by the blast radius."

"Okay. The grenade'll give us a five-meter fist," Kowalski said. "The cloud's about two, three meters thick."

"That's a ten-meter opening give or take, if you plant the grenade in the center of the cloud. The inversion will look like a doughnut in the surrounding region, with the smoke from the blast in the center."

"How long will it remain open?"

"Moments," Hathaway replied.

"Thank you. Out."

Kowalski looked back. The men were nearly finished assembling the launchers. It would take about one minute to load and site the weapons. They had two RPGs for each. "Moments" wouldn't give them enough time to fire both and reload. They'd have to fire one to punch a hole in the smoke, then send the other rocketing through it.

The sergeant took another hit of clean air as the Jeep rattled farther up the increasingly steep and winding path, then got back on the radio with Parks.

"Sir, did you hear that?"

"I did."

"We'll need a radar countdown to flyover," Kowalski said. He glanced at the GPS mounted between the seats. "We're at elevation 3971 feet, speed forty-five miles an hour."

"We can enter the data but if you slow down or speed up that will give you a plus-or-minus factor."

"I understand, sir. I doubt we'll be speeding up. We just need enough time to clear the air and I'm hoping you can give us that. Can we get a countdown from ninety seconds?"

"You'll have it," Parks said.

The Jeep held close to a consistent speed as Kowalski watched the GPS. When he was certain they wouldn't make the window on top of the volcanic peak, he punched up the map to determine the highest point they could reach on the western slope, one where the wind currents were steadiest. Data from the Pearl Harbor Meteorological Center suggested the edge of the Lualualei amphitheater valley. The highest point, with 360 degree visibility, was nearly three-quarters of a mile away. Kowalski informed NWAD of the change, then told the driver where to turn off the relatively wide path to an incline of glassy basalt that was somewhat smoother, an ancient flow that had hardened where it had been set down. Speed would not help them now, though the sergeant appreciated the slightly less lumpy ride. He was sure the SEALs holding the large, unwieldy M-72s across their laps were glad as well.

The whine of the Hawker had become a loud roaring, caught in the numerous valleys and thrown back as a multidirectional drone. It passed as they ascended, meaning that the next sound they heard would be the Angel in pursuit. When it came, the distant hum was unlike the sound of Hathaway's craft. There was something cleaner about the Angel. It reminded him more of the purr of a microwave oven than the chugging of a gas-powered generator.

"You've got about three minutes until the Angel is in your neighborhood," Parks informed him.

Kowalski acknowledged the update. Before it got too loud he went on the point-to-point radio to the other Jeep, told the tail-gunner to have his men set the new HD-4 grenades for a timed air-burst instead of concussion. The 'high dispersal' grenades created a central burst, surrounded by minicharges to send shrapnel as far as possible, as forcefully as possible.

Because this path was a natural formation in a dry, remote area there were no road-cuts, no structures or trees, no barriers other than low scrub on either side of them. Visibility was limited only by the haze, which was shifting less and less the higher they climbed. The temperature remained constant, around eighty degrees, controlled by the volcano and not by offshore winds. Perspiration kept Kowalski's bandages damp, alleviating some of the tug.

But the discomfort inside grew, the pressure of the responsibility that he had assumed. It wasn't doubt. Kowalski had helped cap wells and on two occasions had been there to assist in extinguishing blazes. He had been a member of LASER since its inception. Yet he had never had this kind of task, made a decision this important. As his dad used to say when they watched the Cowboys play on TV, *"A coach can be as confident as all get-out, but on any given Sunday . . ."*

"Closing on two minutes," Parks said.

Kowalski turned to the driver. "Let's stop here."

The Jeep snapped to a halt. His legs and ass thanked him. Kowalski was also glad that the Pearl guys weren't giving him grief about chain-of-command. Situations like this reminded him that there were professionals outside of LASER who cared less about ego than about the mission.

"Cut the engine," Kowalski said.

The driver did. The other driver did the same. Now there was nothing but the whisper of a soft wind and the fan-like hum from the oncoming Angel.

Kowalski motioned the men from the jeep. He went to the GPS and brought up a detailed view of the area. Then he got back on the wireless. "Sir, we are in grid 1-10 on map four. What's the Angel's heading?"

"She's coming from the northeast, just passing over grid—hold a second—grid 8-36, according to Mr. Emens."

Hathaway cut in. "She will cover one full grid every ten seconds, Sergeant. You better move it."

Kowalski pulled off the headphone. He needed both ears for this one. He eased from the car, scraping an injured leg on the Jeep, and snarled in pain as he limped toward the men with the launchers. They had just finished loading the grenades and were standing by the Jeep.

"Set up and fire the inversion shot ASAP," he said.

"Where?" one of the men asked through his oxygen mask.

"The highest angle you can get!" the sergeant snapped, jabbing a finger up. "Do it *now*!" Except for the adjustment he had made to the warhead there was nothing the soldier needed to do now except push the timer on the grenade. He stood the M-72 on its blast shield, pushed the timer, dropped to a knee away from the Jeep, and hoisted the weapon to his shoulder. The other soldier stood back several steps and

Kowalski did the same. It was instinctive; if the mechanism failed to launch for any reason, the few paces wouldn't protect them from the explosion.

But the rocket didn't fail. The grenade soared off with a very loud pop. The operator did not wait for the charge to detonate. He jumped to his feet, hurried to the ordnance locker in the back of the Jeep, and carefully retrieved a second rocket for immediate reload. Meanwhile, the other soldier knelt to take his shot. The next rockets would explode on impact with the Angel.

Assuming their target and the smoke cooperated.

The RPG exploded five seconds after launch. The boom echoed through the circular valley and thick, cottony gray clouds were flung from the ivory-white core. Kowalski was eager but calm as he watched the now-empty heart of the explosion suck ash toward it, clearing a ring around the center. But the calm vanished as the ring reached its maximum diameter, a thin wisp of clear air beneath the thick, unaffected layer of smoke above.

They couldn't see the sky above. The plan had failed. Kowalski's brain went into sift-mode, the place it visited before panic set in. The Texan had gone there since his school days, whenever he faced a test question he couldn't immediately answer or a baseball pitcher he was afraid to swing against, both of which would have earned him whuppings from his father. The sergeant went skipping through his memory, through all his resources, looking for help. He remembered once seeing crows circling the last gasps of a well fire, watching for prey that might have been chased from its den, or else choked or incinerated and easy to pick at. He knew that they were crows because of their distinctive, warbling *"clawk, clawk"* cries. He heard them but he could not see them, exactly. Just the underside of their shadows cast on the white smoke.

Cast from above by the sun.

The hum of the Angel grew louder. The two SEALs were poised and waiting for instructions.

It was ten A.M. Kowalski knew where the sun was. The hole where the RPG had burst was closing slowly because the air was so quiet.

"Wait for my signal," the sergeant said confidently.

"Are we still going to fire, sir?"

"We are absolutely," Kowalski replied. "And we're going to bring that sucker down."

He looked up at the gray-white tester, ignored a fresh rumbling under his feet, concentrated on the skies. He had to keep reminding himself that the Angel would not announce itself with the same sound as other planes, that it was softer and less resounding—

He realized he had tossed the headphone away. The countdown might have helped. There was no time to recover it, though. He would have to lead the plane slightly, compensate for the fact that the shadow would be lower than the actual aircraft. He stood beside the men.

"I'm going to give two firing commands," he told the men. " 'One' is for you." He tapped the head of the man on the right. " 'Two' is yours. Understand?"

The men repeated the instructions. Kowalski barely heard. There was a loud, high, sustained whistle like the sound of a hang-glider approaching overhead. A very big one. Parks had told Kowalski about the unique wings of the Angel and he assumed they were making the sound. The jet had to be damn close to be doing that.

Then he heard another sound. This one was less melodious: it was like someone snapping their fingers extremely fast, the sound of the turrets discharging. Kowalski watched to the north, for the first hint of a darker shape moving over the smoke. He was once again in a kind of alert calm. He had two shots, not just one, and he was determined that one of them would hit the mark.

Kowalski saw a thin, thin line of rain to the north and smiled slightly. At least that part of the plan had worked: the Angel's projectiles were melting moments after they were fired. The aircraft continued to fire, oblivious to what was happening. The rain moved toward them, about thirty feet in front of them. That was a good sign: extrapolating up-ward, the Angel was exactly where he thought it would be.

Beneath the clacking of the guns the sound of the aircraft itself changed. It was more resonant. The Angel had obviously cleared the wall of the valley and was moving toward their position. He saw the hint of a shadow and watched it for a moment. There was definitely something moving above the smoke. The image grew in proportion to the ever-increasing volume of the object. Kowalski painfully turned sideways so that he was between and not directly behind the weapons. If one of them spit past the blast door he would probably be cooked anyway, but this was where he wanted to be.

The shape was vague and amoeba-like until it was roughly at a two-o'clock position. That was when it started to look like a cylinder with wings. He waited. The hole they'd punched was beginning to fill but that didn't matter. He would have to fire before the Angel reached it.

"You both have a track on the thing?" Kowalski asked.

Both men answered in the affirmative. He knew that. He had watched them eyeball the shadow, find a landmark in the smoke in front of it, and use that to line up the shot. The men were professionals.

The aircraft was just passing through the one-o'clock position. It was time.

"One!" Kowalski shouted.

The launcher to his right hissed, the rocket fired, and the grenade was skyborne on a column of reddish white exhaust. The soldier stayed put so as not to distract his companion. It appeared the grenade was on a clean intercept course. Kowalski decided to take a chance with second.

"I want the second targeted at the wing, not the fuselage," the sergeant said.

"On it," the soldier replied. He glanced briefly to the right and adjusted his aim accordingly.

Kowalski watched as the shadow and contrail both headed toward the noon position.

"Two!" he shouted.

The second grenade shot toward the target as the first one covered the final leg of its ascent. It hit the Angel on the undercarriage, halfway between the horizontal center and the portside of the shadow. It caused the image to shudder and wobble and sent a small fireball earthward. The blast dissipated well before it reached earth. There was a small shower of debris in the valley, but the men had no idea what kind of damage it had caused. Apparently it was not enough: the jet was still airborne, its sounds and speed undiminished.

Now Kowalski was nervous. He wondered if it had been smart to commit the second grenade to an even smaller target. The men watched the rocket disappear into the smoke as the aircraft passed through the noon position.

They heard the second blast, saw a fresh fireball, and watched the big charcoal-colored shape as it shot south.

In two distinct pieces. One was the fuselage. The other was a very large section of wing.

"Yes!" Kowalski shouted.

"I suggest we move," the soldier on the right said as he was rising.

It was a good idea. The wing was on their side of the aircraft and tumbling length-wise like a reaper. The Jeeps had been left running, the drivers behind the wheels. Kowalski scooped up his headset as he climbed awkwardly into the seat and the vehicles shot up the road. He looked back and saw the silvery wing as it broke through the smoke, drawing it downward in angry little wisps. The wing hit not far south of where they had been standing, on the edge of the valley, ribs and metal skin cracking as it hit the hard rock. Before it had even settled, the fuselage came through the smoke, a large diving shark of a thing, headed toward a collision with the northern slope of the valley. It made a glancing first impact, then continued downward. They could hear it cracking its way downward, throwing up rock and pieces of itself as it fell.

It was an inelegant takedown but it was a successful one.

There were high-fives in the second Jeep. They were well-deserved and Kowalski shot them a thumbs-up. They gave it back to him. As LASER had proved, successful operations always erased the rivalries between the services.

Sergeant Kowalski told the drivers to stop. The volcano rumbled as if reestablishing alpha dog priority against the noisy intruder. The sergeant put on his mask to get a few particle-free breaths. Then he put the earpiece on and swung the microphone back in place.

The line was still open. Radar and the Hawker would have given NWAD the news, but the sergeant wanted to tell him anyway.

"Rear Admiral Parks, sir," he said. "We took a wing off the Angel."

"What's the eyewitness report?" Parks asked, giving Kowalski his moment in the sun.

"She is *so* down, sir."

TWENTY-FOUR

Norco, California

There was no cheering when the team in the bunker received the news of the Angel's destruction. Corporal Emens continued to sit at the radio and both Scott and Bryan waited behind him. For them the mission was not over. Two LASER operatives were still in the field.

It wasn't exactly a Pyrrhic victory for Parks but it was a heartbreaking one. An exercise that had started with so much promise had ended better than it might have but far, far worse than it should have.

The interpreter explained the developments to Chan, who used General Scott's radio to talk to Shanghai. Their pilots had reported seeing the three explosions and the senior captain in charge of the mission seemed satisfied. He ordered his squadron to turn back. After a midocean refueling they would return to the base heroes. They had faced the superior force and stared them down.

They can have that victory, Parks thought. It was not so much a win as it was not another loss. That wasn't the same thing.

Then Emens heard from the patrol boat that had successfully collected the three LASER jumpers. The room was utterly silent as they reported that a parachute had been

spotted riding the waves some two miles off the Oahu coast.
They called for a rescue chopper out of Pearl while they
headed toward the area. The spotter noted that it was one of
the paragliders the LASER team had used.

The helicopter arrived first and two divers jumped in.
They said that the chute belonged to Lieutenant Black.

She was "whipped but alive," as one of them put it.

A small cheer rose from the LASER section of the
bunker. Parks smiled. The interpreter informed Chan, who
smiled and bowed his head toward Bryan, then told the general he was glad for him.

"We have saved all of our comrades today," the Chinese
pilot added, "including those who were not yet drawn into
our drama."

The translation was approximate but the sentiment was
true. Their actions had averted a possible war.

None of this absolved Chan or Shanghai from what they
had done the day before. Happily, that was not Parks's problem. Except for one phone call he had to make in private, his
job was done.

As Parks was leaving the bunker, the medic onboard the
Navy chopper informed Scott that the officer they'd recovered had suffered a mild concussion apparently sustained
when her helmet struck the aircraft; burns on her arms,
though her jump suit had taken most of the flash; and severe
lacerations where the tether had slapped her cheek and neck
after the blast tore it loose.

None of it was life-threatening.

"Except to a Captain Gabriel," the medic quoted her as
saying. "She says she's going to mess him up for leaving her
alone."

They also found pieces of the solar panel embedded in
her suit and would be saving those to return to NWAD. It impressed Parks that the plane had obviously taken that hit,
too, and survived.

They had built a good aircraft. That was something.

Parks left the bunker, surprised by the bright daylight. He

had lost all sense of time in there. He stopped by a bank of vending machines to grab coffee and a package of cookies before going to the office he had appropriated. Though no one said anything but good morning, people gave him anxious glances, which meant word hadn't gotten out about the Angel. That was good. The announcement should come through channels from Secretary Whittle. He should also be the one to let the FAA know it was safe to fly. Parks couldn't begin to imagine the delays and confusion all of this had caused, though he had a feeling he would find out in the hearings.

But that was for later. Right now, he let his brain close down a little and his muscles relax. He didn't realize how tense he'd been until he closed the door, sat behind the desk, and started to tremble. He felt a tightness in his throat and pressure behind his eyes but he refused to let himself go. Until he made the call to inform the secretary that the test of the Angel had been concluded, he was still on the clock.

Whittle had heard about the "termination" from the National Reconnaissance Office. The NRO was tapped into all the major U.S. bases and, like NWAD, had seen the results on the radar from Pearl.

"Need I tell you how Paul Ponce has taken this?" Whittle asked.

"Mr. Secretary, I don't think anyone is happy with the way this program ended up," Parks said.

"You're wrong about that," the secretary replied. "The Guardian Angel Program is sure to be continued, though I have no idea under whose aegis. The good news for you is Ponce and the Congressional Armed Services Committee are not likely to go after your head. How can they, when it was an act of God that set the Angel lose? We can and will argue that those who were adversely affected disobeyed restrictions that were clearly in place. And the Angel did prove itself well beyond all the parameters NWAD had established."

"I'm not sure I'm gratified," Parks said.

"You know how these things work. Take what's there and be grateful," Whittle replied sharply.

The secretary was correct, of course. But that didn't make him right.

"What happens to the Angel itself?" Parks asked.

"I've been on the phone with the commanding officer at Pearl. Recovery Operations will secure the crash site as best as possible, document the wreckage, and then begin bringing the pieces in. They'll be stored at the naval station until final disposition has been decided."

"You know, sir, that Hank Hathaway is the man to head the postmortem unit."

"I'm sure his involvement will be considered at some point."

That was as bloodless an endorsement as the rear admiral could have conjured. Hathaway could certainly forget leading the investigation. He'd be fortunate even to be on it.

Or maybe he would *be lucky not to be part of it,* Parks thought. Scapegoating took many forms, from banishment to bringing you in. There was nothing quite as demoralizing as being blamed for, then hooked to, a misfire, then having your nose held to it day after day. Apart from the one warning their exchange was cordial. Parks was hardly a neophyte: that had nothing to do with any kind of mutual appreciation society. It had to do with CYB. Cover your back was a more inclusive form of cover your ass. The ramifcations tended to be more severe. The men might need each other to fudge the checks-and-balances failure during congressional hearings, and Whittle would want to be sure the rear admiral and he were not in adversarial positions.

Unless the navy secretary were perfectly in the clear, Parks knew. Then the rear admiral would be entirely on his own.

A call from Pearl informed him that Dr. Hathaway had landed safely and would be phoning soon. Parks decided to remain in the office to brief him. He chewed slowly on a cookie, drank some coffee, and let the rest of the day's stress wash out of him. It came through shaking fingers, a renewed tightness in his throat, and pressure behind his eyes that was more insistent now.

He was surprised to find his brain humming *God Bless America*. He didn't know if it were being facetious or not. Probably not. The good guys had pulled off some magic, the plane and its destruction, and though the bad guys had tried to use it for a partisan agenda they had failed. The drama was all part of America, of being American. When everything had been toted, even if he lost his command and his commanding view, Rear Admiral Edward Redmond Parks would still rather be a goat in San Diego than a pilot-hero in Shanghai.

That was enough to bring the tears, a mix of relief and pride and also gratitude that the only blood spilled today had been some of his and some of Hathaway's.

TWENTY-FIVE

Pearl Harbor, Hawaii

"And I thought the Angel got trashed."

That was Sergeant Kowalski's assessment as looked at a newscast from Coronado, the first from the air now that general flights had been resumed.

The sergeant was dressed in a hospital gown and propped in a bed at the Branch Medical Clinic Makalapa. He had come here to be checked out, and if everything was okay, he would be released. Lieutenant Black was in the bed beside him, not propped, not watching TV. She was sedated and when she was awake didn't bother to say much or open her eyes. What she did say generally had the mumbled phrase "screw the Angel hard" worked in.

After a well-earned rest, General Scott, Major Bryan, and Rear Admiral Parks had flown from Miramar the next morning to see the heroes of the Angel "deprogramming," as it was being called with the understatement and misdirection that was characteristic of the military. Lieutenant Commander Chan had flown with them on the 737 along with Deputy Consul Jian. The administration had agreed to release the pilot but did not want a Chinese military aircraft coming to California. The Chinese refused to allow him to fly on a commercial airline, saying it demeaned his status. The compromise was that he would be escorted from the continental United States on an American military craft and turned over to a Chinese military plane at Pearl. Bryan was glad those negotiations had gone on while he slept. They were the kind of games that made his temples tight. He knew from Scott's pleasant demeanor that the general had not been involved, either.

Parks had not said much during the flight, but Bryan knew that a lot of the fallout from the Angel test would land on his head. Bryan didn't feel too bad for him, though. The Act of God nature of the tsunami would be factored in and he'd be sent on his way with a nice pension.

Considering that people died, it could have gone a helluva lot worse for Parks, Bryan thought.

Lieutenant Commander Chan was also getting off lightly. The administration probably just wanted to make this whole thing with China go away. Let Shanghai and Beijing have bragging rights that they faced down the U.S. military and won. The DoD would get behind a cover story about the tsunami causing problems with air security and sell that to Congress and the public. Then, quietly, they would resurrect the Guardian Angel and send it back up. And the next time the Chinese or anyone else decided to venture into American airspace without permission they would not be getting out again.

That was the difference between Washington and Beijing. Better to lose some face than to lose your head.

For Bryan, the most important aspect of the mission was that LASER had done what they set out to do. Not in a pretty way, not in the way they'd intended, but with the threat ended and all members relatively intact.

The biggest downside was for Kowalski. He had aggravated his leg wound and bought himself extra ward-time. The fact that he would have to spend even more time in bed was killing the sergeant. He wanted to be out and about, thumping his chest and soaking up congratulations from anyone wearing a uniform and any Hawaiian lady who was not. Bryan assured him there would be time enough for that. The ladies in Corpus Christi were just as impressionable as the *wahines*. Kowalski was unconsoled. His seat was heavily bandaged and whatever impressions he made would unfortunately stop there.

The only upside for Kowalski was that he could visit and keep a fraternal eye on Black. The woman was awake most of the time but with a slowed, drug-induced perspective. She spoke occasionally, mostly to ask about aspects of the mission. The sergeant was happy to brief her. The other jumpers also stopped by, though the bulk of LASER was still in Coronado helping with the cleanup efforts.

Bryan himself was sorry to have missed out on the finale, though he understood the significance of his own role. He joined General Scott and Rear Admiral Parks at Hickam for the departure of Lieutenant Commander Chan. The deputy consul would be returning to Los Angeles on a commercial flight.

Before boarding the Chinese mid-size Han transport, Chan—through Jian—said that he was grateful to be able to return home to his family. "And I am glad," Chan added, "that all of your people will be seeing their families as well."

Parks thanked him.

"I believe we have all contributed to international peace this day," Jian said. "I commend you for your part."

No one responded. From the slight twist to Scott's mouth, Bryan could tell that they were thinking the same thing: *If you had kept out of our business, none of it would have been necessary.*

Chan boarded with a bow to Jian and a handshake from the others. An unmarked military vehicle took Jian and an aide to Kapolei Oahu Airport. The three officers waited until the Han took off, then went to the rear admiral's car. He had dismissed the driver, preferring to navigate on his own.

"Old family habit," Parks had explained. "We Parkses have always sailed our own boats."

The men drove back toward the Hale Koa Hotel. Parks

would drop off his companions and then continue to the Pearl communications center. He had a video conference scheduled with the recuperating Captain Flynn and the navy secretary. While the events were still fresh—and with Congress and the FAA sure to demand it sooner rather than later—Whittle wanted to assemble as careful a timetable of events as the chief scientist and the rear admiral could provide.

It was strange, parting after a crisis like this. The men had been put together in a tight, tough situation but they had hadn't really bonded. Their lives had not been at risk, and they each had had separate areas of responsibility. There was no sense of *"If you're ever in San Diego give a shout."* The men knew they would probably never see one another again.

The future didn't change Parks's sense of now, which was a feeling of gratitude. There was a warm breeze and an even warmer sun as he got out with them and stood in the visitors' circle at the front of the hotel. The ocean gleamed behind him. It was placid and the rear admiral wore it well. Unlike Scott, who needed a theater of operation, Parks was born for the base. There was nothing wrong with that. It just made the men very different.

Parks saluted the general, then offered his hand to him, and then to Bryan.

"It's been a privilege and an education to watch you work," the rear admiral said. "Thank you both." His tone was almost as warm as the weather. Ultimately, no officer likes having other officers help clean up his mess. Parks could have made the good-bye a formal affair.

"We were glad to be able to contribute, even though it was a little outside our charter," Scott said.

"No. You saved my ass figuratively. And Captain Flynn's literally."

"Have you spoken with him?" Scott asked.

"I will be soon," Parks said. "But I hear he's coming along and he was sorry he couldn't be with us through this."

"My attitude, sir, is that we're all in this together," Bryan said. He added, "Just like the Chinese diplomat said, only without the bullshit."

Parks gave him a wry smile, then looked at his watch. "Gentlemen, I have a postmortem process to begin."

"Don't let them bust you up," Scott said. "Test programs always go wrong. Remind them of that."

"I will," the rear admiral replied. "Truthfully, General, I'm not worried about me. I'm worried about putting this behind us, fixing the bird, and putting it back in America's skies. If the Chinese didn't show us anything else, they showed us how vitally important that is."

"I like your attitude," Scott said.

The rear admiral left with a smile of gratitude.

"General, isn't this all a little bass ackwards?" Bryan asked as they watched him go.

"What do you mean?"

"The Lone Ranger's the one who's supposed to ride off while the grateful townspeople wave their thanks," Bryan said.

"Oh, we're definitely part of a town," Scott said. "A damn fine one. And I hate to say it, but you chose the right reference."

"What do you mean, sir?"

"The rear admiral will be lone enough."

"The hearings?"

"Yes, but not just that. He plans to do an Angel maneuver on these boys. I was talking to him on the flight over. He's decided to fight to keep control of the project. He feels that the Angel's performance actually vindicates his team. Their job was to design and field an effective machine, not mount an intervention."

"He thinks he has a chance? Do you, sir?" The men had started walking toward the side of the hotel, toward an outdoor tiki bar.

"I do, if he aligns himself with the hawks," Scott said. "And I wouldn't blame him."

"For selling out? I would, sir."

"To the contrary. I think he'd be falling on his sword for

the good of the nation. No one knows the Angel program the way he and Hathaway do. If it means forming an alliance with the devils to see it properly finished, and the homeland protected, I have to admire the man."

"But what are we protecting if we *do* sell out, sir?" Bryan countered.

"Ah, the purity of ideals," Scott said as they went to the bar. "We're talking about a master plan, national survival. Speaking of survival, I'm going to call my wife and let her know where I am. Then I'll treat you to a beer and pretzels while we hash out the core issues of integrity versus necessity."

"Mrs. Scott doesn't know you're in Hawaii?" Bryan asked.

"Are you kidding?" the general asked. "Of course she does. I mean I'm going to let her know where I'll be sitting. Her plane should be landing in about a half hour. First commercial flight here from Los Angeles. And while we wait, you and I have some work to do."

"Sir?"

"The Scott Slammers versus the Bryan Batboys. Baseball."

Bryan smiled. "Yes, sir."

There were a few people in the outdoor bar. Scott took his cell phone off to the side, beside a potted palm, to leave a message for his wife. Bryan sat on a stool and ordered a ginger ale. He wasn't much of a drinker, and it was too early for the beer or two he would otherwise be having. Though he had to admit the Rold Gold pieces would probably taste a little livelier piggybacking a Coors.

The major sipped the ginger ale.

Maybe life is *about compromise,* he thought. Sometimes to enhance a moment, at other times for a long-term impact. Sometimes to catch your opponent off-guard and sometimes to present yourself with an unexpected challenge, a fresh stimulus, a different way of looking at things.

Bryan looked across the sea when he heard what might

have been Mrs. Scott's plane coming into the airport. Something so ordinary and taken for granted had to be fought for and won back.

Like liberty, he couldn't help but think. Stripped of the specifics, that was fundamentally what the past few days had been about. Maybe Parks had it right. Guys used to lie about their birthdate to get into the army. The rear admiral wanted to remain at the front, regardless of what it took to get there.

The general was right. That battle was worth the compromise. Unlike Parks and unlike Scott, who had to readjust his sights after losing NATO, Bryan had never had to endure anything like that.

The major downed the ginger ale quickly, then asked for another. He was thirstier than he'd thought. Then he did something out of character. He changed the order to a beer. Not for the taste of the beer but for the taste of compromise. It wasn't what he wanted but it wasn't as bad as he'd expected. And damn if it *didn't* make the pretzels taste better.

DATE DUE
